I0775574

THE PALISADES

A Novel

GAIL LYNN HANSON

First Edition: October 2023
Published by Slippery Fish Press
Print book interior designed by Kirkus Book Prep

Library of Congress Control Number: 2023908620

ISBN (hardcover) 979-8-9882874-2-1
ISBN (paperback) 979-8-9882874-0-7
ISBN (eBook) 979-8-9882874-1-4

Gaillynnhanson.com

for Tim

I specialize in murders of quiet, domestic interest.

— AGATHA CHRISTIE

PROLOGUE

On July 4, 1922, a fire burned the last of the legendary movie studio Inceville, which had produced silent movies in a crevasse of the Santa Monica Mountains, its mouth gaping to the sea. Only a weatherworn church from the set remained. That same year, a town was born from the ashes, christened Pacific Palisades by the Reverend Charles H. Scott, a religious-intellectual commune perched on a cliff overlooking the Pacific Ocean.

In that same year, Frances Gumm (Judy Garland) was born in Grand Rapids, Minnesota. Also that same year, Frances Lillian Mary Ridste (Carole Landis), just three years old, half-Norwegian, was left by her father and moved by her mother from Fairchild, Wisconsin, to Southern California. And in that same year, a girl, all Norwegian, was born on Chicago's West Side to Lutheran parents who loved God more when she survived a near-fatal childhood illness.

In 1942, Angela Lansbury, age seventeen, moved from London to Hollywood via New York to debut in the award-winning film *Gaslight*. In 1946, Judy Garland, just four feet eleven inches tall, starred with Angela in *The Harvey Girls*. In 1945, Carole Landis, known as the "Ping Girl," a more beautiful (some would say) but lesser known Marilyn Monroe, starred in a small role on Broadway with future novelist Jacqueline Susann, who later wrote *Valley of the Dolls* (1966), based on the tragic lives of Carole Landis and Judy Garland. And in 1947, the girl from Chicago, also four feet eleven inches, moved to Southern California, to the Palisades—her inspiration, a film about going west, starring both Angela and Judy.

In 1948, Carole Landis, age twenty-nine, died of a Seconal overdose after throwing a Fourth of July party at her home in Pacific Palisades, not accidental. In 1969, Judy Garland, age forty-seven, also died of a Seconal overdose in London, accidental. The Palisades lived on to shelter movie stars and the wealthy. And the girl from Chicago married rich, mingled with actresses, and like Angela, lived a very long time.

Jesus was in the room. He was everywhere, Father said, living inside of them because they were believers.

The Bible remained at the head of the bed where Dorothy lay, as if the book itself held power to heal her. Her mother's cool dishrag fingers touched Dorothy's forehead each hour, checking for fever. Mother leaned in from afar, never sitting, never asking Dorothy how she felt, distracted by Paul, the beautiful baby perched on Mother's hip, always hungry. Dorothy felt more like an object to be maintained than a child to be loved.

The Bible's black cover was soft and worn. It smelled nice, leather and paper. The onionskin pages with dingy edges, more so near the back, in the New Testament, marked where Jesus came in. The pages crackled, making Dorothy feel tingly and sleepy.

Dorothy only left the house to go to church, one her parents started with two other Norwegian Lutheran families. They'd walked door to door, asking people to join them in planting the church, as if they were planting a seed that would grow into a fruit-bearing tree rooted deep in their small community west of Chicago. Saint Paul's Lutheran Church, named by her mother, had no money and no building, so the faithful group met in the mortuary rent-free.

The children's church, Sunday School, was held in the basement, where a single light bulb shone too brightly against the floor and offered nothing to the dark corners. Alongside a wall, Dorothy lay on a mattress with a dusky-yellow stain. The cement walls cried from various leaks, glistening in the low light. If she squinted, the water became diamonds.

Dorothy was certain a dead body, its juice seeping out, had rested on her mattress. It smelled sour, like Paul's spit-up and mildew. Would she die there, too? "Better not stain a good mattress," Mother might say.

For two hours each Sunday, she listened. Above, an organ vibrated, shaking the light bulb, making shadows quiver. Singing —Mother's voice was high and shrill, and Father's, low and steady, much lower than his speaking voice.

Below, Mrs. Larsen read about slaves and the Red Sea, blood and bravery, miracles, blindness, lameness, washing feet, wells, throwing stones, a baby, a garden, an apple, a snake, a donkey, palm leaves, and a robe of many colors, which Dorothy liked best. They sang about God holding the world in his hands and how Jesus loves children. But Dorothy did not sing. It hurt her chest to breathe deeply.

The children whispered about the other room, the one down the hall, dark, where the door was kept closed. The room contained dead bodies in coffins or laid out on tables. The grown-ups dressed them up nice with makeup and fancy clothes so that they didn't look so dead. One boy said dead bodies shouldn't be kept out loose because with all the Jesus talk upstairs, they might come back to life, like Lazarus.

Dorothy kept an eye on that doorknob. She had a good view from her mattress. Once, she saw it turn. Another time, a girl said she smelled something nasty. Green gas seeped from under the door; Dorothy was sure of it. That same day, an older boy told a younger one that he would lock him in there if he didn't hand over everything from his pockets. The little boy, bright fear in his eyes, emptied his pockets—a piece of swirly taffy, a dime, two blue marbles, and a dead beetle with an iridescent green shell like a jewel.

Dorothy was sure she'd be put in that room. She often tried to sit up, but Mrs. Larsen always coaxed her down, pressing her body into the stain. She hoped she really would be dead, the door locked, and her coffin shut tight. She didn't want to wake there, Jesus or no Jesus. But mostly, she hoped her body would not leave a stain.

Dorothy's sickness was a test of faith. Her parents memorized all the parts of the Bible that spoke of faith, how faith, even a little faith, a mustard seed, would be rewarded. One day her parents would say, "Now pick up your mat and walk." And she would. She would do it because everyone believed.

The sickness had started with a lingering cold that dropped to her lungs, a cough, a deep bark, fevers, and finally, pain with every breath. Empyema, it was called, where pus collects in the lining of the lungs, caused by bacteria. The only treatment was to drain the fluid and hope the body would recover.

Weeks passed. Life moved around her. Father sat on the edge of her bed most evenings, reading and looking into her eyes with identical eyes, pale blue and round. He prayed even when her mother's faith faltered, reading about all the people Jesus healed. But when her fevers rose, Mother insisted they do something.

When the doctor came, her parents shuffled back as he entered the house. Tall and thin, a tree in winter, the man dressed only in black, black hair, a black bag, a black mole on his cheek, and one black thumbnail. His face remained somber, as if he led the dying to the other side and found his job very sad, or maybe he didn't care for what he was about to do.

A rib, a floating rib, would have to be removed in order to access the lung. Maybe the rib wasn't connected to anything and could be plucked out without much trouble. Dorothy brightened at the thought, but Mother gasped.

The doctor asked for whiskey to ease any discomfort.

Father, eyes wide, brows raised, said, "We don't keep whiskey in this house, sir."

Mother panted. The hollow of her throat pushed in and out. She paced, Paul bouncing on her hip, while staring at Dorothy's body.

Dorothy closed her eyes, sorry she had caused so much trouble. With her father's presence, she lifted her heavy lids. He brought her hand to his lips, smiling with such tension Dorothy feared his face might break.

The doctor said, while opening his bag, "I may have some in here." He produced a small bottle, filled the dropper. "One, two, three." It spread across her tongue. She felt power in the burn.

Her mother's face, contorted and old, and her father's, serene and hard, both looked alarmed, as if she'd done something evil, so she closed her eyes and listened to the rain and low rumble of thunder rattling the china in the cabinet nearby. She liked how the rain made the street shiny.

Mother opened the window and left the room, but her father stayed; the scent of his aftershave lotion rode the cool breeze. He took both her hands and held them firm inside his own.

The doctor lifted her nightgown and touched her side. Father squeezed tighter. The first sting of the blade, the shock of pain, caught her breath. Mouth open, jaw tight, as if to scream, but no sound left her body.

Father said, "Though I walk through the valley of the shadow of death, I will fear no evil."

The pleasure of him holding her was greater than the pain. His deep voice and warm hands anchored her. Father's hands were the hands of God. Jesus held her hands. If it took a rib to hold God's hand, then it was worth it. God had removed a rib from Adam to make Eve, after all.

What would her rib look like? What would the doctor do with it? Her mother made ribs for dinner a week ago. She hadn't eaten, but she'd examined the curved bone, white beneath the meat. Would hers have meat, too? Mother always collected the bones in old newspaper for the dog next door. When Dorothy played in the neighbor's yard, she'd find them again, dry and clean.

The doctor worked. Father prayed. Thunder grumbled. Would Mother throw her rib to the dog? Would he chew it clean?

A nasty smell, musty, like spoiled meat, engulfed them. Father let go. Dorothy opened her eyes to see him cover his face with a white handkerchief. Her abandoned hands, suddenly cold, grasped, only to find the stiff edge of her mattress.

The doctor's hands were streaked red. He, too, held a sour look, dark brows spiked like caterpillars, white lips pressed tight. A metal pan, a shiny tool, the blood, it all should have alarmed her. But she was not alarmed until she realized the putrid smell rose from her own body. The shame, Father disgusted by her body. She closed her eyes and held still, as if obedience might contain the odor.

A week later, Dorothy sat on the davenport with a picture book of farm animals. The room seemed different, everything turned. Father hung his hat with the black and white feather on the peg by the door. A broad smile spread. He walked to her and clutched her hands. "My girl, you are feeling better?"

On a Saturday afternoon in June, Dorothy walked to the front porch, where her mother and Mrs. Larsen stood talking. Mother held a broom as Paul played with a green toy car at her feet. They screamed. Paul cried. Mother picked him up, held him close, and stepped back. Mrs. Larsen laughed. "Welcome to the land of the living."

She hadn't died, or had she? Had she been resurrected like Jesus? Mother stared while cradling Paul's fuzzy head. Dorothy waited for her to smile, maybe laugh like Mrs. Larsen. But she merely leaned forward, touching Dorothy's forehead with icy fingertips.

Once she was back in bed, Paul crawled up and patted her head with fat outstretched fingers. Dorothy laughed as he touched her face with sticky hands smelling of bread. She reached to hug him, but Mother pulled him back. "Don't get him sick. One sick child is hard enough."

Her sickness was punishment. What sin? Sneaking cookies, forgetting prayers—or was it wanting love from anyone besides God himself? "A jealous God," Mother said. Dorothy touched the tender tip of Paul's finger. Being jealous felt a lot like being mad. She hoped Mother would sit with her, but she took Paul and left the room. And so she knew how God felt and was sorry she'd made him angry.

PART I

CHAPTER 1

DOROTHY

Dorothy Anderson grew up in a home where movies were strictly prohibited. Card playing, dancing, secular music, alcohol, and socializing with Catholics were also banned, but the only thing that mattered to Dorothy was the movies.

As a sophomore in high school, Dorothy was going steady with a lean, blue-eyed senior who'd presented her with his class ring, which she found rather ugly. One summer night, in 1939, they secretly met at the downtown theater to see *The Wizard of Oz*. Judy Garland was almost Dorothy's exact age. Her voice, her lips, the curves of her body—Dorothy realized how Hollywood and a camera could turn an ordinary girl into a movie star and that people, men in particular, loved movie stars. It didn't matter that the movie star did not return love because it was about *being* loved by many people, an abundance of love, rich with love, love that could be stored away, even wasted. Dorothy wanted not one man, but thousands.

In 1940, when Dorothy's boyfriend left for basic training, she went to *One Million B.C.*, alone. The theater-release poster featured a blonde woman dressed in a skimpy red garment slit up the thigh. *See The Most Exciting Adventure in a Million Years.* The actress, Carole Landis, head flung back, eyes closed, large-mounded breasts prominent, spilled over the arms of a dark-haired man with a square jaw and bare chest, who ran from an enormous green dinosaur.

In the following months, Dorothy focused on her body. She practiced a new walk, loose and sultry, tilted head, pouty lips, a coy smile. Styling her white-blonde hair in voluptuous curls and staining her cheeks and lips with her mother's lingonberries, she decided she was beautiful, too.

Her father inspected her at breakfast, over his glasses. Her full figure was well developed, which bothered her parents, she knew, by the way her mother insisted she wear a sweater in summer. She was short, four foot eleven, like Judy, but that was easily corrected with heels.

In 1943, Dorothy graduated from Saint Olaf's College in Minnesota, where she had studied English literature and piano. Her postcollege mission plans in the Orient fell apart when both China and Japan instituted policies that denied American travelers, so instead, she moved home with her parents and brother, Paul, to teach English at the local high school. Dorothy had been relatively content with her mother cooking and washing (it's what her mother did best), but deep down, she itched for something more.

Dorothy had become an exceptional pianist. She played church hymns at Saint Paul's Lutheran Church. Saint Paul's had finally raised enough money to build a modest structure, moving from its temporary, yet lengthy, location at the mortuary. The rectangular barn-shaped building, painted white, was nothing like the small, yet impressive, Catholic cathedral across the street, but they got money from headquarters.

Despite her parents' rules, Dorothy was a grown woman and continued to spend her free time at the local theater. In 1946, *The Harvey Girls*, starring Judy Garland and Angela Lansbury, was featured. Dorothy sat in the dark theater, eating popcorn and drinking Coca-Cola. Dorothy had become a big fan of both actresses because Judy was short and musically talented, and Angela seemed mature and independent. Angela looked old, even then, but Judy was pretty, with her petite figure, full and shapely. She imagined they'd be friends if they ever met. Dorothy had thought a lot about Hollywood, and with this film about going west, she felt even more compelled to do the same.

A week later, her Aunt Hedda, her father's sister, called and asked to speak with her. "You're twenty-four now?" Hedda asked in her cool California style, breezy and loose, as if she were on vacation. "I've been thinking about you lately, wondering how long you plan to live at home."

Dorothy glanced at her parents sitting side by side on the davenport, watching her. "I have a job here and everything."

Hedda said, "It's the everything part that sounds dull. How about California?"

Stylish Aunt Hedda. Oceans and movie stars. Hollywood.

Although Dorothy's parents were not happy with her decision, they were comforted by the fact that Aunt Hedda was not wild. However, they didn't know that she was on the periphery of things that were.

Hedda had become acquainted with a prominent family, Walter and Judith Fiske, by way of Dorothy's paternal grandfather, who knew Walter's father, Charles Fiske, from his ties to the Chicago West Side. Hedda and her husband were often invited to Judith's lavish parties in Brentwood, where she also came to know Walter and Judith's children: Esther, Eugene, and Frank.

Once in California, at a party, Hedda handed Dorothy a hand-cut crystal glass of pink punch while eyeing Esther, who stood alone, hunched and homely in a shapeless brown dress. "She's too big."

"Yes, she is." Dorothy sipped.

Hedda flipped her hair from her shoulder. "Men don't like big women. And she's bossy."

"Schoolteachers often are." Dorothy scanned the room. A beautiful blonde with curls framing her face and deep-red lips, lingonberries, was surrounded by jovial men. The woman touched her bare neck and sipped sparkling champagne, aloof to the desperate faces that fought for her attention. "I know what men want."

Hedda raised her eyebrows. "Don't ever let your father hear you say that. He'll blame me."

Dorothy giggled, still watching. A pale-pink dress, silk, sleeveless, clung to the woman's full breasts. She looked familiar. "You have to let men think they're in charge, let them decide some things, make it sound as if all the good ideas are theirs, and then they'll do whatever you want."

Hedda studied the blonde woman. "And where did you learn this?"

"I've watched a lot of movies." Dorothy looked back at Esther. "Poor thing." She set down her cup and pulled at the sides of her dress, trying to make it sit properly. "Men like petite women. It makes them feel more powerful."

Hedda smirked, as if she agreed but would never say. Her husband, equally stylish and handsome, whispered in the blonde woman's ear. The beautiful woman's lips moved as he laughed, wide-mouthed, like the martini glass he held too high.

Dorothy looked again. "Wait. Is that—"

Hedda nodded. "Yes."

"She's . . ." Dorothy could not find words. She wanted to stand closer, inspect every bit of her. She wanted to be her.

"Gorgeous, I know, and separated. She's with Rex Harrison." Hedda raised one brow. "She lives a few minutes from here."

Coy and seductive, Carole Landis flirted and swayed as she sipped her champagne. The handsome men surrounding her, with their Hollywood hair and smug smiles, competed for her attention. One man stood out, dumpy, short, too young to be balding, with sagging jowls and tapered fingers.

"Have you met Esther's brother, Eugene?"

Dorothy recalled meeting him but had forgotten the encounter as if it had been an incident on the periphery. "No, I don't believe so."

Dorothy sauntered toward the men, knowing Hedda would follow. She straightened her back, trying to add an inch, then paused to let Hedda pass.

"Eugene, this is Dorothy, Inga and Rolf's daughter. She's recently moved here from Chicago."

Dorothy gave Eugene a quick, flirtatious smile—he was a man, after all—but she studied Carole. For a moment, their eyes met, blue, before Carole turned to face a window with a view of the gardens. Pale, luminous skin, with impossible pouting lips, Carole gazed beyond the glassy pool.

Eugene's relentless smile, such eagerness, no effort needed, Dorothy looked away.

"You smell nice," he said while stepping a bit closer.

Dorothy barely heard, so focused on Carole. They looked alike—the hair, the eyes. Carole was taller, of course, but Dorothy had smaller feet.

Eugene handed Dorothy champagne. "I studied theater in college. Mother thought I'd make a good actor, so I gave it a try, but I prefer painting." Dopey-eyed, pants pulled to his ribs, Eugene lifted his cheeks higher, revealing more teeth.

Dorothy couldn't figure them out. She decided that his face was misaligned. Glancing around his parents' lavish home, she saw that everything was gold and gilded, Judith's magnificent jewelry twinkling with every gesture. "I studied piano and literature."

Eugene handed her a silver cocktail napkin embossed with a cursive *F.* "I'd like to hear you play. Maybe this coming week? I'm free most days."

Carole wandered off arm in arm with a thin woman in a black backless dress. The men, sullen, turned to one another, amused, as if someone had told a dirty joke. Admiring Carole's hourglass figure from this new angle, lustful, they nearly panted. Dorothy waited for them to notice her.

Dorothy and Eugene began dating the following week, not because she enjoyed him, though he was pleasant enough, but because she could not resist the context in which he inhabited. For months, Dorothy told Hedda that Eugene was a stuffed shirt, but she finally gave in when he presented her with a large diamond and a promise of a house in the Palisades. She grew to appreciate his useful qualities—his incapacity to get angry, his disinterest in her excessive shopping, and his compliance with their social calendar.

Eugene's parents bought them a house on Via De La Paz. Dorothy liked the sound of it, fancy and exotic. She practiced letting it roll off her tongue. Judith decorated it and approved of an eventual second story. Walter, Eugene's father, gave Eugene a few apartment buildings to manage, which he did from home. Dorothy kept teaching because she had nothing else to do and didn't want to spend all day in the house.

In 1948, a few months after the wedding, including a month in Hawaii, a gift from Eugene's parents, Dorothy fixed a plate of eggs and bacon for Eugene as he read the newspaper.

Eugene cleared his throat, then softly said, "Carole Landis died."

Dorothy felt her body stiffen before setting down Eugene's breakfast. She didn't want to appear overly interested in movie stars. Judith said it was uncouth. But once Eugene went to putter in the garage, she took the newspaper to her bedroom.

Carole had been found facedown on her bathroom floor, dead of an apparent drug overdose. She'd been not so secretly having an affair with the married Rex Harrison. Two suicide notes were reported, one to her mother and one to Rex, who had denied their relationship.

Dorothy sat on her bed with the paper. More news revealed

details of Carole's life—she had only wanted to be married and have children like normal people, but the endometriosis had prevented this. Dorothy wiped a tear from her cheek. She wished she could have been there for Carole as a true friend, to talk things through, come up with a solution. If Carol had only known that a true friend was nearby, a friend who could relate in so many ways, maybe she could have been persuaded to keep going, to find a new man, a better man, one who would appreciate her and love her for her true self, a woman almost too beautiful for this world—beauty can be a burden—but a woman nonetheless, one who just wanted to be a mother.

Dorothy touched her stomach. She was still not pregnant. To her surprise, she enjoyed being with Eugene. Her mother had no trouble, so why should she? The only explanation was that Eugene could not provide the essential ingredient.

Dorothy bought Eugene looser pants with an array of belts to hold them up, hoping a bit of fresh air and less constriction would resolve the problem. Eugene never knew this, of course; he simply followed her orders, chuckling, happy to please.

When a new jewelry store opened in the village, Judith suggested it to Eugene, to cheer Dorothy up. Over the years, he shopped there often, Carson's Fine Jewelry, named after the owner, whom Eugene grew to trust for his good taste and upscale clientele. Dorothy was regularly presented with an array of fine jewelry. Eugene treated her with extra kindness, taking her out every Friday night, buying her even more jewelry, and agreeing to attend formal benefit dinners so that she'd have plenty of places to wear it. The jewelry became her obsession, a distraction; it filled a void, and this allowed Eugene to live in relative peace, painting and eating while Dorothy shopped, watched movies, and read murder mysteries.

In 1964, Dorothy turned forty-two. After nearly eighteen years of marriage, she realized that she would not have children. At forty-one, her cycles had changed. She cried privately and avoided the children's department at Bullock's, where she'd spent years buying a slew of irresistible dresses, an angora baby blanket, a white bunny with floppy ears. It helped, buying things, as if the act itself might make a baby come. The collection became quite large, an entire wardrobe for a baby girl's first year. Diapers, for the baby smell. Baby lotions and baby creams labeled with cute baby bees or fuzzy baby animals. Baby shoes for all occasions. Baby books. Baby hats. A baby raincoat with baby galoshes. All of it hidden away. When the sense of loss overwhelmed her, she thought of Carole Landis, because beautiful women sometimes didn't have children, even though they were the ones who should.

The Fiske properties continued to increase in value. Walter sold some, bought more. The numbers worked in his favor, so Judith and Walter moved into a larger home in Brentwood. The house was impressive but not as lavish as the home across the street, which had recently been purchased by Judy Garland. Judy had separated from Sid Luft, so it was just her and the children. Joe was eight, Lorna eleven, and Liza had already gone to New York. Judith sent an extravagant bouquet of flowers to welcome them and received a very nice note in return.

One day, Judith called. "Dorothy, come over."

Dorothy painted her lips, spritzed her neck, grabbed her pink sunglasses, and drove three minutes to Judith's house. Judith led her into the back sunporch, which overlooked a swimming pool surrounded by palm trees intermingled with birds-of-paradise, hibiscus, and bougainvillea. The maid brought iced tea on a silver tray. With a sly smile, Judith handed Dorothy an invitation. Dorothy admired the engraved silver lettering.

Astonished, Dorothy looked at Judith, who smirked with such delight that Dorothy thought she might burst. "Are you going?"

"Of course! Who wouldn't?"

The invitation, signed by Judy Garland, included a smaller reply card with a thick envelope already stamped.

"It's her son's birthday, Joe. Walter wouldn't care a thing about this, so you're coming with me."

Dorothy felt a flutter in her chest. She giggled and nodded until Judith told her to stop.

Dorothy spent weeks shopping. After trying Saks, Neiman Marcus, and Bullock's, she found the perfect thing at a small boutique in Brentwood—a halter dress in blue-and-white gingham. Eugene seemed uninterested but suggested she wear her ruby earrings.

"Eugene." Dorothy removed beauty products from a thick shopping bag with a gold-ribbon handle and set them on the dining table. "Do you realize that Judy and I were born only three days apart?"

"Isn't that something." Eugene ate a cold sausage left from breakfast. The grease shined his lips. He wiped his face on his sleeve, then burped.

Dorothy smeared lotion on the back of her hand. "Too bad about the drugs, but she's better now."

Eugene stifled a belch. "Is she?"

"Oh yes, after Carnegie Hall and her own show. It was the greatest comeback. You know, I saw *The Wizard of Oz* when I was seventeen and she was seventeen, of course, and with my name." Dorothy looked at the ceiling. "The irony. It was a tiny theater back home. It got me thinking about California."

Eugene chewed; a piece of sausage fell from his mouth. "I'm very glad you saw it."

"People said she wasn't pretty, but I don't know what they meant—she was gorgeous on the big screen. And that voice, well, there just aren't words."

Eugene took Dorothy's hand. "You're as pretty as her."

Dorothy pulled away. "All those men married her for her money. Men can be so greedy." Dorothy admired the gigantic tangerine opal, a fire opal, on her finger (Mr. Carson said it was one of a kind). A smooth, rounded dome, alive, like a baby's forehead. It flashed red and orange under the chandelier, changing with the light, growing. "But not you, darling."

On the day of the party, Dorothy wore rubies and red heels. She bought Joey an expensive red firetruck and had it gift wrapped, paid extra for premium paper and ribbon.

A maid wearing a black and white uniform opened the door. Dorothy and Judith were ushered through a lavish entry hall of marble, silk, and flowers to the back, where little boys were squeezed into jackets with bulging buttonholes and girls were decorated in bows from ponytails to shoes. The children screamed and ran around in cone-shaped hats. Dorothy loved the energy, the laughing children, all dressed up like dolls.

The adults stood a distance away, drinking champagne. Judith talked and laughed with her friends. Dorothy didn't drink alcohol during the day, so she looked for Judy. The maid piled Dorothy's gift on top of a mountain of others. Dorothy stepped over to make sure the card had not slipped off. When she turned to rejoin Judith, a clown wearing large red shoes blocked her way.

"Excuse me," Dorothy said, taking a step back.

"I'm the only one who's supposed to dress up, lady," he slurred. "Are you *Dorothy* or something?" Lifting his foot, he said, "Look, we both have red shoes." His rancid breath, tinged with alcohol, blew across Dorothy's face. Pointing at her shoes, tipping his head back, and opening his mouth wide, cackling, the dangly thing wobbled in his throat.

Dorothy scanned the other guests, who all wore subdued, elegant dresses.

"Are those real rubies, *Dorothy*?"

"Of course they are! Aren't you supposed to be playing with the children?" Dorothy straightened her rings. "Does Miss Garland know that her clown is drunk?"

"Judy?" The clown tipped his head back again and screamed with laughter. People looked. "I work all her birthday parties. I take the job because the drinks are abundant."

Dorothy looked past him. "Where is Miss Garland?"

"Who knows?" The clown staggered away, knocking the sofa table with his big shoe.

Dorothy looked down at her shoes, the crisp gingham of her dress, and the flash of her rings. The clown, from across the room, pointed. Children appeared confused. Women turned to each other and covered their mouths. It had seemed like a good idea—clever, even—not to dress in costume, of course, but to dress in theme. But now heat radiated from her face.

Dorothy wandered around admiring the furnishings and knickknacks until she found a pretty powder room. The wallpaper, large tropical birds, the pink toilet and sink, the glass faucet handles with ornate brass, and the gilded mirror offered a pleasant retreat in which to fix her lipstick. She took a thick floral guest towel and tucked it inside her purse. When she opened the door, she bumped into the clown.

"What is it with you, lady? You're so small, I can't even see you. Might step on you with my big shoe." He lifted his foot and snickered, spraying Dorothy with spit.

"I'm the same size as Miss Garland. For your information, we are also exactly the same age. And my name *is* Dorothy!"

Shrieking, the clown struggled for breath, then slapped his knee. "This might be the funniest thing I've ever seen. Maybe she can help you find your way home! Judy is probably down there." He pointed down the hall. "She should get a load of you." He stumbled back to the party.

Dark and quiet, the hall clearly led to the family's private quarters: yellow carpet, blue walls, landscape paintings. She secured her rattan basket purse in the nook of her elbow, glanced at her shoes, then walked toward a large gold-framed mirror. The doors were all shut but one at the end. As her image became larger and clearer in the approaching mirror, she thought about what she might say: *Excuse me, I must have gotten lost. I was using the mirror. I was intrigued by all the fascinating art in the hall.*

Dorothy poked her head in the open door. The room glowed pale green, indistinct, like an underwater landscape. Gold drapery, seagrass, billowed around tall glass doors leading to the backyard, obscured by another layer of gauzy fabric. Through the sheers, Dorothy made out the faint sparkle of the pool. An impressive canopy bed, adorned with dozens of tasseled pillows anchored the room. A chandelier reacted to a current of air. The crystals, barely visible through the vague light, vacillated with hesitation.

Dorothy stepped in and took a deep breath. Perfume? Alcohol? She would remember everything. The wide dressing table, much like her own, displayed framed photos of the children, a porcelain Scottie dog, and a pair of earrings. She picked one up. Diamonds, of course. Or emeralds? Hard to tell through the haze. She set the earring down with the slightest clink, then paused, relishing the moment. She turned. A small figure in a large chair sat motionless.

Judy, wearing a long emerald dress, blended into the spring-pea walls and velvet cucumber lounge chair where she slumped, asleep. Dark lashes rested upon her cheeks, black-cherry lips parted, but her head was turned at an odd angle. A glass of champagne fizzed on the side table, alongside a few prescription pill bottles. Her darling bare feet hung free above the ground.

Dorothy whispered, "Miss Garland?"

A step closer revealed her slack face, lipstick painted beyond her lips, severe arched brows, a dark half circle under one eye, and an ivory comb slipping from her hair. Diminutive and smudged, mousy-faced, Judy opened her eyes and looked around, blinking as if she'd fallen asleep by mistake. Her head stopped at Dorothy. Gasping, she looked her up and down. "Dorothy?"

Dorothy stepped closer. "Yes! Judith Fiske must have told

you I was coming. It's wonderful to finally meet you." Dorothy sashayed to Judy, holding out her hand.

Judy reached for the champagne, downing it in one giant gulp, burped, dropped the glass, and wiped her mouth with the back of her hand before laughing in short, flittering giggles that bubbled around the room.

"We are the same age and the same height." Dorothy slipped off her heels. "See?"

Rolling and spinning, Judy's eyes would not hold still.

"You're the reason I'm here. I'm from the Midwest, too. I know about going west, like *The Harvey Girls*." Dorothy waited. "I also play the piano."

Judy pushed the arm of the chair with her elbow, but it slipped, so she slouched back down.

Dorothy turned back to the photos on the dresser. "Your children are so talented. Lorna sang beautifully on your Christmas special." Dorothy swallowed the rock in her throat. "My husband and I couldn't have children. I wanted a girl. Singing lessons, dance lessons, acting lessons." Dorothy turned back to Judy, whose eyes had closed again. "I even bought her a necklace. Carson's wrapped it in a silver box with a pink bow. An aquamarine, for a child, to match her eyes." Dorothy felt her eyes moisten. "I still keep it in my bedside table."

Judy snored through her cavernous nostrils.

"Joey must wonder where you are." Dorothy looked toward the door. "His party?" She stepped into her shoes.

Judy's jaw went slack, her throat pulsed, taffeta bunched around her waist, and her feet, like those of a child with painted red toenails, twitched.

Dorothy remained. Everyone needed a rest now and then, a glass of champagne, a pill to calm the nerves. It's a lot of work, throwing parties and raising children. And Judy deserved her privacy.

Judy pulled her head up and opened her eyes, which whirled a full rotation before focusing. "Dorothy, go home."

CHAPTER 2

RADICAL RED

This first time with a new client would be awkward for many, even the most experienced of caregivers. Ruth gazed at Esther's flesh—filled with blood, leaching fluid and oil, rising and falling with breath. She placed her hand on it, felt heat and the fuzz of fine hair. *Peach.* But to Ruth, it was nothing. Working as a caregiver to mostly wealthy, private clients for nearly twenty years, starting in 1986, she'd seen it all. These people needed her. And this woman, another old body—tired, damaged, a dead leaf, shriveled, hanging on until that gust of winter wind—needed Ruth in typical ways, such as the maintaining of her body and home, but the impending relationship would, more accurately, resemble an exchange because Ruth also needed Esther.

Water dripped from the tarnished chrome bathtub faucet, each white lever indicating *Hot* or *Cold* in bold black lettering. Plunk. The sound echoed from the cast-iron walls of the tub, glazed in conch-shell-pink porcelain the color of healthy gums. Competent and gentle, Ruth was good. She knew this. Plink. The disturbance expanded into perfect rings, a target. She was thorough, yet discreet; old people trusted her. Plunk. Little waves. A small window faced west, toward the ocean, where an amoeba of bright-green moss crept from one corner, thriving in light and humidity, a successful display of photosynthesis and human neglect. Plink. The problem—too much time to think thoughts Ruth didn't like, the ones she wished would float away. *Milk and blood. Tea with sugar. Knives and needles.* Or she was sometimes bored, often restless. But not today, not with Esther Fiske.

Esther sat in the bathtub, where pale rolls of fat, which might have been cute on a baby, encircled her middle. White hair looped to form a loose bun. Her knees bent so that the flesh of her calves hung heavy, pulling away from bone. Her shoulders commanded like a man, yet sloped forward like an unloved woman.

Water ran down her pale and freckled back, glistening beneath the harsh bathroom lights, skin that had avoided the Southern California sun, unlike her ruddy face and hands, marred by liver spots. Ruth wiped away bubbles with a peach cloth frayed on one corner.

Ruth had a view, across the hall, into the bedroom, where she admired Esther's neatly made twin bed, the pastel quilt folded back smoothly (Ruth was good with beds). A pillow, a warm meal, only now did Ruth have these things, usually, but not as a child, not when she needed them most. Two mothers, and both times they'd left. Good mothers, real mothers, love their children even when they're ugly or stupid, or both. Fully known and fully loved. Cherished. She'd seen it in movies and books. But it didn't matter now.

A two-inch scar, white and raised, angled up the left side of Esther's back.

Generally, Ruth cared. She wasn't a bad person, or didn't want to be.

Tiny white dots lined each side, stitch marks, where the needle had poked through.

Ruth touched the scar, felt the sharp sting of the needle. *Hotpink thread.*

"You see that scar?" Esther croaked, the sound deep and ragged.

Ruth looked again, a cut, precise. She avoided it as if it might be tender.

"Empyema. I had it when I was four. That's where they drained pus from my lung."

Ruth stayed clear but continued to wipe Esther's back, admiring the clean skin, a taut fabric defying age. Scars on bodies were normal, especially on old people, but scars from knives made her uneasy. *Green goo.*

"My sister-in-law, Dorothy, had it, too, almost died from it. Strange. Children don't get that sort of thing anymore."

Ruth's brother's pocketknife—the curved blade, the wicked point, and the smooth wooden handle—he'd carried it every-where, fiddled with it, picked his cuticles bloody. She'd felt almost nothing, a diluted sting, a soft prick. Physical pain dimin-ishes when one is distracted by something worse. A vet can hold his hand in ice water longer while watching scenes of combat than of Julia Child chopping onions. "No, I don't think so." Ruth's hands shook with her thoughts. She steadied them between her thighs.

"No antibiotics back then." Esther bowed her head.

Ruth pressed the cloth against Esther's neck until she moaned with pleasure. Esther had never married. It made Ruth hesitate to think that she was the one to offer this, that most likely no one had ever touched this intimate spot where a pink birthmark, a jagged moon, crept into her hairline. She had seen movies where bodies were identified by some unique mark. Morbid—she knew she was morbid, all those murder mysteries she had read to old blind Miss Miller.

Ruth wrung the cloth. She already knew a lot about Esther Fiske. Esther had spent her whole life as a schoolteacher, sharing this house with her elderly mother until she died, a woman named Judith, a very wealthy woman and much more attractive than her daughter. Watching them for years, Ruth knew about all the Fiskes, where they lived, marriages and births, the money, and habits they held dear, until they became part of her own life. Fantasies morphed into memories. A whole history manufactured in Ruth's mind. Creating, editing, Ruth constructed her entire backstory, one in which her name was also Fiske.

Ruth had never been officially licensed as a caregiver. After working fifteen years as a hotel maid, she worked for six more as an assistant's assistant at the state-run nursing home. Back then, no one cared about the licensing. It was hard to find people to clean up the messes. She ate what they ate, chewing pointlessly, and thought often of how it would feel to be that old, still eating the mush, the grayish beans dissolving in her mouth, the way they slid down the throat. She had decided one day, when a tinny pear had slipped over her tongue, the syrup pooling in her cheek, that she'd never be there. Up at Pacific Palisades, standing on the cliff, in full view of the ocean, where everything is green and pretty, air infused with citrus blossoms, a breeze in her face, she'd jump.

In 1986, "Management" terminated her. Too many residents were dying under her care. Turning to leave Management's office, she'd glanced back to see him standing behind the desk with his fat pink hand holding a file folder to his chest. She'd said, "They're all dying. You are dying." Management, mouth slack, eyes fearful, had looked at her as if she were an apparition.

Sometimes Ruth missed the nursing home, a little. It seemed those old people were better when she was around. They'd look up, straighten their shirts. They'd look a little less tired, a little younger, kind of like real people again, not just bodies. But the freelance work had proved better—no other employees, no bosses, no extra human interaction.

Esther lifted her thick, soft arms, propping them on her knees so that Ruth could wash beneath. Heavy, blue-veined breasts hung into the water, pitiful, never having fulfilled their purpose. One hand drooped down. A ring with a large red stone surrounded by diamonds hung on to the knuckle. *July.* Not the red Ruth had seen on front doors in magazines, with snow and Christmas wreaths. More like fruit, juicy fruit, shiny and warm under the California sun in the farmers' market where she'd taken a private client week after week until he died by her side watching baseball on TV just an hour after his tea, which he liked sweet, a taste Ruth also appreciated for a variety of reasons.

With a final breath, he'd fallen against her shoulder. Ruth had rested her cheek on his spotted bald head, where it remained for twenty-eight minutes (Ruth liked even numbers). She had known, of course, as the bat cracked, that it was only a game, that the world cared nothing for them. But Ruth liked games, so she had waited while a mantel clock ticked. His head had become heavy. A bird had chirped outside. When his face fell into her lap, she shifted, straightened the body, placed the arms neatly, and then the world had begun again.

Ruth focused on the ring. Esther would not die today. Again, the ring, the medium-red stain of a cranberry, just a hint of blue, not too much yellow. But no, not quite. Then, pleased with herself, she thought, *Bloodred.* Rich and thick, saturated, a gorgeous color.

Esther glanced at Ruth, then at the ring. "My mother's." Straightening it, she said, "She liked anything red. It's from the Mogok region in Burma, best rubies in the world. We called it the Crimson Flame, but the official color is Pigeon Blood." Esther expelled a breathy laugh. "My father bought her anything she wanted."

The exquisite stone sitting on the withered, androgynous hand of an old woman made the hand look unworthy. Something welled up. The ring, almost rude, intense, shifted like an elegant woman in a red, silky dress standing in a shabby room.

Esther's eyelids fell, heavy. "It should stay with the bloodline when I pass."

Feigning disinterest, Ruth whispered, "It's nice." But it wasn't nice. It was extraordinary.

Esther's eyes closed. Her chin dipped and her body swayed. Ruth put more soap on the cloth and worked the lather from elbow to wrist, then wiped it over her hand. The ring fell, landing with a faint tink on the bottom of the tub.

Esther's eyes remained closed, so Ruth reached into the water and slipped her hand under Esther's thigh. As she held the ring, the diamonds flickering wildly, it snarled at her. She rubbed the stone on her pants, then slid it onto her finger, taming it. Platinum, heavy, too heavy for white gold. She pushed it into the front pocket of her pants, then stood to get a towel.

Esther woke with startled eyes. "I must have dozed." She chuckled while Ruth moved to wash her legs and feet. "I feel like a baby. It's so embarrassing."

Ruth placed a cloth over Esther's scant pubic hair. "Just think of it as a spa treatment." Ruth hated the loss of dignity, when the body becomes a burden, the shame. *Candy clouds.* And since no option existed to truly root out this feeling, which Ruth had also experienced about her own body, she had learned to simply cover it up and look away.

"I guess, but I was never into that sort of thing. Not like some women, not like my sister-in-law, who just got her eyes lifted." Esther's eyes widened. "She's eighty-three!"

Dorothy. "Maybe she's lonely."

Esther shook her head. "Never. She lives in a fantasy world filled with handsome men and movie stars. She thinks she's friends with Angela Lansbury, who lives near here, you know." Esther looked at her hand. "What was I saying?"

Ruth peered into Esther's downturned face, looking blankly into the water. "Dorothy, you were telling me about Dorothy."

Esther looked up. "Dorothy, yes, did I mention her name?" Esther waited a moment, searching Ruth's face. "She got wrapped up in the Hollywood scene and the money. She likes my last name." There was a hint of snobbery in the way Esther raised one brow. "Dorothy was my brother Eugene's wife. I had two brothers, Eugene and Frank. They've passed." Esther's face flushed. One earlobe, too long, was covered with bubbles.

Ruth said, "Is the water too hot?" But she wanted to keep talking about Dorothy. She'd been watching her, driving by her house regularly.

Esther looked back into the water as if deep in thought or, more likely, void of thought. Her feet ballooned with the water distortion, purple veins and twisted toes.

Ruth said, "When did Eugene pass?" But she knew. *May 20, 1996.*

Esther raised her head. "Nineteen ninety-six, I think."

"Do you see Dorothy much?" Ruth had been patient, but it was now about time for Dorothy to need someone. Eighty-three was the downturn year, a bit of forgetfulness, that extra effort to rise from a chair, a weak knee. Ruth would never be eighty-three. She would be eighty-two, then eighty-four. She was never thirteen, or any odd number after that. Next year, she would be sixty-six, again.

Esther wiggled her toes. "Eugene was such a nice man. Just a nice person. Never hurt a fly."

Ruth agreed. His face, even dead, the skin waxy and bulging over the collar of that ridiculous tuxedo, had looked kind. He was kind. The year before his death, just seven words had passed between them. Ruth wished it were six or eight, but it was, unfortunately, seven that had formed his question. Thoughtful and patient, he'd waited for her answer.

Esther turned to look at Ruth. "Doesn't seem like that type is around anymore. Everyone has to prove something or be some-thing. What's wrong with just being nice?" Esther wiped soap-suds from her arm. "Eugene just wanted to make Dorothy happy. Like my father that way, but not as ambitious. Never needed to be." Esther laughed. "He got so fat."

Ruth shifted because the ring bit into her hip.

Esther slumped to hide her bare chest. "He always had food

dribbled down his front. It drove Dorothy crazy. She'd be dabbing his shirt while he waited, just pleased with the attention." Esther stared at the black mold spreading across the pink wall tile. She touched her finger where the ring had been. "They seemed happy even without children. Dorothy blamed Eugene. Something with his sperm count. I wouldn't know." Esther shrugged. "He had three front teeth. Have you ever heard of such a thing?"

Ruth looked to the window, then back to Esther. "Maybe you should invite Dorothy to dinner. It's not good for either of you to be alone so much." Ruth smiled with her lips closed to hide her offensive teeth, eroded and stained by sugar and smoke. "I'm happy to cook."

Esther nodded. "We haven't gotten together in a while."

Sitting on the side of the tub, facing Esther, Ruth pulled a strand of hair from Esther's cheek and tucked it behind her ear. She wished someone, anyone, would have done this for her, just once, such a small thing. That someone might care enough to notice a stray hair, a tear, a bruise. "I could make some of your recipes."

Esther's mouth gaped, revealing a crooked smile. "Your eyes." She swallowed. "They're extraordinary."

Ruth's green eyes had been described as evil, divine, and everything in between. She looked away, sensing they might betray her in some way, but then she looked back at Esther because it felt nice to be seen for something good, something attractive.

But Esther's face contained fearful curiosity, as if admiring something she shouldn't, the complex shading of a bruise or the luxuriant color of blood. Ruth saw Eugene clearly now in the face of his sister, kind, loving. *Why Dorothy?* Remembering that Dorothy had not been his first choice.

Esther looked to the window and shifted her body as if needing relief from a vision that was too intense to endure for long. "That would be nice."

Ruth gripped Esther under both biceps. She was still strong in her arms, all that lifting of bodies, dead or alive, even though her legs felt weak and her lungs were no good. Esther planted one foot onto the bath mat, then the other. Ruth reached for a towel. A necklace, which Ruth kept hidden under her shirt, dangled in front of Esther's inquiring eyes. Esther, gazing into the stone, smiled, then nodded. Ruth assumed Esther was still thinking about dinner, but her face held something more, a serene look of deep satisfaction, which seemed an exaggerated response for Ruth's simple suggestion.

Ruth tucked her pendant back inside her shirt before she discreetly wrapped Esther in the towel. The remaining Fiskes together in one room—Ruth let the satisfaction settle before giving Esther a gentle squeeze. "Yes, just like the old days."

CHAPTER 3

OUTRAGEOUS ORANGE

Esther and Ruth spent that afternoon in Esther's 1970s kitchen, dark oak and yellow, looking through dog-eared recipe books, the cardboard corners soft and split, the spines cracked, red-and-white check, that familiar book everyone's mother had but Ruth had only seen on TV.

"Paprika was exotic back then." Esther set the book aside and reached for an index card box. After flipping open the gray metal lid, her large fingers ran through the handwritten cards. "Swedish meatballs!" She pulled out a grease-stained card, blue ink smeared. "Mother's recipe." Looking at Ruth, she said, "Could we make these?"

Ruth placed her hand on Esther's back. *Heat.* "Why, sure we can."

Esther's breath quickened. Ruth removed her hand because she was never sure how people felt about touch. A light brush could agonize, whereas a heavy blow might numb, but most excruciating was nothing at all, so Ruth returned her hand because she was Eugene's sister, after all.

"Mother's grasshopper pie!" Esther held the card. Smiling, she put her thumb on a green fingerprint stain, biting her lip when it trembled.

Ruth inhaled the faint scent of Esther's rose lotion. "That sounds fun." And it did. Ruth had never baked with her mother, more accurately, her foster mother, who had always been at movie auditions. She'd been in a couple of obscure movies back then but wanted desperately to play the part of "Eve" in an upcoming film. Ruth heard about Eve all the time; everything was about Eve. Ruth was only seven. She saw the film, *All About Eve*, alone three years later, in 1950, with Eve played by Anne Baxter. From then on, Ruth had (privately) referred to her foster mother as Eve.

Esther set the recipe card on the counter. "We're all Scandinavian, my family and Dorothy's. Dorothy knew our food, lutefisk and lefsa. She didn't come from any real money, and her mother, Inga, didn't care for the Hollywood scene. Too religious. But my mother thrived here, the glamour, the parties."

Ruth leaned against the counter. "Where's Dorothy from?" *Chicago.* Ruth knew how to keep old people talking. Listening had always proved useful.

Esther looked out the kitchen window into the tropical overgrowth of her backyard. "Chicago, like my father. Dorothy's father worked for the telephone company. It was a good enough job, but there was no . . . accumulation of wealth. My father was in real estate; the money built up. Then he came to California and did the same thing. I grew up over in Brentwood. We lived across from Judy Garland, although I was out of the house by then."

Ruth looked to the window where Esther's eyes had been. She noticed the blooms of a red hibiscus tree. She'd wanted the ruby slippers, not because they were pretty—*red sequins picked from Eve's costume, glue, scuffed Mary Janes*—but because she'd imagined the freedom of clicking her heels and traveling to Oz, or to anywhere.

"Oh yes, we were in the middle of it all. Dorothy attended one of Judy's parties. She even saw her bedroom." Esther turned to look at Ruth. "It was green."

Ruth picked up the meatball card and scratched lightly at a crusty stain. Ancient crust. 1950, perhaps? Ruth felt a memory form in her mind as if fragments floating in space suddenly aligned.

Ten years old, her lacy yellow dress, finger knuckle-deep in grasshopper pie. Dorothy had pressed her thumb to a meatball, testing for doneness, then carelessly picked up the recipe card. Aunt Esther shooed her away; then Judith told them both to stop fussing and let the maid finish.

Later, when Esther was resting upstairs, Ruth rolled pale meat between her wet palms The precise mixture of beef and pork made a sticky sound like a paint roller. *Horsemeat. Bad children get horsemeat.* The strong taste of meat can conceal. Meatballs are perfect containers for hidden things, vessels for pills. She smashed the meat, then formed it again, rolling, the sound. *Humans are just meat.*

Ruth noticed the color variations in the meat—red, white, pink. As a child, she had three friends. They'd run the schoolyard, whinnying, kicking grass, and swishing their tails. Ruth was a black stallion with a long mane. Her friends, palominos. When Ruth was almost ten, she'd drawn her birthday party invitations with kittens, rainbows, and horses. Eve had been distracted with another audition, but Ruth didn't mind planning the party herself. Their neighbor, Miss Miller, brought cupcakes decorated with pink frosting and jellybeans. A tea party—Ruth wore a dress and braided her hair. She borrowed fancy china from Miss Miller's cabinet and wrote her friends' names on place cards with her calligraphy pen. She waited with Miss Miller in the living room. After a while, Miss Miller took a thick book from her purse and read about a ten-year-old orphan who was treated cruelly by her aunt and sent away. *Jane,* Ruth liked that name. An hour passed, then another. The house remained quiet. The frosting on the cupcakes hardened, but Miss Miller kept reading. When the light changed, dimming, she closed the book and said, "Should we have a cupcake?" Miss Miller lit ten candles, five on each small cake, and sang. She gave Ruth a gold poodle pin with a rhinestone collar and sparkly red eyes. "Ten is a special year, Ruth. Ten is when a girl is her truest self." Ruth watched the pin catch light. "Ten is like a little window that opens between childhood and adolescence. Fresh air comes in. The sun shines bright. Everything is crystal clear. When you grow up, remember how that feels. It can direct your whole life."

The next day, three palominos galloped around while the chain fence surrounding the playground dug into Ruth's spine as she pressed her back against it. Clara, the one who'd first sat with Ruth at lunch and shared her Jolly Ranchers, pranced up with tiny hands bent down at the wrists. "Our mothers don't like your mother." Clara became a girl again, kicking the dirt with her saddle shoe. "She's trashy."

Ruth said, "She's going to be a movie star." The palomino reared back and pawed at the space between them with hand-hooves. "Something's wrong with you, too. You can't play with us." Ruth sank down and wrapped her arms around her bent knees. "She's not my real mother." Clara ran away. Ruth's stomach plunged, not from Clara's words, but from her own.

When she'd stood and turned from the playground, gravel crunching beneath her foot, to look through the fence, her face pressing against it hard enough to leave marks, smelling the iron, she noticed a pale-yellow convertible with plenty of shiny chrome parked on the street under a large palm tree. The driver, a nearly bald man with plump, smooth skin, watched her. Reaching his hand through the car window, he held something out. A few feet away, a gap in the fence offered an escape. Ruth had used it before. She slipped through and approached the car, noticing the red leather interior and oversize silver hood orna-ment, an airplane, maybe an eagle, flying at high speed. As she turned to look at the man, the thing he held flashed in the sun, a small foil-wrapped square. He said, "Happy birthday, Ruth," then reached it out farther. Ruth wondered how he knew her name, then stepped closer. It flickered as he twisted his wrist. A gold wedding band encircled his finger. He said, "There's mint cream inside." Ruth took the candy. The gold foil was banded with pretty green and pink tropical paper and printed with the words "The Niumalu Hotel, Honolulu, Hawaii." She still had that wrapper, her bookmark for years, smelling it when she needed to escape.

Ruth placed the last meatball in a bowl when the doorbell sounded a fancy chime. She went to the door.

A diminutive blonde woman wearing orange sunglasses the size of sand dollars waited outside. Dorothy held a wide smile. "Hello, Ruth."

Ruth stepped back. Dorothy's voice, the edge of it, revealed a tone more consistent with meeting again than meeting for the first time. And Dorothy's eyes, knowing eyes, examined Ruth's face as if Ruth had done something that only the two of them knew about. This notion initiated a new scenario. Ruth endured a wave of panic upon realizing the consequences. Dorothy seemed to recognize her.

Dorothy moved into the house with tiny steps. High wedge sandals strapped to her feet resembled the hooves of a pig. The white straps cinched, cutting off circulation, making her toes a dark-purplish color, *dead*. Nails were painted coral, *flamingo*, like the smoked salmon Ruth had just bought at Gelson's. A bright floral top flowed to her knees. Her hair was fixed big and smooth, rolled under, firm like a helmet. Cheeks flushed fuchsia. Eyes, pale and milky blue, tender, contrasted sharply with the dark outline of plum, enhanced with black mascara. Eyebrows curved into steep arches. Lips, *Watermelon Laffy Taffy*.

Adorned. Decorated. Dorothy sparkled like the one Christmas tree—plastic—Ruth remembered as a child, before her foster father left, dripping with globs of tinsel and flaking red metallic balls. But Dorothy's jewelry did not look cheap.

The loose skin of Dorothy's hands, veins rolling over tendons, led to an exquisite bracelet. At least an inch wide, the piece was embedded with large sapphires and showcased diamonds forming geometric shapes. Dorothy moved the bracelet down her arm, placing it precisely on her thick wrist, then walked past Ruth toward the kitchen.

Ruth followed in Dorothy's trail of perfume. *Expensive.* Keeping the right distance, but always close enough to hear and be ready—her clients had appreciated this.

Dorothy squealed, "Swedish meatballs!"

When Dorothy and Esther finally settled in the living room, Ruth heated the oil, then waited for it to smoke before adding the meatballs. They sizzled, releasing the musty scent of rendered fat. Esther had taught her to gently nudge them with a wooden spoon, careful to keep the brown crust intact. Ruth mashed the potatoes and stirred the lingonberry sauce. Real food, mostly loving intentions. Ruth felt good.

Dorothy's voice drifted into the kitchen. "How is Ruth working out?"

Esther said, "Wonderful! She's only been here a few times, but she's good, trustworthy. We talk. It's nice."

Ruth stepped closer to the entrance of the dining room, where she could hear better.

Esther whispered, "She's had a hard life."

"Oh?" Dorothy sounded eager.

Ruth knew the type, those who enjoy hearing of others' pain. She had only mentioned a few things to Esther, nothing big.

Esther said, "She didn't have proper parents. She told me she learned to cook quite young because she had to. And she smokes."

Dorothy made a tsk-tsk sound. "Not in the house?"

"No, outside. She sneaks out, but it drifts in, and she smells of it."

"She does look rough," Dorothy said. "Her skin's not good.

She looks kind of Mexican with that black hair. How did you find her?"

Ruth looked down at the ragged ends of her hair. *A witch. A stallion.* She imagined Esther's thoughtful eyes adrift, as if trying to remember.

"Actually, she found me. I was at Gelson's, having trouble with the cart. You know how those wheels stick. She fetched a new one and moved my things."

"You don't know a thing about her." Dorothy's rings clinked on glass.

Esther said, "In the parking lot, she loaded my groceries. I took her business card."

Dorothy cleared her throat. "She has a business card? What's her last name?"

Esther hesitated; the silence lingered. "I don't recall it just now."

"Well, I'd want some references. I saw her looking at my jewelry."

Ruth stepped into the dining room to replace the silver salt and pepper shakers she'd used in the kitchen. *Fiske, Ruth Fiske.*

The living room was just across the main hall. Ruth moved to the side, near the hutch, where she was hidden from their view, but she could see the women in the reflection of the mirror hanging over the buffet table.

Esther glanced into the dining room, then turned her attention back to Dorothy. "Of course she was looking at your jewelry! Eugene spoiled you."

Dorothy looked to the dining room, to the salt and pepper shakers. "You have some nice pieces, too. I read in the *Palipost* about jewelry being stolen from estate sales in the neighborhood."

Esther leaned forward. "Dorothy, you should consider hiring her." She glanced into the dining room.

Dorothy crossed her arms. "I don't need a caregiver!"

Esther pulled her skirt over her knee. "Think of her as a personal assistant, a lady's maid, like the English upper class."

Dorothy chuckled. "Well, maybe. I would like a driver. Several people at the club have personal assistants, just to cook and clean and manage things, that's all."

Ruth stepped back into the kitchen, to the stove, where she shifted the meatballs and calmed herself with a few deep breaths as Miss Miller had taught her. She would dismiss Dorothy's initial expression of recognition. Things were going precisely as Ruth had hoped. Esther had hired her, and now Dorothy would, too. Besides, even if Dorothy had recognized her, it didn't mean she knew who she was.

Ruth continued to poke at the meat. *Proper parents.* She wasn't sure what Esther had meant, exactly. If mothers were supposed to be Betty Crocker, and fathers were supposed to come home each night, then no, she did not have proper parents. Ruth rarely spoke of herself with clients but had told Esther a few things because she'd asked. It had been nice to hear words outside her head, for once.

Ruth popped her head into the living room. "Dinner's ready."

"Wonderful, Ruth." Esther's face beamed, and for a moment, Ruth felt something. An image of Eugene's smiling face appeared in her mind.

Esther and Dorothy stood and moved into the dining room, where Ruth pulled out the chair on each end of the large dining table.

Once they were seated, Esther looked at Dorothy's wrist. "You're wearing the bracelet. Mother adored it. When Eugene was born and Father gave it to her, I was only seven. Mother screamed. I didn't understand that she was happy. The sapphires are two carats each. Cornflower Blue is the best color."

Dorothy looked at Ruth, who stood in the doorway leading to the kitchen. She flicked her hand. "Go on, Ruth."

Ruth looked down and noticed the floor where a silver metal strip separated the linoleum flooring of the kitchen from the wood of the dining room. When Ruth was seven, her brother had told her he wasn't actually her brother. That mean smirk, eyes wicked, eager to say it, not like he was sorry or anything. Eve ran around in a costume she'd slept in while fighting remnants of an elaborate hairdo. Her brother pulled her aside and pinned her to the wall. Wet lips moved to form words, breath thick with Orange Crush soda. A stray cat, she was a stray cat, like that tabby one they found with one eye and a chunk of ear missing. His parents took her because they got paid. She was a foster kid. Ruth had walked away, throat tight, the room spinning. The ground had broken. Falling, her body hardened for impact. Glancing across the room to their mother, his mother, slamming dishes into the sink, clown-faced with garish stage makeup, Ruth saw, when Eve's exasperated raccoon eyes fell on her, that it was all true.

Ruth returned to the kitchen to sprinkle candied pecans across the two salad plates and add a bit of blue cheese. Esther said Dorothy loved blue cheese. *Pretty*. They'd be pleased.

Ruth wiped dressing from the edge of the plates before taking them to the dining room. Dorothy lifted her hands, which twinkled in the light of the chandelier. Ruth draped a napkin over her lap like she'd seen done at nice restaurants when other clients had treated her, but she was distracted as she watched the spectacular bracelet slip up Dorothy's arm. To wear something so beautiful, hold it, feel its weight, Ruth ached. She returned to the kitchen but stayed close to the door.

Dorothy said, "Did you get your estate figured out?"

Esther said, "No. I only have the one niece, Frank's daughter. Poor Frank. Wanted a boy. Mother hoped to dote on a whole slew of grandchildren, and all she got was this one, who just isn't very nice. Sorry, I know you said it was Eugene who had the problem."

Dorothy cleared her throat as if to dismiss the topic of whose body was infertile. "You've told me what she is."

Esther paused. "Did I?"

"So that won't work. She and her girlfriend would blow it all on art. A Georgia O'Keeffe painting." Dorothy chuckled.

Forks scraped plates.

Dorothy said, "There's always charity. I've promised Saint Olaf's a large amount. The head of the school flies out and takes me to dinner. They're dedicating a building to me, the Fiske Atrium. We're designing it together. It will have—"

"Maybe I'll give everything to you since I'm sure to go first," Esther interrupted.

Ruth returned to the stove to stir the deep-red sauce. A little attention, dinner, is that all it would take? Ruth knew, of course, that she had little to offer Dorothy, no atriums or placards bearing the Fiske name. But Ruth knew her skills.

Ruth mashed the potatoes with a fork. This niece, Frank's daughter. Ruth hadn't known about the other niece, the gay niece. Dorothy's opinion of her was to be expected. Ruth wasn't surprised, but it did make her think of David.

Ruth dropped a few pats of butter into the mashed potatoes, then added some milk. Thick and creamy. Ruth watched the yellow butter swirl into the potatoes as she stirred. In 1968, Ruth had watched the playground from her car, window open. Alone, her son, David, had leaned against the fence. Eleven and skinny, her own dark hair fell over his eyes. A few boys sauntered toward him. *Good,* she'd thought. *It's good to have friends.* The boys laughed and kicked gravel. One threw a rock. Blood ran down David's chin. He spat into his hand. Another bounced off his head. As he staggered away, more boys closed in on him. Blood ran through his fingers and down his wrist. A boy yelled, "Fag! He's a fag! Got no mama. Poor little fag with no mama to wipe his ass!" The boys hooted and made the circle tighter. David slid around, trying to escape, but every time he got close, another rock came, so he limped to the center, crouched down, and wrapped his arms around his head. A boy with orange hair stepped closer and shouted, "Disappear!" David pulled tighter into a ball. Orange raised a large rock and slammed it into the back of David's head. He fell over, and his hands went limp. Ruth opened her door and vomited. Wiping her mouth, she looked up. Orange. Teachers broke up the circle. The nurse helped David. The school grounds emptied. When school let out, she followed Orange home. On the front porch, there was a bench, a sleepy dog, a wooden sign with WELCOME carved into it, and a milk box. After being stricken with a strange illness, Orange died the following day. His siblings also became sick and died, all but one, who was allergic to milk. The authorities blamed an isolated outbreak of bacteria "of some sort." But the kids that day saw too close a connection, too-perfect timing, too much justice to have occurred without superhuman intervention. David became known as "Demon David" and was left alone.

Tortured for years with the belief that his thoughts held destructive power, David had found relief within the Catholic Church, which offered redemption through exorcism. He had marked the occasion with a cross tattooed on the back of his neck.

CHAPTER 4

THE BOOK OF RUTH

The next morning, after a fairly late night with Dorothy and Esther, Ruth slid open the narrow window of her apartment to place a dense ball of Wonder Bread, formed between her fingers, on the concrete ledge three stories high because she believed that even the most detestable creatures are worthy of human kindness.

The pigeon hesitated, bobbed his head, then turned so that his red eye focused on the bread. The bird's yellow, scaly feet stepped closer. His greenish-blue, iridescent neck shone in the sunlight. Closer, the pigeon used his bright, red eye to inspect the bread. Quick, he flashed its redness at Ruth, then back to the bread, snatching it with his beak.

"I'm Ruth." She set another bread ball on the ledge just as someone knocked, more accurately, pounded on her door. Ruth turned to look at the door, where a sunburst mirror, circa 1970s, was permanently glued. Ruth held her breath and waited with her hand still hovering near the window.

The mirror had come with the apartment. Ruth hadn't noticed it until after she'd moved in because when she'd first toured the space, the door had been open, hiding the mirror. It wasn't until she'd settled that she'd finally noticed the gilded rays of varying lengths bursting from the center circle where it had framed her face. She'd imagined herself to be an angel with a halo, or sometimes a goddess, and on other days she was the Statue of Liberty. But Ruth had finally settled on Sunshine Girl because a kind man had called her that when she was a child.

The knocking, now softer, came again. "Ruth, are you in there?" The woman's voice was tinged with panic. Ruth reached to the back of her head and dug at a vertical scar buried beneath her black hair until she felt it weep with blood.

Ruth had lived in the building for twenty-five years, alone. The four-story concrete structure in east Los Angeles, built in 1937, was used as a jail until 1970, when it was converted into low-income housing. Ruth had moved in right after her own thirty-day stint in prison during the summer of 1981. A new neighbor, the insistent woman at her door, had moved in just a month ago.

High-pitched and frantic, the voice penetrated through her door. "Open up, Ruth! It's important."

Ruth looked back at the pigeon, which jutted his neck in and out while shuffling his feet along the ledge. She glanced at the blood beneath her fingernails, then pushed herself from the kitchen chair. As she approached the door, her face, encircled by the sun mirror, looked old and angry, with deep crevasses vertically dividing her forehead.

Ruth opened the door. Her neighbor, the same size and shape as Ruth, a ripe pear, midsixties, mixed race, with long, straight, platinum-blonde hair and curled purple eyelashes, stood in the hallway wearing a long, colorful, tropical-themed dress. She wore layers of necklaces, bracelets, and rings composed of shells and beads. All of it looked cheap.

The woman stepped toward the doorway, rattling the shells. "Ruth, I need you to come over to my place. I've had a vision. I need to read your cards right away."

Ruth closed the door, holding the knob firmly until only a small gap remained. "I can't right now."

The woman moved her face close to the gap. Ruth inhaled an odd mixture of exotic spices and floral scents. *Coconut.* The woman leaned in closer so that her crooked, amber teeth were framed by the open crack. "I won't charge you this time. Your life depends on it."

Ruth had concluded that this woman was not only crazy but also a very convincing scammer. "I don't believe in your witchcraft. Go away."

Through the crack, one of the woman's eyes expanded; the purple eyelashes spread wide. "Ruth! Please! It's about your future. I've seen it. We're soul sisters, remember?"

The woman was convinced that she and Ruth had been sisters in another life, but Ruth didn't believe in things like that because her son, David, had told her it was evil. Ruth shut the door and walked back to her table, where she took another slice of bread from the bag. She squeezed honey from a plastic bear-shaped bottle onto the bread, sat down, rolled it up, and took a bite.

Two rooms created her third-floor apartment, a bedroom (with a bathroom) and a living/dining/kitchen area. Ruth sat in one of two kitchen chairs that she'd placed around a square metal folding table with a brown plastic covering that was perpetually sticky. She took another slice of bread and formed more balls. She tried to make them the exact same size and shape, like hail, because it was satisfying for Ruth to accomplish this small task, which most people would find tedious, useless, or boring. Ruth stood to line them up on the ledge, then waited for the pigeon to return. It wasn't long before he appeared from somewhere above with a swoosh of his wings before settling to eat.

Ruth looked into the pigeon's eye. "You have pretty eyes. Most people wouldn't like red eyes, but I do because they remind me of Red Hots." Ruth spaced the remaining balls evenly along the ledge. "You probably wouldn't like them. They're pretty spicy." Ruth watched the aqua iridescence of the pigeon's neck shimmer in the sunlight. She thought of a Hawaiian lagoon she'd seen on a day she'd also looked pretty, her eyes done up with purple shadow and liner. "I used to take care of a woman named Olivia at the nursing home where I worked. She gave me a book called *The Color Purple*. She said it was good." The pigeon snatched up another bread ball. "I like thinking about colors."

Ruth glanced at her TV, where *The Oprah Winfrey Show* was playing. "Oprah just got a crayon named after her. No surprise, it's called 'The Color Purple,' described as 'vibrant blue violet.' But I like yellow. Your feet are very nice, too. I'd say bumblebee yellow." Ruth took a cigarette from the right pocket of her cardigan and a lighter from the left. "The original Crayola crayon name from 1903 wasn't yellow; it was 'Lemon Yellow.' Nothing is ever *just* yellow." Ruth lit her cigarette while watching Oprah. "Anyway, I finally got around to reading the book. The main character, this poor woman, Celie, had a hard life, with a lot of bad things happening to her, so she talked to God, wrote letters. David always told me that God waits for us, but I don't know what he meant."

The pigeon looked up and down, then all around, until Ruth set more bread on the ledge. She smoked while staring out her window, beyond the littered street, the graffiti-covered cement wall, and the railroad tracks, up into the blue sky. "I don't know how to talk to God."

Ruth stood and opened one of five kitchen cabinets that she'd painted pineapple yellow. Everything in her apartment was some shade of yellow, except for the walls, which were pale blue. She pulled a box of Lucky Charms from her cabinet. Most of the marshmallows, marbits, had been eaten, so she took out a handful of healthy pieces to lay them on her table. "Can I call you Marbit?"

Marbit flew in, landed on the table, and pecked at the cereal.

Ruth sat in her chair and watched a thin figure wearing

baggy pants and a black hoodie stumble across the street. The figure fell into the gutter and rolled onto his back. "David always said God is my true father, but I believe my father, my real father, was a pretty good man. I'm not mad at him for leaving me. I did the same thing." Ruth took one last drag, then flicked the cigarette out the window. "Families repeat stuff."

Ruth heard footsteps in the hall. She held her breath. Scraping sounds came from the door. "Ruth!" Then, quieter, the woman whined. "Can't we be friends?"

Ruth went to her door and pressed her forehead against the sun mirror. She watched her image disappear as her breath fogged the glass. Her voice came out low and rough. "Leave me alone."

In a hushed voice, the woman, just inches away, said, "You don't understand, Ruth. I'm here to help you. Listen to me. I know things." Her voice lowered. "I know everything."

Ruth pounded the door with her fist. "You're a nutcase!" She walked back to her kitchen table, now covered with pigeons feasting. They simultaneously looked up. A few flapped their wings, then resumed eating. Marbit was larger than the other pigeons, and their feet were pink, not yellow. None of the other birds, unlike Marbit, had a thin white collar like a necklace.

Ruth turned when she heard footsteps. The neighbor woman stood near her open door, which Ruth had failed to lock. One eyelash had partially released and hung askew. Her white-blonde hair draped over her shoulders, and her lips were dark pink and tense. Her fingers were tipped with long orange nails curled into claws, and a green crystal, which hung around her neck, swung back and forth as if tracking time.

The woman looked at the pigeons, then back to Ruth. She raised one finger; the orange talon ticked at Ruth. "I'll get you evicted for this. Those are sky rats, don't you know? They're rats!"

Ruth looked at the pigeons. A few wandered around her kitchen. One was on the counter. They were beautiful—all the colors, the opalescence like a fish scale, a pearl, or maybe the mysterious flash of precious metal. She didn't want to think about what it really reminded her of, but then she did—the bittersweet memories of her children's eyes.

The woman stepped closer. "I know everything about you, Ruth. Everything. I know that they set you up here after you were released." She folded her arms across her ample chest, squeezing up her cleavage. "And I know why you got fired from the nursing home. Going from one prison to the next." She tipped her head back and flipped her hair off her shoulder. "I'll tell the landlord you're feeding rats. I'll tell. He'll evict you, and you'll never find another place!"

Ruth pulled another cigarette and the lighter from the pockets of her sweater, sat down, and crossed her legs. "That was a long time ago." She lit the cigarette and took a long drag before handing Marbit a piece of cereal.

"The rats, Ruth, the rats." The woman tapped her sandaled foot. Her toenails were also orange, and her sandals were hot pink and clunky. "Your only way out is to just fly away like one of your birds. Just fly away, Ruth. Go ahead, Ruth, jump." The woman flicked her hand at the window. "Jump, like your son. Jump and see what happens."

Ruth felt a rush of heat fill her face, a familiar sensation. The heat came every time someone mentioned David with cruel intentions. She removed the cigarette from her lips, then turned to the woman. She opened her mouth as if to speak, but instead, she pressed the burning orange butt to her tongue, where it sizzled a moment, then smoked. She felt no pain because the scar tissue that had formed there, the result of a cruel joke, had left it numb but not tasteless. Ruth scraped her tongue along her bottom teeth to rid it of ash, then spat on the floor in front of the woman's feet. Marbit jumped onto her shoulder and picked at her black hair. "David was a priest. Priests don't jump."

The woman's face contorted, then seemed to melt, as if the

heat inside Ruth, now subsiding, had been transferred to her own face. Ruth recalled that scene from *Raiders of the Lost Ark*. She liked Harrison Ford. He seemed different than most men.

Ruth picked up a Lucky Charm, a pink heart. Ruth thought of another movie, one of her favorites, maybe her very favorite. She hummed a song from *Mary Poppins*. More pigeons came into the apartment, eating and pooping. Another jumped on her other shoulder, and several gathered at her feet. Ruth hummed until the words to "Feed the Birds" came. Ruth sang and swayed her body. The pigeons appeared unfazed, as if Ruth were a tree in the wind. Ruth looked at the woman and smiled.

The woman backed away and ran from Ruth's apartment.

Ruth turned to Marbit; he'd jumped back onto the table. "My friend, Olivia, from the nursing home used to sing to me." Ruth continued humming. Marbit shifted from foot to foot. "Once, she asked me to shave her head. She sat down on her huge butt and rested her hands on those strong thighs and said, 'Do it.' Soon enough, her gleaming brown scalp surfaced. She smiled in the mirror and I smiled back, both of us looking at her reflection. She was beautiful! She said she felt free. Born again, like a brand-new baby. She wanted me to try it, too, but I told her I couldn't because I had a big ugly scar on the back of my head. That's when I started telling her things."

On the table, one pigeon started pecking at another. A gray feather flew up.

Ruth lit another cigarette. "David was *almost* a priest. He was still training." She sucked the blood from beneath her fingernails. "He said God loves everyone, even bad people who don't care about him." She took a long drag. "Surely, he loves some people more." Ruth blew smoke from the corner of her mouth. "David said I can't think a thought without God knowing it. My thoughts aren't too good. They just appear." Ruth turned to the window when a police car screamed by. "I read the whole Bible. I guess I wanted to impress David. I didn't even skip the parts where all the names are written one after the other. I couldn't pronounce them, but I still let my eyes fall on each one."

Marbit seemed interested in another pigeon. They pecked around and eyeballed each other.

Ruth watched ash fall from her cigarette. "There's a book in the Bible with my name. Something about a woman getting a new family, a new mother."

Some pigeons made their way to Ruth's harvest-gold couch, which backed up to the blue wall separating her apartment from her neighbor's. Marbit, turning back to Ruth, kept moving his head from side to side while staring at her, his red eye searching.

"I knew another woman when I was young, my neighbor, Miss Miller. She had a lot of books, mostly murder mysteries. She's dead now. I did just what she told me. I hope it didn't hurt." Ruth reached out to touch Marbit's head. "Why do pigeons have red eyes? Looks like blood."

Marbit flipped a piece of cereal in the air.

Ruth heard someone in the hall. A small piece of paper slipped through the crack beneath her door. It appeared blank. Ruth went to pick it up. She turned it over to find the word "MURDERER" written in bold, black ink. Ruth felt her stomach twist, *Orange*, before wadding it up. She looked at Marbit. "People are really lonely. It makes them do strange things like talk to themselves or wear purple eyelashes. I'm never lonely. I like to be alone." Ruth threw the paper in the trash, then looked at the wall over the couch, where she'd taped many of her drawings. Some were crooked, and the spacing wasn't right, but Ruth liked to look because they gave her hope.

Ruth found a white crystal-ball-shaped marbit on the table —a new addition for 2006. She rolled it between her fingers. "She's wrong, that crazy woman. I do have another place to go. A really nice place." Ruth believed this just as she believed everything David had told her, but her hand trembled.

CHAPTER 5

MANGO TANGO

A couple of weeks later, while Ruth was cleaning up after Esther's breakfast, the phone rang. Ruth answered it because Esther was upstairs. Dorothy said, "Is this Ruth?" Ruth confirmed, so Dorothy continued. "I'd like to hire you, Ruth, not like Esther, not as a caregiver, you understand, but as an assistant." Dorothy emphasized that last phrase, slow and clear.

Ruth smiled while rolling her thumb over the wheel of the lighter in the left pocket of her cardigan sweater. *Lady's maid.* "Of course."

Ruth had been in lots of old people's homes throughout the years, but when she stepped across the threshold into Dorothy's front entry, pausing in the stillness, faced with a menagerie of shiny objects, she realized how good it felt to finally be inside this house, which she'd driven by for years, watching Eugene and Dorothy coming and going, to movies and restaurants, to Gelson's. And then watching just Dorothy after Eugene had died.

Dorothy was proud of her things. Ruth could tell by the way

she watched to see which items would make her pause, so Ruth was careful. But she knew her eyes would catch. She loved things that shone or sparkled. As a girl, she had longed for the crystals her teacher hung in the classroom window and shiny wrapped candy in the drugstore.

The air in the living room loomed dim and cloudy, sitting for years, disturbed only by the breath of an old woman. The mauve carpet, a strange mix of bluish purple and pink, frayed where it met the parquet floor, where Dorothy had discreetly placed her canary-yellow sandal. *Lemon Drop.* Gray flesh infused with spider veins burst from around the straps.

Ruth, finally where she believed she belonged, would have little time for other clients, besides Esther, of course.

Ruth returned her focus to Dorothy's foot. She had rubbed countless old feet back to life, black, white, pink, sometimes gray. Her hands were good, warm, and strong, they all said. When the blood returned with color and heat, they'd sigh, and Ruth would know she'd done good.

Ruth looked up, into the living room. An ivory sofa with a smeared stain, as if much effort had been spent to remove it, sat forlorn beneath a faded Asian screen. The coffee table displayed a large art book with a bald man screaming on a bridge in front of a red sky. *Fever dream, swirly, moving.* Ruth tilted her head. *Horror.* Art should be pretty. Art should be what we want. Flowers, fruit, forests, oceans. Ruth's drawings, her quaint houses, precise and perfect, which she'd taped to the walls of her apartment, made sense. Everyone wants that, a handsome home filled with lovely things. But her eyes wouldn't leave the screaming man. Something rose in her chest—fear, grief, a mirror, a truth—and for a moment, Ruth was comforted by the thought that all people suffer.

A gilded mirror hung over the fireplace. Layers of drapery offered additional levels of security. Small side tables nestled against chairs with curvy legs, exhibiting countless figurines, mostly geishas, and plump children in baby-doll dresses or overalls. A large antique doll with a white porcelain face, rosebud lips, and blonde human hair sat in a green chair, a doll Ruth would have loved as a girl. *Jane.* At the nursing home, demented residents had squeezed dolls to their chests, soft, ratty ones with yarn hair.

Dorothy, standing behind Ruth, her voice low and rough, said, "That's Tiffany."

Ruth turned around. Dorothy stared at the doll, her face maintaining a silly expression, as if someone had slapped her awake. The corners of her mouth turned up, revealing just the tips of her incisors, and her eyes became wet. She panted slightly; her chest moved up and down. Ruth had seen this look before when a woman she'd cared for had recalled her dead child. The woman's eyes had fixed on nothing, a blank wall, with her face weighed down under some invisible force. Ruth cleared her throat. "Dorothy, you are quite the collector."

Dorothy straightened her cheeks, smiled, and jingled her bangles. "I like nice things."

Ruth was used to dark rooms, pulled shades, and dirty carpeting. When people got old, even wealthy ones, the things that once seemed nice, were nice, remained because of how they once were. The once-pristine fabric of the sofa was extraordinarily expensive, so it remained. The coffee table was Henredon, even with the outdated height and the 1960s hardware, so it remained. And the hand-painted Rococo lamps depicting pastel scenes of the French countryside, giant lampshades, dented and infused with dust—they remained because they were once good.

Ruth turned to look across the foyer and into the dining room, where an enormous crystal chandelier hung over the dining table.

Dorothy's rings scraped the switch plate. Light sprang from the crystal, refracting into rainbows along the walls of the dining room, which were lined with ornate gold mirrors. Ruth stared into the cluster of light hovering over the expansive table, scratched but still good, until she felt a breeze in her mouth and her eyelids flutter. Turning back to Dorothy, stunned by the brilliance, she had no words, so she closed her mouth and clenched her teeth against dark thoughts. *Cover your stupid, ugly face.*

Dorothy grinned and stepped closer, as if Ruth's reaction was to be expected, considering such an impressive display.

Ruth turned away. Her face had revealed too much. *Pumpkin.* But everywhere she looked, the warm glow of a silver tea set, the glossy wooden buffet, a gold-rimmed teacup, she paused. Her insides, a murky pond, stirred to reveal what hid beneath— green muck, jealousy, the need to possess, to defy her life and create a new one. A golden baby spoon flashed in the china cabinet. Beauty can be owned.

Dorothy stepped closer to Ruth. "Ruth? Is the chandelier too bright?"

Ruth composed herself. Old people want you to see their things to prove they had a life. Simple souvenirs, a child's room, lined up, neat clutter. But Dorothy did have nice things, expensive, irreplaceable things.

"The chandelier. Overwhelming, isn't it?" Dorothy placed her tiny hands on the curve of a dining chair and tapped her opal ring. Tilting her head back as if admiring a great monument, she said, "It was Judith's, Esther and Eugene's mother. I wouldn't dare leave it when she died." Dorothy grinned. "The realtor got angry when I took it." Dorothy paused, as if Ruth were to say something. "Judith had visited the Hall of Mirrors, the Palace of Versailles, you know?"

Ruth nodded but still looked up into the lights.

"Anyway, Judith wanted a chandelier just like that, so my father-in-law found an artisan in Paris who copied one of those chandeliers exactly, but smaller, of course. Notice the slightly almond hue of the crystals." Dorothy pointed at the small crystal bowls, the edges fluted like a flower, under each candlelight. "You know it's French by the shape of the bobeche."

Ruth continued to gaze into a teardrop crystal and thought

of Eve. Eve habitually wore a pinkie ring with a tiny white opal. Once, Ruth took it, wore it around, pretended. Pretty, the swirls of pink and green magically appeared in the light. She'd felt different, more valuable. When Eve caught her, a four-inch gash to the back of her head from orange-handled sewing scissors left a scar where hair never grew again. The Frankenstein slash required explanation, the story changing with her mood, with the state of her digestion. The truth was too humiliating, to be hated by one's mother. Eve was not her real mother, of course, but abandonment, by her birth mother, was worse than any physical assault. So in some sense, Eve was better than nothing. The blow had caused Ruth to drop the ring. It fell to the dizzy black-and-white tile. The opal broke. Opals are fragile, like the skull of a baby. A piece bounced away, landed near the toilet, winking. Ruth had touched the back of her head, wet; her hand, red. It crusted over. After her brother's bath, she dunked her head. The dingy water turned rust.

Ruth reached to the back of her head and ran her finger down the firm ridge of her scar. It felt similar to the cartilage edges of her ear. She watched as the crystals of the chandelier turned when a weak breeze, tinged with the scent of urine, moved through the room. Various shapes and sizes clustered tight. *Woozy.* Anchored in the center, in the very heart of the spectacle, was a long shard resembling an icicle, more like a weapon than a thing to be admired.

While looking up, Dorothy said, "I have the maid clean each crystal, one by one. I taught her to take a cup of lemon water and carefully move it from crystal to crystal. Then she wipes them with a soft cloth. Afterward, well . . ." Dorothy, the powder and rouge on her face glistening, caught in a state of ecstasy, as if witnessing the face of God, whispered, "It's spectacular."

Ruth slid her hand from her hair and returned it to the right pocket of her sweater, where she kept one cigarette. A fall from a tree. Jagged rock. A slip in the tub. Sharp corner. A careless tumble. Barbed wire. How does a girl get a gash on the back of her head without a weapon? There was no abuse in 1951. The child deserved it. A private matter. Silence. Later, Ruth told people another face had grown there, a cyclops. The eye peeked through her hair, always watching. "It comes in handy," Ruth explained to those who had not already turned in fear. "But Mother insisted the face be surgically removed." A quick part, fingers prodding, she would say, "The eye was here, where it dips in. Do you want to feel?" And so she was left alone.

Ruth watched light swell and quiver along the walls. Dorothy's voice went on, muffled, as if some words were said aloud while others were whispered inside her head. The chandelier, a thing created just for light and beauty. Ruth, adrift on emotion, swayed.

Steadying herself against a wall, Ruth stepped back into the foyer and glanced down a dark hallway with two shut doors. "Are those the bedrooms?" A storm, cold nausea, swept through her body, yet she wanted to see because one of them would be, should have been, hers.

Dorothy peeked around the corner. Her cheeks dropped. "You don't need to go down there," she said, her voice a low whisper. "My suite is upstairs."

Ruth noticed an old magazine cover, framed and hung on the wall near the stairs. The magazine was entitled *URD*. A drawing of a woman in a full-length olive-green dress and long, blonde hair with a decorative band around her head poured something from a bucket. Light, it looked like pouring light.

Ruth leaned in and noticed two white swans in the background. "What's this?"

Dorothy stepped closer. "Ah, yes. It was Judith's. A very rare find. This was a popular women's magazine in Norway in the 1940s and 50s, intended for the cultural elite. *Urd* is sometimes written as *Urth*." Dorothy paused. "Hmmm . . . those are all the letters of your name." Dorothy's eyes moved around the magazine, then back to Ruth. "Anyway, she is the goddess of fate in Norse mythology. The myth states that she is always present when a baby is born, to decide their future." Dorothy returned her focus to the illustration. "I never learned Norwegian, but Judith was fluent. She always had the new edition on her coffee table, but I just liked the art."

Ruth thought about rearranging the letters of her name, *Hurt,* then wondered what this goddess had thought of her being born out of wedlock, and if that's what had started all the bad in her life.

Dorothy headed up the stairs. Her feet slid onto each step, ankles wobbly. She gripped the handrail to pull herself rather than using her thighs. A fall down the stairs was always feasible. Lots of movies had that scene. *Dolores Claiborne.* Ruth followed her.

Dorothy tried to catch her breath.

Heart trouble?

Dorothy said, "Here's Eugene's office," as if he were in the next room.

A brass coatrack stood guard near the door, hung with several baseball caps, sweat-stained and cheap, with the plastic mesh back and the foamy front advertising things. The adjustable straps were still fastened to the size of his head. Ruth stared too long because Dorothy's face changed, smile gone, jowls quivering. Her lower eyelids went slack; the red inside shone, bright and gruesome like Marbit's. Dorothy looked up and down the coatrack before quickly running her eyes around the room.

A large wooden desk anchored the space, displaying extravagant desk things, a sharp gold letter opener, a leather pen holder. On the wall behind it, a cartoonish painting of a family hung, subjects all in a row, distorted, the paint lumpy.

"Eugene painted," Dorothy admitted before redirecting Ruth to the window.

But Ruth kept looking at the painting. "Is this your family?"

"It's supposed to be Eugene's. His parents, Esther, Frank, and here." Dorothy pointed to one of the boys, whose teeth stuck out like a rodent's. "He painted himself." She flipped her hand. The gold band of her ring caught the light. "Eugene never looked like that."

Ruth knew all about Eugene—what he looked like, that one of his three front teeth was dead center, and that he had died—because she'd watched him, from a distance, for years.

After Ruth was fired from the nursing home, she read the obituaries to kill time. If they mentioned the living relatives, the survived-by people, then she knew a widow might need help. She'd track this in a small spiral notebook and attend the funerals in a black dress she kept clean. Sunglasses, hair up, she stood near the back. It wasn't hard; the ones crying were spouses and children. If anyone asked, she was "an old friend," and this would inevitably lead to Ruth offering her business card for eldercare services. But she didn't find Eugene this way.

Ruth continued to study the painting. "It's nice." By habit, her own colored pencils were still kept sharp and in rainbow order. As a child, she'd taken a new color each day from school for her houses, which she created with help from *Good House-keeping*. When Ruth was nine, she had lined up her best drawings of pretty houses, hoping Eve might notice. They were good, too good. When her brother saw, he took out his little thing, held it like a weapon, and pissed all over them. She tried to save what she could, crawling to sweep them up, but a kick to her chest stopped her. As she lay on her back, with the hard press of his knee pinning her shoulder, sneering, glaring with mineral-blue eyes, the sea before a storm, he pissed in her face. Hot, surprisingly hot, fresh, young piss. She squeezed her lips, but it seeped in.

"He has an ocean view. You can see there." Dorothy tapped her berry-pink fingernail on the window. Dorothy's face went silly again, slapped, mouth ajar, one side drooping as if she might be suffering from a stroke.

Through the palms and shiny grapefruit leaves, a small spot of blue lingered beyond the cliff rising from the beach. Above the heat of LA and the fog of Santa Monica, Pacific Palisades was like a perch for those with means—with foresight.

Dorothy pulled her face together and moved to the door. "Come see the master suite."

Before leaving, Ruth scanned Eugene's office. Two matching leather chairs sat on an oriental rug with a frayed corner. *Chewed?* Tall shelving held children's books. Near the door, a rectangular hole cut through the floorboards. The furnace clicked. Air shifted up through the hole. Ruth inhaled. *Urine.* At the nursing home, she'd breathed it daily. *Accidents.* Old people sat in their own filth. It wasn't easy to know right away. Four hours on the skin and it turns, sour milk—no, more pungent, ammonia. It wasn't the burning smell that took her breath, but the profound loss of dignity, their downcast eyes, the shame.

A Baby Ruth candy wrapper lay inside the floor vent. Seeing her own name made Ruth pause. Her life had always been disjointed, but now, she felt different, as if something had snapped into place. "We should get a cover on that vent. Someone could twist an ankle."

Dorothy looked at the hole. "Eugene likes to keep that open. He says it allows for better air circulation."

Ruth glanced behind her as if Eugene was watching.

Dorothy walked down the hall and into the master suite. Ruth followed. Peach. *Jelly Belly Peach.* A closet with bifold mirrored doors stretched across a wall. A well-worn tufted chaise faded in the west window, like a lounging woman draped with silky nightgowns. At its foot sat heeled slippers with feathered poofs. The blond-wood dresser glittered with jewelry. Ruth stared at the spilled treasure chest while Dorothy's eyes glistened with pride.

"Do you like jewelry?" Dorothy smiled, a temptress, blue eyes sharp with desire.

Ruth looked away, fearing her face would betray her. "Yes." Helpless, she glanced back. Her eyes caught on ruby earrings.

"I've collected over the years." Dorothy seemed to notice

where Ruth's eyes landed. She handed Ruth a ruby earring. "I wore these to one of Judy Garland's parties."

Ruth took it. "Really?" Cool and heavy, it looked like it might taste sweet.

Dorothy picked through the remaining jewelry on her dresser. "We were friendly. She was having a rough spell, but we spoke awhile in her room, and then she was all right. We had an instant connection. I think she appreciated that I didn't fawn over her. Celebrities want to be treated like normal people. She was tired, and sometimes champagne can affect people. But I knew—one look at her face, and I knew she was glad I was there. A friend had come right when she needed it, not a fan, but a true friend, and I was grateful I could be that for her. Despite the medications and broken relationships, pure Judy was still inside. I saw it. Judy would always be eighteen and lovely, no matter what the world did to her." Dorothy's voice turned quiet, and her cheeks twitched. "Judy would always be Judy."

Ruth closed her mouth, which had watered a little, then swallowed. "I dressed as Glinda, the good witch, once, for Halloween."

Dorothy looked up. "Do you like *The Wizard of Oz?*"

Ruth swallowed again. "I like how she, Dorothy, I mean, got to go home in the end."

Dorothy's face went blank. "Home?" Dorothy fondled a diamond bracelet while watching the ruby in Ruth's hand. "Everyone likes coming home." She set the bracelet down and looked up to Ruth's face. "Well, anyway, I'm glad I could be that for Judy, a true friend."

Ruth gazed again into the ruby. *Heavy.* She closed her fingers around it and tightened her lips. Dorothy was teasing her. But Ruth was better at this game. She set the earring back on the dresser.

"Eugene bought me a lot, but now, I buy for myself. I'm worth it." Dorothy caught herself in the mirror and pursed her lips. "My jeweler makes custom pieces for me."

Ruth noticed the earring again, now safely out of her reach. The slick surface of each facet reflected flashes of cherry light.

"Hard to find two that match." Dorothy held the other earring in her outstretched palm. "But my jeweler is very good." She set it down next to its mate. "Esther has the most sublime ruby. It's truly breathtaking. Have you seen it?"

Ruth looked away, into a mirror. There were no mirrors in prison. Ruth hated mirrors like she hated knives; both had been cruel. That month, July 1981, had been a relief. Food, shelter, clothing, although she wished the jumpsuit hadn't been orange. Brownie day was good. She'd sneak a second one into her pants, and then her underwear looked like the residents' diapers at the home. Once, another inmate asked what she'd done. Ruth said she'd taken jewelry from a pawnshop. The woman had laughed. "Were you gonna sell it back to them?" Ruth looked down. A fly floated in her soup, with translucent wings like opals. The back door in the alley had been left open. Seeing no one, she'd gotten curious with the jewelry, put a few pretty things in her pocket. The inmate tipped Ruth's bowl, spilling the soup onto her lap. "You've done worse. I can see it in those green devil eyes." When the burning subsided, Ruth plucked the fly from her thigh and laid it on her palm. It staggered to its legs and flew away. Upon release, Ruth was warned, "There's no leniency with repeat offenders." So she moved on to estate sales in nice neighborhoods.

Ruth noticed Dorothy's bed, a poof of peach linens, tone upon tone of peach. Lots of pillows, another potential hazard, but mostly just dangerous for babies.

Ruth knew that apricot was different from peach, tangerine was another shade altogether, and then there was melon. Ruth didn't mind peach, even though it was a little like orange. But instead of mixing red and yellow, you mix pink and yellow, and the difference between pink and red is just white, so white makes orange turn peach. *Peach Jolly Rancher.*

"You won't need to be in here unless I need something."

Dorothy glanced back at her jewelry. "I keep this out since I wear it every day." Dorothy searched Ruth's face.

Ruth touched the bed. "This color is so warm, so elegant."

Dorothy looked at the bed. "Yes, I love mango."

Ruth returned her hands to her pockets and gripped her lighter. "Mango, yes, that's it."

Dorothy straightened a decorative pillow edged with ivory lace and ribbon. "I enjoy naming colors."

"I do, too." Ruth's neck softened. "I like naming them after candy." Embarrassed by her comment, Ruth's cheeks flushed hot. She looked away.

Dorothy sat on her bed and cocked her head to look up into Ruth's face. "Do you have a sweet tooth, too?"

A side of Dorothy emerged that Ruth hadn't expected, something real, an old lady who liked sugar. "Yes, I do."

"Eugene loves his sweets. I buy loads of Halloween candy, but he eats as much as he hands out." Dorothy chuckled, then sighed.

Ruth looked over her shoulder, then back to Dorothy, wondering why she kept referring to Eugene in the present tense. Eugene seemed real, too. They were real people who ate cheap candy and played silly games. Ruth took a step back. "I bet Eugene was a very nice man."

Dorothy struggled to swallow. She nodded. Even more real now, she appeared small and vulnerable, as if the shiny packaging were falling away and what remained was kind of ordinary. Dorothy, head down, fiddled with her wedding rings.

Ruth watched the diamonds break light into colors. She had loved one person. Her son was a grown man, thirty-two, when he'd found her again. They'd walked the beach. He was delicate but handsome, anyone would say, and had a really good job gardening at the Self-Realization Fellowship Lake Shrine in the Palisades. Looking up at the cliffs, Ruth had said, "Where the rich people live." *David.* She'd not named him, but she liked the name because she'd never known a David. An inverted cross tattooed the back of his neck; she noticed it as he gazed at the ragged edge. It confused her. He spoke about finding God like finding a father. She hadn't had the courage to tell him about his father, yet. David had said, "It looks like someone ripped the earth away, like breaking bread." Ruth thought it a clever thing to say, but she liked everything he said. She loved his carved face, his whispery voice, the mud caked to his pants, and the way he touched her hand, as if it were precious, as if she were forgiven. Offering him a peach Jolly Rancher, she said, "I'm going to live up there someday." He placed it on his tongue and closed his mouth while studying her face, serious as if he believed her. Leaning to kiss her cheek, eyes blue and green marble, shimmering, a mermaid tail breaking the surface, the peach scent warm and strong, he said, "I bet you will."

Dorothy's head popped up. Her focus snapped toward the doorway, and her face opened in shock. She pointed. "Did you see that?"

CHAPTER 6

EUGENE

Eugene believed he could hear the waves crash if he held his breath. He sat at his desk, watching the palms sway and the citrus swell, turning pinkish yellow and heavy, a little more each day. It was 1995, late March.

Sleepy. The dust swirled in the fading afternoon sun. A single sheet of paper lay in the center of his desk, a rental agreement. He took his brass pen from its holder and signed it. Replacing the pen, he moved the paper to his empty outbox before resting his right cheek on the desk. A whistle in his nose and a gurgle in his stomach broke the silence. He'd already eaten the tuna fish sandwich Dorothy had made for him that morning, with Ruffles and a pickle. Eugene liked to eat the pickle last. Strawberry sherbet waited in the freezer, but his head was too heavy.

Drifting, thinking of what he might paint next, he heard a sound, a slight movement along the floor, the faintest crinkle of paper. He raised his lids to enjoy the blue sky and passing clouds, like approaching ships with great sails.

The sound alerted him again. Lifting his head, he noticed the oily print of his profile on the blotter. Dorothy would not be happy. Squinting, he saw two mounds, just like Alfred Hitchcock's self-portrait sketch. Dorothy had loved *Dial M for Murder*. Eugene drew a nose, lips, and finished the curve of his head, adding three lines for hair. After signing, he released the sheet. He was smiling, planning a frame while reveling in a great sense of accomplishment, when the crackling sound came again. He looked over his desk.

Near the door, shiny black eyes stared back at him. Large round ears, pink inside, a long snout, white whiskers, and a tail. "Well, hello there." The rat held a silver candy wrapper in its mouth, taken from Eugene's hidden stash. Eugene shifted his foot, and the rat scampered behind a chair. He stood and walked around his desk. Down on all fours, he said, "Do you like candy, too, little fella?" Eugene crawled closer, peering into the shadows. The rat darted, bouncing alongside the bookshelves, then disappeared into the floor vent where a wooden slat had been chewed away.

CHAPTER 7

ATOMIC TANGERINE

A couple of weeks passed. Ruth had been making excuses to stay later at Dorothy's house to avoid her neighbor, who'd become relentless in her pursuit to intimidate Ruth if she wouldn't comply with her requests to have her future told. But Ruth also wanted to be at her apartment because she had developed an authentic interest in pigeons— researching and reading, running her own experiments to observe their intelligence and behavior, noticing changes in poop color and consistency based on what she fed them, and so on. She missed them when she was not there and worried about their safety.

While at Dorothy's, Ruth had tried her best to gain Dorothy's trust by doing everything right. Ruth listened to her babble on about her past boyfriends and breakups, her clothes, her eight sets of china for all occasions, her special relationship with Judy Garland, and of course, her jewelry. Ruth had mentioned almost nothing about her own life, and Dorothy had never asked. As uncomfortable as it made Ruth to talk about herself, she knew she would need to equally participate for their relationship to grow. The easiest way for Ruth to live in Dorothy's house was for Dorothy to invite her, and then she could simply wait until Dorothy died. Old people can die in a variety of ways. Ruth had learned over the years that most people never questioned the exact manner of death in a person over eighty. Although Ruth preferred to live alone, she could endure sharing for a while. But to make things clean, the best-case scenario would be for Dorothy to leave her the house, officially, in her will.

Ruth prepared a proper tray, then she served Dorothy tea with the Fiske silver and Dorothy's wedding china in the living room. Dorothy sat on the sofa with her ankles crossed. She stared into the cup as Ruth poured her tea. When Ruth backed away, Dorothy picked up the floral cup and sipped with her eyes fixed upon the gold tweed drapery opposite the sofa.

Ruth stood near the window. "Should I open the curtains?"

Dorothy, still focused on the window, said, "No."

Ruth dabbed at the mantel with the feather duster Dorothy had insisted she use. Dust billowed up, then settled. "Are you sure?"

Dorothy sat motionless. Her profile revealed her age, the turkey neck, the melting jowls.

Ruth picked up the teapot. "It's a beautiful day."

Dorothy finally looked at Ruth. "OK, maybe open them a little."

Ruth struggled with several cords, pulling back the layers until, finally, a few inches of sunlight spilled through.

Ruth wondered if Dorothy was unhappy with her. She'd been good, done everything right, but Dorothy was still sharp. She noticed everything—the arrangement of the cookies, the temperature of the tea, the way Ruth folded towels.

Dorothy flicked her hand. "Ruth, go fetch my wrap, the periwinkle one on my chaise."

Ruth climbed the stairs and entered Dorothy's bedroom. The jewelry had been put away. She searched the bathroom for medicine bottles, but there were none. Drawers were filled with makeup—Chanel, Estée Lauder, Lancôme. A mirrored tray with a lacy brass edge sat on the vanity, crowded with perfume bottles.

Something sparkled. A pin. Ruth picked it up, tanzanite, flickering; the lavender-blue color was undeniable. She pushed it deep into her pocket, picked up the wrap—*Sour Blue Raspberry Hubba Bubba Bubble Gum*—and headed for the stairs. Pausing at the entrance to Eugene's office, she noticed the family portrait again, crude and cartoonish.

Stepping in, Ruth removed a hat from the rack. A jagged brown stain remained on the inside rim. Lifting it to her face, she breathed in the distinct scent of a dirty head. She plucked out a gray hair and twisted it between her fingers, silver and shiny, a fine wire. So intimate, holding a piece of him. She dropped it, then kneeled to peer inside the floor vent—dust bunnies, more candy wrappers.

Ruth stood and walked to the window. She opened it a crack, cranking the handle, then reached into the left pocket of her maroon cardigan sweater to retrieve her lighter while simultaneously pulling a single loose cigarette from her right. She smoked each cigarette in thirds because one-third, six drags, was all she had time for when she'd worked at the nursing home. Ruth blew smoke out the window, six drags, then turned the butt and pressed it to the end of her tongue, where it created a tiny sizzle. She experienced no sensation there, on its tip, where the scar tissue had proved impenetrable to further violence. Ruth replaced the remaining two-thirds in her right pocket.

Moving behind Eugene's desk, she opened a drawer, hoping to locate estate documents, maybe a will, but a few paper clips and rubber bands were all she found. Another drawer revealed a pencil. She tried one more and found a young girl wearing a tattered, rust-colored headscarf with intense green eyes staring up at her, as if looking into a mirror of her youth. Ruth hadn't seen it in years. *National Geographic*, June 1985. She lifted it from the drawer. The pages felt soft yet unspoiled. *Haunted eyes tell of an Afghan refugee's fear.* Remembering now, the girl was just twelve, maybe thirteen, an orphan. Ruth replaced it and closed the drawer when a faint pang, as if she were about to be scolded, drew her attention to her stomach.

Moving to the shelves, she took down a red book. *Ferdinand.* The pages were stained. She sniffed. *Chocolate.* Reading, she sat in a leather chair. It creaked with age, stale breath expelling from the cushion. Ruth picked at a split in the arm, where she imagined Eugene's hand resting. A sense of well-being descended upon her because, like Ferdinand, she also enjoyed gazing at the sky and smelling flowers.

Eugene had read her this book. She saw it clearly now, her yellow dress, braids tied with matching ribbon, which reminded him of sunshine. She was his Sunshine Girl, after all.

Ruth noticed a small closet concealed behind the open door leading into the office. She stood and opened it to find a row of canvases lined up, resembling a loaf of sliced bread. Ruth flipped through them. They were undoubtedly Eugene's work. She pulled out a small canvas, something she could easily fit in her bag, depicting a rat. The rat was sitting on his haunches. Ruth brought the painting into the light from the window. She looked closer. Yes, the rat was smiling and holding a blue, red, and silver mini candy bar.

Ruth stepped into the hallway, then paused when she heard Dorothy speaking. Ruth took a few cautious steps down the stairs, then waited. Dorothy's voice sounded pleasant and sweet, as if talking to a child. Ruth continued to descend the stairs and tiptoed down the short hall until she could peek around the corner into the living room. Dorothy had turned to the corner of the room near the fireplace, to the large blonde doll seated there in the chair.

"Tiffany, what do you think of Ruth?" Dorothy paused. "Yes, me, too."

Ruth noticed that the doll's hairstyle had changed to braids, and her dress was different, yellow and lacy. She waited.

"We'll need to keep an eye on her for sure. I'll count on you, sweetie."

Ruth took a few quiet steps back to the stairs. She'd had clients like this before. They were usually harmless, but it would add new challenges, especially if Dorothy needed to make important decisions pertaining to her estate. Questions of mental capacity might arise.

Ruth moved back toward the living room with firm, noisy steps, then entered. "I found your wrap."

Dorothy stared absently through the column of light from the window.

Dorothy said, "Why are all gardeners Oriental?"

Ruth placed the wrap around Dorothy's shoulders.

Outside the window, an old man wearing a wide-brimmed hat and loose white tunic meticulously trimmed the rhododendrons with a sharp weapon. Pink petals fluttered to the ground.

Dorothy sat on the sofa.

Ruth had never thought much about race but wondered why Asian people's skin was called yellow.

Dorothy pulled the wrap farther around her shoulders. "I love oriental things. The food is just OK. But I don't trust the people, the Japanese."

"Why?" Ruth felt stupid as the question left her mouth.

Dorothy flipped her hand. "The war, of course! My plan was to go to Japan on a mission trip after college. I was to teach English and Christianity. But it never happened."

Ruth refilled Dorothy's tea.

Dorothy reached for her cup. "Do you know who Paul Tibbets is?"

Ruth's stomach fluttered. Her ignorance was cumbersome.

"You may have been too young. He flew the *Enola Gay*. Hiroshima." Dorothy sipped with a slurp. "He dropped the bomb."

"Yes, of course." Ruth thought it looked more like a roasted marshmallow than a mushroom. Or maybe a Peep, the original ones, with wings. Ruth had bought herself a package of Peeps on her fifteenth birthday. The wings were missing. The clerk said the wings took too long to make, so they just made them without wings now. Ruth had left the drugstore, sat on a bench, opened the package, and bit off a head. With sticky fingers, she split the body in half, then stuck one piece to each side of another Peep. Birds should have wings, so they can fly from danger.

Dorothy looked back at the gardener, working his small brown hands around the shrubs. "Eugene flew with him, with Paul Tibbets."

Ruth's voice sounded low and hoarse, as if she had spoken before clearing her throat. "Eugene was a war hero?"

Dorothy gazed at the window; it seemed she might fall asleep. "Yes. He was."

Ruth, somewhat overwhelmed by this information, felt honored standing in his house. Ruth set the teapot on the coffee table and took a step toward the window to conceal her face when her eyes became moist with emotion. She waited for Dorothy to say more, to reveal the details only a wife might know, but Dorothy's face remained hypnotic and resolved, eyes obedient, as if taking in a broad horizon. "Pigeons were also war heroes. I've been reading about them lately. They saved many soldiers in WWII by carrying messages and locating those stranded in lifeboats, lost at sea." Ruth looked out the window. "With their remarkable navigational skills and ability to see ultraviolet light, they always find their way home."

Dorothy still stared at the window as if she'd not heard Ruth. "They called the bomb 'Little Boy.' Eerie, don't you think?" Dorothy lifted her eyes to the ceiling, fluttered her lashes. "I love irony." She looked at the window, at the gardener. "He's worked for me for twenty-five years and I don't know his name."

A jagged line of sweat ran down the gardener's cheek. Had his family survived? One hand resembled a chewed piece of gum, the skin rutted like the rind of a Sumo orange, the kind

Olivia had preferred because they were easy to peel. Ruth, curious now, said, "Should I ask him?"

Dorothy pushed at her cuticle.

"I'll pretend I'm going to my car and ask." Ruth went to the door, turned two deadbolts, and removed the chain. Her car was parked on the street. She walked slowly. A few feet from the house, hopefully out of Dorothy's view, Ruth pulled her cigarette and lighter, two-thirds left, from her pockets, lit it, and slipped it between her teeth. Six drags.

Ruth slipped the warm cigarette into her pocket and brushed her tongue against the back of her teeth as she approached her car. A police car slowed, then stopped a few feet away.

The officer rolled down his window. He inspected the large dent on the side of Ruth's car. "Do you live here?"

"I work for Mrs. Fiske." Ruth turned back to find the gardener watching.

Firm-faced, he said, "I'd like to see your ID."

Ruth retrieved her purse from her car. Fingers fumbling, she handed it to him through his window. Backing away, she steadied herself against the car, glancing at the house. Was Dorothy watching?

A few minutes passed, and then the officer, a large man with good posture and an oversize head, stepped from his car, boots squeaking. "Does Mrs. Fiske know you have a record?" He moved toward the house. "I'd like to speak with her."

Ruth noticed a rosary dangling from his rearview mirror. "I've changed. By God's grace." David had said those same words to her on the beach.

The officer waited, as if the presence of God would become visible on her face.

Ruth thought of crossing herself, trying to remember how David had done it. Chest, then head? Shoulders, left to right? The officer watched her hesitate. Starting with her heart, she circled her hand around, ending at her forehead, then bowed like a Japanese person.

Only one thing marred her official record. A commandment, yes, but not the worst one. Ruth wondered as she bowed again if the Ten Commandments were in order of importance. Is murder ever justified? Is theft ever necessary?

The officer took Ruth's right hand. She flinched. *Raw.* She initiated touch, always. Her body slipped with the loss of control. Her hand contracted into a fist. *Sting.* The officer enclosed it inside his own. *Pressure. Heat.* She looked at the sky. A fluffy cloud. *Cotton Candy.* An old prop plane, lemon yellow, flew by. Ruth imagined a bomb falling from it, landing on him, forcing him to release his grip.

He moved Ruth's hand from her forehead to chest, shoulder to shoulder, left to right. "It goes like that."

Ruth offered a faint smile. She looked at the sky again, as if God were watching. Her heart lifted.

He handed Ruth her license, nodded, his chin softer. "We were asked to be extra vigilant. The old ladies around here are worried about their trinkets getting stolen." He returned to his car and drove away.

Ruth placed her hands on the hood of her car. They burned. Sky reflected in the windshield. Clouds split. A sunbeam blinded. Adrenaline returned to its lair, leaving exhaustion in its wake. A moment later, still weakened, she walked back to the house. The gardener had returned to the flowers. She bowed. He bowed. She bowed again. "What's your name?"

Ruth closed the door and fastened the locks. "Akio."

"Akio. That's right." Dorothy sipped her tea. "The Japanese were awful, you know. My first boyfriend from high school came back and wasn't the same." She looked at Ruth. "From the war."

Ruth, relieved that Dorothy had not mentioned the police, steadied her trembling hand on the back of a chair. "But you found Eugene."

"Yes, I did." Dorothy's face relaxed. "I made dinner every night. Eugene liked to eat. I lost twenty pounds after he died."

Ruth sat in a stiff French chair and noticed the yellow metallic flecks woven into the fabric. As a child with no friends, Ruth had often gripped the chain-link fence surrounding the playground at recess, just like the gorilla at the local zoo. She had recalled the poor beast looking depressed the day she'd been invited by a classmate with a tenderhearted mother. His tough black fingers had curled around the bars. A dried tangerine peel lay at his feet. Noting the defeated look in his eyes, Ruth had wanted to do something, free him, give him something sweet to eat. One day, on the playground, a ball had bounced, swing chains rattled, children had laughed, a jump rope had whipped the concrete. While gripping the steel fence, an endless repetition of diamonds, until her fingers turned purple and her face glazed with tears, she'd noticed, once again, the yellow car like a banana split parked on the street. This time, the man smiled and waved.

Dorothy said, "What did that policeman want?"

Ruth looked to the window. She grasped her hands and tried to rub away the lingering heaviness of the officer's grip. "He thought I needed help with my car." Turning to Dorothy, she said, "He's Catholic. He had that necklace thing on his mirror."

Dorothy laced her fingers. "The Catholics will end up in eternal damnation, you know."

David. Ruth couldn't imagine it, would not believe it, but asked anyway. "Why?"

"Worshipping Mary. Confessing to a priest. Earning salvation by works. And then the obvious . . . when men aren't allowed to marry."

Ruth didn't understand, so she kept looking out the window, watching Akio clip, again noticing the scarred hand and wondering about the pain, the burning—how the skin had tried its best to close itself and be smooth again. Scars are ugly, failed efforts to heal, a reminder of violence. Ruth scraped her tongue against her teeth as if to rid it of something.

Dorothy leaned over and grasped Ruth's hand. "Stick with me, Ruth. I'll show you the way. Lutherans talk to God directly. Jesus, Ruth. Jesus is all that matters. No priests, no rituals, just Jesus. He is the light of the world. He will forgive you. You will be free. He loves you."

Light, forgiveness, freedom, but mostly, love. Ruth's mind soared at the possibility that there was a solution, an antidote, for her life. She picked at the chair fabric. Her breath quickened as a warm gush rolled through her chest. The feeling was unrecognizable. She couldn't tell if it were good or bad, if she was panicking or experiencing, could it be, hope?

Dorothy stroked Ruth's hand, gentle and warm. "You'll be new, reborn. Your past will be wiped away."

Ruth pulled her hand away. If her past were wiped away, then her children would be also. She scratched her cheek, then moved her hand to the back of her head where the scar, ever reliable, grounded her.

Dorothy leaned in closer. "Like a newborn baby."

Ruth twisted her hands, focusing on her white knuckles. The feelings of warmth had dissipated, leaving her body cold and tight. In 1955, Ruth had wiped blood from the head of her newborn baby girl, *Jane*, before her brother took her. Just a child herself. *Fifteen.* The confusion. Her bleeding had begun at thirteen. A teacher helped but never explained. Blood seemed bad, scary. But babies were good. How did a baby get inside of her? So stupid, Ruth shook the question from her head, but the jagged memory remained in her throat until she swallowed.

"Don't listen to that policeman. You just cry out to Jesus." Dorothy leaned back and folded her hands in satisfaction. "They've been patrolling lately. There's a thief working the estate sales. We've all been on the lookout."

Repeat offender.

Ruth shifted her eyes to the coffee table. The screaming man on the art book stared back like that Halloween mask from the movie *Scream* that she'd seen everywhere with the elongated face and grotesque open mouth. The one that made her uncomfortable because it was just how she felt sometimes. She felt it now as she thought of David screaming for her from hell, from eternal damnation. When she looked up at Dorothy, so calm, so pleasant, Ruth felt heat rise in her face. She wanted to take that book and slam it across Dorothy's stupid, clownish face. How dare she speculate on David's eternity.

Dorothy looked at the book. "You know Munch? He's Norwegian. His sister was in a lunatic asylum near where he painted this, Oslo. One day he saw the sky turn bloodred at sunset. He heard a scream." Dorothy studied Ruth's face. "It's supposed to represent anxiety in modern man."

The wavy red sky, the blue river, the bridge, and the ghostly man, a child's nightmare. Ruth said, "Eugene could have painted that."

Dorothy sat on the sofa. "Eugene hated that painting." Her face drooped with concern. "It scared him."

Ruth felt her emotions shift. She was scared, too. Scared of going home each night to her apartment, concrete and overly fortified, where her neighbor tormented her daily. Scared of returning to prison, where she'd been teased for her skin and teeth. And sometimes, she was scared of Dorothy, because in her presence, she felt a familiar awareness of being toyed with.

They sat in silence. Dust passed through the shaft of sunlight. It drifted around the room. Ruth followed one piece to see where it would go. Up, up it flew, across the room. She thought of Eugene flying a tiny plane. It soothed her, that feeling of flying, adrift. Eugene's funeral was well attended, a fancy affair for sure, exotic flowers, thick-papered programs. A large photograph of Eugene in uniform had been displayed on a table. Lots of people, but no one wore black, so Ruth stood out. She'd watched Dorothy, glittering with jewelry, white-blonde hair, blue eye shadow to match her dress. Ruth had gotten close, smelled her nice perfume, but Dorothy had never looked at her. Plastered grin, no tears, Dorothy had clearly enjoyed the attention. She was hosting a party. In contrast, Esther, tall and broad like a man, with little makeup to disguise her heavy features, had worn a loose beige dress and cried, shoulders bouncing. She used a cane, winced, and dabbed at her cheek with a wad of tissue. Their eyes had caught. Esther lingered on Ruth's face until a man in a light-blue suit took her arm. They trailed behind Dorothy, whose lips, unnaturally pink, were so bright against the soberness of the day that it seemed rude. *Laffy Taffy.* They were the color of the pink Watermelon Laffy Taffy warming in Ruth's pocket.

Dorothy stood and walked toward the kitchen. "Let's go to the den."

Dorothy led Ruth through the kitchen to the cozy room tucked in the back of the house, where books covered one wall and two wingback chairs, one plaid and the other pale pink, faced a large TV. Ruth scanned the room—a piano, knick-knacks, piles of magazines, and mail.

Dorothy rested her hands on the back of the pink chair. "Eugene and I spent a lot of time in here. I taught high school English. I've kept all the books."

A DVD collection occupied the shelf above the TV—the entire series of *Murder, She Wrote.* The surrounding books looked old, some '80s paperbacks. Ruth recognized a few names, such as Hemingway and Dickens, but didn't know much about them, so she stayed quiet, hoping Dorothy wouldn't talk as if she did.

Dorothy said, "Do you read?"

Ruth quit school before eighth grade. She darted her eyes around until they stopped on a collection of thumb-size enameled clowns playing instruments and juggling balls. In front of the plaid chair, black velvet man-slippers with a gold crest on the toe were positioned accurately. "I don't have a lot of time, but I like mysteries."

"Me, too!" All the lines on Dorothy's face turned up. She directed Ruth to a barrel-shaped table between the chairs, encircled with open compartments filled with books. She gave it a spin. The table whirled around like a lazy Susan, ticking like a roulette table. "It's English burled elm, very expensive."

Ruth's brother had renamed their lazy Susan, fitted into a corner cabinet under the kitchen counter where Eve had kept the stockpot, "Dizzy Ruth." Once, he'd told her about a fun game where she'd need to crawl inside. He'd said it was just like a carnival ride and she'd even get a prize, candy, if she stuck with it. He'd spun her, ignoring her pleas to stop, cackling, until she threw up and then secured the cabinet door. After two hours, her bladder gave way. Three hours later, she was released by Eve, who'd backed away, fingers to her lips. "My God, Ruth, have some respect for yourself." Ruth crawled out, covered in her filth. Eve folded her arms. "How pathetic, the cabinet was open."

Dorothy grinned, displaying all her teeth, even and slightly yellow, as if she were a child showing off a new toy. "Agatha Christie. I have all sixty-six books."

"I haven't read those." But Ruth had read them all aloud, in sequence, through *A Pocket Full of Rye*, to her nearly blind neighbor, Miss Miller, who died, as she watched, in 1957.

"My goodness! You must start here with the first one, *The Mysterious Affair at Styles*." Dorothy turned the table, then slipped a book from the shelf. "It's a first edition, 1920. Eugene found it for me. It's signed." Dorothy opened the cover to reveal an attractive signature.

Ruth recalled Miss Miller's living room, the green floral sofa, her torn stockings, the Depression glass candy dish filled with saltwater taffy, her pretty pink ring. "I can't take your signed copy." Ruth had a first-edition signed copy of every Agatha

Christie written through 1956, including the six Mary Westmacotts, all boxed carefully in her apartment.

"Of course you can; books are meant to be read, and jewelry is meant to be worn." Dorothy, chin down, eyes serious, looked at Ruth as if they shared some secret, then turned and swished her hand across her bookshelves like a game-show host. "Then we'll move on to Dickens."

Ruth sensed Dorothy's emphasis on the word *jewelry*, or was it her imagination? Ruth fondled the teardrop shape of her pendant necklace through her shirt, making sure it was hidden. The prison doctor had diagnosed her with paranoia, possibly schizophrenia, neurosis, depression, and anxiety. Ruth had suggested PTSD. He'd laughed. "You weren't involved in combat." Then he'd tipped his face down, reproachful. "You're insulting our veterans." His final conclusion: "You are a sociopath." He'd offered her drugs, but Ruth had flushed them because she wanted to remember, to remember her babies.

Ruth turned to a long table that stretched across the back of the room. It displayed a village of small cottages with thatched roofs, English streetlamps, and cobblestone paths. A wagon of tiny vegetables delighted Ruth. One house bore a crooked sign, THE OLD CURIOSITY SHOP. Another, M. FEZZIWIG WAREHOUSE.

Dorothy twisted around a worn wing of Eugene's chair. "My Dickens village. It's my version of a dollhouse."

Ruth peered down a street with charming shops. She wished to be small and walk around, maybe get some ice cream. Once, as a child, at school, through the chain-link fence, Ruth had watched the man in the banana-split car, habitually parked on the street opposite the playground under the same large palm tree, place a green plastic spoon in his mouth, move his lips around, swallow, then wave. *Dairy Queen.*

Dorothy pointed out various scenes from the books. Stories Ruth hadn't heard of, except for Scrooge, which she watched on TV most Christmas Eves. She liked Mr. Scrooge, not just at the end, but all of him, because he was lonely, and lonely comes out in different ways. She'd imagined being Tiny Tim's mother, cooking the goose and pudding. Every year, she cried, wept aloud (no one would hear), even though she knew Tim would get well, because she was just so damn happy about it. "I like when Scrooge buys the giant turkey for that family with the crippled boy."

"Tiny Tim." Dorothy looked at the village. "There's hardly anything sadder than a sick child."

Ruth thought of that boy, *Orange.* It bothered her to think what she was capable of. Just a child, and his siblings—she'd not thought that through. She'd not thought at all. Her body had moved until it was done. A mother will protect her child at all costs.

Dorothy turned from the village, sat, and rested her hands on the piano—a baby grand with yellowed keys. She smoothed her hands across, her rings dragging as if feeling for flaws.

At that moment, a piano played, not from within the den, but from outside. Dorothy leaned across the piano to reach the window. She pulled the heavy drapes back. After listening a moment, she played along—something romantic.

Soft light filtered through the inner sheers. Dorothy's white-blonde hair glowed. Her rings, twinkling, clicked lightly on the keys while her tiny hands spread and moved with ease and precision. The unseen piano continued while Dorothy paused to listen. Then she played while the other instrument was silent. Back and forth they went, as if talking.

"That's Robert, my neighbor." Dorothy stood and curtsied. "My parents bought this piano for my twelfth birthday. I played the organ at church, then studied music in college. Everyone said I was very good."

Ruth looked out the window. The silhouette of an older man sat at a piano; a bald patch crowned the upper back portion of his head. He continued to play with small square hands. Ruth already knew of him because she'd attended his wife's funeral.

"It's our little game." Wearing a sly smile, Dorothy stepped to the window to cinch the curtains. "We've been doing it for years." She fondled the pendant hanging from her necklace, a pink crystal lying over her heart.

Ruth again touched the stone around her own neck through her shirt, feeling the pointed tip and rounded mound.

"Playing together, I mean. That's all." Dorothy paused to listen. "Chopin. He's very good—if you like that sort of thing." Turning to the window, she said, "They moved in shortly after we did. He's widowed now." Dorothy cocked her head. "He's Scottish."

Dorothy left the room. Ruth followed. She glanced down the hallway Dorothy had previously dismissed. Her hands turned cold and sticky. *Clouds, candy, candy clouds.* Back then, just thirteen, looking up through the window while lying on her bed, waiting for it to stop, Ruth could see clouds, a bird, a plane. It helped, to think about something else. To be anywhere but inside her body. *Reality is slippery, like memory.*

Dorothy sat in the living room. "Eugene and I always went out on Friday nights. I enjoyed that, going out. We'd sometimes do dinner *and* a movie." Dorothy rearranged her wrap. "Why, it's Friday, isn't it? Let's go out!" Dorothy's face lit with hope. "There's a good place in the village. They have regular American food."

CHAPTER 8

THE BOOK OF RUTH

Ruth opened the window of her apartment to set a pile of Corn Pops on her kitchen table, then sat. Marbit flew in, landed on the table, and pecked. A couple more pigeons joined him.

Ruth looked down at her hand, where she was wearing Esther's ruby ring. "Esther said it should stay with the bloodline." Ruth straightened the ring, then looked into Marbit's eye. "They call the color Pigeon Blood."

Two more pigeons flew in and landed on the table.

Ruth lit a cigarette. "I like it this way, pretending things aren't complicated. Dorothy and Esther see me as a stranger, which is true. But I do like to imagine this was how it always was, making family recipes and chatting about old times." Ruth fiddled the cigarette with her thumb, then took a long drag. Marbit jumped onto her lap. "Esther would have been a great mother to someone." Ruth touched Marbit's foot.

The neighbor woman screamed, the sounds penetrating through the wall. Ruth looked at her drawings. Houses—beach cottages, mountain cabins, country estates, all places Ruth would have liked to live. They fluttered with the breeze from the open window. Ruth shifted her eyes to her gold couch, lumpy and stained. The pigeons kept eating as if they hadn't heard.

Ruth stood and walked to the stove. Marbit jumped from the table to follow her.

The woman cried, then whimpered.

Ruth looked down at Marbit. "You hear that?" She put on a pot of water to boil and tore open a box of Kraft Macaroni and Cheese. "That woman is crazy with a capital *C*. We need to stay away from her." Marbit, at her feet, searched around the floor.

Ruth poured in the noodles and thought of that first dinner when she'd met Dorothy. "While we were making dinner, Esther said there are only two books of the Bible named after women. I knew this, of course, but hadn't really thought too much about it. 'Ruth and Esther,' she said. Esther looked at me like I was supposed to say something. Then she asked about David. 'Do you have children?'" Ruth stirred with vigor, creating a whirlpool. Marbit looked up at her and pecked at her pant leg. "I told Esther, 'My son was named David for no reason in particular.' But she said there are always reasons for naming children and that David was a king in the bloodline of the true king, Jesus. David was the great-great-grandson of Ruth, the Ruth of the Bible."

Ruth stopped stirring when the water foamed up. The woman moaned through the blue wall, then a door slammed. A moment later, the woman pushed Ruth's door open and ran in. Ruth's hand shook. She swore she'd locked the door. Blue eyeliner smeared down the corners of the woman's eyes, blood ran from her mouth, and a fresh black bruise spread over her cheek. Now both of Ruth's hands were shaking, and her mouth hung ajar, as if she wanted to speak but forgot how.

Ruth turned back to the stove, where she pretended to read the directions on the Macaroni and Cheese box but kept glancing up at the woman.

The woman looked at the pigeons, then, with a rattle of her beads, sat at the kitchen table. "He's a monster, that man, but I need him. He's the father of my children." The woman kicked away a pigeon on the floor. "I have a boy and a girl, just like you."

Ruth wiped at her own cheek. Still gripping the macaroni box, she said, "What do you want from me?"

The woman pressed her eyelash in place, then used her nails to comb through the ends of her white-blonde hair. "Ruth, I told you. I'm Urth. Urth, the Norse Goddess of Fate. And I've seen things in my dreams." She looked hard into Ruth's face. "You're going to fall . . . and die."

Ruth glanced at Marbit, then back at the woman's dark skin, maybe Asian, maybe Latino, but light, like she had some white in her, too. "Earth? Like the planet?"

"No. U-R-T-H. I told you, we're soul sisters."

Ruth backed away, near the window. She realized the woman was crazier than she'd originally suspected, and the only way to deal with her was to play the game, but be better. "You know, I was here when they filmed *Nightmare on Elm Street*—1984. Down in the basement, in the boiler room. Have you ever been down there? It's *the* boiler room."

Urth's face sunk away like a scared little girl. "I don't like horror movies." Urth stood and stepped toward the door. "You are very strange, Ruth, very strange."

Ruth went back to the stove to stir her pot. "Freddy Krueger was a bad mistake. In one of the later movies, they explained all that. How his mother worked in an insane asylum and was violated by all these psychopaths. Freddy was a mix of a bunch of very bad people." Ruth looked at the floor, to Marbit. His eye moved over her face. Ruth used to worry about David. That he'd turn out bad, too. But he didn't. He was very good.

Urth continued walking toward the door with her arms folded, as if she were cold. She paused to look at Eugene's painting of the smiling rat hanging on the wall over the couch mixed in among Ruth's drawings. "Stop feeding those sky rats, Ruth." Urth looked around. "There's shit all over the place!"

Urth moved her feet around, trying to avoid it. "I'm going to tell, and then you'll be sorry. Then you'll wish you'd have stuck with me, listened to me." The flesh of Urth's face turned hard as she dropped her chin and widened her eyes. "I know things, Ruth. You should be my friend. We're the same, Ruth, you and me; we're part of the same whole. Yin and yang, Ruth and Urth." She turned and left.

Ruth went to shut her door. She looked at her reflection in the mirror for a moment, her fear framed by the golden sun. Where would she go if Urth was right and she was evicted before Dorothy cooperated? Ruth swallowed to moisten her throat, then went back to the stove. She reached down to touch Marbit's head, her hand still shaky, then drained the noodles. "Esther said the Ruth in the Bible was a great hero, a woman full of loyalty for her mother-in-law. I just have Aunt Esther and a stepmother, if you'd call Dorothy that." Ruth picked out a noodle, bit it, then threw the remaining half on the floor. A flock of pigeons ran over. "Dorothy's mean, but I need her to trust me. I'm trying to be patient, to not get angry. I don't think I can be like the Ruth of the Bible. Or maybe that Ruth didn't have such a challenge as this."

Ruth tore open the cheese packet and dumped it into the pot with some water. She stirred it into an orange paste, which she didn't like to think about. No milk or butter, but it was still OK. "Esther said I was made in God's image. A reflection?" Ruth glanced back at the sunburst mirror. Had she locked the door? She searched through the pigeon crowd for Marbit—he was easy to identify with his yellow feet. "She said God doesn't make mistakes. It would seem unlikely. But when I look around and see all the bad and suffering, I can't help but wonder if God turned to some other world and left us burning on the stove." Ruth poured the noodles into the cheese paste. Marbit looked up at her. "I was a mistake. There is no arguing that fact. It happens all the time. I don't really care now." Ruth's throat tightened. "But as a kid, I just wanted to be wanted."

Ruth plopped a spoonful of macaroni on the floor for Marbit. "Dorothy must have had a tough childhood, too. It comes out later. The marks become visible with old people, like veins on the backs of hands. The fat hiding those veins melts away, and there they are. Been there all the time."

Pigeons had migrated onto the counter.

"Olivia had big veins like a swollen river, brown like the Amazon. I saw a nature show about it once." Ruth became fixated on the concentric layers of feathers encircling Marbit's neck. "She didn't care where I came from."

Marbit stayed close to her feet. His beak was coated with orange cheese goo.

"Why are the people with the hardest lives the most kind? I'd like to be kind. Olivia said I was, and so maybe it's true. I keep her words handy when other things pop in my head, like being hated by two mothers, or when I see dark hallways and the rest of it." Ruth ate a spoonful of macaroni from the pot, scraping her teeth along the wooden spoon. "Or when I think bad things about Dorothy."

Ruth took the pot to the table. "David said God never wants us to hurt each other." Marbit wandered over. "I think he meant that people get hurt enough by their own families, so why make it worse?" Ruth scooped up more macaroni. "Miss Miller was good to me; Olivia was, too. Miss Miller read to me, as long as she could, and Olivia sang. Kinda like mothers do." Ruth put another blob of macaroni on the table. Marbit flew up. "Although Miss Miller did get me thinking a lot about murder."

CHAPTER 9

ELECTRIC LIME

R uth sat in the living room, waiting, while Dorothy changed for dinner. She didn't want to go to dinner because crowds made her uncomfortable. Dorothy's feet scuffed around overhead. When Dorothy had put on her heels, the sound changed to the familiar click, click across the bathroom tile. Ruth didn't want to see the screaming man on the cover of the book anymore, so she stood and wandered down the hall, past the limey-green bathroom she'd used only a few times since she'd learned to "hold it" while working at the nursing home. The phrase "hold it" always popped into her head when she felt the urge to go. She stood at the bathroom door and looked down the hall. The next two doors, one on the left and the other at the end, had always been, and remained, closed. The sound of drawers rolling penetrated the ceiling. Ruth continued down the hall to the first door. She grasped the doorknob and turned until the door opened. Ruth peeked inside to find a regular-looking bedroom. Through the dim light, it appeared to be decorated in floral yellow wallpaper and bedding. A strange-looking group of dolls, mouths hanging open—*Screaming,* she thought—occupied a long narrow bench against the far wall. She wanted to go in but heard the clicking of Dorothy's shoes down the stairs, so she closed the door and ran into the bathroom.

"Ruth, Ruth!" Dorothy's voice rang out from the living room.

Dorothy's heels clicked across the parquet flooring of the entryway. "Ruth!"

Dorothy knocked on the bathroom door. "Are you in there?"

Ruth flushed the toilet and opened the door. "Are you ready to go?"

Dorothy looked around the bathroom. "What were you doing in here?"

Ruth said. "I needed to use the bathroom. I can't hold it all day."

Dorothy laughed. "Of course not." But her eyes still moved around the walls as if to make sure nothing was missing.

Dorothy wore a teal linen blouse, and matching blue stones dangled from her ears. Dorothy's toenails, freshly painted red and shiny, peeked through heeled sandals. The jagged ends of Ruth's own black hair rested on the front of each of her shoulders. And her own deformed toes, nails coral and chipped. *That damn second toe,* too long and twisted.

Dorothy finally looked at Ruth. "They have regular American food at this restaurant. Did I mention that?"

Dorothy smelled good, as always. Ruth said, "Yes, you did. I like American food best."

Dorothy smiled with approval. "Yes, American food is always better."

The restaurant, tired, like a Holiday Inn from the 1970s, but nicer, more fabric and dim lighting, was packed with white-haired people at 5:30 p.m. When the hostess led them back, Dorothy fixed her eyes upon a man sitting alone at the bar. Dressed in a tweed dinner jacket, hair combed slick over his head, he wore sunglasses, as if recovering from cataract surgery.

A bottle of Visine sat next to his stemmed glass, filled with dark-red wine, black cherry, *Tootsie Pop cherry.* He turned to Dorothy, raised his hand, hello.

"That's Robert," Dorothy whispered.

Ruth put her hands in her cardigan pockets, grasping the lighter. "The piano man?"

Dorothy nodded. Her face appeared bright and flirty as she smiled and fluttered her lashes.

Ruth had hoped to sneak out for six drags. "Should we ask him to eat with us?"

"He won't." Dorothy paused as she approached him. "Nice to see you, Robert."

"And you, too," Robert replied with a Scottish accent. Removing his sunglasses, he inspected Ruth, squinted, then shook his head.

What part of her did he remember? Their eyes had locked briefly at his wife's funeral. Looking back, so long ago, over ten years, 1995, surely Robert wouldn't remember. But Ruth's underarms became damp.

Robert's eyes remained fixed on Ruth. "I am, ah, meeting a friend."

Ruth pulled her eyes from him when the hostess led them to their table. The waitress, a plump Black woman, filled their water goblets.

Dorothy unfolded her napkin. "He was really looking at you."

"Do you think?" Ruth sipped water. She thought it odd that Dorothy noticed Robert's reaction but did not seem to remember herself. Dorothy was there, too, at Irene's funeral. Maybe Dorothy did remember. Dorothy's face held steady and pleasant. Ruth couldn't tell.

Dorothy opened her menu. "He never takes off those glasses."

"Maybe he's hiding something." Ruth had worn dark glasses, many times. It wasn't the physical pain that hurt. What truly hurt, and still hurt, with the occasional flutter in her gut as a reminder or the lowering of her eyes at harmless things, such as blue eyes or adolescent laughter, was the humiliation. Not the humiliation of a grown seventeen-year-old boy striking her face with a closed fist, while bad enough, it was the devaluation of not being protected, of not being rescued, of not being loved.

"Yes, he's hiding his eyes. Anyway, he eats here every night and is always meeting a friend, a lady friend." Dorothy fiddled with the large aquamarine stone on her finger. "But there is no friend. He wears that same jacket, sits in that same stool, and orders the same thing—dry spinach salad, lentil soup, and plain chicken breast with red wine. It takes him three hours to have dinner."

A long strand of gray hair hung from the back of Robert's head, draping across the tweed. *Braveheart?*

"He walks in front of my house every night at five fifteen and back again at eight thirty." Dorothy shook her head. "It's sad how lonely he is."

Ruth crunched a cracker and thought of how many Hungry-Man Salisbury Steak dinners she'd eaten over the years, brownie first. By the end of the week, her trash was lined with green beans.

"I'm never lonely. I'm too busy to be lonely. I've got so much to do." Dorothy sighed. "Tomorrow I need to buy stamps." She believed this, because certainty anchored her face with an ease that would not easily accompany a lie.

Ruth said, "Does Robert have children?"

Dorothy kept her eyes down on her menu. "No. There was something wrong with his wife."

Ruth thought of Irene's funeral, the elegant white tulips, the fantastic dessert table. "Has he been widowed awhile?" *Scottie-dog cookies.*

Dorothy finally looked up. "Irene died years ago. She was very odd. Sometimes Mother Nature should just be left to run its course."

Ruth's instincts took charge—she imagined stabbing Dorothy in the throat with her fork and twisting until things inside snapped. "And some people are so cruel it would be better if they were never born."

Dorothy blinked while examining Ruth's face. "Sometimes the people who love us are cruelest of all."

Ruth suddenly felt bad about the fork. She tried to erase the image from her mind, but it kept busting through. "Yes, I think you're right. I wonder why."

Dorothy focused on getting food into her mouth. Ruth struggled with the bones in her fried tilapia.

Dorothy said she hated fish. "The smell gets stuck in my hair."

Ruth covered the carnage with her napkin. She'd thought the fish a good choice, the price moderate compared to Dorothy's steak.

They splurged with chocolate mousse. Dorothy scolded the waitress when her coffee was forgotten, because she wanted it with the dessert, not after. She inspected the bill. "You notice I don't need reading glasses. My eyes are perfect." She made check marks on the bill, then laid her credit card down. "Sometimes they try to add things to the bill. You should always check it."

Ruth swiped her finger along the dessert plate to get the last of the mousse. "That's a good idea."

"Well, that was nice." Dorothy rested her hands on the table. "How about a movie?" Eyes light and watery, her lids blinked as if recalling a pleasant memory.

Ruth licked her finger. "What's your favorite movie?"

"Oh my, there have been so many. The old movies were so much better than what they make now." Dorothy admired her rings with a tilt of her head. "Did you ever see *One Million B.C.*?"

Ruth shook her head.

"Carole Landis's first big film. Everyone said we looked just alike. It was 1940. I was just eighteen."

Ruth imagined Dorothy as young, sweet, round, and innocent, as all girls in books and movies seemed back then. They never made books or movies about girls in real life—or about girls like her. Everyone acted. Eve had pretended to be someone else. Even now, Dorothy pretended. Ruth had imagined, too, that certain things never happened, that she lived on Gilligan's Island.

In 1940, Ruth was born, left, and then, thirteen years later, left again. Her body was bought and sold as if everyone had wished her to disappear. At seventeen, she saved everyone the trouble, leaving everything, even her son. Hawaii. *Elvis and Angela.* She had liked the huge ocean separating her from that life, as if her past had been a tangible thing she could bundle up, set down, and abandon.

Once home, Dorothy stood in the den, flipping TV channels with the remote while Ruth watched. *"Gaslight!* This is one of my favorites! Angela Lansbury—1944. She's eighteen. It was her screen debut. It won a bunch of Academy Awards." Dorothy hurried to the kitchen. "I'll make popcorn!"

Ruth went to the Dickens village, leaned close, and imagined eating a muffin from the bakery. Tiny Tim had fallen over. She righted him. A pleasant feeling caressed her shoulders and trickled down her back. To fix something felt good. She straightened a pine tree and turned two villagers to face each other.

Dorothy returned with a steaming bag of popcorn and two bowls. "Ruth, would you get the Cokes?"

Ruth went to the kitchen. Next to the sink, Dorothy's wedding rings, which she wore on her right hand, twinkled on the counter. They caught the last light coming through the window. The sun, a rich yolk, the light spread thick, sank into the ocean, changing the sky to swirly sherbet, pink and yellow.

Ruth reached for the rings. The large round diamond was at least four carats, and the wedding band comprised a full circle of diamonds, not just chips. They scattered the light, broke it into colors. She dropped them into her pocket, got two Cokes in small glass bottles, and returned to the den.

Dorothy divided the popcorn into bowls and wiggled to get comfortable in her chair. Her feet hung free, so she let her shoes slip off and stretched her purple toes. "Aren't you going to sit?"

Eugene's chair—the faded plaid and the flat seat cushion with a ridge in the middle remained, as if he'd just gotten up. Ruth hovered over the edge, then released her weight onto the chair. Leaning back, she rested one hand on the frayed arm and noticed the faint scent of men's cologne.

Smiling, Dorothy looked at her, excited for the movie, but then her face changed.

"What is it?" Ruth sat up.

Dorothy kept staring, as if overtaken by something profound. "It's just you, in his chair."

Ruth sprang up. "I'm sorry, I can sit somewhere else."

"No, sit down. It's nothing." But Dorothy kept inspecting her.

Ruth turned to the TV. "The movie's starting." Sometimes the slightest thing will trigger old people's memory. A smell, a taste, a gesture. It was best not to let their thoughts linger long.

Dorothy said, "Ingrid Bergman is so beautiful. She's Swedish."

On the TV, Paula (Ingrid Bergman) was being swept off her feet by Gregory (Charles Boyer) in Italy.

Dorothy held a wad of popcorn between her fingers. "Now, watch carefully—there's a reason he is so insistent on living in Paula's aunt's London home. The aunt was a famous singer and very rich with precious jewels."

Ruth moved her eyes to watch Dorothy's tiny hands work around each other. Her dry skin rubbing made a sound like fine sandpaper. The rings were risky, but Ruth felt good with them in her pocket, filling the void. Ruth touched the back of her head, fingers prodding for the bald ridge. She scratched at it, then noticed blood under her nails. Sucking her finger. *Iron.* She'd try them on at home.

Dorothy whispered, "The aunt was murdered."

Paula and Gregory walked through the abandoned house. Paula became agitated looking at her aunt's possessions, so Gregory suggested they move everything into the attic, where they would not invoke disturbing memories.

Dorothy pulled at her ring finger with her thumb. "He's trying to make Paula think she's crazy, forgetting things."

Ruth looked back to the TV. "He's not very nice after all."

"I don't want to spoil it for you, but the jewels are not in the attic." Dorothy turned to Ruth with a wicked smile. "They are in plain sight."

Ruth's face flushed hot. *Repeat offender.*

Dorothy pushed from her chair and walked toward the kitchen. "Men can be so greedy. Always wanting something, our bodies, our money . . ."

Ruth stood. "Where are you going?"

"I need to use the bathroom, and I want to get my rings. I take them off when I make food. Sit back down or you'll miss the clues."

Ruth started for the kitchen. "I'll get them for you."

Dorothy waved her away. "No, you sit down and enjoy the movie. I'm getting up anyway."

Ruth stepped in front of Dorothy, bumping her. "Go to the bathroom and I'll get your rings."

Dorothy pressed around Ruth, pushing her, and headed into the kitchen. Ruth followed.

Dorothy turned to Ruth with chilly eyes. "Ruth, I've got it." Her voice had a hard edge. She went to the sink. "I set them here." Looking around. "I took them off when I made the popcorn because the oily steam sticks to the diamonds."

Ruth got down on all fours. "Maybe they fell?" *Eve.* She recalled Eve's broken opal, the yellow drips dried to the toilet, the jolt, pain, then long strands of her black hair on the floor.

She cowered, a child again, then imagined the orange sewing scissors in her own hand, her big, strong Hungry-Man hand.

"No, Ruth, they wouldn't be on the floor." Dorothy stared into the sink.

Shaking away thoughts, Ruth got up. "Go to the bathroom and I'll keep looking."

Once Dorothy left the kitchen, Ruth placed the rings in the drain of the sink, careful to push them on a small ledge to the side where they wouldn't slip down. When she heard the toilet flush, she searched the counters again as Dorothy returned. "This is terrible. I'm so sorry."

Dorothy looked like a child about to cry. "I can't believe it. Eugene bought me those rings right before he died. They were an upgrade."

Ruth softened with the mention of Eugene. Curiously, she felt sorry for Dorothy—or was it for Eugene? The way he'd painted his family and hung it in a special spot, even though it was hideous. How he'd read children's books to no one. How he'd endured this woman. "We'll find them, don't you worry."

Dorothy's eyes darted around. Her face shrank and turned inward, like she was hiding. Ruth cocked her head. "Dorothy?"

Dorothy stepped closer to Ruth, her face wild and silly, as if to tell her a secret. "There's been someone taking things in this house for years."

By instinct, Ruth stepped back. She had no one coming after her now, but she still felt like it, like someone was just around the corner. Maybe it was just a habit, or maybe not, but that part that wouldn't forget loomed continuously, like it had to be there, even if it was bad, almost like she'd miss it if it were gone.

Dorothy scanned the counters. "I thought it was my cleaning lady, but it kept happening when she returned to Mexico."

Ruth noticed a Cheeto on the floor, wedged in the crack between the refrigerator and adjacent wall. "What things?"

"A spoon, lipstick, jewelry, even a pair of my panties. Eugene thought I was crazy, but sometimes I see things out of the corner of my eye." Dorothy looked at Ruth, then shifted her eyes while keeping her head steady. She waved her hand to the side. "Right here, I see something flash by."

Unseen things frightened Ruth more than most people—the dark, closed doors, things covering her head—but she wondered if Dorothy was right. A thief in the house? Ruth considered delusion. "Have you had your eyes checked?"

Dorothy pursed her lips. "Of course, Ruth!"

Ruth had dealt with hallucinations before, a sign of dementia.

Dorothy laid her hand on Ruth's upper arm, then leaned in. "I haven't told anyone else because they'd think I lost my marbles. But I thought you'd believe me."

The warmth and light pressure from Dorothy's hand, the faint wind and stale scent of her breath, reminded Ruth of Olivia. Being touched breaks something down between people. "I do. I believe you, and I'll keep a close watch out."

"Good." Dorothy patted the back of Ruth's hand, the other still pressed on Ruth's arm.

Dorothy's gentle touch, her childlike eyes searching for reassurance, and the tender comfort in her voice, a mutual exchange resembling affection, as though they were members of the same team, friends, maybe family, muddled, then relieved the perpetual tension residing in her chest. It softened, like taffy in her pocket. But then sadness tarnished the moment because Ruth realized what all those kids got every day of their lives. Love. But mostly, Ruth was perplexed that she cared about Dorothy's feelings at all.

Compelled by the warmth of Dorothy's hand and the grief in her eyes, Ruth reached into the drain. "Let's check in here." She felt around, huffing and twisting, then lifted the rings with a smile. "Here they are!"

Dorothy snatched her rings. "How in the world?"

Ruth felt the sudden loss. "Maybe you wiped the counters and swept them down?"

Dorothy's face changed again, firm and scolding. "No, I didn't."

Ruth watched Dorothy slide the rings on her finger. "Maybe you forgot?"

Dorothy crossed her arms, the rings twinkling on the hand that clutched her arm. "I can't imagine I would do that."

Ruth regretted returning them. "Well, you must have, because how else would they get in the drain?"

Dorothy paused. Her expression transformed once again, a bit of shame veiling her face. Eyelids heavy, she gazed into the drain. Lips tight and cheek quivering, she said, "I guess you start forgetting when you get to my age."

Ruth placed her hand on Dorothy's back. Moving in slow circles, Ruth felt heat rise from the hump between her shoulders. "It's OK, Dorothy. That's why I'm here." Ruth had regained control but remained curious about Dorothy—how quickly her mood changed, how she snapped, then softened, how Dorothy treated her like a confidant and then, suddenly, a servant.

CHAPTER 10

BANANA MANIA

The next day, Ruth drove Dorothy to the market where Dorothy had shopped for the past fifty years. Dorothy held on to the seat belt that crossed her chest as if preparing to jump from a plane. Fortunately, it was a short drive, a straight shot down Via De La Paz. Ruth had been there many times, knew the store well, was ready for the time it would take. She parked with a stop that made Dorothy's head fly forward.

"Here we are." Ruth got out. She went to Dorothy's side, opened the door, and reached for her hand.

Dorothy slapped Ruth's arm. "I've got it." Her purse strap pulled the loose skin of her forearm. The sapphire bracelet flashed. One of her legs shaky, she said, "This knee has never been the same since I twisted it. It's weaker."

Ruth chose a large cart and followed Dorothy into the produce section. Dorothy inspected five of each fruit before selecting one. Apples were searched for bruises, oranges squeezed and smelled, even onions were scrutinized for unseen soft spots. It took a full forty-five minutes. But Ruth didn't mind because last time Dorothy bought her candy and doughnuts.

Ruth watched the other shoppers, noticed their expensive

clothing, glamorous. Jewelry flashed outrageously in the artificial light.

Dorothy moved into the cold section. She picked up hazelnut coffee creamer and handed it to Ruth. Eggs, she checked for breakage. "I can't stand yogurt. Yuck! I like good cheese, though." She picked up a white chunk. "Danish cheese."

In the frozen aisle, Dorothy inspected the packaging to choose between brands. "Do you eat corn dogs?" Dorothy smiled. "I'll get a box for you, too."

Next, they went to the butcher counter. "I'm picky with meat." Waiting for her beef to be ground fresh, Dorothy glanced across the store, to the deli counter. Ruth followed her gaze to another old, pear-shaped woman with large sunglasses.

A wide grin spread across Dorothy's face. "There's Angela."

"Who?" Ruth looked more closely.

"Angela Lansbury." Dorothy pushed her hair up.

"From *Murder, She Wrote?*" She looked old. She'd always looked old.

"We're friends. I always figured out the murders." Dorothy turned to Ruth. "I have an ability to solve mysteries from all my reading, Agatha, film noir." She looked back at Angela as she approached. "I taught high school, you know. I always knew when those kids were lying. Those kids needed me, needed a positive influence in their lives."

Ruth had also needed a positive influence in her life. Miss Miller had been good to her, as good as any real mother, but there was only so much she could do. Finally, she just opened the cage door and shook until Ruth flew away.

Angela lifted her hand and wiggled her fingers. Dorothy did the same, eyes bright and young, remembering something. A favorite childhood Christmas gift, a first boyfriend, a beach vacation? Things Ruth could only imagine as good, because those things had not been in her life due to their lack of existence or their distorted nature, and therefore they were not pleasant to her, but painful. But she imagined these things in

Dorothy's life and saw them in her cheerful eyes and in the way she tried to straighten the hump of her back as Angela approached.

Seeing the youth emerge in Dorothy's face, Ruth recalled the year she was desperate to have a dollhouse for Christmas with a family of dolls, sisters. Relying on Santa, she sketched a design, which she placed in an envelope to take to the drugstore, where Santa letters were collected in a wooden box bound for the North Pole. But her brother snatched the letter from her fingers, ripped it to pieces, and told her that his parents were tired of pretending to be Santa Claus just for her. By fifteen, she'd had many "boyfriends," as her brother called them, but they were his friends, not hers. At seventeen, her solo beach vacation to Hawaii, where she ended up working as a hotel maid for five years, included very little beach time. So when she thought of these things, these clichéd things, about what might make a person's eyes light up and turn young and hopeful, it was only from movies.

"Nice to see you, Dorothy." Angela glanced at Ruth.

Ruth would have liked an introduction but did not expect one. The truth was, she'd already met Angela, forty-five years before.

"When are you returning to Ireland?" Dorothy asked.

Angela kept looking at Ruth. "In a few weeks. I needed some sunshine."

Angela's cart contained a neat pile of fresh vegetables. Crusty bread peeked out like an advertisement for healthy eating. Dorothy moved around to the front of her own cart, trying to hide the two family-size boxes of corn dogs.

Dorothy pushed the cart toward Ruth. "My assistant takes care of my cart." She looked at Ruth. "Go on, Ruth. You know what I need."

Ruth took the cart and backed away, not sure where to go. Angela smiled at her, parted her lips, and lifted one finger, as if she were about to say something.

Dorothy stepped into Angela's view of Ruth. "Well, have a very nice trip. I hope to see you again before you leave." Dorothy glanced back to Ruth and discreetly shooed her away.

Angela waved again, then walked away.

"That was exciting," Ruth said.

Dorothy still watched as Angela turned down an aisle. "Yes. She's a wonderful person, an excellent actress."

"I noticed you have all the *Murder, She Wrote* DVDs. Maybe we could watch them sometime."

"Yes, maybe we could." Dorothy's face changed again, sadder, as she stepped up to the meat counter. "I would never eat that stuff in the case. You break it open, and it's all brown inside."

In the bakery section, Dorothy piled boxes of bear claws, doughnuts, fritters, scones, and muffins into the cart. "My mother made excellent doughnuts." She picked up another box and gazed through the plastic lid.

The crusty sugar sparkled. The glaze dripped seductively.

"She knew just how sweet to make them. The kitchen smelled so good. She used real lard, of course." Dorothy lifted her head. "I can hear it sizzle, even now. Brown sugar, that was the secret."

Ruth remembered, too.

She always mixed the batter wearing Grandma Judith's embroidered apron, blue birds and pink tulips, to protect her dress, the one Grandma sewed from a McCall's pattern for her tenth birthday. The skirt flared out, and a ribbon wrapped the waist. The sleeves were capped and trimmed with lace. Big white buttons ran down the back. Ruth chose the fabric, silky and pale, like lemon cream pie.

"You can have some. These are way too big. I cut them up and freeze them. I only eat a small piece with my coffee." Dorothy paused. "Is there anything else you'd like?"

Ruth hesitated, not sure if Dorothy was really being nice. "Could I get root beer?"

Dorothy looked surprised. "Root beer?"

"I mix it with milk. It's really good. Do you remember *Laverne and Shirley?*"

Dorothy's face wiped blank.

"They always made it with Pepsi, but I like it with Root Beer. Did you watch that show?" Ruth liked how everything always worked out in the end and how Laverne and Shirley were like sisters.

Dorothy grabbed another box of pastries, chocolate croissants. "I don't remember it much."

"It was so funny. The way Laverne didn't shave her legs because she said the stubble held up her pantyhose." Ruth laughed. Her mouth fell open without restraint until she noticed how Dorothy stared at her teeth—or was it the scar on her tongue?

Dorothy crossed her arms; the sapphire bracelet flashed. "All right, but it sounds terrible to me."

Ruth led Dorothy to the soda and snack aisle. She reached for the generic brand of root beer. "This kind is just as good and so much cheaper!" She'd done good. "Who needs a fancy label?" Ruth turned to find Dorothy standing next to Angela, who was holding a bottle of Sanpellegrino. She had apparently slipped into the aisle while Ruth's back was turned.

Dorothy glanced at Angela, then said, "Well, hello again! My assistant here is making a recipe for me with root beer. It's a very nice dessert, very complicated and quite unusual, but light, very light." Dorothy turned to Ruth. "For heaven's sake, Ruth, get the good kind."

Ruth replaced the one with the black and white label and reached for the swirly letters and foaming mug. She stared at the pretty root beer label but watched from the corner of her eye as Dorothy whispered something to Angela. Dorothy shook her head and cleared her throat, even though it didn't sound like it needed clearing. Angela smiled politely at Ruth, then reached for another bottle of water.

Ruth, head down and face hot, said, "Dorothy, we need more milk."

Dorothy sighed and looked again at Angela, who pretended not to notice. She whispered to Ruth, "Go get your milk and meet me in line."

Attempting to be quick, Ruth spun the cart around but bumped Angela's hip. "I'm so sorry, sorry, sorry."

"It's all right." Angela looked into Ruth's eyes, then dropped her gaze to the stone around her neck. Back at Ruth's eyes, Angela squinted as if trying to read fine print. "You're the one, *Blue Hawaii*."

Dorothy watched. "What? What did you say?"

Ruth tucked the pendant inside her shirt, then moved away, down the aisle. She grabbed a gallon of whole milk and set it on the bottom of the cart. Still scolding herself, she took a sharp turn, left wheels caught air, the jug tumbled out, the cap popped off, and milk poured over the floor with a glug, glug. Everyone looked. One man scowled because he had to maneuver his cart around the spill. Ruth grabbed another milk, placed it in the cart, and moved into an aisle.

Ruth composed herself. Dorothy would never know. But then a woman cried out, "It was you," followed by a disturbing thud. Ruth looked back. Angela lay in the puddle of milk. She caught Ruth's eye for the briefest moment before Ruth stepped behind a tower of bananas.

People rushed to help. The manager ran in with towels. But it was Dorothy who appeared from nowhere, pushing people aside. Ruth had never seen such vigor. Angela took Dorothy's hands, and the manager lifted from behind. As Angela stood, Dorothy's bracelet fell into the puddle.

Dorothy said, "Miss Lansbury, are you all right?"

"Please, call me Angela." She looked back. "Your bracelet. I'm so sorry. Did I break it?"

The manager handed it to Dorothy.

Dorothy inspected it. "It's only the clasp."

Angela wiped her milk-soaked pants with another towel. "It's beautiful. I'll pay for the repairs. I insist."

Dorothy waved her hand in the air. "Of course not. I'll take it to Carson's."

Ruth stepped out. She stared at the floor and dug deep into her pockets, where she clutched her lighter with one hand and broke her cigarette in half with the other.

Dorothy held her face tight, her voice low. "Ruth, what are you doing? Why didn't you help?" Dorothy turned back to the puddle. "What kind of imbecile spills a whole gallon of milk and walks away?"

Angela's eyes focused on Ruth's neck, searching. She finally smiled at Ruth then turned to go.

Ruth whispered, "I'm sure it was an accident."

"If you spill something, Ruth, you need to tell someone to clean it up! Didn't anyone ever teach you that?" Dorothy looked at the milk jug in her cart. "You must have seen who did it."

Ruth rolled the wheel of the lighter. "No. I didn't."

Dorothy moved toward the front of the store, but Ruth still stared at the puddle. A young boy with a mop smeared white across the floor. He didn't know how to mop. Back at the nursing home, "Management" always called Ruth because she didn't get queasy. She'd even cleaned up her own mess after her first baby came, Jane, blood still flowing from between her legs. Something else had fallen. She'd screamed. Another baby? Prodding it with her finger, no, a hot, blood-soaked sponge. She'd put it in the trash, then wondered if it was a vital organ. The knife, a pocketknife, had remained on the cement, the rusty blade glistening red. The baby had lain in a box, wrapped in a grease-stained towel, with a long red cut on her head where the knife had grazed the skin. Ruth had touched the wound. Squeezing her eyes, she'd wondered what would have happened if he'd pushed a tiny bit harder. She'd leaned down to kiss the diagonal red line. Mothers do this, to stop pain. Her baby's mouth had worked, but at the time, Ruth didn't know that she wanted milk.

Ruth followed Dorothy to the checkout line, all the candy, the packaging, so shiny. Dorothy dug through her purse, then took her time writing out the check, signing her name slowly, like an autograph. Ruth scraped her tongue across her lower front teeth, then reached for a pack of Skittles. She slipped the candy into her coat pocket. *Eternal damnation.* Like David, Ruth had suspected for years that her thoughts held destructive power. David had confided, expressed his concerns, confessed to the murder of a young classmate who'd bullied him, the weapon— his thoughts. Ruth knew, of course, that none of this was true but could not bring herself to tell him that she, in fact, was the murderer. In hindsight, she should have, and she knew this. It might have saved his life, one less item to heighten his pile of burdens. And while she could see the irrationality of these thoughts in her son, she could not see the absurdity in herself. The facts held firm; people around her died. Sometimes the cases were explainable, and sometimes not.

The next day, Ruth prepared tea while listening to Dorothy and Robert play piano. She grew fond of the ritual, with its formality, and the security provided by consistency. They played most afternoons, sometimes for hours. Ruth became accustomed to their language. Not that she understood, but she could interpret the mood, like listening to a foreign language. It wasn't hard to distinguish love from hate, peace from war, and to identify loss and longing. The music became emotion. The touch of their hands, the timing, the personal inflections, convinced her to pause, to notice. Listening more each day, ideas formed to create the story between Dorothy and Robert. Was it a love story? She hoped not.

Ruth walked into the den with the silver tray, placed it on the coffee table, and handed Dorothy a linen napkin she'd pressed earlier that morning. "Was that 'Lavender Fields' just now?"

Dorothy placed the napkin across her knee. "Very good, Ruth."

Ruth did the wash on Monday mornings. Dorothy liked her sheets ironed with the jasmine-infused water she'd bought at a gift shop in Santa Monica. The bottle was too pretty to pass up. Ruth enjoyed this gentle work that allowed her to imagine a life of quiet cleanliness and order. The jasmine steam rose as she pressed out wrinkles with the heat. So satisfying to see them go! The hum of the clothes dryer often lulled her into pleasant drowsiness, as if someone safe were stroking her hair.

Ruth said, "Earl Grey?"

"Maybe Darjeeling today." Dorothy seemed bored, her face droopy. "Ruth? Why don't you sit down and take a break? It's a lot on Mondays, with the wash and pressing."

"I'm fine. You enjoy yourself." Ruth felt she had already crossed a line by going to dinner and watching movies with Dorothy, but she knew this moment would come. It always did. When there was nothing to do but just talk. Her clients wanted companionship more than anything else. Most often, it was the real reason she was hired, but Ruth was always cautious not to overstep that boundary. She busied herself preparing Dorothy's cup.

In her low, stern voice, Dorothy said, "Ruth, sit down."

Ruth looked up and waited a moment.

Dorothy cleared her throat, then said, a little sheepishly. "Please. Won't you join me?"

Reading Dorothy's face, the pleading look in her eyes, which harbored a weak fear, perhaps, that she might always have tea alone, Ruth set down the sugar tongs.

A strange feeling rose up. Ruth was not sure what it was, this feeling of being wanted. And even more strange, Ruth noticed, was the sensation of her own wanting. When Eve left to follow her dream, Ruth had been surrounded by men, her brother, her brother's friends. She was thirteen, her brother eighteen, so he was in charge. Knowing what she was, a foster kid, understanding what that meant, she realized that her real parents existed somewhere, but they had not wanted her. Even these new parents had not wanted her, and her brother—she resisted calling him that—had never wanted her. But now, her chest lifted because she was wanted, even if it was only for tea with an old woman.

Dorothy relaxed her face with what appeared to be relief. "Go fetch another cup, my dear."

Ruth nodded. She liked being called "dear."

Ruth went to the kitchen, returned with a cup, and sat in Eugene's chair. She sipped tea, indulged in a cookie, and used a pressed napkin that she would wash again, but she didn't mind. "What are you reading now?"

Dorothy stirred her tea with a tiny spoon. "Another mystery. That one I picked up at the market. It's not very good. Not like the old ones."

Ruth set down her cup. "I finished *The Mysterious Affair at Styles*."

Dorothy reached down and spun the barrel table, ticking as it whirled around. When it stopped, she removed a book. "Did you have it figured out?" She handed *The Secret Adversary* to Ruth. "There's always money, an inheritance, and poison."

Ruth watched the table spin, which caused a slight wave of nausea. "I couldn't figure it out, but I enjoyed seeing it all in the end."

"I identify with these characters, the matriarchs. You might, too. There is usually a maid." Dorothy cleared her throat. "You'll get better. Keep reading."

Ruth didn't mind the maid reference. She enjoyed service work, and she already knew all of Christie's endings. When Ruth had read them to Miss Miller, they'd both guessed the whole way through. And Ruth had liked the time it took, an excuse to be out of her own house.

Robert played his piano. Dorothy cocked her ear to the window.

"He is very good," Dorothy said. "'Prelude to the Afternoon of a Faun.' It's kind of sad, don't you think?"

Ruth nodded.

Dorothy looked at the window. "Do you ever get sad, Ruth?" Dorothy looked down at her hands while rubbing them together. "I mean, really sad."

Ruth waited a moment. "Sometimes, but I'm happier when I'm here . . . with you."

Dorothy remained focused on her rings as if she hadn't heard.

CHAPTER 11

EUGENE

Eugene sat at his desk, folding paper airplanes. He experimented, attaching different items: a paper clip, a bit of candy inside its shiny wrapping, a tack. He created a design strong enough to hold the item and still sail to the hallway.

At first, it took a whole day. Then the rat would come earlier. And after a few weeks, within an hour, the rat ate the candy, took the shiny gift, and scurried down the vent.

Dorothy had given Eugene a miniature coin collection for his birthday. Eugene drilled a small hole through the penny and threaded it with a thin shoelace from his dress shoe. Tying a slip-knot, he attached it to the plane with the candy. If he were lucky, the rat would poke his head through the loop while reaching for the treat.

The snare tightened. Eugene, delighted, had created a tiny collar with his penny charm. The rat fought, chewed, and pulled with its paws, but if there was one thing Eugene had learned in basic training, it was proper knot tying. The little penny collar was so cute that Eugene, once again, felt a great sense of accomplishment.

Through his window, the pale sky, a thin line of corrugated clouds, he watched a shorebird fly west. His heart burst open with love, which spilled to warm his chest. He looked back to the rat, still pulling but gradually becoming more interested in the Junior Mint wrapper attached to the plane. His snout twitched and his tiny paws worked. "Lincoln. Can I call you Lincoln?"

Eugene placed a snack-size Twix in his mouth, attached the gold metallic wrapper to a paper airplane, and launched it through the doorway. Delivering treasures. A single earring— what would she do with it now? A diary key, finishing nails, a sequin swatch of cloth snipped from Dorothy's New Year's Eve gown; she'd never wear it again.

Opening another candy wrapper, Eugene closed his eyes and drifted. What would Dorothy make for dinner? What movie would he take her to on Friday?

Eugene heard something. He opened his eyes. Lincoln sat on his desk and nibbled the last of his candy. His eyes, like little balls of shiny black licorice, shone warm and thoughtful. With tiny teeth, grains of salt, Lincoln seemed to smile, so Eugene smiled back. Lincoln wiped at his long snout with his paw. Delighted, Eugene wiped his own nose. Their eyes locked. "Hello, Lincoln."

Lincoln worked the candy.

"Do you know about Abe Lincoln? Can I tell you about him?" Lincoln's white belly spilled over his feet as he sat on his haunches. "He was a very tall, skinny president. His profile is there on the penny. Look down and you'll see it." Eugene placed another piece of candy in the center of his desk. The rat crawled to it and ripped the paper with keen familiarity. "Common people are the best in the world—that's the reason God made so many of them." Eugene opened a Kit Kat and crunched. "You know who said that?" Crunch. "Abraham Lincoln did. The greatest president. The one who preserved the

Union and freed the slaves." Eugene swallowed, then burped silently so as not to scare Lincoln. "You should know where your name comes from."

CHAPTER 12

SHOCKING PINK

A silent agreement had been established. Dorothy seemed to know Ruth had secrets, but she never asked. Dorothy seemed unconcerned with Ruth's past, never questioned, never pried. She even gave Ruth a key so that she could come and go as she pleased. But Ruth would always wait in the foyer to announce her presence.

Once day, as Ruth closed the front door, Dorothy came down dressed and ready to go. She clicked her heels around the foyer, then stopped in front of a mirror in the central hall leading to the bedrooms to push at her hair. "You'll need to drive me to the village, to Carson's. I want to get my bracelet repaired and cleaned." She handed it to Ruth—the one from dinner at Esther's house, the one Angela had accidentally broken, sapphires like a flawless September sky.

Ruth took it. Cool and heavy, it flashed around her fingers. Astonished, she swallowed her desire, but it sat in her throat, swelling as if angry hands squeezed.

Dorothy gave Ruth the maroon velvet box. "Here, I have trouble getting it in there."

Ruth fumbled with the box while trying to hold on to the bracelet. "It does seem tricky."

"Wait. Put it on." Dorothy's face held something clandestine, the look of someone talking about sex or murder.

Ruth gazed into a sapphire.

An important meeting, just the two of them. A birth gift was very special, Eugene explained as he lifted it from the box. The bracelet, giant and so heavy around her dainty wrist, it felt like a handcuff. Mesmerized, Ruth pranced around the house, flinging her arm, looking in every mirror, rebraiding her hair just to see it flash. The blue stones with her yellow dress looked nice. Eugene laughed. "It will be yours someday."

Ruth flipped open the lid and slipped the bracelet into the box. She snapped it closed with a muffled thump. "No, that wouldn't seem right."

"Wouldn't it?" Dorothy raised her brows.

Ruth held out the box. "I never wear other women's jewelry or clothing. I guess I'm a bit superstitious."

Carson's Fine Jewelry, founded in 1948, was written in gold cursive across the glass door. Mr. Carson faithfully served the stars of Hollywood for special occasions, bridal sets, and designer watches until his retirement. The store sat on the corner of the main street, unchanged, generic, but classy and discreet.

Dorothy waited for Ruth to open the door. A thin, well-groomed man in his forties wearing a filmy scarf greeted Dorothy with a strangely high voice. Lightly grasping her hand, he then led her, as if drifting on calm waters. "Mrs. Fiske, wonderful to see you. Wait a moment. I'll get Mr. Halabi."

Dorothy turned to Ruth. "He's so handsome."

"He's pretty." And Ruth meant it. He was a beautiful man.

Dorothy looked again as he walked away, hips swaying like those of a runway model. "Mr. Halabi wouldn't hire one of those. He's very conservative. Although he might be Muslim."

Ruth wasn't following Dorothy's thoughts, but she'd already assumed gay people did not make it on to her "good people" list. Ruth was pretty sure Dorothy would not put her on the good list, either. She imagined Dorothy having an actual list, how fitting it would be to her character, and how few names it would contain. Mostly fictional people, perhaps, like characters in movies.

Glass cases and fresh flowers abounded; salesclerks, mostly older, clad in suits and dresses, hands loosely clasped, wore aloof smiles, as if they weren't concerned with selling anything. Ruth peeked into a case.

A moment later, a very tall, astonishingly handsome Mr. Halabi emerged. His shiny black hair formed a gentle wave across his head. Deep, rich skin spread smoothly over his forehead, and his cocoa eyes with dark, thick lashes, sultry and exotic, enticed. He held out his elegant hand to Dorothy, who batted her mascara-clumped lashes and accepted his help up a small step to the main floor of the showroom.

No one looked at Ruth, which was fine with her. She stood near a crystal bowl filled with tiny metallic-wrapped twisted candies. Staring into the case, she leaned closer. Her pendant swung from beneath her shirt and tapped the glass. A clerk cleared her throat, eyeing it. Ruth dug out a handful of candy and backed away. The clerk stared at the stone as if it might be dangerous. Ruth looked down. The little bomb exploded with yellow light.

"So nice to see you." Mr. Halabi enclosed Dorothy's hand with his own, making a sandwich. "How can I help you, Mrs. Fiske?"

Dorothy pulled the box from her purse and set it on the counter. "I need the clasp repaired." She removed the bracelet, then darted her eyes around to see who was watching.

"It's spectacular. Cornflower Blue, so rare." Mr. Halabi reached for the bracelet but paused with his hand hovering over it. "May I?"

"Of course." Dorothy slid it toward him.

Mr. Halabi took a small magnifying glass out of his suit pocket and held it to his eye. "Fantastic. What is the history?"

"It was Eugene's mother's birth gift. My father-in-law had exquisite taste." Dorothy's eyes scanned Mr. Halabi's suit as he inspected the stones.

Ruth sucked her candy. His manicured nails with perfect white moons; his impeccably fitted dark suit; the red silk cloth that peeked from his breast pocket; his fine shoes, so shiny; and the sweet scent of expensive men's cologne created the illusion of a perfect man with a plastic smile that could've had a lot behind it or nothing at all.

Mr. Halabi, the bracelet draped over his long fingers, said, "It's very dirty, and some stones are loose."

"Yes, it's quite old." Dorothy folded her hands on the counter. "Do you want to know how it got so dirty and broken?"

Mr. Halabi's lips tightened, and he slouched slightly, as if annoyed.

"Angela Lansbury did it, by accident, in Gelson's." Dorothy spoke loud enough for everyone to hear. A few salespeople turned to look.

"Interesting." Mr. Halabi looked back at the bracelet. "She is a client of mine as well."

Dorothy cleared her throat with a decisive cough. "We're friends. Did Mr. Carson ever tell you the story of how we both wanted the same pair of earrings?"

Mr. Halabi, still holding the bracelet, looked closer to inspect the inscription inside. "No, I'm afraid not."

Dorothy touched her ear. "I got the earrings, but we've been friends ever since."

"I see." Mr. Halabi's eyes were still focused on the bracelet. "I'll need to keep it a week or so."

Ruth watched him, the desire in his eyes, the sly, soft-spoken manner in his voice. The bracelet was, in fact, should be, hers. Ruth stepped up next to Dorothy. Placing her hand on her shoulder, she whispered into Dorothy's ear, "Why don't we just wait while he fixes it?"

Dorothy looked back to her bracelet, then up at Mr. Halabi. "I thought you could fix it while we wait."

He replaced it in the maroon box. "I'm sorry, but it will take some time to properly repair and clean such an intricate piece."

Ruth turned to face Dorothy, took her hand, and said, "Dorothy."

Dorothy returned Ruth's gaze. She appeared frightened, like that day in the kitchen when her rings were missing. "What is it, Ruth?"

Ruth looked, unflinching, into Dorothy's eyes. "I don't think you should leave it today."

Dorothy nodded slowly, turned to Mr. Halabi, and grasped the box. "I've never left it with anyone."

Mr. Halabi's expression went slack. He suddenly looked older. "I'm always here when you're ready." He flashed Ruth an evil eye.

Once outside, while walking to the car, Dorothy explained to Ruth that Mr. Halabi was the new owner as of the last ten years, since Mr. Carson retired. "He's very handsome, don't you think? Middle Eastern, though. Do you trust the Arabs?"

Ruth's apartment building was full of people from different backgrounds. She didn't distrust Mr. Halabi because he was Arabic, but because he had asked to touch the bracelet instead of just picking it up.

Ruth opened Dorothy's car door.

Dorothy swung her purse onto the floor and plopped down with a sigh. "He's such a nice-looking man, but I think you're right. I didn't want to leave it. Maybe I can have someone come to the house to fix it."

Ruth walked around to her side of the car and got in. "I may know of someone who could do that. I'll check on that for you." She turned to Dorothy and smiled.

Dorothy folded her hands in her lap. "Good. Thank you, Ruth. I'm glad I didn't leave it."

Ruth started the car and pulled away from the street.

Dorothy reached down to open her purse. She touched the maroon box, then zipped her purse closed. "His wife is pretty, blonde. She had several miscarriages—ten, I think. But now they have two boys. They go to a school for learning problems." Dorothy's sour-cranberry lips, thin and tight, spat, "They're kind of retarded."

Ruth ran a stop sign. A car honked. She'd been called that word, *retarded*, so often that she thought, many times, that she was. Such a painful word, like the word *ugly*. *Ugly* is an ugly word. *Retarded and ugly, only good for cleaning messes.*

Dorothy made a dry, sticky sound with her mouth, her tongue peeling from the roof, as if she were tasting something sour. "You know, they didn't keep children like that when I was growing up. They were there, and then they weren't."

Ruth coughed. Dorothy would've rejected her, too. She needed a cigarette. A cigarette would burn through the thin skin on the back of Dorothy's hand in seconds. Tender skin, like the tip of her seven-year-old tongue when she'd touched it to the glowing orange coil. Her brother had said it was sweet. But it had sizzled and tasted smoky, like an ashtray. "Hot tamales!" Slapping his knee, he'd pushed it back into the dash of the car. It was more painful than childbirth; tears had flooded her cheeks because the burning wouldn't stop—the searing pain, her mouth open, a silent scream as he cackled. She'd let her tongue spill out of her open mouth, saliva dripping to her lap. Eve had turned from the front seat, "Close your mouth. You look stupid like that."

Dorothy turned to Ruth. "They put them in special homes. Are you OK?"

Ruth coughed again. "I just need a little water." *A foster home?* When Ruth was fifteen, she'd delivered Jane in the garage. The baby wouldn't come out, so her brother had used his pocketknife. The panic had infused through his face, distracting her from the pain. So strange to see him afraid. He'd cared enough to save her, and oddly, part of her felt loved because of it. Terrified the baby would break, Ruth never held her. Less than an hour together. The thought shattered Ruth's heart. Later, mopping the blood, she'd watched the baby's tiny chest heave, red and wet, a violet hand, and a cut across her head. Slipping back into the garage, clothes changed, he picked up the box and darted his eyes to Ruth. "Her name is Jane," Ruth said. Her brother nodded, face white with shock, as if he might honor this statement, then left. Ruth watched a red puddle form between her feet. Hunching from the pressure in her pelvis, exhausted, she lay on the cool cement and thought of the orphan Jane from Miss Miller's book. Cheek pressed flat, iron, minerals, gasoline, she dipped her finger in the blood. Eyes closed, red room, Bing cherries in June, no girl should be imprisoned with ghosts or locked in an attic. She wrote, on the cement, "Jane Was Here." Brontë's Jane was poor but clever. And Jane found love. Bleeding for weeks, she couldn't sit, then a foul smell, green goo in her underwear, and chills. He held his nose when he got near and called her revolting. Finally, she got a mirror and looked. She would do what needed to be done. Eve had a sewing kit. She found a needle and thread, decided on hot pink. Eve had used it for a costume. The first poke—are there words? Excruciating, but she managed, tears streaming, hands shaking, to cinch the skin, sliced clear to her behind, back together. She wanted to keep going, poking and pulling, sewing it all shut so nothing would ever go in or out again.

Ruth saw a large palm tree ahead. She pressed the gas.

Dorothy turned her head to watch the road. "It was better that way. Why burden the whole family when you could always try again? You must know all the family history before you marry so that this kind of thing can be avoided."

Ruth imagined the car crashing into the tree, a few coconuts falling on the hood, and Dorothy's bloody skull cracked open, her mouth ajar, teeth missing.

Dorothy held her seat belt. "Ruth, why are you driving so fast?"

Ruth was used to the way old people talked, generational stuff, but Dorothy's cold nature proved monstrous. Then a vision came of Miss Miller sitting on her sofa, listening to Ruth talk about how she'd wanted to go back to school but was afraid. Miss Miller had sat next to her. With their sides sealed together, the warmth, Miss Miller had reached her arm around Ruth, and so Ruth had laid her head on Miss Miller's shoulder.

Ruth took a deep breath and slowed the car.

Dorothy went on about how Mr. Halabi had taken such a special liking to her. She spent so much money in his store, more than some celebrities, he'd said. "I'm his number-one VIP."

Ruth felt Dorothy watching her.

Dorothy said, "Do you wear mascara?"

"No, not usually." Ruth turned to Dorothy. "Why?"

Dorothy looked concerned. "You have long lashes."

Ruth looked back to the road. "I hadn't noticed."

Dorothy leaned closer. "Yes, they're quite long. You're lucky for that."

Ruth pressed the gas pedal hard, forcing Dorothy's head back against her seat. Ruth focused on the freshly painted yellow lines dividing the street. When she was seventeen, her second baby, David, with those beautiful eyes and long lashes, had been born without assistance. She'd spent time with one of her brother's friends. He'd never hit her. She was already pregnant but told the boy the baby was his. As her stomach swelled, he changed, too, wanted her to act like a real mother, maybe get married. But the only thing Ruth knew about mothering was that mothers leave their children.

Dorothy said, "Eugene had long ones, too, but it doesn't matter so much on a man."

CHAPTER 13

THE BOOK OF RUTH

Ruth watched dust float around her apartment. It sparkled in the sun. She got that sleepy feeling again that reminded her of listening to Dorothy and Robert play piano. Marbit flew down to the window ledge. He flashed his red eye, then tapped his beak on the window. Ruth stood and opened it. She took a few Cocoa Puffs from the box sitting on her counter and placed them by Marbit's feet. "David said God is love, like God equals love. I like thinking about that, even if it's hard to imagine." Ruth lit a cigarette. "Something seems true about it."

Ruth sat at the table and looked Marbit in the eye. "I need to say something about that kid, *Orange*. I think about him and his brothers and sister every day. He pops into my head, and then I think about his mother, and my throat gets so tight I can't swallow. He had a mother, and I ruined her life. Killing is wrong. I say this as a confession. David said I should." Ruth swallowed hard. "David never knew what killed that boy!" She flicked ash on the floor, then looked at her drawings on the wall. "He thought it was all his fault, his bad thoughts."

Marbit ate the last puff. Ruth poured more onto her table. He bobbed his head up and down, then pooped.

Ruth lit another cigarette. Marbit flinched with the sound of the lighter and the flash of orange light. "To be honest, I would do it again. To see your child hurt so bad, tortured, humiliated, just because he was different." Ruth ate a puff. "They didn't understand him. You'd do the same."

A knock, slow and steady, sounded on Ruth's door. She looked at the sun mirror. The knocking continued. It was a different knock. Her stomach fluttered when she realized it might be the landlord. Ruth stood and tried to shoo Marbit out the window, but he just kept dancing around the table and eyeing her hand like it might contain new treats. "Go on out for now." Ruth finally picked up Marbit, soft and warm. Ruth cradled him to her chest and buried her face in his neck, then set him on the ledge. "I'll be back. Go hide around the side there. Go on."

Marbit waddled down the ledge, hiding his body, but peeked his head around the side of the window. Ruth smiled; she couldn't help it. "Go on, sweetie. I'll be right back."

The soft, slow knocking continued. Ruth went to the door. "Who's there?"

No one answered, so Ruth opened the door a crack. Urth stood on the other side in a fur coat and large orange sunglasses studded with rhinestones. She smiled and pushed her way inside. Ruth backed up.

Urth sat on the couch and propped her feet on the coffee table that Ruth had found at an estate sale on the last day, when everything was half-price. "Now let's talk about what you've done."

Ruth remained by the door.

"I saw you, Ruth. I'm watching you all the time. You think Dorothy doesn't know exactly what you're doing?"

Ruth, hand still on the doorknob, said, "Are you following me?"

Urth admired her long orange fingernails. "I've got my ways. A goddess has special powers. I can see things that have happened." Urth looked up at Ruth. "And I see things that haven't happened yet." Urth curled her fingers, forming a loose fist to line up her fingernails across her palm. Her pinkie nail displayed a gold glittery sun decal. Urth held it up to show Ruth, then gave her a sly smile. "I know you want to be good, Ruth. I know you try."

Ruth moved from the door to stand at a comfortable distance, next to her table. She thought about David. How he'd explained God's nature, working all things for good. A spider crawled across her drawing hanging on the wall above Urth's head—a yellow cottage nestled into a hillside where patches of wildflowers mingled with tall, arching grasses. She'd drawn that picture in prison and imagined it was where she'd raised her children.

My babies are God working all things for good. God loves them, so they are good, and God loves me, so maybe I'm good, too. It's hard to imagine, me and good. It would be funny if it weren't so stupid.

Urth crossed her legs, then straightened her long pink and orange floral skirt around her ankles. "Your children are good, Ruth. Mine are good, too. But you are absolutely not. You're bad, very bad, Ruth. You're a thief. Nobody likes a sneaky thief."

Ruth was wearing Dorothy's aquamarine ring, so she placed her hand in her cardigan pocket, hoping Urth would not notice.

Urth twisted her hair around her finger while watching the bulge of Ruth's hand twist in her pocket. Ruth slipped the ring off, then wrapped her cardigan tightly around her body and folded her arms. Ruth looked at the window. Marbit peeked around the corner.

Urth spotted Marbit, then flicked her hair over her shoulder. "Just one little call to the police, Ruth. One call, and they'll know about everything. Everything you've ever done."

Ruth held her hands out. "What do you want from me?"

Urth looked to the window, then back to Ruth. "I want to be your friend. I want to help you see who you really are. You'll never be anything different. You're not like those people. You're not rich, or pretty, or even educated. You're nothing, and Dorothy hates you. Can't you see this?"

Ruth felt her throat tighten and bits of anger bubble up in her chest. She steadied herself by gripping the cool metal back of her kitchen chair. "My son was a priest. He said to show mercy for people who hurt us or for people we don't like." With a screeching sound, the chair, reacting to the intensity of Ruth's tightening grip, moved a few inches across the floor. "He said to love and all will be well. A perfect God can't do anything imperfect or unloving. God will help me. He'll put me where I'm supposed to be."

Urth stood. "David wasn't really a priest, Ruth. You know that." Urth shook her head. "You're supposed to be right here with me." Urth reached out her orange nails. "We need to watch out for each other. You understand? I'm your people, Ruth." She turned and sashayed to the door, her long skirt swishing around her feet.

Ruth stepped back. "I don't even like you. You're mean! I'm nothing like you, nothing at all!"

Urth's head fell back while she laughed and walked through the doorway. She turned to face Ruth. "Poor Ruth, can't see the truth. Look in your sunshine mirror. Look and see what's there."

Ruth ran over, slammed the door, and turned her lock. She went back to open the window. Marbit flew in and landed on the table. Ruth poured out some Cap'n Crunch and sat down. A flock of pigeons followed him and scattered around the apartment. Marbit walked across the table, closer to Ruth, his toenails scratching the vinyl tabletop. He paused in front of her, bobbed his head up and down, then turned his head to give her a good look.

Ruth reached out to touch his back. "David said we do what we know. That's when he forgave me for leaving him. To be forgiven for that was the greatest thing that ever happened to me. We cried, but I was so happy. This flood blew through me like a big, warm tropical storm that you just want to run through and get as wet as possible. That's what it felt like. Love, I guess. David said we are surrounded by God's love all the time, but I don't feel it, not here. But up in the Palisades, maybe. Would you come live there with me?"

Ruth turned to look when an intense scratching sound came from the blue wall where her drawings hung.

CHAPTER 14

JUNGLE GREEN

In the past weeks, Ruth had neglected Esther, not because she'd wanted to, but because Dorothy was taking all her time. Dorothy always needed something cleaned or ironed. She wanted items rearranged on high shelves, cupboards cleaned, and new shelf paper in each dresser drawer. Ruth had used the opportunity to look for official documents pertaining to Dorothy's estate, but she hadn't seen anything interesting other than a few stamped envelopes addressed to Angela Lansbury. Ruth again asked about the bedrooms on the main floor, but Dorothy dismissed her question, saying they'd get to that last. Ruth had expected this to happen because lonely people don't know they're lonely; they just think they need a lot of help with things. But that morning, Esther had called and begged to see them. She'd not been feeling well.

Ruth opened Dorothy's car door. "It will be nice to spend some time with Esther."

Dorothy's face pouted. "She's so grouchy and boring."

Ruth got in and started the car. "We don't need to stay long. I'm sure she's been lonely."

They passed the local high school.

Dorothy tapped the window. "*Carrie* was filmed there. Sissy Spacek. Did you like that movie?"

Ruth was still tormented by nightmares of things falling on her head, pig's blood, pumpkins. She glanced at the school. "It scared me."

Dorothy looked at Ruth. "It was clever how Carrie had that power with her mind, how she could hurt people with her bad thoughts."

Ruth watched the high school shrink in her rearview mirror. Maybe it was true. Wasn't that what people said—Wayne Dyer, she'd watched him for hours on PBS—that thoughts could determine your future? Something like that. Ruth dug at the scar beneath her hair. *If you change the way you look at things, the things you look at change.* Certainly, it could work both ways, good thought, good things, bad thought . . .

Dorothy admired her rings in the sunlight coming through the window. "I've read some Stephen King. *Dolores Claiborne* was kind of funny, but I don't really enjoy horror, do you?"

Ruth looked back to the road. "No, I like happy movies."

Dorothy sighed. "Is Esther dying?" As if inquiring whether or not it might rain.

"She might be." Ruth wiped at her cheek, remembering something. "Sometimes people are just ready to go."

Dorothy cleared her throat. "I'm not afraid to die. Why would I be afraid of going to heaven?"

Ruth stopped at a light. Her left blinker ticked as if time were running out. A bomb exploded in Ruth's mind, containing an image of David screaming in a lake of fire. Why had this thought appeared while speaking of heaven? Death had always presented itself as quiet and easy, but she feared for David. She was still terrified that Dorothy might be right about the Catholics.

"Are you afraid?" Dorothy asked.

Many times, death had felt like a good option.

Dorothy pulled down her visor to look in the mirror. "Do you believe in Jesus?"

Ruth had never been to church. Only good people went to church, and if you tallied the facts of her life, it would not look so good. "What does that mean, to believe in Jesus?"

Dorothy slapped the visor up. "No one ever taught you? I might be afraid then, Ruth. You can't go to heaven unless you believe Jesus has saved you from your sins."

Ruth looked at Dorothy. "I thought you just needed to be a good person and you'd get in."

Dorothy patted Ruth's shoulder. "It's OK, Ruth. A lot of people think that."

Ruth, curious now, said, "So bad people get in if they just believe?"

In a low, authoritative voice, Dorothy said, "Yes."

Ruth turned onto Esther's street. "That doesn't sound right."

Dorothy laughed. "It's not a country club. People aren't voting on you."

Ruth pulled into Esther's driveway.

Inside Esther's house, the air pressed down, heavy and stale. Ruth followed Dorothy up the stairs.

Dorothy hesitated at the entrance to Esther's bedroom, as if death were contagious. Her face hardened, and her lips were sealed shut. Afraid to die? That would be normal, of course. But to Ruth, it was nothing, maybe not nothing, more like the end of a mystery, satisfying, with answered questions.

Esther, wearing a pink terry-cloth robe, lay in bed with several pillows propped behind her. She smiled weakly. "Dorothy, I haven't seen you in weeks. Ruth said you've been busy. And Ruth." Esther's smile grew. "I'm so glad you came, too."

Dorothy slid into the room. "Yes. I've had a lot to do."

Esther's face drooped. "I'm tired, and my legs are weak."

With hesitation, Dorothy sat on a chair next to Esther's bed while Ruth cleared away dishes from her nightstand.

"You're not dying yet." Dorothy leaned back in the chair. "I can tell."

Esther tried to sit up a little. "How?"

Dorothy's eyes moved around Esther's face. "By the color of your face. The skin gets kind of yellow. You're pale, but you're not yellow."

"Then I won't die today." Esther chuckled.

Ruth stepped into the doorframe. "Can I bring up some tea?"

"That would be nice." Dorothy cleared her throat. "Use Judith's china."

"Nancy, your neighbor, brought by some pumpkin bread a couple of days ago. Should I slice it up?" Ruth asked but nearly gagged, thinking of it. *Orange slime.* "She made it special because you used to like it when you'd get together."

Ruth went downstairs and found the china behind the glass of an enormous cabinet—pale-pink rims with gold flowers. She stepped out back for six drags, then prepared the tea tray and climbed the stairs, but she paused outside Esther's door.

Dorothy wasted no time. "Have you gotten your finances in order?"

Esther's voice cracked. "Not yet."

"Let me handle it. I'm in perfect health, and I'm good with money. When Eugene died, everyone asked me what I was going to do, as if I couldn't handle the finances. I have people, my broker, my attorney, my accountant. And when I go into Wells Fargo, they all know me. Eugene would approve."

"I miss Eugene," Esther said, her voice wavering.

Ruth peeked in.

Dorothy stood to look in the mirror. "When I take my checks to the bank, all the people working there smile and wave."

"I never got to say goodbye." Esther's voice broke. She looked to the window. "He died so suddenly."

Dorothy touched up her lipstick with a broad sweep across her bottom lip. "The president of the bank sends me a Christmas card. He signs it with real ink, not just a stamp."

Esther folded her blankets down, then ran her big, knobby fingers across them. "Such a kind man. A good brother, so gentle. Loved his candy."

Ruth still waited by the doorway. They hadn't noticed her there. Remembering Eugene, the china rattled in her hands. Cream puff had dripped from his chin at Irene's funeral during that pleasant moment before Ruth had answered his question.

Dorothy sat back in her chair. "He certainly had a sweet tooth. All those stories of the Curtiss Candy Company. He always talked about the factory tour he'd gone on when he was six. I heard it a million times. The giant vats of chocolate, how he licked the side where it dripped because they told the children not to touch. As if his tongue didn't count!" Dorothy released a mellow, affectionate laugh. "He was a good man."

The tray was getting heavy, so Ruth set it on a small table outside the door.

Esther said, "I've left something for Ruth."

Ruth waited, listening. She'd never brought up anything pertaining to money with Esther. She rarely did with any client because a certain point would come when she just knew by the way they'd start talking—"Do you like this silver ice bucket, Ruth?" or "Food prices have really gone up. Here's a little something extra." They'd wait for her reaction, and so Ruth would oblige. It usually wasn't much, maybe a few knickknacks or an extra twenty dollars.

Dorothy's voice snapped back. "Really? How much?"

Esther hesitated; her throat cracked. "Not much. I hope she'll fix her car. It's not safe."

Dorothy said, "She needs to fix her hair and get some clothes that fit."

The doorbell rang, which startled Ruth. She moved into the doorway. "I'll get it." Ruth went downstairs. A woman about her own age, with short, dark hair and a heavy, square jaw, stood outside. She wore no makeup or jewelry, other than a dull coin thing around her neck on a leather strap. Her baggy pants were held up by a fanny pack.

"I'm Andrea, Esther's niece. Are you her nurse?" She stepped inside. "I need to see her."

Ruth moved away. "She already has a visitor right now."

Andrea jutted her neck back, then squeezed past Ruth to climb the stairs. "Who?"

Ruth waited in the foyer. "Dorothy Fiske."

Andrea stomped louder. "Oh, Jesus." She was near the top. "Dorothy's trying to scratch up the last of my family's money."

Ruth started to follow her; then, remembering to check the stove, she went to the kitchen. After turning it off, Ruth hurried up the stairs. Andrea had already taken the tea tray from the table. Ruth stood in the doorway.

Esther turned her head, then shifted her body. "Andrea? Is that you? I didn't expect to see you. Did I forget?"

"No, Aunt Esther." Andrea took Esther's hand. "I wanted to see you. My mom said you weren't well."

Dorothy's eyes turned slick with ice. "Hello, Andrea." Her voice resonated, low and slow.

Ruth said, "I'll get another cup."

"Grandma's china. How nice." Andrea's voice contained the singsong of insincerity.

Ruth returned with the cup. While Andrea interrogated Esther about her health and business affairs, Dorothy sipped tea, eyeing her over the rim.

Esther fumbled with the bread. "It's good bread. Don't you think, Dorothy?"

Dorothy's eyes had not left Andrea's face. "Yes, very moist."

Esther leaned to look around Andrea. "Ruth, have a piece. Come sit."

"No, thank you." Ruth wanted Andrea out. She didn't care for these women. She'd never washed their armpits or tolerated their insults.

Andrea gave Ruth a stern look, then turned back to Esther. "Could we talk privately?"

Esther's cheeks dropped. Breadcrumbs fell from her lips. "Why?"

Andrea sat on the bed. "We need to discuss the estate."

Dorothy clicked her cup in its saucer. "For heaven's sake! That was subtle."

Esther struggled to sit straighter while Andrea took away her bread.

Dorothy stood with a huff. "I'll wait downstairs."

Ruth followed.

Once in the hall, Dorothy said, "The nerve, talking about her estate when the poor woman is clearly on her deathbed. Who would do such a thing?"

After an hour, Andrea reluctantly agreed to drive Dorothy home. Ruth went back upstairs to bathe Esther.

Holding Esther's biceps firmly, Ruth lowered her into the tub. "How does that feel?"

Esther blew air from her pursed lips. "Ouff. A little warm."

"It's the temperature I always make it." Ruth fastened Esther's hair into a bun.

Esther sank down into the water, hunching her back. "So funny for Andrea to come 'round like that. She wants me to change my will."

Ruth worked on Esther's feet, rubbing them with a cloth.

"She's the only blood relative." Esther turned to Ruth and waited. "As far as we know." When Ruth made no comment, Esther continued, "I loved Frank, but I loved Eugene more." Turning away, she said, "I shouldn't say that."

Ruth stroked her back. "You can say whatever you want."

"People get crazy when it comes to money. They come out of the woodwork." Esther stared into the water. "Maybe everyone will get a big surprise."

Ruth squeezed soap onto the cloth.

"I was supposed to take care of you, not this." Esther touched her ring finger, fondling the knuckle. "But this is OK, too."

Ruth guided the cloth over Esther's scar. "I'm not sure what you mean."

Esther sighed. "It doesn't matter now. We still ended up together."

Ruth shriveled inside. *Bittersweet.* Confusion unsettled her mind. "What was Eugene like?"

"Very pleasant—he did what he was told. Kind of melancholy, though. He was always searching, looking for something, driving around in that yellow convertible he loved so much." Esther watched her hand float on the surface of the water. "He'd spend hours polishing the chrome and conditioning the leather seats. He wanted to care for something. He was good at that, caring for things. And always liked silly games and puzzles. He loved giving secret gifts to people, even if it was just a pretty leaf or a lucky penny he'd found on the street. He'd slip little treasures under my bedroom door, then run off. He was such a sweetheart."

Ruth wrung the cloth and folded it neatly before setting it on the edge of the tub. "I know he painted."

When Ruth was twelve, the librarian had handed her a flat metal box tied with yellow ribbon, Eagle Prismacolor Colored Pencils. The librarian had said, "These are extremely expensive." She'd given Ruth a look as if she should be grateful. "Someone left them for you." The librarian had waited, hands laced, as if Ruth might explain, but Ruth stayed quiet because, at the time, she hadn't known who'd sent them.

Esther wrapped her hands around her bent knees. "Well,

yes. He wasn't talented and not much of a looker, but we may have underestimated him."

Ruth sat back on her heels. "I'd like to have known him."

"I wish you could have." Esther slouched. "I'm tired, Ruth."

Ruth rested her elbows on the edge of the tub. "We'll make it a quick bath."

Esther kept looking at her knees. "No, I mean, I'm really tired."

Ruth touched Esther's shoulder. "I know you are."

Esther turned to look into Ruth's eyes. "Can you help me with that, dear?"

Ruth waited a moment, understanding now, Esther's words paired with that pleading look of helplessness.

Esther reached back and touched Ruth's hand, which was still resting on her shoulder. "Maybe we can help each other."

It was not the first time someone had asked this of her. Miss Miller, being Catholic, couldn't do it herself, as if God didn't already know her intentions. But Ruth hadn't known, only seventeen; how could she have? She just made tea as Miss Miller had instructed.

Ruth's stomach sank as her chest lightened, because she could do something for them that no one else would. "You know, Esther from the Bible was a beautiful queen."

Esther said, "Yes, I guess she was."

"She saved her people, her family, from destruction. Even though everything looked like a bunch of coincidences, it was God working all along."

Esther looked into Ruth's face. "You've grown into a beautiful woman, Ruth. I'm glad we met."

Ruth touched Esther's scar. Her throat tightened. "You've made my life better." Ruth turned on the hot water. Esther closed her eyes, her face flushed.

Ruth left the bathroom, then paused at the entrance to Esther's room. She walked in, opened the top drawer of the dresser, and removed a small box from Carson's.

Digging further, she took out the things she liked, sparkly things, then ran her finger through the dusty film accumulated on a small, framed photo of Esther, Frank, and Eugene. Young, they huddled on the beach, laughing. A mirror hung behind the dresser, highlighting her cratered skin from the chicken pox she had scratched bloody. Her black, stringy hair with fizzled ends resembled a broom. She pulled her lips back, revealing yellow teeth with brown in the cracks. Sticking out her tongue, its bull's-eye scar, white rings seared through pink, gave the impression of something evil, an alien, a snake, or a queer tattoo that a rock star might use to shock her fans. She placed the photo and jewelry in her bag.

The sound of water prompted Ruth to return to the bathroom. It spilled over the side of the tub. Ruth turned off the faucet and wiped the floor. Esther's breasts floated like white buoys. With her head propped against the wall, she snored.

Ruth went down the hall to Judith's bedroom. The ceiling slanted at odd angles, as if the space had been an afterthought. A twin bed covered with a white spread fringed in pom-poms divided the room. A French country scene hung over the bed. A couple of Victorian chairs, blue velvet, were placed near a window overlooking the backyard.

Ruth gazed at the ocean, pale like Esther's eyes. The garden below had overgrown into a lush jungle. Oranges and lemons hung heavy from outlandish trees while others rotted in the grass. Esther's potted orchids lined the side of the garage, flourishing despite neglect. Esther hadn't hired a gardener for years, so Ruth had called Akio, who had started that morning and still worked through the overgrowth with a machete.

Ruth would have liked a house like this with a room of her own, a nice view, a spot of blue. She would have liked to live with her mother, her real mother—or the mother she had first imagined her to be, before they met. She recalled a woman in the nursing home, years ago, who had liked to talk. Ruth had fed her applesauce and massaged her swollen, gray feet. She'd had a child out of wedlock and left the baby with a Catholic church. They'd told her records were kept, so her name would be forever recorded as the child's mother. She'd paused, as if Ruth might ask why it was important that her name be remembered. But Ruth held the woman's foot and waited for her to continue. A child would inevitably look for his mother, she'd said. She wanted him to be able to find her. Ruth had asked, "Did he find you?" The woman, smiling, pointed to a photo on her dresser.

Ruth's attention fell again on Akio, hacking through the jungle. She then turned to the closet. Judith's clothes hung in dry-cleaning bags. She tore off the plastic and touched her face to a plain green dress still holding the faint scent of sweet perfume. Shoes with thick heels and square buckles, elegant, expensive, crowded the floor while lacy, feathered hats lined a shelf. On the dresser, a wedding photo of Judith and Walter, an attractive couple with white teeth and smooth skin, watched. Ruth put the photo in her bag. Drawers contained silky underwear and socks, but one was filled with letters and cards. She stuffed them into her bag.

Esther called from the bathroom. "Don't let Dorothy take the ruby. It's yours."

Ruth looked at the door but couldn't stop stuffing things into her bag. She needed them. They belonged to her now.

"Ruth, I knew the moment I saw you . . . I'd never hire someone"—Esther's voice faded—"without proper research."

Ruth dug deeper in the drawer. A card, separate from the rest, lay on the bottom of the drawer, something a child had made. A drawing of a family, more than stick figures, as though someone, the child, had tried. A mother, father, and three children, two boys and a girl.

Esther choked. "I'm so glad you found me . . . And Jane, don't worry. She'll be well taken care of."

Ruth paused. No one knew about Jane but him. Her throat went tight. She looked up. *Jane? My girl.* How could Esther possibly know about Jane? Then Ruth became distracted by the card in her hand.

Dear Mother,

Happy birthday!! I love you because you take care of me and make me safe. Father has a present for you. He said it could be from me, too. He said I couldn't tell you but here is a hint. It is red and sparkly. It is the best in the world! You wear it on your finger. I'm the short one and my smile is crooked because Muffy bumped my arm when she was chasing a fly.

Love, Eugene

Ruth looked at the drawing. The short boy had three yellow lines for hair and a sweet face with a crooked smile. She placed it in her bag and returned to the bathroom.

Esther's head floated facedown between her thighs. Her white hair spread, ethereal, like the graceful tentacles of a jellyfish. Her broad back shone, clean and smooth, except for the scar, which protruded like a white worm. Ruth sat on the edge of the tub and touched the worm, running her finger along the ridge.

Ruth's stomach rumbled; it was dinnertime. She returned to Judith's room, removed her clothes, and slipped a pale-pink beaded evening gown over her head, cool and heavy. She stepped into a pair of silver heels. She selected earrings, a necklace, and three rings from her bag.

Returning to the bathroom, she opened the drawers. The expensive makeup, probably Judith's, looked old, but Ruth didn't care; the bottles were pretty, with fancy gold lettering. She covered her face until her pockmarks were filled, her lashes thick, and her lips bloodred.

A sound, the deep gurgle of bubbles, followed a bovine moan. Ruth turned. Esther had slipped onto her side, curled into a fetal position, head half-submerged, eyes open to slits. A bubble escaped her mouth and rose to the surface, another, then two more. Ruth reached into the water and gently pushed Esther's head under. Esther's hand twitched. The tip of her tongue slipped through her teeth. Another bubble. Her eyelids widened—blue panic—then slowly drifted down.

The world had stopped, but it would begin again when Ruth was ready. She kept her hand on Esther's submerged head and listened to the plink, then plunk of the dripping faucet, steady, keeping time. She counted the drops silently until she reached eighty-eight, then removed her hand and wiped it on her dress. She watched a moment as Esther's head floated back to the surface. It remained facedown.

Ruth went downstairs. She liked the click-click of her heels and the tightness of her calves. All of it, the weight of the beaded gown, the sticky fullness of her lips, the dark fluttering of her enhanced lashes. As she lifted her hands to see the rings, magnificent color danced in the low light.

Ruth made herself a tuna fish sandwich with Ruffles and a pickle on Judith's china. She mixed root beer and milk into a crystal wineglass. In the dining room, through a veil of dim light provided by the elegant chandelier, she ate while gazing out the front window at the dent in her car.

Ruth had also been left with the Catholics who facilitated a foster program. After her talk with the woman at the nursing home, she waited almost five years, then checked. She wasn't sure she really wanted to know the woman who'd left her. It took another two years until the Catholic church confirmed—a Ruth, just Ruth, had been left in their care as a newborn in 1940. However, they had been unable to give Ruth the name of her mother without the mother's permission. Ruth had left her phone number with them and was assured that they would try to locate her. If her mother agreed, they'd release her name to Ruth.

When Ruth finished eating, she reached into her bag and pulled out the photo of Eugene, Esther, and Frank on the beach, then went to the kitchen for scissors.

CHAPTER 15

MISS MILLER

In 1957, Miss Miller, eighty-two and nearly blind with cataracts, asked Ruth, seventeen, to come every day and read to her—Agatha Christie, in sequence, starting with the first, *The Mysterious Affair at Styles*.

Ruth agreed because it was a place to go, even if it was just next door. Miss Miller had the original British printings, not because she was British but because they were regularly sent to her by someone who was.

Murder and mayhem filled Ruth's days instead of math and literature because she'd quit school at thirteen. With her parents gone, no one cared. So her education was entirely devoted to studying the dark mysteries of the human psyche.

Miss Miller could see only enough to get around her house. Ruth was glad for this because her stomach had begun to swell again. She knew what to expect, gagging, overwhelming fatigue, bloating, and heaviness, then a flutter, a kick. It terrified her to think of how the baby would come out and, worse, that it would be taken, like Jane.

Ruth asked Miss Miller if she had children, but she said no, she'd never married, as if that mattered.

She told Ruth her story. Born in New York City to her single mother, she traveled across the entire country to teach school in California. In 1900, everyone else was going for the gold, but she went for a fresh start. Enchanted by the high altitude and clear mountain air, she lingered in Colorado for a couple of years. While visiting the rugged Sweet Home silver mine, situated over eleven thousand feet above the sea, she met a fellow New Yorker, a nun, Mother Cabrini, who was caring for the workers and their families. This tiny Italian nun later became Saint Frances Cabrini after establishing numerous hospitals and orphanages around the world and discovering a healing spring with her walking stick, like Moses. She had the most extraordinary blue eyes.

A miner had given Miss Miller a clear, pink stone. He'd said, "Inca Rose—we usually throw this stuff in a pile, but this one's real pretty. Blood of dead Indians turned to stone."

Miss Miller held out her hand. The dark-pink stone, vitreous, with a pearly luster, like rock candy, was mounted to a gold ring. Miss Miller said, "There are mines in Argentina, but the rarest, most beautiful stones came out of Colorado. Around that time, Tiffany's sent out their top mineralogist. He declared that Sweet Home produced the finest gem-quality rhodochrosite in the world."

Ruth's chest stirred as if a frog kicked and squirmed there. A gush, her heart warmed from a tropical tide, love, perhaps, mouth salty, for Miss Miller? The stone throbbed and glowed. It reached to her.

A whispery wind swirled, and then a voice, mellow and weak, Miss Miller said, "It is the foremost ally in healing childhood wounds."

Ruth wanted the ring.

Miss Miller turned her pale face toward the light from the window. "In Colorado, Mother Cabrini established the Queen of Heaven Orphanage and a beautiful summer camp for the girls on Lookout Mountain, up on a cliff overlooking Denver.

That's where she discovered the healing spring. It's never stopped running."

Ruth liked how nuns were called *Mother*. She pulled her eyes from the stone to watch Miss Miller's thin lips cinch and expand.

Miss Miller turned back to Ruth. "Mother Cabrini was canonized in 1946, and just a couple of years ago, they mounted a twenty-two-foot statue of the Sacred Heart of Jesus on Lookout Mountain. I wish I could see it. Maybe you can find a picture of it and tell me what it looks like."

Ruth envisioned the giant Jesus perched on the tip of a tall mountain and a spring of sparkling water flowing down from his feet.

"Mother Cabrini and I met again, thirty-six years later." Miss Miller patted the sofa seat next to her. "Right here in Los Angeles. I helped her establish the Villa Cabrini Academy over in Burbank. Just girls. It was a good place to teach and end my career. I enjoyed it."

Ruth imagined a place with just girls.

Miss Miller, eyes lost, said, "Ruth, go fetch a book from the shelf. *A Daughter's a Daughter* by Mary Westmacott. Do you see it?"

After a few pages, Ruth knew the author. She recognized the voice and said, "It's Agatha."

Miss Miller said, "Very good."

The story was distressing. Miss Miller had meant well, but Ruth still longed for a mother, even if heartache was inevitable.

The next day, Ruth found a new book on the kitchen table. Wrapped in brown paper and tied with string, the return address, England. She opened it—*A Pocket Full of Rye*. Looking up, contemplating the crucifix hanging over the doorway, she wondered, as she did every day, if passing beneath it would change something.

Miss Miller's voice sounded from the living room. "Bring it here, dear."

Ruth took the book to the small living room, where Miss Miller sat in a blue chair. Her stockings were torn, and she wore a pale-green dress stained down the front. Stray hair frizzed from a loose bun. Milky eyes, skim blue, sat useless behind horn-rimmed glasses.

Miss Miller folded her hands. "Title, please."

Ruth touched her swollen belly, a watermelon. The baby pushed her ribs. Miss Miller stared blankly through her window to Ruth's bedroom window next door. Her face wilted as if she remembered something troubling. Ruth had pulled open the curtains earlier, as usual, because she liked the light, and Miss Miller liked the heat.

Ruth opened the book. The signature, *Agatha Christie*, pressed into the paper with a sure hand and saturated black ink. She brushed her fingertips over the name, felt the indentation.

Miss Miller's voice held a bit of impatience. "Are you going to read?"

Miss Miller had her read slowly. She did not want to miss anything. Ruth didn't mind. She liked the game, the puzzle, but the stories lacked emotional consequence, as if murder were normal.

When Ruth paused between chapters, Miss Miller asked, "Where is your father, Ruth? Your *real* father."

Ruth looked up. "I don't know."

"You need a father. A woman cannot provide the kind of protection you require, and certainly not a blind one." Miss Miller directed her eyes at Ruth's stomach.

Ruth closed the book.

By habit, Miss Miller pushed her glasses up her nose. "My father was lazy, I heard, and too rich to bother working. He was American but moved to England after I was born. Probably wouldn't have been very good at working anyway."

Ruth held the book to her chest. "You never met him?"

"No, he had another family after me, but I correspond with one of his daughters." She looked at the book, a shield across Ruth's chest. "I was unintended." Miss Miller swiveled the Inca Rose around a hidden hinge. *A poison ring.* It opened, not like a book, but spun a half-turn radius like a switchblade. She held it out to Ruth. "Here's a picture of him, Frederick Alvah Miller."

Ruth set the book down and leaned closer. A tiny portrait of a white-bearded man was fixed inside. She looked up and into Miss Miller's pale eyes. "You kept his name?"

Miss Miller chuckled. "He wasn't going to get rid of me that easy!"

Ruth leaned back and cradled her stomach. "I was unintended, too."

CHAPTER 16

EUGENE

E ugene removed the vent cover on the floor of his office because as Lincoln grew larger, he was having trouble squeezing through. Lincoln watched from a chair.

Eugene turned to him. "You are free to go. I cannot hold you against your will."

Lincoln stopped eating his candy and looked up.

Eugene sat in his own tufted leather chair. "I will not enslave you."

Lincoln wiped his head, causing a little ear flap to kink down. *Was it hurting him?*

Then his ear flap flipped up, and to Eugene's relief and utter delight, Lincoln stayed.

Eugene moved his paints and canvases from the garage (against Dorothy's wishes) to his office. He painted Lincoln, his sweet rat face shaped like an eggplant, his white muzzle with black whiskers, and his big belly smeared with chocolate (just like his own). He knew, of course, that Dorothy would never allow a rat to stay in the house, so it was all the more fun. Eugene talked until the sun glowed warm and dense. In the matching chair, Lincoln snuggled next to a small pillow needle-pointed with golf clubs (Eugene did not play golf).

Dorothy had bought an entire collection of classic children's books over the years, with hopeful expectation. Eugene enjoyed them. Once it was clear no baby would come, he asked Dorothy if he could keep them on his own bookshelf. Her face broke open, releasing salty tears as if Eugene had sealed their childless future. Later, he moved them.

"Lincoln, I'm sad today, but I don't want to burden you." Eugene grunted as he reached for a red book. "This is my favorite." He cleared his throat.

Lincoln peeked from behind the golf pillow.

"I have Cool Whip." Eugene, beaming, opened the lid of the white fluff he'd brought up from the kitchen. Digging into the center, extending his hand, he offered a glob to Lincoln, then licked his finger and lifted the book to read. "There was a little bull, and his name was Ferdinand . . ."

An iridescent-green hummingbird bumped the glass of Eugene's office window while dancing around a red feeder.

"At least I got to name her—my baby girl."

Lincoln cocked his head.

"I felt pressured. Really pressured."

Lincoln nibbled his candy.

"All that colorful light shining down through the stained glass, the incense, and bloody Jesus staring down at me." Eugene took a deep breath. "I couldn't leave her without a name, so I pulled a few candy wrappers from my pocket. The panic, the pressure—Lincoln, you can't imagine."

Lincoln froze. He appeared concerned.

"I looked to my clenched fist and opened my hand. Kit Kat, Mounds, or Baby Ruth."

CHAPTER 17

LASER LEMON

R uth had called the ambulance after Esther "passed out in the bathtub." Ruth hadn't felt sad, and this bothered her some, because it might mean she was a sociopath, as the prison psychiatrist had told her—lack of empathy, absence of emotional connection, stealing. Urth was definitely a sociopath—controlling others with threats, using charm to manipulate, impulsive, possibly violent. Dorothy, also a potential sociopath, had whimpered a little at the news, dabbed her eye for an hour or so, and then asked Ruth to organize her sock drawer. Dorothy liked folded socks, not sock balls, which were "crude and lazy." Ruth used the opportunity to search again for official documents of any sort, but she found nothing. She'd also helped herself to large citrine earrings that had been sitting alone on Dorothy's dresser. She'd dropped them into the right pocket of her cardigan next to her new cigarette.

A few days later, on a Monday afternoon, with the wash and ironing done, Ruth entered the den with a tea tray, where Dorothy sat reading a book with a bloody knife on the cover. Dorothy had been keeping the drapes pulled back a few inches. The light had changed with the onset of autumn—softer, more golden.

Dorothy slipped her finger into the book to keep her place, then inspected Ruth's hips. "Ruth, your pants are always so tight. I think you need a larger size."

Ruth touched her hips and pulled her shirt down to hide the bulge in her pants pocket—a blue topaz tennis bracelet left on the coffee table earlier that morning.

Dorothy wrinkled her nose. "And why do you always wear those oversize cardigan sweaters?"

Ruth wrapped her sweater around her body while looking down at her black tennis shoes.

Dorothy shook her head. "Black, brown, gray, navy. Ruth, you always look like a bruise."

Ruth looked up. "I feel more comfortable like this. I don't like to stand out."

Dorothy crossed her legs and rolled her ankle. "Honestly, Ruth, how about wearing something a little cheerier once in a while?"

Dorothy inserted a bookmark before setting her book on the burled elm side table. "Sit down. Do you remember the first Agatha Christie I gave you?"

Ruth walked around the coffee table. "It's still my favorite."

"Well . . ." Dorothy smiled like she had a surprise to share.

Ruth sat in Eugene's chair and poured Dorothy a cup of tea. She nibbled the edge of a Pepperidge Farm Cookie in the shape of a shell dipped in chocolate (like soap from the Coco Palms Resort in Kauai).

Dorothy glanced from side to side, then leaned toward Ruth. "Don't you see? *The Mysterious Affair at Styles.*" She looked into the corner behind Ruth, as if checking for spies. "Poison."

Ruth wasn't sure where Dorothy was going with this.

"Esther was poisoned," Dorothy whispered, as if someone else might hear.

Ruth tried to interpret Dorothy's face. Was she serious? "They think it was a stroke."

Dorothy picked up her teacup, crossed her ankles, and

sipped. "A stroke from the poison. From the tea, or was it the pumpkin bread?"

Ruth realized they had been watching a tremendous amount of *Murder, She Wrote* and reading lots of Christie, but she had never expected this. "I made the tea."

Dorothy offered a wicked smile. "I guess that makes you a suspect."

Ruth chewed another cookie, then swallowed. "I did leave the tray on the upstairs hall table when I answered the door. I went to the kitchen to turn off the stove, and when I returned, Andrea had already taken it in."

"Yes! Precisely what I was thinking. I don't trust Andrea." Dorothy's eyes twinkled. She set her cup down and rubbed her small hands together, as if she were crafting a plan.

"Maybe the bread?" Ruth could play.

Dorothy looked hard, squinting. "Yes, the bread. Mr. Poirot says nothing is insignificant. We should consider the neighbor, Nancy."

Ruth bit her lip. "But there would be no motive."

They both sat for a moment, thinking. Ruth was enjoying herself. This was what girlfriends or sisters might do—pretend, gossip, get all worked up for the pure fun of it. But she wasn't sure Dorothy was pretending.

Dorothy raised her index finger. "Unless Nancy and Andrea worked together."

"Ahh, yes." Ruth nodded with enthusiasm.

"Andrea must have dropped something in her tea. We should have checked the cups. Had them tested." Dorothy shook her head at the oversight. "Who else was in the house that day? Let's write this down."

Ruth reached for a pen and paper. "Well, George came in to change the burned-out bulbs."

Dorothy slapped her thighs. "George! George has been working on her for years!"

Ruth clicked the ballpoint pen. "What do you mean? He's

her handyman."

"You don't know?" Dorothy paused, ate a cookie, sipped her tea—her way of building suspense.

Ruth's pen hovered over the paper. "What?"

Dorothy set down her cup and smiled. "George asked her to dinner once."

Ruth tapped the pen on the paper. "Like a date?"

"Yes, exactly like a date." Dorothy smirked, as if she'd said something scandalous. "He knew about her money, of course. Everyone knows the Fiske name."

"So there was motive?" Ruth wrote "George" on her paper. "Maybe she'd left him something in her will?" Ruth ate more cookies.

"Yes. You may be right about that. She was very generous. I'm positive you'll get something, too." Dorothy cleared her throat in a superior way.

Ruth said, "Akio was there, too."

Dorothy sipped. "Who's Akio?"

Ruth swallowed her cookie. "Your gardener."

Dorothy set down her cup. "Oh yes, Akio. Why was he there?"

Ruth scribbled something on the paper. "Esther asked me to hire someone, so I called him."

Dorothy seemed to think for a moment, tilting her head and looking at the floor. "Did he come in the house?"

Ruth put her hand in her pocket and ran her finger along the facets of the citrine stone. "Well, yes. He did. He left mud all over the kitchen floor."

"Just like Styles!" Dorothy sat taller, rubbed her thighs. "What did he want?"

Ruth touched her chin with hesitation. "He asked where the spigot was."

Dorothy frowned. "Why'd you let him in?"

"I guess that wasn't so good." Ruth sank into her chair. "But he's very nice."

Dorothy straightened her back. "We need to make a time-line. Let's put all the events in order."

Ruth drew a line across her paper. "Remember, I went downstairs to get another teacup for Andrea."

Dorothy glanced at the paper. "Was anything out of the ordinary?"

Ruth looked at her shoes, thinking. "No. Except he asked me if you and Esther were related."

"Really?" Dorothy leaned in.

Ruth looked up, excited. "Yes, he saw the name 'Fiske' on her check."

Dorothy's eyes expanded. "Check?"

Ruth felt she may have done something wrong. "I was just paying him. Esther had already signed it, so I was making it out like she told me."

"Well, this is a mystery indeed." Dorothy slid her cup to Ruth. "More tea."

Ruth stood to pour. Dorothy's mind confused her, but she liked the game, the comradery. Ruth didn't see all the connec-tions, the motives. Frankly, it was ridiculous. Surely, Dorothy knew this. But Ruth was getting better at understanding how Dorothy's mind worked, and besides, she knew how Esther died.

Dorothy sucked in her breath and pointed at the floor near the entrance to the kitchen. She whispered, "Did you see that?"

Ruth, still holding the teapot over Dorothy's cup, looked to where Dorothy pointed. "What?"

Dorothy lifted her feet up to the coffee table and gasped. "There! I saw it again. Something by the door." Dorothy pointed. "There, on the ground!"

Ruth set down the teapot and went to the kitchen. She walked through the dining room and circled back to the den, then shrugged. "What did it look like?"

Dorothy, eyes wide, moved her hand back and forth near the side of her face. "I'm not sure. Just a movement out of the corner of my eye. A pitter-patter."

Dorothy finally put her feet down and stood. She walked with caution, almost on tiptoe, into the dining room. Ruth followed. Dorothy turned and put her finger to her lips. "Shhhhhh."

Dorothy stopped, straightened her back, and looked up at the chandelier. In her normal voice, as if nothing were wrong, she said, "We need to clean the crystals."

Ruth looked toward the dazzling light while trying to follow Dorothy's abrupt change of topic. "Now?"

Dorothy reached up and pulled a crystal; the chandelier swung like a ship on rough waters. "Yes, go get some lemon water and a soft rag."

Ruth went to the kitchen and returned with the items.

Dorothy pushed her hip against the table. "We'll need to move the table."

Ruth realized this meant that she would need to move the table. "I'll try." Ruth pulled until it moved a few inches.

Dorothy kept uselessly bumping the table with her hip. "You're getting it."

Ruth managed to slide it to the wall, breathless and dizzy, coughing.

"If you'd stop smoking, it wouldn't be so hard." Dorothy stood directly under the chandelier, which spanned nearly three feet. She reached up and touched one of the larger crystals, the size of her palm. "Each one needs to be dipped and wiped individually."

Dorothy had caused the whole chandelier to spin and sway. Ruth looked up to the spot on the ceiling where the fixture was anchored and noticed three jagged cracks extending from the ornate brass plate. The ceiling surrounding the plate was stained yellow, and the plaster was bubbly. A feeble attempt had been made to paint over the blemish. The twelve-inch shard pointed down from the center, with its wicked tip directly over Dorothy's head.

"Now, see here, all the dust." Dorothy fingerprinted each crystal. "And the grease."

Ruth touched Dorothy's arm. "Dorothy, maybe you shouldn't stand right under it."

Dorothy laughed. "Eugene hung this himself."

Ruth looked up. She was certain that four cracks were now on the ceiling. "I'd feel better if—"

"Eugene was pretty handy when he wanted to be." Dorothy pulled harder on the crystals.

The chandelier's swinging arc became wider. Ruth stepped back.

Dorothy remained under the rocking chandelier, as if she were performing a circus trick. She turned in a circle with her arm stretched out. "He hung all the pictures in this house."

The pictures hung at odd angles, too low or pulled away from the wall.

Dorothy motioned. "Come here, Ruth."

Hesitating, Ruth stepped under the chandelier and held up her glass of lemon water.

"Now swirl it around. Come on, Ruth. Use your wrist."

When Dorothy got tired of standing, she moved into the living room to sit near the fireplace, where she could still watch Ruth swirl.

Dorothy yelled, "You're going to have to stand under it!"

An hour passed while Dorothy corrected Ruth's technique. Light scattered over the room from the disrupted crystals.

Ruth turned to the living room. "I can't reach the top without a ladder."

Dorothy gripped the armrests of her French chair. Her face appeared solid and motionless, with only her lips moving as she spoke. "You can trust Eugene. I realize you didn't know him, but he always did a good job, followed through, took full responsibility."

Ruth nodded. "It seems that way."

CHAPTER 18

SCREAMING GREEN

The following Friday night, Dorothy and Ruth went to dinner, to the same restaurant, to eat American food. Robert sat erect at the bar. They ordered the same as last time, fried tilapia and skirt steak with chocolate mousse to share. Dorothy reviewed the bill, commented on the dim lighting, the drafty air, Robert's mystery date, and the cool weather.

Dorothy signed the bill and set down the pen. "What should we watch tonight?" She took a last sip of coffee. "We're almost through *Murder, She Wrote*, 1995, I think." Dorothy looked at Ruth. "The year Irene died."

"Irene?" Ruth pretended not to know.

Dorothy set down her cup. "Yes, Robert's wife. I thought I mentioned her name."

Ruth took a long drink of water and avoided eye contact. "How did she die?" Ruth knew, of course.

Back in her sleuthing mood, Dorothy let her words hang. "It was strange, very strange."

Ruth watched ice rotate in her glass, remembering Irene's eyes, identical to her own. Ruth recalled Eugene's desk, the magazine—*1985*, National Geographic, *"The Afghan Girl."* Everyone had marveled at the profound fear in the girl's stunning eyes, but Ruth knew what it felt like from behind those eyes. You don't have to go to Afghanistan to find that girl. Fear is fear, beautiful eyes or not.

Dorothy set her napkin on the table. "Should we watch something else tonight?"

Ruth picked her tooth and sucked a glob of food from under her fingernail. "How about *Charlie and the Chocolate Factory*? I like the older one."

Dorothy's eyes flickered in the candlelight. "Ahh yes, Roald Dahl, such a wonderful author for children."

Ruth looked up from her finger. "Who?"

"Oh, Ruth." Dorothy rolled her eyes. "*Matilda*? *James and the Giant Peach*? Surely, you've read those."

Ruth's cheeks burned. She hated being ignorant. If she'd stayed in school, had a mother who read, maybe things would have been different. Looking toward the bar, her throat tight, she watched Robert eat his lentil soup. The thin gray strand hung down his back. "Does Robert cut his own hair? He seems to keep missing a strand." Ruth thought of William Wallace from *Braveheart*, Mel Gibson's hair, the wildness and random braids, then refocused on Dorothy's question. The shame, even Wallace was educated.

Dorothy patted Ruth's hand. "I know it wasn't your fault. But guess what? It's never too late. I'll be your teacher. How does that sound?"

Ruth's eyes blurred, so she turned her head away. Robert chewed dry spinach. Dorothy's hand rested on her own, warm and comforting. She tried to breathe normally, swallow, and let her eyes dry while gazing at the dark-gray carpet, wisely chosen to hide dirt and food stains. Ruth thought about darkness, how it conceals things and how the things are still there but just look gone. She lifted her head to gaze into the candle flame, which wobbled in the center of the table, separating her from Dorothy. Light, we want light, but we are too afraid of being seen because our stains would be revealed. Ruth looked past the flame and into Dorothy's watery eyes. Was she getting emotional, too? Ruth hoped she was not alone with this feeling. "I'd like that very much."

Eugene had read all of Roald Dahl to her in his office each night. The chair was so big, but cozy. He'd promised her a birthday party with ponies for everyone. Mother was designing her cake shaped like a doll with yellow hair. He always had candy, the good kinds with nougat.

Dorothy said, "I've got an idea. Tomorrow, we'll go to the bookstore in Santa Monica and get all the best of Roald Dahl. That's about fourth grade. It's nothing to be ashamed of. Ruth—these children's books are truly the best."

Ruth nodded. "Dorothy, you've been so kind to me."

Eugene had picked up the yellow ribbon from the chair. It had slipped from the end of her braid and lay across the golf pillow in his office. He liked yellow, too. Forming the bow, struggling a little to get it just right, he'd said yellow was a happy color. Good things were yellow—sunshine and sand, honey and lemon pie, sunsets and baby chicks, butter.

Dorothy cocked her head. "It's my pleasure. Tonight, let's watch *The Mirror Crack'd*. Angela Lansbury plays Miss Marple. Elizabeth Taylor, Rock Hudson, and even Pierce Brosnan are in it. 1980."

Ruth's heart softened. Dorothy cared. They could be friends.

Dorothy smoothed her hand across the tablecloth. "It's based on Christie's book. You probably haven't read it yet."

Ruth said, "I'm about to start *And Then There Were None*."

"You mean *Ten Little Niggers*." Dorothy's voice, quite loud, caused the couple next to them to look.

Ruth's eyes dropped to the fish bones on her plate. *Olivia.*

Dorothy straightened her rings, then gazed into one with a large blue stone. "*Ten Little Niggers* is the real name. I have both versions."

Ruth shifted her eyes to her empty coffee cup.

Dorothy looked at the couple next to them, who pursed their lips while giving her the stink eye. Dorothy blinked a few times, then turned back to Ruth. "What a grumpy-looking couple. Why go out if you're just going to be grouchy?"

Ruth recalled that Miss Miller had had the original, but she'd told Ruth it was an impolite word used by uneducated people. It's not that Ruth hadn't heard the word plenty of times. In fact, it was a favorite of her brother's, but she'd never heard it used so nonchalantly, as if the word was completely normal, as if Dorothy had no idea of the pain that word had caused many people.

Dorothy lifted her hand to the waitress, then pointed to her coffee cup. A Black waitress with ample hips and long blue fingernails, who had not served them dinner, sauntered over. Her face held the look of someone ready to strike. Ruth dipped her head lower and hunched her shoulders forward, moving back into her shell.

The waitress filled both cups, then stood firm. Ruth got the impression that she might not leave.

Dorothy looked up at her. "Where's our waitress?"

The Black woman said, "I'm your waitress now." She put one hand on the shelf of her hip, her nails like talons across her tight white pants. "Do you like your coffee black?" Her voice got louder with that last word.

Dorothy blinked again. She seemed confused. "Yes, I do. I always take it black. Thank you."

The waitress moved away, back toward the kitchen, where several staff members had been lined up, watching. They snickered, and one high-fived her.

Dorothy took a sip. "Anyway, it's a shame Agatha got pressured like that. Everyone today is screaming about censorship, and then they make her change her title." Dorothy patted Ruth's hand. "I'll give you the original."

Ruth moved her hand away and tried to see the staff from the corner of her eye.

Dorothy pulled her cup in closer. "The coffee is good here, very dark." She took another sip, creating a faint slurping sound. "Anyway, it's her most popular book and *the* bestselling mystery of all time. Isn't that ironic for a country that's become so liberal? Especially here, where schools are making unisex bathrooms. It's awful!" Dorothy's eyes fixed on the red lipstick stain on the rim of her coffee cup. "It was also her most difficult book to write."

Ruth needed more water. She coughed to stop a different waitress who scurried by.

Dorothy slid her hand across the white tablecloth as if trying to iron it with her hand. "As I was saying, *Ten Little Niggers* is taken from the old nursery rhyme. Didn't your mother ever sing that to you?"

Dorothy had now stopped all surrounding conversation. Robert turned. Tiramisu formed a mustache on his upper lip.

Ruth whispered. "My mother didn't sing to me or read." Ruth's chest sank with humiliation and tangible sorrow she wished to rip out or swallow away with cold water.

"It goes like this." Dorothy clapped her hands and sang the rhyme, which, painfully, required her to say the N-word over and over again.

Ruth could not sink any deeper into her chair. Trapped. Eyes glared from all directions. Scolding faces, hatred, separation, and disgust emanated toward them. Unaware, Dorothy smiled as if recalling a pleasant memory while Ruth scraped her tongue across her teeth over and over until she tasted iron. She wanted to run outside, light a cigarette, walk, anything but sit in that chair where the vinyl seat had made her butt sweat. She looked into the candle flame and breathed like Miss Miller. *Bumblebees.* And then she was calm. *A citrine bee flew from a sunny tulip to a golden daffodil before zooming into a lemon-cream cloud, and then away it went into the mustard sunset.*

Dorothy finally finished with the last line. "He went out and hanged himself, and then there were none."

A buttoned-up restaurant manager with a firm expression

approached. "Miss Fiske, may I kindly ask you to refrain from using that word? You are offending the other diners."

"What word?" Dorothy held her mouth open, surprised.

The manager cleared his throat. "I'd rather not say."

Dorothy's defiant face shone in the dim light. She smiled slightly. "You must tell me what word you mean."

The manager's eyes darted to Ruth, then back to Dorothy. "The N-word, Miss Fiske."

Dorothy continued to smile. Her face relaxed as she leaned back and looked squarely at the manager. "It's a historical piece of American literature, Mr. Andrews." Dorothy's voice turned firm and low, as if she were getting serious with a lesson. "I was teaching my companion about the traveling blackface minstrel shows in America and about its origin from Frank J. Green's original 1869 book entitled *Ten Little Niggers*."

Ruth focused on the air moving in and out of her nostrils. *School buses, corn, American cheese.*

The manager threw his hands in the air and walked away.

Dorothy let out a huff, then laughed. "My word. What an awful man."

Ruth looked back to the flame. *Baby ducks, bananas, golden pearls.* She swallowed hard. Her throat was sticky. "In 1962, Crayola renamed the Flesh crayon Peach because some children were confused."

Dorothy wrinkled the peach flesh between her brows. "What does that have to do with anything?"

Once home, Dorothy searched around the den for her DVD of *The Mirror Crack'd*. "I know I have it here somewhere."

"I'll make popcorn." Ruth went to the kitchen. She put a popcorn bag in the microwave, then pulled half of a cigarette from the pocket of her cardigan and opened the window. She lit the cigarette, started the microwave, then moved back to the window. She had two and a half minutes.

Dorothy had given Ruth her own snack shelf for her Cheetos, powdered doughnuts, and candy. Her collection included Sour Patch Kids, Snickers, Twizzlers, and her favorite, which was hard to find, so Dorothy had bought her a bunch, Fun Dip. Dorothy's emerald earrings sparkled on the counter. She picked one up. Gorgeous, the green foil of an Andes mint.

Ruth gazed into the stone. In 1995, nearly six years after she'd inquired with the Catholic church, they called to inform her that her birth mother was willing to connect. Ruth met her mother at a Denny's on the outskirts of LA. Ruth ordered eggs with pancakes. Her mother, smooth olive skin, dark hair pulled tight, ordered coffee. Irene wore all black and no jewelry; her intense green eyes protruded in a ghoulish way. Yet, evidence of her former beauty was apparent in her chiseled, symmetrical face and fine skin. Ruth saw no resemblance. Ruth had tried to look nice with a new blouse—gray floral, wash 'n' wear, no ironing needed, and burgundy lipstick. Ruth had looked old for fifty-five, or maybe just tired. She'd brought a gift, a sketch of the view from the bluff, the Palisades, just water and sky, which she'd created with her colored pencils. She'd placed it in a large envelope with the word *Mother* written in black, dead center. But Irene gasped ever so slightly when they greeted. A subtle yet undeniable expression of disappointment, possibly even alarm, cloaked Irene's face, drawn, like someone getting off the red-eye to attend the funeral of a relative they'd never met. Ruth had planned to talk about normal things, but Irene came right out with it: "I never loved your father." Ruth noticed a blood spot suspended in her sunny-side-up egg. "My womb came out with you. You just held on and ripped it right out like you didn't want to be born. Punishment for my immorality. And then, the irony of it all." Ruth's insides fell. She knew she wasn't wanted, but not this. She'd hoped for a different reason. Sick? Poor? Irene went on, "Some women marry for money." Ruth dissected the red spot; blood seeped into the yolk. "Do you know who your father is?" Ruth couldn't manage words. She pushed her drawing deep into her purse until it crumpled. Finally, Irene scribbled his name on a napkin and slid it across the table. "You should be looking for him, not me."

When the microwave beeped, Ruth set the earring down, then extinguished the cigarette on her tongue before slipping it into her pocket, one-third left. She poured the popcorn into two bowls, then took Cokes from the fridge and Twizzlers from her snack shelf.

"I found it!" Dorothy called from the den.

Ruth hurried to the den and settled into Eugene's chair.

Dorothy pointed at the TV. "There's Angela."

"They made her look really old." Ruth chewed a red rope.

"Miss Marple was an old woman, smart and clever. But they should have put some lipstick on her." Dorothy reached for the popcorn. "Did I tell you about those emerald earrings I wore tonight? They're on the kitchen counter. Did you see them?"

Ruth twisted her red rope, which had become sticky in her hand. "I didn't notice. Should I get them for you?" She grabbed a handful of popcorn.

Dorothy watched Ruth's face. "I can get them." But she remained, holding Ruth's gaze a few seconds too long. "I don't need them right now." She turned to the TV. "Angela bought them for me."

"Angela Lansbury?" Ruth mumbled through her mouth stuffed with corn.

"Yes, we were both at Carson's, and she had already picked them out but I didn't see her, so I was trying them on when Mr. Carson said Miss Lansbury had already spoken for them."

Ruth took a long swig of Coke. "So what happened?"

Dorothy's smile spread like lemon curd on a warm scone. "When Angela saw them on me, she looked stunned."

Popcorn fell from Ruth's hand. "Stunned?"

Dorothy's eyes darted around Ruth's face. "She was in awe."

Ruth burped.

"So she let me have them because they looked exquisite on

my ears. I have exceptionally well-formed ears." Dorothy pushed her hair away from her ear for Ruth to see.

"Wow." Ruth touched her own ear.

Dorothy straightened her rings. "And that's how we became friends. Actually, they match your eyes." Dorothy leaned closer. Her face soured, the skin pinched around her eyes, as if she were remembering a past sorrow or had just eaten a lemon. She recovered, leaning back. "What color would you call them?"

Ruth flushed. This was the second compliment she'd ever received on her appearance. The first was in 1957, at the Hawaiian Village Waikiki Beach Resort (formerly the Niumalu Hotel), room 14A, where he played his guitar, sitting on the bed, hair black and slick. He asked, "What do you think?" She stood in the doorway, holding a rag. "Come here and s'down." Ruth sat next to him. He looked up from his guitar. "What color are your eyes?" Ruth said green. He shook his head. "Just green? I see a twilight sky and a tropical cove, teal water." He peered closer. "And treasure! Gold, emeralds, sapphires, and pearls. You've got the whole world in those eyes. I wanna know what a girl with eyes like that thinks of my song."

Elvis had a soft spot for pigeons.

Dorothy said, "Did your parents have green eyes?"

Ruth touched the corner of one eye, pulling the skin down like a tired child. "My mother did."

"You should try them on." Dorothy found the remote and restarted the movie. Elizabeth Taylor, heavy and aging, batted her lashes and swooned at Rock Hudson.

Robert's piano began. Dorothy paused the TV. "*Les Misérables.* I'll add it to your reading list. Tenth grade." Dorothy listened. "He's waiting for me." She pushed herself from the chair and shuffled to her piano, played something, then returned. "He's OK now. We understand each other."

Ruth twisted around to watch Dorothy return from the piano. "But how?"

Dorothy sat in her chair. "I just know, Ruth. Music is

communication through emotional language. Instead of your brain, you use intuition, like solving a mystery. Have you ever just looked at someone's face and known everything?"

Ruth had, in her mother's face at Denny's, then again in her father's a few months later. Everything she'd wondered about, had hoped was not true, to her disappointment, had become clear.

Dorothy took a sip of Coke; the air bubbles gurgled down her throat. "I know Robert very well."

In the movie, Angela recited "The Lady of Shalott." Dorothy joined in.

> *She left the web, she left the loom,*
> *She made three paces thro' the room,*
> *She saw the water-lily bloom,*
> *She saw the helmet and the plume,*
>
> *She look'd down to Camelot.*
> *Out flew the web and floated wide;*
> *The mirror crack'd from side to side;*
> *"The curse is come upon me," cried*
> *The Lady of Shalott.*

Dorothy paused the movie. "Tennyson. A woman is cursed to live alone in a tower, weaving her web, her art. She can only see the outside world through a mirror. She weaves the images she sees on her loom. But they are mere shadows of the world. When she sees the handsome Lancelot and looks out the window to see Camelot, the mirror cracks. She escapes on a boat but freezes to death. Lancelot sees her dead and finds her lovely."

Ruth tried to understand. "What does it mean?"

"There are different interpretations, of course, but many scholars, including myself, agree that it's about the dangers of isolation, about not living in the real world, and the risks." Dorothy looked at the darkened sheers covering her piano window. A quiet ballad seeped through the walls.

Ruth said, "Sounds like she should have stayed in the tower."

Dorothy gazed at the window. "But if no one ever saw her art, her beauty, it's as if she never existed."

Ruth looked toward the window. "So maybe it's worth the risk even if it doesn't work out?"

Dorothy shifted her eyes to her piano.

"Do you think the piano—you and Robert—does it help with that? I mean, that you can hear each other?"

Dorothy blinked with intention, then folded her hands. "You're smart, Ruth. Has anyone ever told you that?"

Another compliment. Ruth felt her shoulders lift. She smiled, then, aware of her teeth, she pulled down her lips and lowered her gaze to the carpet. "No one has ever said that."

Dorothy patted Ruth's knee. "Well, now someone has."

The movie continued. Dorothy nodded off, and so Ruth went to the kitchen and scooped up the emerald earrings.

Looking in the bathroom mirror, she realized that Dorothy was right; they did match her eyes. A thrill vibrated inside her as she watched them sparkle. Was she smart? The green stones, rich, heavy; she liked the weight of them pulling her ears.

Ruth took off one earring and became fixated, once again, on the color. That day at Denny's, Irene had told her she was dead. Not, *You're dead*, but rather, *I'm dead*. A sinister smile had spread, revealing more teeth, straight white teeth. "Do you smell that?" Irene had asked. But Ruth only smelled bacon and syrup. Irene continued, "My flesh is rotting."

Ruth said, "It looks OK to me."

Irene's green eyes flashed. "I'm in hell. We both are." Ruth could not argue. Her life had felt like hell, was hell much of the time, but she was reasonably sure that she was not delusional. Irene's lips turned thin and pale. "We both died when you were born, and now you've come back to torment me." Ruth had stabbed a piece of egg, swirled it in the runny yolk until it was glazed orange, put it in her mouth, and swallowed, as if to prove her wrong.

Ruth returned the earrings to the counter. She brought Cheetos and a pack of Fun Dip back to the den.

Dorothy's chin rested on her chest. Her back curved down deep, like a bird with its head tucked under a wing. *This is how she'll look when she's dead.* Ruth watched the movie, sucking orange cheese goo from under her nails. She licked at her Fun Dip stick, alternating between the green and pink sugar pouches. She was proud of herself for not taking the earrings. It had become too easy. She'd wear the jewelry around her apartment, but after a few weeks, each piece would lose its luster. She'd take something new, but the same thing would happen again.

Dorothy lifted her head and blinked before turning to Eugene's chair. "Eugene? Is that you? You look different."

Ruth noticed the vulnerability in Dorothy's face. It no longer held firm with effort, but rather, it looked childish, soft and tender. Ruth watched Dorothy as she waited for a response, her eyes wondering and dreamy. Ruth became curious, now noticing her own feelings, also warm and dreamy, enhanced with the sugar coating her tongue and the familiarity of a well-worn chair that was now hers. She wanted to stay in that moment because it felt good and safe.

Dorothy's faded blue eyes whirled around, trying to focus. Ruth knew she should say something to reorient her, but she remained still and quiet.

Ruth thought how Dorothy was mostly kind, and even when she wasn't, Ruth sensed she didn't realize her cruelty. She was acting, like all people do, to cover wounds or scars. But not now —right now, Dorothy looked real.

"You always had a thing for Elizabeth Taylor. You liked her dark hair . . . her violet eyes." Dorothy closed her eyes. Her head bobbed.

Pigeons, unlike humans, can see ultraviolet light.

"And you married me for my money." The words left Ruth's mouth, her voice low like a man's, before she could stop them.

Dorothy abruptly lifted her head and opened her eyes wide. "And Irene, why Irene?"

Ruth lowered her voice even more. "Irene meant nothing to me. I love you and always will."

Dorothy smiled, but her eyes remained unfocused. "I know you do. I am the fairest of them all." Her lids drifted down.

Ruth leaned back behind the wing of her chair. In a very low, manlike voice, she said, "But remember, darling. You must not forget our daughter. Take care of Ruth. Get the estate in order."

Ruth peeked around the wing. The twitching flesh of Dorothy's face struggled against old memories swirled with sleep and her aging brain. Dorothy, confused and helpless, wanted reassurance, so Ruth reached over and patted Dorothy's knee. "It's me, Dorothy. It's just me."

Dorothy's eyes opened wide. "Oh my goodness. I must have drifted for a moment." Dorothy looked at the Fun Dip pouch in Ruth's hands. "You found your candy." Dorothy, more alert, nodded with approval.

Ruth licked her dipping stick. "Thanks again for the shelf."

Dorothy stretched her short legs out straight for a moment, then lowered them. "It's so late. Would you like to stay over?"

Ruth studied Dorothy's face. Everything she'd done was for this moment, and here it was, an invitation to stay. Maybe for just one night. It was a start. But something felt weird. She wanted to check on Marbit because she'd not seen him that morning. "Thank you, but I need to get home."

Dorothy's mouth gaped with disappointment. "My parents never let me have girlfriends sleep over."

Ruth stood and brushed sugar from her pants. "Why not?"

"They thought they'd tell me about sex. Like I hadn't heard it all at school." Dorothy chuckled. "I'm not such a prude, you know." She flashed her gold fillings. "I had lots of boyfriends. Several wanted to marry me. I have a way with men. I know how to make them feel special."

Ruth felt creepy, like when the boys had touched her.

"It helps if you're petite. I was also curvy—well, I still am." She ran her hands along the sides of her waist. "And naturally blonde. It's an ego thing. Men need to think they're clever and strong and needed. That's it. They're quite simple."

Ruth wrapped the wings of her cardigan around her body, then crossed her arms. "I never had much luck in that department."

Dorothy crossed her legs and laced her fingers around her knee. "But you have a son?"

The Fun Dip stick wedged in Ruth's cheek ticked downward. *And a daughter.* Ruth was not ready to share David. Sixteen years later, his death was too raw, the images too vivid.

Dorothy smiled. "Esther told me. You must have mentioned it to her. I didn't realize you two had gotten so close."

Ruth had spoken about David to Esther. Their last exchange had revealed secrets. Ruth removed the stick from her mouth. "I'll tell you about him another day."

CHAPTER 19

UNMELLOW YELLOW

A few days later, Ruth's snack shelf was empty, so she searched remote cabinets. She'd never checked the high ones, the ones above the refrigerator. She found a stepladder, which opened with a startling squeak. Ruth steadied it on the floor, then climbed.

What luck! A great collection of potato chips, Fritos, even pork rinds filled the high cabinet. Why'd Dorothy keep the good stuff hidden? Ruth reached for a bag, the ladder groaning under her shifting weight.

Dorothy's heels clicked behind her. "Ruth! What are you doing?"

Ruth turned. Dorothy's face looked more frightened than angry. "I was hungry, and my snack shelf is empty." The Cheetos bag crinkled in her hands.

Dorothy touched her temple. "Why would you think to look way up there?"

Ruth stepped down and closed the ladder with another jarring screech.

Dorothy flinched, then took a step back to lean against the counter.

"Dorothy? What is it?" Ruth set the Cheetos on the counter.

Dorothy's breath quickened and her eyes expanded, as if she'd spotted a snake on the floor. "That's the last sound I heard before Eugene died."

Ruth set the ladder aside. His ghost was everywhere. "I'm sorry. Was he using this ladder?" Ruth looked from the ladder to the Cheetos. The lettering looked different on the bag, and the stamp read, "Best by November 18, 1996." Ten years old.

Later that evening, Dorothy seemed herself again. Ruth made popcorn while Dorothy looked for a movie.

"Ruth!" Dorothy screamed from the den.

Ruth hurried to the doorway.

Dorothy, sitting in her chair with a desperate look on her face, said, "*Please Murder Me!*"

Ruth steadied herself on the doorframe. "What?"

Dorothy pointed to the TV. "Angela Lansbury, Raymond Burr—1956."

Ruth relaxed her shoulders. She walked into the den, where a black-and-white film, accompanied by dramatic, ominous music, blared because Dorothy had turned the volume up high.

Dorothy shooed Ruth back to the kitchen with a flick of her hand. "Hurry! Get the Cokes."

Ruth ran back to the kitchen and returned with the popcorn, Cokes, and a bag of M&M's in her teeth.

Dorothy's eyes flashed with the flickering TV. "It's film noir. A French term for crime dramas. The German Expressionist movement in the 1910s and '20s started it all. But the heyday for film noir in Hollywood was the 1940s and '50s."

Ruth felt her life was film noir. She poured a handful of candy into her mouth.

Dorothy said, "Did you ever see *The Maltese Falcon* or *The Glass Key*? Both were based on novels by Hammett."

Ruth tried to seem interested, but she wanted Dorothy to stop talking so that she could listen to the movie.

Dorothy took a swig of Coke. "Watch. Angela is good in this one."

But Dorothy couldn't resist; she continued with lessons on classic Hollywood filmmaking. "The first true film noir was *Stranger on the Third Floor*, 1940. I had to hide all these books under my mattress because my parents would have been appalled." She peered around her chair to look at Ruth. "Surely you've read *The Postman Always Rings Twice*?"

Ruth shook her head.

Dorothy sat back. "I have all these on my shelf. I'll look later."

Ruth and Dorothy watched in relative silence. Ruth felt herself dozing but wanted to see the end of the movie. She opened her eyes to see Angela Lansbury (Myra) shoot Raymond Burr (Craig), then put the gun into Craig's hand, but Myra was defeated with evidence on a secret tape recorder.

"I like when there is justice in the end, don't you?" Dorothy rubbed her thighs.

"Me, too." But Ruth had found that justice was complicated.

Dorothy grabbed the remote and turned off the TV. "It's so late, Ruth. Why don't you spend the night? You can take the guest room down here."

Ruth yawned. "Are you sure?" Marbit had been well fed that morning, and Ruth was tired.

Dorothy stood. "Of course! I'll get you a nightgown."

Overhead, Dorothy rummaged around; the mirrored bifold doors squeaked and the drawers dragged open, then slammed shut.

Ruth stood and went to the piano. She passed by Dorothy's writing desk, which sat adjacent to the window facing Robert's house. Her eyes caught on an envelope lying there, which had been addressed to Angela Lansbury, written with a calligraphy pen. She picked it up, thick, and turned it over, but the envelope had already been sealed. Ruth set it down and sat at the piano. What could Dorothy possibly be writing to Angela about? She played one note, then another. Why would Angela care a thing about her? She ran her hand up and down the keys like a child. Dorothy had proved stranger than Ruth had originally thought. *Delusional?* Robert's piano sounded through the window. He copied her. Ruth ran her hand along the black keys in a dramatic sweep, dark and creepy. Robert did the same. Silence. Then he started a new piece, something simple and quiet.

"Schumann." Dorothy stood in the doorway.

Ruth jumped up.

Dorothy walked toward the piano. "It's OK. Sit down."

Dorothy slid in next to her.

"He's playing 'Kinderszenen.' It means 'Scenes from Childhood.'" Dorothy looked at Ruth. "The name of this piece is 'Pleading Child.'"

Dorothy played.

Watching her hands move along the keys made Ruth feel safe.

Dorothy touched Ruth's back. "Are you tired?"

Ruth felt the heat of Dorothy's hand. A pleasant tingle moved up her back and into her neck. "I'm OK."

"He's playing the most famous one now. 'Träumerei'—it means 'Dreaming.'"

Ruth listened, soothed.

Dorothy moved her hand back to the piano and played a few notes. "Like a child's dream. Do you hear those four notes repeating but a little different each time?"

Ruth did. She liked how they changed but were still kind of the same.

"Schumann was a genius, but he had breakdowns. Many famous artists have mental problems. It's what makes their art so good." Dorothy looked at the wall behind the piano, where one of Eugene's paintings hung.

Ruth looked up at it. A bowl of fruit. It was pretty good. The apple looked like an apple. The banana looked like a banana. Once, Ruth had sent a drawing into a contest she'd read about in a magazine. Using her Prismacolor pencils, she'd drawn a house made of candy, as the contest rules instructed. She'd won a five-dollar gift certificate to Dairy Queen, and her drawings were printed in the December 1952 issue of *The American Home.*

Dorothy stared at the painting. "Eugene was very stable mentally." She moved Ruth's hand into position. "Let me teach you."

Ruth pulled back. "No. I can't."

"Sure you can." Dorothy played a simple version of "Rock-a-Bye-Baby" with one hand. "See?"

Ruth put her hand on the keys and followed the notes Dorothy played.

Dorothy whispered, "There you go."

Fumbling, yet fun. This is what people did together—talk, eat, and play music. Ruth eased in, tasted a normal life, and it felt good.

"Now close your eyes and hold out your hand." Dorothy placed something cool and heavy in her palm. "Open them."

Dorothy's face beamed with joy; her eyes were lustrous and cheeks flushed.

In Ruth's hand lay the emerald earrings. A rush went through her body.

Dorothy closed Ruth's hand around the earrings. "I want you to have them."

Ruth looked at the tenderness and sincerity in Dorothy's eyes. "But, Angela . . ."

"I know, but they match your eyes perfectly." Dorothy's smile stretched across her whole face.

Ruth opened her hand. The emeralds twinkled, then blurred.

Dorothy said, "What is it, Ruth? What's wrong?"

The shame, the joy, Ruth's jumbled emotions bled into each

other like a strange soup that would have been better if a few ingredients had been left out.

"Let me help you." Dorothy put one in Ruth's ear. "Are you crying?"

Ruth wiped her cheek. "I'm sorry. It's just, no one has ever done that to me before."

"Given you a gift?"

"No, not that." Ruth rubbed her nose. "No one has ever asked me to close my eyes and put something in my hand. I've only seen it in movies. But I always wanted someone to do that to me."

Dorothy squeezed both of Ruth's hands, as if she were about to go on a special date. "Go look in the mirror."

Ruth went to a small mirror by the doorway leading to the kitchen. The reflection of Dorothy watched from behind.

"Now shake your head so they sparkle."

Ruth shook her head back and forth but continued to look at Dorothy in the mirror. She didn't want to think about Irene anymore. But when she looked in the mirror and saw the one thing pretty about her, she saw Irene.

Dorothy turned to her chair to retrieve something. "I found you a nightgown. I've never worn it because it was too long. It's Lanz of Salzburg." Dorothy held the gown up to Ruth, light blue, covered with purple and yellow seashells. A white sailor collar encircled the neck, with a shiny satin bow in the middle. "I had to order it special from the Vermont Country Store. The seashells are so cute. And the cap sleeves. See the grosgrain ribbon trim?" Dorothy held up the hem, then turned to grab another gown from her chair. "I also have this one. Isn't it precious?"

The second gown was covered in *Peanuts* characters, with buttons up to the neck and elastic to cinch the wrists.

"I love the *Peanuts* gang. See the sweet red ribbon across the chest?"

Ruth scanned the gown. "I liked the Thanksgiving one where they make popcorn and toast."

Dorothy ran her thumb along the ribbon. "*It's the Great Pumpkin, Charlie Brown* is my favorite."

Ruth's stomach twisted. "I don't like Halloween." When Miss Miller could still see, they'd made Ruth's Halloween costume together. Miss Miller had suggested she dress as Dorothy Gale from *The Wizard of Oz*, but Ruth wanted sparkles, so they decided on Glinda. Miss Miller had bought the pink fabric and silver trim and made a wand with a shimmering star.

Dorothy examined the tag hanging from the sleeve. "It's a girl's size sixteen. They only came in children's sizes, but I think it should work." Dorothy rubbed the fuzzy flannel between her fingers. "Which *Peanuts* character do I remind you of?"

A strange question, another game. Ruth looked at the gown. "I'd have to say . . . You won't be mad, will you?"

Dorothy's face lit up. "Of course not! I love them all. They're complex. Schultz wrote it for children, but it says a lot about real life."

Real life? Was Dorothy's life real, or was hers? Maybe neither? Both? She just liked the part for kids. "I'd have to say Lucy."

Dorothy chuckled. "I can see that. Remember when she had the psychiatry booth and sold advice for a nickel? She gave everyone terrible advice!" Dorothy smoothed her hand across the gown, still smiling.

Ruth looked at the gown, at Charlie, and thought of Eugene. "What about me? Who am I?"

Dorothy rubbed her chin. "Well, *hmmm*. That's a bit more difficult. You're smart and sweet, so you could be Marcie."

Ruth took the gown, sat, and laid it across her lap to admire the characters. *Safe.* The quiet hum of the refrigerator, the soft gown draped over her knees, Dorothy's voice, the innocence, a childhood she would have liked. "I'm Charlie."

Dorothy sat in her chair. "A boy? How so?"

"I get sad sometimes." Ruth stared at the little bird, Woodstock, on the gown, portrayed in bright yellow. After Ruth's daughter, Jane, was taken away, Ruth cut her hair short, wore pants with a button-down shirt, and went by "Ralph." The diagonal slash on the back of her head had shone white and proud against the surrounding dark hair. Former doubters had come to believe her cyclops tale. But it had only seemed to entice her brother. He'd said, "Do you stand to piss now?" After becoming pregnant again, with David, she let her hair grow and returned to being Ruth. Maternity pants did not exist in 1957.

Dorothy placed her hand on Ruth's. "I know. I see it in your eyes. Ruth, if you ever want to talk . . . I can't fix everything, but I thought the earrings might cheer you up. It's always helped me when I'm sad, to put on something pretty."

Ruth removed the earrings and set them on the coffee table. "I can't take them."

"Sure you can." Dorothy handed them back.

Ruth refused. Looking at the carpet, she had never expected to feel so vulnerable, a mollusk.

"I'll save them for you, for when you're feeling better." Dorothy rubbed Ruth's hand. "Now go change into your nightgown."

Ruth undressed in the living room. The gown only reached her knees and the sleeves were barely below her elbows, but the fabric was soft and cozy.

As Ruth returned to the den, Dorothy gasped and said, "Isn't that cute!"

The guest bedroom was down the dark hallway. Dorothy stopped at the first room; the door at the end remained closed.

"What's in the other room?" Ruth asked before thinking.

Dorothy gave her a stern look, as if Ruth had said something inappropriate.

"I'm sorry. I was just curious."

Dorothy looked at the closed door. "It's just storage." She walked into the guest bedroom and switched on the light.

The wallpaper, the bedspread, a soft chair, even the rug, all flowers. A yellowing lace topper lay across an old bureau containing a mirrored tray, which displayed perfume bottles and tiny figurines of kittens.

"It's all Laura Ashley." Dorothy touched the bedspread. "I bought every one of the matching pillows, the boudoir, the lumbar, and these cute triangle ones."

Ruth dug her bare feet into the fluffy rug and touched the bed. White eyelet fabric hung from the canopy.

An antique wooden table held a group of singing dolls about a foot tall, with mouths drawn open in circles. One wore a black hooded cloak. A man held a boy on his back. Another was wrapped in a robe, topped with a sleeping cap, and held a candle. And finally, a ghostly man stood draped in chains. Ruth stepped closer. The faces looked real. "*Christmas Carol?*"

"*A Christmas Carol*, Ruth. There is an *A* before the word *Christmas*." Dorothy straightened Bob Cratchit's hat. "Aren't they adorable?"

"They look so real." Ruth was charmed.

Dorothy folded her hands and stepped back to admire them. "Byers' Choice. They're all handmade in Bucks County, Pennsylvania. They're extremely collectible and expensive."

The white-gowned figure of the Ghost of Christmas Past; the black hooded one of Christmas Future; and the jolly bearded giant in a green fur-lined robe, the Ghost of Christmas Present, captivated Ruth. "I like them." Ruth wished to live in a world where people still went caroling.

Dorothy touched the red velvet dress of a doll. "I've always wanted to go to the factory. They give tours through their life-size Victorian village, with cobblestone streets and shops like Dickens's London. There's a doll museum with an enormous display. Hundreds of dolls. I've seen pictures."

Ruth imagined it and felt genuine elation like a child might feel upon seeing a special gift. "What fun!"

Dorothy's face fell a bit. "Eugene had no interest, and besides, it seems like a thing for women."

Ruth touched Tiny Tim's crutch.

"Pennsylvania is so far." Dorothy chuckled, but the sound lacked enthusiasm.

Ruth stepped to Dorothy, leaned close to her face, and said, "I could go with you, as your assistant." A moment later, Ruth slumped, afraid Dorothy would think she'd crossed some boundary.

Delight smeared Dorothy's face. She grabbed Ruth's wrist. "Well, there's an idea. How exciting to take a trip! We could also visit the Hershey factory. It's not too far from there."

Ruth tried to maintain her pleasant expression, one she'd learned to uphold under any circumstance, but positive feelings rushed in without effort. She was happy.

The Scrooge doll, long-faced, sported a pink flush beneath molded cheekbones and a pointy, crooked nose. "Their eyes are nice."

"Yes, such humanity." Still smiling, Dorothy turned down the bedding and fluffed the pillows. "We'll talk more about our trip in the morning." Dorothy stepped past Ruth into the tiny bathroom with a telephone-booth shower and pedestal sink, dusty pink. "Here's a new toothbrush and a brand-new bar of soap." Dorothy opened a box lined with satin to reveal a creamy oval bar engraved with the letter F. Her face plumped with pride. "You can use it."

Ruth reached out her hand, then hesitated. "Are you sure? It's so pretty."

"Of course. Soap is meant to be used." Dorothy looked around, admiring her surroundings. "There is a whole stack of towels in the closet." She glanced at the small crystal chandelier hanging from the ceiling. "I took that one from Judith's house, too."

Ruth gazed into the twinkling light.

"I was afraid the cleaning help would take it. They were all Black."

Ruth couldn't pull her eyes from the light. Olivia, the Black woman Ruth had taken care of at the nursing home, was, in her real life, a singer from Barbados who entertained tourists. Olivia was always smiling, so Ruth had thought her mind had gone. Eventually, she'd realized the woman was just happy. She'd said, "I know you've had a tough go, Ruth." Ruth had ignored her until Olivia said, "Honey, you and me, we're the same." Ruth had finally noticed her maple-syrup eyes. "You've been hurt real bad. I can see it." She'd sung softly to Ruth about the sea and the stars. They'd held hands. Sometimes this had made Ruth cry. And sometimes Ruth hadn't known who'd held whom, which felt good. When Olivia died, Ruth wept in the supply room because they weren't supposed to get emotional around the residents.

Dorothy sauntered back to the bedroom with the confidence of a movie star. She flipped her hand. "We have chocolate croissants for breakfast." Dorothy patted the bed, grinned, then whispered, "Bedtime."

While getting into bed, Ruth's heart gushed, and not because of the croissants.

Dorothy pulled the sheet up to Ruth's chin, followed by a fuzzy blanket, and finally the comforter. The word *comforter* stuck in Ruth's mind because it was how she felt at that moment. Dorothy's small hands worked the fabric, pulling and straightening it across Ruth's body. Ruth felt warmth gather within her. Dorothy appeared delighted to do this. She watched Dorothy's face, content and peaceful, and Ruth felt such comfort that she believed the feeling to be love.

"There we go." Dorothy sat on the edge of the bed and looked into Ruth's eyes. "How do you feel?"

Ruth had never been tucked in before, given a brand-new nightgown and fancy unused soap. She took a deep breath, then slowly let it out. "Good. I feel good." With her head cradled into the pillow smelling faintly of lavender, Ruth closed her eyes against the soft blue light. She felt Dorothy get up—the bed moved slightly—then heard her door close with a gentle click. Her thoughts drifted.

Eugene had tucked her in every night. He'd stroked her head with his tender fingertips and kissed her cheek, his lips soft and warm. "I love you" were the last words she'd hear before closing her eyes.

Turning to face the doll of Christmas Present, who held a tiny sprig of holly, Ruth imagined him alive, returning her gaze with his elf-like face. Relaxed, heart slowing to a steady rhythm, Ruth closed her eyes and drifted to "Träumerei" playing inside her head.

Ruth woke when she heard a voice, Dorothy's voice, through the wall. Feet shuffled around in the room next door. With the clank of a metal trash-can lid, the sound of sliding drawers, and a few whispers and murmurs, Ruth's pleasant feelings dissipated. The other door latched, and then Dorothy clicked her heels down the hall, past Ruth's room.

Ruth focused on the dim shine of the doorknob. A couple of months after Denny's, Ruth had attended Irene's funeral. The reception was a genteel affair with white tulips and fine china. She'd hung around the elaborate dessert table, nibbling Scottie-dog shortbread cookies and candy-coated almonds. Someone had said her father's name, the name she'd memorized after Irene had slid her the napkin with his name written with haste in blue ink. So she turned to the kind, familiar, yet much-aged face she'd seen many times as a child, behind the wheel of the banana-split convertible, always parked under the same palm tree on the street just opposite the playground. But for the first time, she realized the uncanny resemblance—the heavy jowls and square, puffy hands. She should have been surprised, possibly shocked, that this man, her father, had watched her from afar throughout her entire childhood, but she wasn't. She had known, somehow, that he was out there and that he cared.

Because at that time, despite all the abuse and cruelness of the world, she was still too young to believe that she could not be loved. When he approached the dessert table, he picked up a cream puff and bit into it. Cream squished out and landed on his chin, then dribbled down to his peach tie. He unsuccessfully dabbed it with a napkin, leaving a white smear. "Hello, there. How did you know Irene?"

Waiting patiently for her answer, not yet looking at her face, he wiped cream from his chin. But Ruth hesitated because she liked the way he looked—the innate kindness, the vulnerability, a certain sweetness, as if the man had never been angry in his life, and she didn't want it to change when she gave him her answer. Contemplating his floppy ears for a moment too long, she said, "She was my mother."

Eugene finally looked up. Seeing her face, his eyes widened and his jowls shook. Was it fear? She knew too well what fear felt like, but she was less familiar with how it manifested in another person. He choked. "Ruth?" Then he hurried away, tripping over a chair. The pain of that moment, the deep tearing of her heart was indescribable. With the turn of her father's back, there was no one. That tiny bit of hope, the weak flame that kept her from the cliff, that had given her a purpose —*he would love me*—had been snuffed out. So she ate a chocolate croissant and listened to the tragic circumstances of her mother's life through shameful murmurs. Irene's condition and the cause of her death had been medically diagnosed—"walking dead syndrome," more officially, Cotard's syndrome, an extremely rare mental illness in which the delusional person believes they are actually walking around while dead. And now Ruth understood Irene's extreme thinness, her strange comments at Denny's, and her tiny sips of coffee—dead people don't eat.

CHAPTER 20

THE BOOK OF RUTH

R uth dumped Cap'n Crunch on her table and opened the window. Marbit flew in with another pigeon that Ruth hadn't seen before. She was smaller, with black eyes and feathers covering her feet like fancy snow boots. *Only males have red eyes.* They ate, working around each other. Ruth sat down to watch.

"Marbit, is this your friend?"

Marbit pecked gently at the other pigeon's beak.

Ruth heard a scream in the hallway. She went to the door to check the lock. Looking at her reflection in the mirror, frightened, her pupils, large black caves, she waited.

Urth's voice came from the other side of the door. "Ruth! Listen! You're going to bleed, bleed to death. The vision came to me just now as I was walking past your door."

Ruth looked back to the pigeons at the table. They kept eating as if nothing were wrong. Ruth got closer to the door. Her breath fogged up the mirror.

Urth's voice came again, deep and ragged. "I can help you if you let me."

Ruth said, "Go away! I don't want your witchcraft." Ruth turned back to the table. This time, Marbit looked up at her. He had a piece of Cap'n Crunch stuck to the top of his head, but he didn't seem to notice.

Urth's voice, again. "Dorothy's going to do it. She's going to kill you, Ruth. She knows who you are. She knows, and she doesn't like it one little bit."

Ruth was startled by a sudden flapping sound. Marbit landed on her shoulder. Ruth looked into the mirror. Her stringy black hair resembled a pirate's. Marbit pecked at her head a few times, then looked into the mirror. He turned his head from side to side, as if admiring himself, then seemed to notice the cereal on his head because he bowed up and down and shook his head all around before finally using his wing to brush it away.

Ruth whispered, "You know who you are." Ruth had read an article explaining how scientists used a "mirror test" to show that pigeons know they are seeing themselves when looking into a mirror. *They are the only birds that are "self-aware."* But when Ruth looked back to the mirror, she hardly recognized herself because oftentimes, she still felt like a little girl.

Urth's voice seeped in again. "Get rid of her, Ruth. She hates you. She's very tricky. You know what to do."

Marbit jumped down to the floor.

Ruth kept looking at her reflection. The shape of her face seemed to distort, as if the mirror were warped.

Urth's voice became softer and smoother. "If you're too chicken, just quit. Stay here with me. We can cook dinner together, watch movies. We can go out."

Marbit flew up and joined his friend on the table. Ruth watched as they groomed each other. Then they huddled up and closed their eyes.

Ruth shouted at her door. "Dorothy likes me! She said I was smart, and sweet, and my eyes are pretty!"

Urth's voice changed again, rough and harsh. "Pack your bags, Ruth. I'm going to the landlord right now, and he hates pigeons. I've watched him lay poison around the building. He tears open the little packets, and the pigeons think it's food. They gobble it up. It must taste good."

Ruth felt sick. She looked back at Marbit and his friend, still sleeping.

"After a few hours, they're all dead, Ruth. It's gross. He tosses them in a trash bag."

Ruth's throat squeezed.

"The babies wander around looking for their parents, and then they find them dead and start making these terrible squeaking sounds like they're crying."

Ruth shook her head, trying to rid herself of the image. *Baby pigeons are called squeakers because of the unique squeaking sounds they make.* Ruth shouted, "I hate you! Go away!" *One rarely sees a baby pigeon because they stay in the nest for two months, drastically increasing their chance for survival.* Urth's beads rattled. Ruth pounded both fists on the door. "I hate you!"

After a long pause, Urth said, "Pack up, Ruth! Once I tell, you're on the streets."

"I've got a new place where you can't come!" Ruth kicked her door, then walked back to the table and sat down in front of Marbit. "I'll pack my bags. I'll pack 'em and never come back because I'm going home, Marbit. Home." Ruth wiped moisture from her forehead.

Marbit bobbed his head. Ruth heard the door to Urth's apartment slam shut.

Ruth slouched and let out a long breath. "I never cried for Esther. The tears haven't come. Why can't I cry? I'm a monster. David said the first step is seeing your own badness, your own sin." Ruth looked up at Marbit. "I did just what Esther asked—like Miss Miller and the others."

Marbit cocked his head back and forth, as if stretching his neck, which shimmered in the sunlight from the window.

Ruth straightened her back. "Dorothy cares for me. I know she does. With all her meanness and the rest, I still want her to like me. I want to make her happy and proud." Ruth lit a cigarette.

Marbit stepped closer to Ruth and looked into her eyes.

Ruth blew smoke toward the window, then scanned her drawings covering the walls. "Eugene gave me those fancy colored pencils. I realize that now. If I had only known back then who he was, that yellow car, him watching, my life might have been very different. He cared for me." She looked at her favorite house, the sweet porch, the palm tree, a yellow car parked in the driveway. "But then I did the same thing, watching David. Why do we keep doing the same things over and over, like it's inherited?"

Marbit jumped into Ruth's lap and nestled in. The feather-footed pigeon flew out the window.

Ruth stroked Marbit's back. "David said Jesus was like a net that caught us all before we hit bottom." Ruth watched a plane fly by her window. "I've always wanted to fly. I hope Jesus caught David when he fell. I imagine that tree, that branch, was Jesus."

Ruth turned to the blue wall when the scratching sound came again, followed by a low-pitched, staccato moan.

Ruth leaned back in her chair and flicked ash on the floor. "All that Jesus stuff seems fine until I think about the bad part of the Catholics—or was that just one man, one bad priest? David said you can't throw out the baby with the bathwater, as if I hadn't heard that old saying before. But it's true. He somehow found God through all the muck." Marbit walked to the edge of the table and poked his beak around. "I'd like to feel God's hand on my shoulder so that I know he's real and it's not just my mind playing tricks."

Ruth closed her eyes. Marbit flew to Ruth's shoulder and cooed. "Why do we need love so badly? I should get over it. It's so humiliating to be unloved. I don't like feeling stupid, either, but to be rejected . . . It feels like I'm half a person. It's like part of me fell away, and now I'm worth less than other people."

Marbit rubbed his head on Ruth's ear. "David said we're made by love, for love. He'd kiss my cheek and say it when he was saying goodbye so that I wouldn't forget—by love, for love—as if it were the only thing that mattered."

The strange sounds from the blue wall became louder. It didn't sound like Urth but more like the low rumble of a growling stomach. The sound left a haunting ache in Ruth's chest.

Ruth watched the wall. "Lonely people don't know they're lonely. They just get uppity and mean, or sometimes they start imagining things."

PART II

CHAPTER 21

DOROTHY

Dorothy's hair got big in the late eighties. She decided to keep it big from then on regardless of the changing fashions. She had her girl tease it way up and spray it firm. Her jewelry collecting and shopping had also reached new heights. At seventy-three, she didn't feel a day past fifty.

It was 1996, and Eugene had finished his masterpiece.

He'd worked in his garage studio for months, or was it years? Giddy, he rushed around, then, with a gentle nudge, urged Dorothy to sit on the sofa. An easel facing the sofa had already been set up. After a brief exit, he shuffled back into the living room with a large canvas draped with a white sheet.

Dorothy had grown tired of Eugene's paint-covered clothing and stained hands. She told him he looked like a painter. He said, "I am a painter."

She corrected him, "You know what I mean—a laborer."

At least this project was over. Like a midlife crisis turned malignant, Dorothy hoped his painting would end for good.

Eugene waited for Dorothy's full attention. Reverently, he pulled the sheet from the canvas. Dorothy felt her blood pressure rise. She clenched her toes and pursed her lips. Eugene smiled with his tongue hanging out, a limp, pink, wet muscle, well trained at pushing food down his throat. He looked back and forth from Dorothy to the painting, then wiped saliva from his chin. "What do you think?"

The painting depicted an old fat woman with big blonde hair. Even the ankles were fat. Bright-red painted toenails bulged around hideous green sandals that Dorothy absolutely did not own. The woman wore copious amounts of gaudy jewelry. The sly smile resembled the Cheshire Cat, wide and cheesy. As was typical for Eugene's work, the paint, garish, poorly mixed, glopped to the canvas as if it had sat around too long under loose lids in hot weather.

"A little like the *Mona Lisa*?" Eugene waited with hope lighting his eyes, like a small boy who'd made something for his mother. He wiped his mouth again, then passed gas.

"Is that what I look like to you?" Dorothy said, her voice low.

Eugene turned back to the painting. "I thought I got your smile just right, and your feet."

Dorothy stood with a huff and left the room.

Later that day, Dorothy read in the den while Eugene banged around the kitchen, rattling chip bags. He appeared in the doorway. "Honey?"

Dorothy lifted her eyes. He was holding a small shopping bag from Carson's.

Eugene stepped into the room and handed Dorothy the bag. "I got you something."

Dorothy accepted it without looking at Eugene's face. Inside were two small boxes. She opened the first to find a large diamond ring. Heavy. Platinum. It sparkled with that new-diamond perfection. Overwhelmed, she smiled.

Eugene took a step closer. "I thought it was time for an upgrade."

Dorothy removed her old ring, slipped the new one on, and held out her hand.

With a hushed voice, Eugene said, "It's over four carats."

Even without children, it was worth it. She let him kiss her hand.

"Open the other box." Eugene smiled.

Equally impressive diamond earrings glittered at Dorothy. "Oh my!"

"The new jeweler, Mr. Halabi, said you needed earrings to match."

Dorothy looked up. "New jeweler?"

"Mr. Carson sold the store last week. His poor wife is sick again."

"I do like this new jeweler!" Dorothy beamed.

"Yes! There! I did get the smile right, my little Mona Lisa."

That evening, Dorothy and Eugene watched the last episode of *Murder, She Wrote*. Eugene made popcorn and got Cherry Coke. Dorothy frowned; she didn't like Cherry Coke. Eugene dropped his cheeks, then hurried back to Gelson's to get regular Coke. Dorothy scolded him when he returned with regular Coke and chocolate cake because she was dieting. However, Gelson's did a nice job with cakes.

In this last episode, "Death by Demographics," a San Francisco radio station owner decides to convert the station's classical format to rock and roll. Tensions rise, and the new program director is disemboweled by a stab from his own fireplace poker. The classical music person was the obvious suspect, but Dorothy and Angela knew better.

As the credits rolled up, Dorothy felt her chest deflate, as if she'd sent an old friend off on a boat, never to return. Twelve years had passed. CBS said the show couldn't compete with the younger generational shows like *Friends* and *ER*. But Dorothy knew better. The show had class. It was enduring. It gave older women a role model in Jessica Fletcher.

Dorothy turned to Eugene. His eyelids drooped. A crumb of cake rested on his lower lip. It wiggled in the wind of each labored exhale from his mouth. Dorothy turned back to the TV. The Pillsbury Doughboy was hopping around a kitchen, giggling about Grands! Buttermilk Biscuits. Eugene opened his eyes to a close-up of a steaming biscuit being effortlessly split open by a woman with taupe fingernails. *Why taupe?* He licked his lips, and the cake crumb disappeared into his mouth. Dorothy stood and left the room.

"Honey?" Eugene called. "Did I miss the end?"

The next day, Eugene rummaged around the kitchen while Dorothy sat in the den. She paused to admire her new ring, wiping it with her sleeve and slowly moving her hand in the light. She went to her piano and played the theme song of *Murder, She Wrote.* Starting with the left hand, then the right joining in, she felt the loss. She wouldn't see Angela every week on TV anymore. This thought hurt, and so Dorothy stopped playing and moved to her desk to write Angela a letter. She took out her best stationery and calligraphy pen but struggled to find words to express her grief. The show had staying power. All ages loved it, not just the old women with nothing better to do. Jessica had been a true role model for widowed women. On and on Dorothy wrote, but like a death, she knew nothing would bring it back. Finally, Dorothy found comfort in the steady flickering of her ring.

Years before, Eugene took Dorothy to dinner and a movie to celebrate her fiftieth birthday. The movie was *Gentlemen Prefer Blondes*, and Dorothy loved every minute. On the drive home, she'd said she identified with Marilyn Monroe because sometimes it was a burden to have such remarkable features. With a serious nod of his head, Eugene had agreed there was an uncanny resemblance. He'd reached over to touch her hand. "You're much more beautiful than her, darling. She is too tall, and her hair is too blonde." Dorothy had believed him, she recalled, because of the intensity of his face and the firmness of his hand grasping hers. "And you're smart and kind." His voice had tightened, the pitch raised. "And to think that you would love an old fuddy-dud like me. I don't deserve you."

After pausing to absorb this memory, Dorothy went back to

her piano and played "Diamonds Are a Girl's Best Friend." Robert joined in, hesitant at first, as if he might not have known it, but he caught on.

Eugene banged around the kitchen and rifled through the pantry. *What could he possibly be looking for?*

She played louder. Robert matched her volume, then rolled along with Bach until the stepladder screeched open, followed by the thump-thump of Eugene's feet climbing. A squeak of metal, the rustling of plastic, a clamp, crash, then a thundering thud shook loose Judith's antique mirror, which hung on the wall dividing the kitchen from the den. Dorothy slid around the piano bench with her back to the keys, to face the crooked mirror, hanging by one corner and swaying slightly. The mirror lost its grip and fell to the floor but remained upright and leaning against the wall where, just on the other side, in the kitchen, something awaited that Dorothy did not want to see.

Dorothy looked closer into the mirror. A jagged crack split it vertically through the center. She heard the faint tick of the mantel clock in the living room. A breeze rustled the palm tree just outside the den window, the one that grew directly on the property line between her and Robert. She stood and walked to the mirror, ran her left hand across the crack, but it felt smooth; eyes closed, she would never know it was broken. She thought of this for a moment, how she could close her eyes and imagine flawlessness, perfection, or anything her mind wanted. When she finally opened her eyes, her ring reflected, dependably sparkled, unbreakable, forever. Sitting on the floor, staring into her broken image, she refused to move.

But when her knees began to ache, Dorothy stood and faced the doorway to the kitchen. One step in that direction, and she would see the thing she did not want to see. So she closed her eyes again. The clock ticked, the palm tree rustled, and so all seemed well until she heard a faint moan.

Dorothy hurried into the kitchen to find Eugene lying on his back, his stomach a giant mound, mouth open and dripping, sweat smearing his temple, eyes blank. Bright-orange squiggly things that resembled shriveled worms surrounded him. Stepping closer, she bent down and picked one up. Twirling it between her fingers, she smelled it, then touched it to her tongue.

Cheese.

Dorothy put it in her mouth and chewed, noticing the orange dust on her fingers. Orange ash also smudged the center of Eugene's forehead, Ash Wednesday, dust to dust. Cheetos. She'd seen the ads on TV with the cheetah wearing sunglasses, but she had never eaten a Cheeto.

The rarely used cabinet above the refrigerator gaped. Dorothy stepped back and lifted to her tippy-toes. It was stuffed full of forbidden snacks, things Dorothy had banned. Potato chips, Doritos, even something called pork rinds. A final breath left Eugene's body, like his habitual sigh before sleeping. She turned.

Dorothy looked at the yellow phone on the wall. *If I call, it will be final.* She wasn't ready, so she moved to the breakfast table, quietly slid out a chair, then sat. *If the body was not moved, if no one knew, maybe it never happened.* She reached for another Cheeto, put it between her teeth, and crunched.

She should have been crying, but Dorothy felt nothing. She loved Eugene, but his body lying on the floor was so absurd that she wasn't sure it was real. How could the world, time, keep moving forward when something so remarkable—a life ending —had occurred? How could everything still feel ordinary? She picked up another Cheeto. If she waited long enough, he might sit up and say, "Hello, darling. I must have dozed off here on the floor. Ha! Isn't that funny?"

Dorothy waited until her eyes became heavy and fatigue overwhelmed her body; then she rested her head on the kitchen table.

Waking to the sound of plastic crackling, Dorothy lifted her head, hopeful. "Eugene?" She scanned the kitchen. The crackling continued. Confused, still groggy, she saw the Cheetos bag moving on its own accord. The bag slid across the floor toward Eugene's head until it stopped next to his ear.

A rat, covered in orange dust, popped out of the bag with a Cheeto between its paws and something glinting around its neck. It crawled onto Eugene's face and sat on its haunches in the center of Eugene's shiny forehead. It nibbled the Cheeto while staring intently at Dorothy. Eugene's teeth protruded. The rat leaned forward, rested its paw on Eugene's third front tooth, and peered into his open mouth, as if it might find more goodies inside.

The room went black. When Dorothy recovered, she felt a goose egg on her temple. Sadly, Eugene remained dead. Dorothy walked, carefully stepping over Eugene to reach the phone. Her hand shook. She recalled her horrific dream, something about a rat. Dialing, gripping the edge of the counter, she said, "My husband has died."

Dorothy busied herself with planning Eugene's funeral. Shopping for new outfits helped take her mind off things, kept her from thinking about living alone. It was like planning a party, but she tried not to think about the reason for the occasion. Instead, she focused on lilies and mums, then decided hibiscus and bougainvillea would be more festive, add more color.

She also decided on her turquoise silk dress and penstemon lip gloss, nails in apricot, and eye shadow in Bahama Blue. She couldn't stand black or gray, but beige was the worst because it just disappeared, like giving up.

The event coordinator at the Ocean Club suggested shrimp cocktail, Stilton blue with red pears, crab-stuffed mushrooms, and a carving station with rare roast beef. Cream puffs and petit fours were selected for dessert because a cake would be inappropriate, advised the chef.

Eugene would wear his tuxedo, the white one. The funeral home lady said it might send a strange message, but Dorothy didn't care; she wanted him to look his best. When it was time to prepare the body, however, Eugene would not fit into the tuxedo that Dorothy had bought for him thirty years prior in anticipation of many formal affairs.

Dorothy insisted, so a seamstress came to the funeral home to measure Eugene's body. The tiny Asian woman had to be coaxed into approaching him. He lay like a gradually sloping mountain, his hands white and puffy, the waxy flesh of his face pulled downward, threatening his ears. The woman measured quickly without touching his body. Her dark, fearful eyes kept darting to Dorothy, who sat in a corner while the old, gray woman who worked at the funeral home cleared her throat and pretended to read.

The seamstress scurried out without a word.

Dorothy watched the door, then turned to the gray lady. "The Orientals are such nervous people."

Later, the funeral home lady called Dorothy to explain that for the tuxedo to work, a large panel would need to be added to the back of the jacket, which no one would see, of course. Panels would also be required for the pant legs and waist.

"Maybe we could get a larger cummerbund," the woman offered. "To cover up the new waistband."

Dorothy agreed. "It will need to match my dress."

The seamstress made an exceptionally large silk turquoise cummerbund, eighteen inches wide and spanning four feet in length, in order to wrap around Eugene's waist. It worked.

Eugene on display, from a seated view in the church, manifested as a bright turquoise mound rising from the coffin like a whale breaking the surface. Surrounded in tropical orange, yellow, and hot-pink flowers, the blue half moon rose from a glossy pewter horizon with brass handles and a white silk interior.

Behind, with the sun pouring through the stained-glass

window, the scene re-created the amateurishly painted mural near the Hispanic beach, a garish splash of color, a smiling dolphin, a green sea turtle. Even the spectators, the guests, men in tangerine pants and women in lime-green blouses, dressed as if attending a luau. Beating drums? The scent of pineapple-glazed roast pig? The sweet tang of a piña colada? Hawaii?

Dorothy had arrived early at the Ocean Club to make sure all the food and tables were done correctly. A miniature rain forest bloomed from the center of each table, dressed in pale-blue cloth like tropical pools. Dorothy had wanted something reminiscent of the Niumalu Hotel in Waikiki, where they'd spent their honeymoon. Gleaming, oversize silverware with the club's emblem engraved into the handle lay precisely two inches from the edge of the table. She straightened a knife that was slightly askew. Pink gold-rimmed charger plates tented with fuchsia napkins gave the impression of sailboats approaching a tropical paradise.

An appetizer table displayed an enormous bowl of pink shrimp on ice. The color made her happy. Pink, especially the right shade, something soft and young, can lift the atmosphere of any occasion. A mound of glossy black caviar was encircled by a ring of precisely arranged water crackers. Cheese wedges, some firm with chalky rinds, others blue and oozing seductively, flanked an ice-sculpture dolphin that sprang from a bed of tightly packed blue delphinium with crests of blue and white passionflower surrounded by birds-of-paradise and yellow cymbidium orchids. A little whimsy never hurt. The crystal stemware twinkled in the sunlight streaming through the commanding picture windows, which overlooked the bluff to the azure ocean beyond. Dorothy again thought of Hawaii, of that second trip when they had returned to give pregnancy one last try, and how Eugene had turned to the window, to the ocean beyond the glass, when he could no longer bear to look

into the enchanting eyes of that peculiar maid who had flus-
tered him.

A tuxedo-dressed waiter—Dorothy had insisted upon white-
tie attire for the staff—approached her with a small silver tray
that balanced a single effervescent glass of pale-gold champagne. "Mrs. Fiske?"

Dorothy, still gazing at the shimmering ocean, thinking of
how strange and small the world can be, turned to him. She
accepted, although she never had alcohol before five. The waiter
bowed and turned to go. She watched him, an older gentleman,
rather handsome, but every man looks good in a tux.

As she surveyed the room once more while sipping champagne at three thirty in the afternoon, her face flushed, and her
focus blurred in a pleasant way. The demanding crystal chandeliers, the hunter-green carpet, the creamy paneled walls, everything scintillating and lustrous—the silverware, the hand-cut
stemware and ice, the gleaming gold rim of the charger plates,
vitreous windows, the ocean, champagne bubbles, and the
radiant fire of her new diamond ring. It was too much, and so
she felt herself becoming light-headed, overwhelmed with shiny,
expensive, twinkling things.

Like a drug, adrenaline coursed through her body. She
always loved that moment right before the guests came when
everything still looked perfect. Standing among it, she became
the very heart of the beauty. They'd walk in with great anticipation, eagerly look around, and be astounded by her good taste
and expensive choices. The orchestrator of such lavishness, such
indulgence, finally, they'd see her for who she was, as she saw
herself, a shining star—Carole, Judy, maybe Angela, but
prettier.

Guests began to arrive. A somber luau, they weren't sure
whether to smile or cry. Dorothy smiled, so most followed suit.
But then a black spot walked in, nonchalant, trying to hide
among groups. Her greasy black hair matched the cheap dress
with floppy pockets. Even black could not conceal the flimsy

synthetic fabric, the ill fit. Terrible cakey lipstick—brown? Cheap gold jewelry, a pinky ring, an ankle bracelet.

Dorothy mingled with her guests, accepted their condolences, but kept a close eye on the woman in black. The woman ate lots of cheese and candied almonds, talked to no one, and stared at the ocean much of the time. Dorothy waited for her to pay her respects, but the woman never approached. Dorothy had seen her before.

The woman put a handful of expensive personalized chocolate boxes in her pocket. Dorothy followed her, and the woman followed Esther when she left with her driver. She watched from the window as the woman got into a light-blue Toyota with a large dent in the passenger door. The Toyota backed out. Black smoke billowed up from the exhaust pipe as it crept around the parking lot, swerving slightly, like a shark scouting for prey, before locking in on Esther's car and trailing it out of the lot.

After the reception, Dorothy retired to her bedroom and stood in front of her full-length mirror. She looked good. Her makeup had held up. Her hair wasn't flat. That was something. But her feet hurt, so she slipped off her heels and rubbed the deep indentations where the straps had pinched.

Exhausted, she lay across the bed with one hand dangling off the side. Closing her eyes, she reviewed the reception. The shrimp ran out. The beef was overcooked, and the pork was too pink. Who was that woman in black? She'd specifically asked that no one wear black. That same dress one year prior, another funeral, where the woman had spoken to Eugene and had eaten all the Scottie-dog cookies. How did she know Irene? Dorothy had ideas, of course. Angela and Agatha would know. Poirot would have it all figured out. But many times, they waited. It was necessary to wait in order to catch the killer. Careful not to give up their hand too soon. They were cautious and clever. Dorothy felt enlivened by this thought.

She opened her eyes to the chaotic 1980s popcorn-textured ceiling over her bed. Popcorn on a ceiling? She'd have it scraped off. More. She was more cautious. She was more clever. More beautiful, more wealthy, more connected, but most of all, she was more patient.

Eugene. His faint scent, designer aftershave, lingered in the sheets. The scent drifted, as if he'd walked into the room. She thought of how frumpy he'd seemed that very first night at Judith's party. His first words, *You smell nice.* His bear hugs. She loved his hugs. His adoration of food. The sweet smile he offered her each morning over coffee. The movies. His unexplainable contentment. How, in his eyes, she saw his heartbreak every time she'd cried over a new baby dress, never to be worn. And then she thought of how his heart did break.

Now, she would eat alone. Watch TV alone. Would she ever go out to dinner and a movie again? Would anyone ever buy her a gift? Hug her? Love her? For the first time since Eugene died, she wept.

Something brushed against her hand. Afraid to open her eyes, remaining still, waiting, she felt it again. Silk? Fur?

A faint voice—an angel, she concluded later—spoke: "Now get up, go to the bank, and take care of business. You've got an estate to manage."

At seventy-four, she was able-bodied and looked good. And who's to say she wouldn't marry again? After all, Elizabeth Taylor married eight times. She looked at her new diamond. Eugene had good taste, in jewelry, at least. Maybe she'd move it to the other hand.

CHAPTER 22

NEON CARROT

During the previous month, Ruth had stayed more nights in Dorothy's guest bedroom than in her apartment. With Esther gone, Ruth had been focusing all her attention on Dorothy. She'd kept the window in her apartment open and bowls of cereal out on the table for Marbit, but she still checked on him daily.

Her own fridge contained lumpy milk, generic root beer, and ketchup. Laundry was difficult. She had to use the laundromat, but it was too far to walk and parking was a challenge, so she ended up not washing her sheets for months. But when she stayed with Dorothy, she always had fresh linens infused with jasmine-scented ironing water, because she did them herself.

Dorothy bought good food. Ruth was happy to cook. She'd fix many of Dorothy's old recipes from Dorothy's mother, Inga, who Dorothy said had died of old age. But Ruth knew that was never true; they always died of something. Dorothy even gave Ruth one of Inga's old nightgowns—a beautiful yellow satin with a matching robe and slippers.

It was early November. Dorothy instructed Ruth to begin decorating for Christmas. Boxes full of decorations were stuffed in closets throughout the house. Each item, breakable or not, was encased in bubble wrap and secured with heavy-duty packing tape. Curious, Ruth tried to turn the knob on the door to the room at the end of the hall, but it was locked.

Dorothy came around the corner. "I told you, Ruth, there's nothing in there."

Back in the living room, Ruth struggled to unwrap a two-foot Santa Claus doll dressed in Bermuda shorts and sunglasses.

Dorothy watched for a moment. "What are your plans for Christmas?"

Ruth held Santa with both arms, hugging him to her chest. "Nothing."

Dorothy sat on the sofa. "I was thinking of asking Robert over for Christmas dinner. I'd like you to cook."

Ruth gripped Santa's leg. "Robert?"

Dorothy smirked. "Does that bother you?"

Ruth's jaw tightened. "I thought you didn't like him in that way."

Dorothy admired her rings. "His wife was peculiar, but I always thought Robert was pleasant. They came to my Fourth of July party only once. My parties were quite elaborate. Everyone wanted an invitation. I served wonderful food. I always thought it was because he wasn't American, but I think it was his wife—something wasn't right. There was lots of talk at her funeral. She was sick in the head."

Sick in the head? Who says that? Something billowed up. Ruth tried to push it down, but it welled and spilled until she just let it happen; the feeling was a verb, to protect, like mothers to children, or maybe children to mothers. Irene was her mother, after all, and her illness was not her fault.

Ruth dug her fingernails into Santa, watching them sink into his Hawaiian shirt. After Irene's funeral, Ruth changed her last name from Saunders, her foster name, to Bernardez, her mother's maiden name. It had felt right at the time. She had still been so hurt, but Eugene was a good man. She'd known it from his face, his eyes, and by the way he'd said hello. She'd wanted to run, too, when she'd met David that first time. Guilt was powerful, a demon, sometimes gloomy and sickening, other times fierce and shrieking. Her whole adult life, it had tormented her, sneaking up at odd or inconvenient times, the sight of a young boy with dark hair, in the presence of any pregnant woman, the hue of the ocean in certain weather, even the color of Wild Blackberry and Margarita Jelly Belly jelly beans when chewed together. Both her babies had his eyes—as beautiful as they were, the color still haunted her.

"I want us to each have exactly forty-five peas." Dorothy handed Ruth a pen and a pad of floral stationery.

Ruth set down Santa and took the pen and pad. "Forty-five?" Ruth wrote *forty-four* because she could not bring herself to write an odd number. She associated everything bad with odd numbers, especially her age. Ten was good—she'd first seen the yellow-car man (Eugene)—but eleven was very bad, Halloween. Twelve was tolerable—she'd done a lot of drawing with her new papers and pencils (also Eugene)—but thirteen was horrendous; he'd (her brother) started coming to her room, and so it went.

Dorothy picked up a figurine of a mouse wearing a Santa hat. "We'll have a roast. My butcher knows what I want. And you'll need to make my mother's recipe for scalloped potatoes. Slice them thin or it's no good."

Ruth scribbled it down. "So, is Robert coming?"

Dorothy set the mouse on the coffee table. "I haven't asked yet."

"Let me ask him for you." Ruth scraped her tongue across her teeth and gripped the pen until her hand ached.

Dorothy looked at Ruth for a moment. "That's a good idea."

Ruth tapped her pen on the pad, relieved that she would have some control. "Dessert?"

Dorothy gazed at a rainbow on the wall, cast through a prism from the chandelier.

Ruth leaned in. "Dorothy?"

Dorothy moved her eyes back to the writing pad. "Yes, let's see. How about my famous winter carrot cake with snow-white icing."

Ruth wrote as instructed but thought of how to keep Dorothy and Robert apart. Ruth had found a safe place, a home, and someone to talk to. What would happen to her if they married?

Dorothy stood and went to the dining room, motioning for Ruth to follow. She opened the china cabinet. "You'll need to shred the carrots first and then mince them. Did you get the knives sharpened yet?"

Ruth imagined scraping each carrot by hand, creating long orange ribbons. "Not yet."

Dorothy took out a crystal cake platter. "Well, it'll be more work, then, but the carrot pieces must be very, very fine."

Ruth wrote "MINCE FINE" on her paper.

"Men have always been drawn to me." Dorothy sat at the dining table, laid her hands on the surface, and straightened a sapphire ring, an exact replica of Princess Diana's wedding ring, a large oval sapphire surrounded by fourteen diamonds. "I wanted a ring like Diana's, so Mr. Halabi made me this. Do you like it?"

"It's beautiful." Ruth had gotten better at hiding her interest. She knew what Dorothy was doing.

"The sapphire cost a fortune because of the color. See how it's not too pale or dark? It's classified as Royal Blue." Dorothy took off the ring and handed it to Ruth.

The ring flashed with sunlight from the window, brilliant blue. Ruth said, "Yes, the color is outstanding."

Dorothy, plastered grin, eyes sharp, waited, as if she wanted Ruth to say more. "Anyway, it was Mr. Halabi's suggestion. He said I reminded him of a Scandinavian princess. He likes that look."

Blue. The ocean, the sky, a blueberry, a jay. Ruth could not think of candy at that moment. She could only think of her children and how their eyes had been that same deep blue flecked with gold, like precious jewels, and how David's eyes had changed as he got older. As the color of water changes with shifting light, the green had emerged in spots, and so they had developed a sort of depth, with layers, which Ruth had studied so many times on their beach walks. Ruth now wondered about the ultimate color of Jane's eyes. She still hoped to see them someday.

Dorothy pushed hair from her forehead. "Men really do prefer blondes. What is the natural color of your hair, Ruth?"

With no photos of herself as a child—no one had bothered to take any—Ruth had no idea. "Brown, I think."

"Why do you make it so dark?" Dorothy looked all around Ruth's head. "Your roots are gray," she said, then looked away, as if Ruth's hair were hopeless. Looking back, she asked, "When will you invite Robert?"

Later, Ruth walked over to Robert's house very slowly so that she could smoke the last third of her cigarette. Once on his porch, she extinguished it, then picked ash from her tongue and slipped the butt into her cardigan. She hated it when people threw them on the ground because her brother had always just tossed them, like the world would clean up his mess.

Ruth knocked.

Robert opened the door. His frizzy gray hair, yellow streaked, was long and wild until he smoothed it over with both hands. He smiled. "Hello. Ruth, aye? Please come in."

Ruth stepped just inside the foyer. The floor plan appeared to be a mirror image of Dorothy's house, but everything was plain and drab. "Mrs. Fiske has sent me to invite you to Christmas dinner at her home."

"Oh?" Robert's face brightened. He inspected her like he

had at the restaurant, his eyes moving over every feature of her face. "I am very busy these days." He walked into the living room and gestured at a beige sofa. "Please sit down."

Ruth stayed in the foyer. "I need to get back to Mrs. Fiske. She would very much like for you to come to dinner."

Robert focused on Ruth's sandaled feet, her toenails thick and yellow, with remnants of hot-pink polish. Ruth's second toe was much longer than her big toe. It made buying shoes difficult. Robert seemed to notice this. "Can you stay for tea?"

Ruth moved toward the door and grasped the knob. "I'm sorry, but I need to get back. Can I tell Mrs. Fiske that you're coming?"

Robert's eyes held steady on Ruth's feet. "Aye. I'd like that very much."

At five o'clock on Christmas day, Dorothy waited in the foyer, wearing a long gown in red velvet.

Her hair and nail lady had come the previous day—a facial, all new makeup. Ruth had driven Dorothy to Saks for the velvet gown, then to DressBarn. "Ruth, you need a black dress," Dorothy had said. Ruth had told her she already had one, but Dorothy insisted she get a new one because the other was probably too tight. When they returned home, Dorothy had presented Ruth with a ruffled white apron and matching maid hat to tie around her bun. "There, now you'll look the part," she'd said.

Ruth tried to smile before letting her eyes fall to the floor, where she noticed Dorothy's glossy, red toenails peeking out from beneath her gown. She kept her goal in mind—Robert and Dorothy would not get close. She wasn't sure how she would prevent the relationship, but she would. She was happy with Dorothy, and so there was no need to bring in a man.

Dorothy said, "Ruth, look at me."

Ruth raised her eyes to Dorothy's face. Her lips also matched the dress, and her soft-blue eye shadow extended all the way to her brows. Ruth scraped her tongue against her bottom teeth while scratching at an imaginary itch in the crook of her arm.

Dorothy tipped her chin down. "This needs to go well. Do you understand?"

Ruth nodded slowly. Her neck made a funny cracking sound as it pushed through the tension held there.

Dorothy reached up and cradled Ruth's chin as if she were a naughty child. "Go on, now, and get ready."

Robert arrived in his tweed jacket and dark glasses. Ruth served tiny sausages on green cocktail napkins and flutes of pink champagne on a silver tray that she had polished that morning.

Dorothy's heels clicked back and forth across the foyer as she showed Robert the *Blue Book*, the social register of Southern California, on the coffee table, where she proudly pointed out "Mr. and Mrs. Eugene Fiske" before sitting in the dining room. Ruth waited in the doorway to the kitchen with her hands folded in front of her waist, as Dorothy had instructed.

Ruth's thoughts drifted to the dolls in her bedroom. She had turned them so that they faced her when she lay in bed. The Ghost of Christmas Future had no face, only a shadowy darkness under the black hood. She tried to think of a face.

Dorothy and Robert eventually sat at the dining table. Dorothy gave Ruth a head nod indicating that she was ready for dinner to be served. Ruth went to the kitchen to plate the dinner. Dorothy hadn't brought up the trip to Pennsylvania again, so Ruth wondered if she'd forgotten or if she really didn't mean it. It hurt to think this, but she pushed it down deep, into the same place she held all her other hurts and disappointments, insults, and abuses. It was crowded in there, a whole life's worth. What if it overflowed and spilled out everywhere for all to see?

Ugly, it would be ugly, and people might slip on the mess and get hurt.

Ruth returned with plates of steaming food and placed them precisely as Dorothy had instructed, in the very center of each place mat. Dorothy shooed Ruth back to the doorway leading to the kitchen with a flick of her wrist, so Ruth resumed her position. She focused on the chandelier since Dorothy had instructed her not to stare at them.

Dorothy swallowed a bite of roast and wiped her mouth with her napkin, needlepointed with a Christmas tree. "What brought you to America, Robert?"

"Aye. I was raised by my two old-maid aunts in Glasgow. When my sister immigrated to Delaware, she wrote to me to come join her for school. I earned my degree in accounting, worked there a few years, but read about the nice weather in Southern California and so came this way when I was twenty-five. Bought myself a Cadillac, then a Mustang, 1967, Acapulco Blue. It's still in my garage."

Dorothy cleared her throat. "Accounting. That seems interesting."

"Well, no, but the money was fine." Robert looked at his plate. "I did some work for Eugene's father, Walter. I'm sure you knew that."

Dorothy cocked her head. "No, I didn't."

"Just a little work with some of his rentals. I didn't do *all* his accounting."

Dorothy glanced to her rings. "I see."

"Yes, he sold me my house." Robert waited, as if this might jog Dorothy's memory. "He bought both houses, yours and mine."

Dorothy glanced to Ruth, then back to Robert.

"Walter had some social connections with Irene's parents. They were quite wealthy as well."

Dorothy chewed with intention, then swallowed. "Is that how you met Irene?"

Robert took a bite, chewed, then swallowed. "Oh, well, not exactly."

Dorothy waited, as if he owed her an explanation.

Robert wiped his chin with his napkin. "We met in the library. She was holding a copy of *Dr. Jekyll and Mr. Hyde*."

"*Strange Case of Dr. Jekyll and Mr. Hyde* by Robert Louis Stevenson," Dorothy corrected.

Robert chuckled. "Yes, of course, very good. Anyway, she asked me if I'd read it. Then, noticing my accent, and Stevenson also being of Scottish descent, as you well know, she asked my name. When I said Robert, she took it as some sort of sign and became obsessed with that book."

Dorothy leaned in. Her eyes were bright. "What a fascinating story."

"We were married six months later, and then I was introduced to Walter Fiske."

Dorothy squinted. "I see."

Robert looked at his plate again. "This is very nice china."

Dorothy touched the rim of her plate. "It's French. A wedding gift from my in-laws."

"Irene liked the finest china." Robert continued to stare at his plate. "We used to take trips to London. She wanted to live there and be British. Her family was Spanish. A real Spanish beauty." Robert shook his head, as if ridding himself of her memory. "In London, we'd stay at the Dukes, a fine place, very expensive."

Dorothy had relaxed some, but she'd turned coy, with a downward tilt of her chin, as if she were gathering facts to be used later for some grand revelation. "Sounds lovely."

Robert looked up at the yellow stain on the ceiling surrounding the chandelier; frowning, he shifted his gaze to the buffet table, where figurines of small children wearing stocking hats pulled an old-fashioned sleigh. "Christmas is for children. That's what they say."

Dorothy looked at the figurines. "Sometimes I wonder what my life would have been like with children."

Robert said, "I would have liked a child."

Dorothy pushed around the food on her plate. "Holidays, birthdays, school, family vacations, all of it."

Robert glanced at Ruth. "Irene couldn't have children."

Dorothy also shifted her eyes quickly to Ruth, then back to Robert. "Eugene had a problem, too."

Robert fiddled with his fork. "I see."

"I wanted a girl to shop for, to dress up, to spoil." Dorothy laughed. "I'd have named her Tiffany after Tiffany and Company, of course."

Robert smiled. "Tiffany would no doubt have been the best-dressed girl in the Palisades, that's for certain."

Ruth, thinking of their shopping trip and her new black dress, understood irony now, after all Dorothy had taught her, after all the mysteries they'd watched, and so she smiled to herself while smoothing down the front of her apron.

Dorothy's eyes lifted. She straightened her spine. "Why thank you, Robert."

"If we'd had children, though, we wouldn't be sitting here tonight, now, would we?" Robert showed his worn, gray teeth.

"No, probably not." Dorothy blinked and touched the loose skin of her throat.

Ruth became lost in the chandelier and recalled a beach walk with David. He'd asked about his father, and so she explained everything as best she could. He already knew the man who raised him was not his father, had suspected it for a while, but he didn't know he was the product of violence. His face changed after she told him, hurt, angry, but not at her. He seemed to swallow something painful; the cords of his neck went tight and his eyes narrowed before he touched her hand and kissed her cheek. *By love, for love.* Glossy-eyed, he looked at her as if she were the hurt one, when all she wanted was to comfort him. What she wouldn't have given to hold his baby self as a secure adult mother. The agony of missing his baby skin against her own, cheek to cheek, was the cruelest of all her pain.

"What do you like to read?" Dorothy asked.

Robert cleared his throat. "The very best book, which I've read several times, is *The Rise and Fall of the Third Reich* by William L. Shirer. Everyone should read it."

"Oh my! I like mysteries and Dickens, Austen, Brontë."

Ruth turned her attention to the center crystal shard pointing precisely over the roast. That feeling, so strange. It was the first time Ruth had been kissed by a man on the cheek. She understood what it could have been, to be loved, or maybe treated kindly, by a man. She kept reminding herself that she was his mother while trying to forget where he'd gotten those beautiful eyes, emerald facets and indigo inclusions, cerulean, turquoise, like those pictures of beaches on wall calendars, like Hawaii.

Robert removed his glasses, took a small bottle of drops from his jacket, tilted his head back, and let two fall into each eye. "Irene and I read Dickens many nights—first I'd read aloud, then her. She wanted to live in those stories."

Dorothy folded her hands and smiled. "How nice. I can see now that your eyes are blue. May I ask why you wear the glasses indoors?"

"My doctor told me too much color TV would ruin my eyes, so now everything's black and white."

"Mine are blue as well, very light blue." Dorothy opened her eyes wide. "Can you see?" Batting her lashes, she asked, "Would you like to see my Dickens village? And my piano?"

"Lovely." Robert's eyes caught on Dorothy's hand. "I couldn't help but notice your ring. Princess Diana?"

Dorothy flicked her finger around. "Yes, Mr. Halabi at Carson's made it for me."

Robert still watched the ring. "Once, at Dukes hotel in London, we were told we couldn't sit at our regular table for breakfast because there was a special guest. I was irritated, and

Irene was, too, but we obliged. Everyone stood when Princess Margaret sauntered in with her long cigarette. She went right to our table and sat down."

Dorothy's eyes grew round and shiny in the low light.

"She ordered a cheap scotch." Robert's face twisted up, disgusted. "We were slow to stand. Irene liked the finest things. She was a princess herself, attended Scripps."

Dorothy jutted her neck back. "Oh! Eugene went to Pomona."

Robert leaned forward. "Ah! What years?"

Dorothy looked at the ceiling. "Let's see. Would have been thirty-eight to forty-two. He was a theater major."

Robert leaned back. "Well now, that is a coincidence. Irene was there in thirty-nine and forty. She never finished." He set down his fork. "She had a very large tumor in her uterus and had to drop out to have it removed."

Dorothy's eyes widened. "Oh my."

"She told me that it wasn't dangerous or anything, just very large. It grew quite rapidly, over a period of nine months or so."

Dorothy stopped chewing and stared at Robert's plate as if she were counting the peas.

Robert mimicked holding a beach ball in front of his stomach. "It just grew and grew. And then she had it removed. She was fine after that. It had made her feet sort of swollen, and she was very uncomfortable at the end. She talked about it often, like it really had an impact on her life."

"I see." Dorothy resumed chewing, slowly.

Robert's cheeks sank. "I guess it did. She couldn't have children after that."

Ruth laughed with a shocking burst of chattering, as if she were a chimpanzee. Dorothy and Robert turned to look.

A tumor? She'd been called many things, but a tumor? An overgrowth of flesh? *That's a new one,* she thought. It really cracked her up. "Excuse me. I was just remembering something funny."

Robert turned back to look at Dorothy, whose lips had transformed into a thin red line. "Irene and Eugene must have known each other. The consortium shared one library, and then, of course, with their parents being acquainted . . . She had the most stunning green eyes, utterly unforgettable." He turned his head again to look at Ruth.

Dorothy's face went blank, as if the room had shifted and she was forced to reorient herself. Mouth gaping. Still focused on Ruth. The stone of Ruth's necklace, unintentionally exposed against her black dress, burst with yellow light.

Ruth, still standing obediently in the doorway, shifted her eyes to gaze down at the stone. He'd loved her at one time, even if fear and guilt had spoiled things. Eugene had loved her, and there was nothing Dorothy could do about it.

Robert sipped his champagne as if to signal a change of topic.

Ruth turned and headed into the kitchen to prepare coffee and dessert. The look on Dorothy's face was undeniable. She knew. Ruth should have felt something with them making connections, but she understood Dorothy well now, so distracted by him, and Robert, clueless. *Steady.* It would pass. Old, feeble minds, their memories held securely in deep ruts, were unable to change the story they had repeated too many times, even if it was untrue. Like most people, they believed what they wanted to believe.

Dorothy, with the voice of a robot, said, "Ruth, we'll take coffee in the den."

"Yes, Mrs. Fiske," Ruth called through the doorway.

Ruth measured the coffee grounds. She rubbed a few grains between her fingers, then watched them fall, like coarse sand, onto the counter. A week after their last beach walk, David fell from the bluff but never reached the beach because his head cracked on a rock that projected from the side. His body, entangled in the branches of a withered tree growing horizontally from the cliff wall, hung upside down, the Cross of Saint Peter righted, his boot wedged between the forks of two branches. He'd bled to death.

Ruth prepared the tray. Dorothy wanted her to use all the pieces of her sterling service, so she included a side of chocolate pralines, but they turned her stomach. She arranged the tray, then paused before leaving the kitchen. When Ruth was seven, her brother had had friends over. He'd said it was a new kind of candy. He'd even eaten one himself. Showed her the inside filled with coconut cream. He knew she loved coconut. "Go ahead, try it." He'd been nice that day, played a game of jacks with her. He picked one up and held it out, smiling, while his friends covered their faces, peeking through spread fingers. She didn't understand because she'd smelled the sweetness on his breath when he leaned in.

Ruth lifted the heavy tray and carried it to the den. She stopped when she saw Robert sitting in Eugene's chair, her chair. Something tightened deep inside her chest, torrid, a twisting that spread up her throat and into her jaw.

"Ruth? Why are you just standing there?" Dorothy sounded disgusted.

Ruth stared at a lumpy praline, the nuts hidden by chocolate. As a child, when she'd bit into the brown oval lump, her teeth sinking in, she'd seen that look on her brother's face. More than a smile. More than ordinary delight had flashed through his indigo-blue eyes with the black fleck of a pirate ship shifting with the violent storm inside his head. His face had radiated pure distilled pleasure. She'd spit, but it was too late, stuck in her teeth. The horrific taste. The house across the street had dogs, big and smelly, with matted fur and ragged, saliva-coated gums. Ruth avoided the yard because she'd stepped in dog poop once and never got the smell off. Ruth recalled that smell as she listened to the cackling laughter of her brother while wiping her tongue with her shirt. She gagged onto the floor. A string of brown saliva swung from her lip. When she looked up, she saw the boys, one slapping his knee, holding his stomach, the other, face steady, eyes blinking thoughtfully, who later, holding her baby boy, believing it was his own, would beg her not to leave.

Ruth looked up and gained her composure before setting the tray on the coffee table. "Mr. McClure, do you take cream or sugar?"

Dorothy watched Ruth, inspected her face as if she'd never seen it before. "Ruth, what year were you born?"

CHAPTER 23

EUGENE

Eugene sat at his desk in a black suit and peach tie, waiting for Dorothy to get ready for the funeral. He hated the color peach, and there was still no sign of Lincoln. Irene, his neighbor, the mother of his only child, his first love, had died.

He looked down at the tie, flipped it over—*100% silk. Strange to think fine things are made from worms. Why not spiderwebs?*

Dorothy clicked around the bathroom. Her heels could be heard anywhere in the house, which was useful information. She appeared in the hallway, her head crowned in rollers. Pausing, her face drooped at the sight of Eugene, an expression he was quite used to. Eugene smoothed his hair down and offered a weak smile. Dorothy let out a huff, then went downstairs. Her hair would need to set for at least two hours, so Eugene opened the side drawer of his desk to find his bag of rainbow gummy worms.

Eugene's fishing pole leaned against a wall. He'd taken it out because he planned to practice casting in the backyard. Rising from his desk, still chewing his worm, Eugene retrieved his pole. He inspected the hook, poked it with his finger. Reaching into his drawer, he took a gummy worm and pierced it, then centered himself with the hallway that led to the master bedroom.

A flip of his wrist, a push of the button, and Eugene successfully cast the gummy worm all the way to the bed, landing it right on Dorothy's pillow. Despite the somberness of the day, Eugene smiled. Slow and steady, he reeled it in. Falling to the floor, it squirmed across the carpet, then bounced onto the hardwood of the hall. As he reeled it in, the sound of the dial so satisfying, Eugene focused on the wiggly worm moving toward him.

He rode a boat in the wide-open ocean, where a giant marlin surfaced to eye his bait. The rocking boat, the glaring sun, Eugene saw the spiked fin emerge from the glistening water. He pulled back. The marlin flipped out. The boat rocked. Eugene pulled harder, but the fish fought back with a powerful twist. The line broke.

Eugene lost his balance and fell into his desk chair. The worm lay still on the dusty floor. If Lincoln came out, he might hook his paw, mouth, or tender snout, which could cause blood loss or infection.

Efficiently, Eugene reeled until the worm popped over the front of his desk. It rested on his blotter, dull and dead. Staring a moment, Eugene thought of Irene. How her face had bloomed with delight when he'd asked her out for ice cream at Pomona. How dark and beautiful she'd looked with firm, young flesh on her bones. How his touch had made her flinch, then cry, because images of her father surfaced from nowhere. The confusion. His resistance. Her insistence, nothing, just her imagination, she'd said, but kept crying. He just wanted to ease her pain. Then the baby, Ruth, grew inside.

Eugene unhooked the worm and twirled it between his fingers, then placed it in his mouth.

CHAPTER 24

SUNGLOW

A month had passed. Ruth hoped that Christmas dinner with Robert was the last "date" Dorothy would have with any man. But it was more than hope; Ruth was resourceful and often underestimated, and so she planned to take steps to ensure this outcome. Ruth believed that she was all Dorothy needed, and Ruth was determined to live out the rest of her life in Eugene's house.

Ruth had decided not to sell the jewelry she'd taken. She liked wearing it around her apartment, and Dorothy paid her enough, but she was curious to see what it was worth. A pawnshop would never tell her the real value, so she took a couple of the best pieces to the fanciest jewelry store in Santa Monica. Realizing it might look strange to pull them from her pockets, she used her good purse, wore her black funeral dress, and tied her hair up.

Ruth pulled open the heavy glass door and walked in. Several salespeople lifted their heads before giving her a quick up and down, but she remained steady and asked to talk to the manager.

A moment later, a stodgy man wearing a dark suit and small round glasses stepped forward. "Can I help you?"

Ruth's purse, which she set on the counter, exhaled the scent of smoke and spearmint gum. "I was hoping to get some jewelry that I inherited appraised."

"Our gemologist is only here on Thursdays." He held his hands behind his back as though he were hiding something.

Ruth opened her purse and held out Esther's ruby ring. "Are you interested in estate jewelry?" She put the ring on her finger. "It's from Burma, but I guess I can come back." Ruth looked out the window. "Or try somewhere else."

The man fixed his eyes upon the ruby. "Let me take a look."

Ruth handed him the ring.

He held a small tool to his eye.

Ruth cleared her throat.

A subtle gasp slipped from the man's mouth, as if he'd just seen a movie star. "Magnificent, the fluorescence." Looking back at Ruth, he said, "Where did you say you acquired this piece?"

Ruth felt a rush of adrenaline move into her limbs. "This was from my aunt, but much of the rest is from my mother, who passed."

"I see." The man, eyes wide, handed the ring back to Ruth, then wiped his brow.

"She loved jewelry." Ruth slid the ruby onto her finger, then pulled the sapphire bracelet from her purse, the clasp still broken. She'd noticed it on the kitchen counter that morning, right next to the coffee pot—a strange place for it, but Dorothy frequently left her jewelry in odd places. "My grandfather gave this to my grandmother when my father was born."

Ruth tried to breathe deeply. The truth felt good.

The man picked up the bracelet. He held his tool back to his eye. An audible breath, scented with coffee, escaped through his lips. "It's fantastic. The color is perfect. I'd guess 1920."

"Close, 1921." Ruth smiled, then brought her lips together.

The man nodded. "The bracelet is worth at least seventy thousand." He paused. "But the ring, old-mine Burma, Pigeon Blood, like seeing the face of God. Maybe five carats." He looked up, breathless. "I can't even begin to explain its worth."

Blood, she agreed. Another rush of emotion flowed through her body.

"I'd need confirmation from my gemologist, but if I had to guess, I'd say at least a million." Sweat ran down the man's temples. "You need these in a safe."

Ruth swallowed, her throat sticky. "I have a safe. I'm up in the Palisades."

The man dabbed his temple with a cloth. "Who's your mother?"

Ruth cleared her throat. "Do you know the Fiskes?"

The man raised his brows. "You're a Fiske?"

Ruth stood tall. "Yes." And she was. The truth, again.

The man's eyes darted to Ruth's cheap purse with artificial leather cracking at the seams. One eyebrow cinched tight. "Why don't you bring the rest of it back on Thursday? Would ten work?"

Ruth hurried from the store. She'd be late. Dorothy would be angry. *Pastries.* Late bearing gifts was better than late empty-handed. Her spirits were high, so she was determined to change Dorothy's mood.

She walked into Gelson's wearing the ring and bracelet, a Fiske. A million dollars glittered from her finger. The ring appeared even more spectacular in the harsh fluorescent lights, a red stoplight. Pigeon Blood and Cornflower Blue. Ruth picked through the produce with no intention of buying. It felt good. Alive, she saw it clearly now, felt intensely, why Dorothy loved wearing her jewelry; she was no longer invisible.

A young woman with perfect legs could not take her eyes from the ring as Ruth selected an apple. An older woman wearing too much makeup stared at the bracelet. She stepped aside and said, "Excuse me," while reaching for a bag of spinach. Ruth had never liked to be looked at before, but now, with this ring, this bracelet, she wanted everyone to see because her body, her very being—Ruth Fiske, was now a rare treasure.

Ruth gazed into the ruby. In 1951, Miss Miller placed the silver crown on Ruth's head Halloween morning, before she left for school. It kept slipping, so Miss Miller added a few hair combs around the inside band. Ruth had never seen, let alone worn, anything so regal. She even walked differently, straight, with a wider stride and lifted head. She was a queen or, in this case, a good witch.

Once at Dorothy's house, Ruth removed the bracelet and tucked it into her purse. She ran inside and set the Gelson's bag on the kitchen counter before peeking into the den.

A deep, ragged voice came from behind Ruth. "You're late."

Ruth started, then turned. Dorothy stood behind her.

Ruth fumbled with her fingers, realizing she was still wearing Esther's ring. "I know. I'm so sorry. I had to run an errand." She held her hands behind her back, trying to remove the ring.

Dorothy looked stern. "What kind of errand?" Her face softened to worry.

Ruth managed to remove the ring and slip it into her pocket.

Dorothy looked Ruth up and down. "Why are you wearing that black dress?"

Ruth hadn't thought about the dress. "I . . . I . . ."

"We talked about color. I've given you lots of nice, expensive things to wear with color."

"I know. I just grabbed the first thing." Ruth tried to distract Dorothy by pulling a white bakery box from the Gelson's bag. She opened the lid and tilted it so that Dorothy could see.

Dorothy's eyes widened. "Éclairs!"

Ruth smiled. "Two for you and two for me."

"Why, Ruth, how thoughtful!" Dorothy touched Ruth's arm. "Should we have them after lunch?"

Ruth paused, still smiling. "What if we had them before lunch?"

Dorothy giggled. "What if we had them *for* lunch?"

"Even better." Ruth got two plates from the cabinet. "In the den?"

Dorothy headed that way.

"What should we watch today?" Ruth sat in Eugene's chair.

Dorothy's face sagged in the harsh light coming through the window. Her eyelids melted into the base of her lashes. "We only have one episode of *Murder, She Wrote* left."

"We watched them all?" Ruth licked her éclair.

"Almost."

"Should we finish?" Ruth took a tiny nibble.

Dorothy stared into the black TV screen. "Eugene died the day after the last episode, in 1996." She put a finger on her éclair, testing its freshness. "It was the last thing we watched together. You never know when the last day will be."

"The last time I saw my son, we walked on the beach." Ruth pointed to the west window. "Down there. Below the bluff."

Dorothy's face changed, soft and sincere. "What happened, Ruth? What happened to him?"

Ruth felt heat in her cheeks. "I don't know. He fell off the edge. It was 1990." Ruth looked at the window. "He'd been working at that Self-Realization Shrine. Gardening. He seemed happy."

The sound of Robert's piano seeped in.

"'Clair de Lune.'" Dorothy took a bite of her éclair, cheek quivering, chewed, then swallowed. "That sort of place confuses people. Mixing Jesus with Buddha." Dorothy flung her hand in the air. "As if anything goes."

Formalized religion confused Ruth. But she wondered sometimes because David was a Catholic. He'd clearly found something there, both good and bad. Miss Miller, too, she'd seemed at peace with her beliefs. Even Esther had maintained a sort of resolve, as if a higher power were in control.

Dorothy set down her éclair; a large half-circle bite mark laced with pink lipstick marred one end. "Where's his father?"

Ruth opened her mouth, but no sound came out.

Dorothy shook her head. "You don't need to tell me."

But Ruth wanted to tell. She wanted to scream out everything that had happened because, after all these years, someone should know all the gory details. Someone should look at her and cry because her story deserved crying. Someone besides her silent, thirteen-year-old self should be shrieking and gnashing teeth.

Ruth pushed until the words came out. "When I was little, I wanted a yellow dress. The same color as a beautiful bird I found dead in my backyard. Its sweet round eyes were half-closed. I closed them the rest of the way, pressing gently with my finger, like I'd seen in movies. I remember because I had a bloody hangnail for months on that finger. I chewed it all the time. It was weird how I chewed it even though it hurt."

Dorothy gripped her napkin and cocked her head but stayed silent.

Ruth picked at a hangnail until blood leaked out. "Anyway, the tiny beak was open just a crack. When I picked her up, her head flopped back really far, so I figured her poor neck had broken. I held her straight and tucked the wings nice and neat by her side. Her belly was soft. I touched my lips to it and felt nothing, but she smelled like earwax." Ruth sucked her bloody finger. "The bird's feet, the toes, they curled under. I remember how much my feet hurt. I'd been sitting on them a long time. But I just kept holding her and stroking her belly as if she could feel. Maybe I thought she would come back, that she wasn't really dead. I even prayed. I asked for the bird to be resurrected. I promised God if he'd bring that bird back, I'd never do a bad thing again. Then one eyelid raised just a hair, and then a foot relaxed. She felt warmer, too. The sun filtered through those yellow feathers, making them even brighter. She was so pretty, that color. Canary yellow."

Dorothy's eyes were penetrating but not scary, so Ruth continued. "I believed and prayed and believed some more until the pink beak opened. That bird was coming back. She got warmer and softer, and her feathers moved a little in the breeze. And I knew then that God was real and he'd help me whenever I asked."

Dorothy's eyes filled with tears. She whispered, "God loves you."

Ruth felt her own eyes strain with emotion. "Then I heard him coming. I looked up into the sun. He was just a shadow, a dark shape, because of the light behind him, but I said, 'She's alive!' But then my hands smashed to the ground with the poor bird inside. My brother, his brown shoe, the frayed laces, mud caked on the toe, a cackle. I felt the tiny bones break, snapping like dry spaghetti, and then the wetness and ruin of it all." Ruth shook her head. Her mouth watered. "A string of syrupy saliva fell to my knee. Funny what you remember. I thought I was screaming, but there was no sound. 'It's dead, stupid!' was all he said before walking away with a yellow feather stuck to his heel. I'd hoped the breaking and wet was the bones and blood of my own hand and not from the bird. But the guts squished out her rear end, and her beak broke off. Blood mixed with the feathers and turned them orange. I hate orange."

Dorothy wiped her cheek. "I know you do, Ruth. I got rid of everything orange in the house."

Ruth looked around the room. No orange.

Dorothy scooted to the edge of her chair. "I can see everything in your lovely eyes. No child should have endured what you did." Dorothy pressed her hand to Ruth's knee. "It's over now. He'll never hurt you again. It's not your fault. Someone should have protected you." She pressed harder. "If you want to scream or cry, it's all right with me."

Ruth melted. She lowered her head and wept. Her body released, as if a gate had opened where all the bad could escape. Things she'd held physically inside her body for years, clawing at her insides, festering in her mind, which she'd held tight, were now gushing out.

Dorothy stood, walked to Eugene's chair, and sat on the edge next to Ruth. She wrapped her arms around Ruth's shoulders, rubbed her back, then held her. "It's OK now. Everything's OK."

To be touched and soothed by a soft female hand and gentle, assuring voice, what a typical child might realize daily from a simple bloody nose, not caused by a strike, or a cruel word, not uttered by a grown-up, felt foreign. A fall from a swing or a word from an insensitive friend were the normal reasons a child might be held or calmed; this realization caused Ruth's heart to deflate because, childhood gone, she was finally experiencing how good it felt to be cared for.

After a long while, Dorothy moved back to her chair and bit into her éclair. "They're good."

Ruth felt more truths, more confessions, emerge inside her head. She wiped her face. "I saw a movie once called *All About Eve*."

Dorothy nodded. "Bette Davis, Anne Baxter, 1950."

Ruth was ten. She'd wandered off, sneaked into the theater. "It was good."

Dorothy licked her lips. "Of course it was. It won Best Picture."

Ruth wiped her face again. "Do you remember the younger one, Eve, when she dressed up in Margo's clothes and pretended to be a movie star?"

Dorothy blinked thoughtfully. "Yes, I remember."

Ruth hadn't understood the movie, but Eve, the film character, was all her foster mother had talked about for months, so she'd wanted to see it. She'd been fascinated by how big the picture was, delighted that she'd found half a box of Dots on the floor, and relieved that she got to sit in the dark without anyone hurting her. "Sometimes I like to dress up, too, and pretend I'm someone else."

Dorothy nodded. "Lots of little girls do that, Ruth. I made lipstick from my mother's lingonberries. I guess I wanted to be in the movies, too."

Ruth shed things she didn't need anymore, heavy, awkward things. She leaned toward Dorothy. "Everything seems better in the movies. Even the bad stuff doesn't seem so bad. Even the bad stuff can look beautiful."

Dorothy nodded again, then smiled. "Yes. Beauty in disguise. Movies have a way of doing that."

Robert played the theme to *Beauty and the Beast*.

Dorothy looked to the window. "I'm going to the beauty shop on Friday. Would you like to come with me?"

"Do you need me to drive?"

Dorothy patted Ruth's knee. "No, I thought maybe you'd like an appointment—or two. We could get your hair colored properly and a manicure. They give wonderful facials. Look at my skin."

Ruth leaned back in Eugene's chair. "Dorothy, I can't afford all that."

Dorothy laced her fingers. "I know, dear. It will be my treat."

Ruth felt herself smiling but tried not to. She wanted to look pretty. Was that wrong? When she was a teenager, the boys covered her face, and for a while, she thought that was how it was done. But movies showed her reality. If it weren't for movies, she'd never have known. "Ok. Thanks."

Dorothy smiled. "You're entirely welcome. I'll set it up. It'll be a 'Ladies' Day Out.'"

Ruth picked up her second éclair.

Dorothy watched as Ruth took a bite. "Will you make us some tea?"

"Of course." Ruth set down her éclair and stood. The ruby ring tumbled out of her pocket and fell onto Eugene's chair.

Dorothy stared at the ring a moment, a scarlet flash on the seat.

Ruth picked it up. "Here you go." She handed it to Dorothy,

then made for the kitchen as if she'd pulled lint from her sweater.

A moment later, Ruth peeked around the corner. Dorothy still held the ring. She slowly moved it in the light. Ruth fixed tea on the tray and returned to the den.

Dorothy held up the ring. "Ruth, this isn't mine."

Ruth poured. "Of course it is."

Dorothy, still staring into the ruby, said, "It's Esther's."

Ruth handed Dorothy a new napkin. "Did she give it to you?"

Dorothy looked at Ruth. "No, but I always wanted it." She slid it onto her finger. The ruby slipped around. "When she died, it was missing. I searched her whole house and finally concluded it had been stolen."

"Let me see." Ruth took Dorothy's hand. "It's beautiful."

"Yes, Burmese, Pigeon Blood. Never treated. The rarest of the rare. Walter gave it to her for her fortieth jubilee."

Ruth poured herself tea, realizing again that she was the true blood relative, a true Fiske, and Dorothy was not. Judith was her grandmother, after all.

Dorothy had not stopped gazing into the ruby. "The fluorescence, combined with the perfect base color, even glows in the dark."

Alive and pulsing, Ruth imagined it sitting in the chest of Marbit.

"Ruth—" Dorothy asked, her voice low and slow. "It fell from your pocket."

Ruth sipped. "Dorothy, don't be silly."

Dorothy looked sternly at Ruth. "I saw it when you stood."

Ruth set down her cup. "It must have been there all along. There are probably all sorts of things in this chair. Have you ever looked?" Ruth stood, gripped the seat cushion of Eugene's chair, and yanked it free. "See. Look at all this stuff."

Dorothy leaned over to look.

Ruth tossed the cushion onto the floor. "A penny, a paper

clip, a pencil, and a peanut. They all start with *P*!" Ruth let out a series of short, fluttering giggles.

Dorothy stood and stepped closer.

"And something that looks like pigeon poop." Ruth snorted. "It's probably a patch of pudding or paste." She ejected a machine-gun laugh.

Dorothy leaned over the chair and squinted. "Why do you keep saying *P*-words?"

"And a pearl!" Ruth's mouth dropped open. She held her stomach. She felt free with her emotional gate now wide open.

"Ruth, stop it!" Reaching into the back corner of the cushionless chair, where something was wedged, Dorothy plucked out a black sphere and held it to the light, a small moon. Her hand shook. "My South Seas black pearl, twelve millimeters!" The large marble, obsidian, rested in her palm.

"Perhaps a pearl plucked from a pendant or pin?" Unable to stop, Ruth screamed with laughter.

Dorothy, still staring at the pearl, said, "It broke off a brooch Eugene bought me for my birthday."

Ruth slapped her thigh. "Ha! Ha! Now you're doing it."

Dorothy's face appeared disjointed.

Ruth smiled. "I love butter and bear claws and banana splits and bread pudding." She waited. "You love . . ."

Dorothy's face straightened. Like Ruth, she couldn't resist a good game. "I love bubbles and books and bobbles and Bloomingdale's."

Ruth said, "I love pie and pajamas and popcorn and Peeps."

Dorothy smiled. "I love pendants and peaches and pianos and pastries!"

Ruth smiled back. "I hate pumpkins and parsnips."

Dorothy was quick. "I hate pack rats and pâté."

"I hate beans and broccoli." Ruth twisted her face.

Dorothy looked serious. "I hate burnt sienna and beige."

Ruth's face settled. "I hate yams."

Dorothy looked at Ruth's pendant. "I hate yellow."

Ruth felt her cheeks drop. "You hate yellow?" She looked down. "Yellow is my favorite color."

Robert played "Moon River." Dorothy looked toward the window. Her lips tightened and her eyes filled, then overflowed.

Ruth, now calm, placed her hand on Dorothy's back. "Come sit. Tell me."

Dorothy sat in her chair and cradled the pearl, her hands like a nest.

Ruth leaned down and rubbed her back. "What a lovely pearl." The depth of the luminous surface moved. Alive. Ruth had always wanted to find a pearl straight from the ocean, something beautiful from nothing, from a speck of sand. *Hawaii.*

"I thought I'd lost it." Dorothy dabbed her eyes with a napkin. "Eugene gave it to me when we were first married. It was part of a brooch." Dorothy looked up at Ruth with such anguish in her watery blue eyes that Ruth's heart softened. "Pearls are living gems. That's what Mr. Carson always said. And the black pearls, the real kind, from French Polynesia, are the finest."

Ruth kneeled on the floor.

Dorothy's moist eyes searched the surface of the pearl. "In 1951, Eugene gave me a brooch—a fish carved from pink coral appearing to swim through golden seaweed; each stalk contained a tiny bead of jade at its tip. Among the weeds, a large black pearl, this pearl, peeked from an oyster carved from mother-of-pearl. The piece was very Asian, the very height of fashion in that moment. He'd presented it to me right before we'd gone out to see Alfred Hitchcock's *Strangers on a Train.* That evening, in the den, Eugene took me on his lap in his favorite chair"—Dorothy pointed at Eugene's chair—"and tickled me until I cried." She smiled, still looking at the chair.

"I hugged his big head to my chest and said, 'I've never sat in your chair.'" Dorothy chuckled. "And you know what he said?" Dorothy looked into Ruth's eyes. "He said, 'Well, now you have.' Then he kissed me. Later that evening, I removed the brooch and noticed the black pearl was missing. I remember staring at the empty oyster. I was overwhelmed with grief. I ran my finger along the smooth interior and felt a rough spot where the pearl had been attached." Dorothy's eyes spilled over. "I knew at that moment that I would never carry a child in my womb. Six years later, I was thirty-seven and still not pregnant. I'd even tried to buy Eugene looser pants, thinking he might be constricted."

Ruth nodded. "Yes, that can happen."

Dorothy looked again at the pearl. "A few years later, in 1957, Eugene said he wanted to take me back to Hawaii to celebrate our anniversary. We'd spent our honeymoon there. I remember thinking, maybe, the tropical air, the fresh pineapple. Eugene was nervous. His jowls always quivered when he was nervous until I settled them with my palms." Dorothy chuckled softly. "I told him it would be different this time. Eugene knew he was expected to perform. Fear had veiled his face the whole week prior. He fumbled around, trying to fold his Hawaiian shirts, and constantly shuffled the plane tickets around, neurotically studied maps. I finally just packed for him. It wasn't the Niumalu Hotel anymore. It was a great big resort called the Hawaiian Village Waikiki Beach Resort. But it's right where the original was. We sunbathed, ate, and spent a fair amount of time in our room." Dorothy gave Ruth a sly smile. "I was sure things had worked this time. Eugene had tried his best."

Ruth knew the hotel well, and also recalled that same year, 1957. The chocolate mint candy, her tenth birthday gift from Eugene, had led her there. She'd just been hired and had been assigned to cover turndown service. Most guests were at dinner, but one evening, she'd stepped into the hall to get the chocolate mints and saw them approach, strolling down the hall, hand in hand. Eugene eager for his chocolate, no doubt. She'd been slipping him an extra under his pillow each night, as she did for many guests. She didn't know who they were at that moment because she'd never seen them close up.

Ruth recalled that Dorothy had been wearing a tropical red and yellow dress. Dorothy had stopped in the hall, then turned to Eugene and said, "Should we go back to the Tiki Room and wait until the maid is done?" Eugene's face had slumped before gazing down the hall, and then he'd said, "I'm sure she won't mind. I'm kind of tired."

Ruth remembered hurrying back into their bathroom to freshen the towels. She'd heard the door shut and the crackle of the chocolate, which Eugene wasted no time in finding. She waited in the bathroom to listen. Dorothy's voice had been hushed but loud enough to hear. "It's presumptuous for the maid to ask for tips like this." Ruth had agreed, but the hotel encouraged maids to hand-sign the form note requesting tips.

Eugene had said, "She's done a nice job with the sheets." Dorothy had nearly shouted, "Look! There's even an envelope." Ruth remembered peeking from the bathroom. Eugene sat on the bed while holding the note. Ruth could only see the shiny crown of his head. Dorothy stepped closer. "What is it?" He placed the note on the bed. "Nothing." But his voice sounded unsettled. Finally, Ruth stepped out with an armful of towels. "Did you have a nice stay?" And then she saw his familiar face.

Dorothy clutched the pearl in her fist and looked down at Ruth, who was still kneeling on the floor. "There was a maid. She had very dark hair, and it was pulled back tight in a bun. When she stepped into our room from the bathroom, into the light from the sunset, streaming in through the window . . . when her face became illuminated . . . her eyes, emerald jewels, had sparkled, a kaleidoscope, surrounded by a sunburst of long lashes . . . exotic and sultry. I'd never seen eyes like that before." Dorothy peered deep into Ruth's eyes. "Eugene's jaw had dropped as if he'd been smacked. When the sunlight shifted, her eye softened to a haunting sea green with flecks of gold, like two eclipses, the irises encircled by lapis rings." Dorothy continued to stare into Ruth's eyes. "I'll never forget those eyes. Then that maid said, 'Elvis is here,' like it was no big deal."

Ruth lowered her eyelids to the carpet. She recalled how she'd tilted her head, as if viewing him from a new angle might clarify something. And then, when she noticed his hands, the ring, reaching for Dorothy's chocolate, she knew, although it had been over six years, of course it was him, the banana-split car. But at that time, she didn't know that he was her father.

Dorothy said, "That maid told us that she cleaned Elvis's room."

Ruth, still looking at the carpet, said, "Wow. It must have been a really nice hotel."

Dorothy nodded. "It was, but it didn't matter." Her face shrank with sadness as she opened her hand to reveal the pearl. "Black pearls are a symbol of mystery. Eugene knew I loved mysteries, of course. But he also told me about a Polynesian legend. Oro, the god of fertility, while visiting the earth on a rainbow, offered a black pearl to Princess Bora Bora. Eugene tried, but I knew, with this brooch—"

Ruth felt her own eyes moisten. "How wonderful to find it again!" She couldn't help it; she wanted to comfort Dorothy, this woman who needed to love a child. What was Dorothy to do with that love? Like hate, it needed a place to go, a home. Ruth wanted to scream out, "Here I am! I'm right here!"

Dorothy, her eyes pink and puffy, said, "I knew we would never have children." She sniffled into her napkin. "And Ruth, I wanted them so badly. Even one, just one child to love." The napkin became a damp wad.

Ruth reached up, took Dorothy's hand, and squeezed. "I understand. I do." *Jane.*

Another tear fell down Dorothy's cheek. "Judy Garland once said, 'If I'm a legend, then how can I be so lonely?'"

Ruth leaned against Dorothy's chair and rested her head on the edge of the arm. "Did she?"

Dorothy wiped her cheek. "I feel that way, too, like Judy."

Ruth let go of Dorothy's hand. "I'm sure it was hard to be so rich and talented."

Dorothy nodded. "Yes, it is."

Ruth smiled at this. Dorothy's healthy self-esteem had become endearing.

Dorothy touched Ruth's shoulder. "Will you take me to her grave? I want to see it again."

Ruth reached up and laid her hand on Dorothy's knee. "Of course."

"The pressures of Hollywood, a child star, those movie producers who fed her the drugs to keep her working, the sexual abuse by the munchkins—although I don't believe that part—they had taken a lovely thing and squeezed it dry." Still holding the pearl, Dorothy opened her fingers and looked as if it might tell her something. "Thank you, Ruth. I know you've been through a lot, too, with your son and all. Life can be hard, but Eugene was a good man. I want you to know that."

Ruth searched her face. "Yes, I believe he was."

Dorothy turned to the window. "I was the one who couldn't have children. You may have guessed that already."

Ruth noticed the pearl's satiny finish in the low light. "I know."

"Carole Landis and I were so much alike. Physically endowed, naturally blonde. We could have had any man we wanted, but the endometriosis." Dorothy closed her fingers around the pearl. "Carole had even prepared a nursery. I'd heard about it later, after she died. People talked." Dorothy looked back at Ruth. "We both just wanted children." She loosened her hand and rolled the pearl around her palm, watching it. "I've always loved black pearls." Dorothy looked up. "Why don't you get rid of your apartment?"

As a child, Ruth's best drawing, created with her Prismacolors, was of a stone house with a sky-blue front door like she'd seen in those magazines. Flowers, green grass, and black shutters. She'd drawn each room, detailed French furniture, airy drapery, and pineapple wallpaper.

"Live here. You like your room, don't you?" Dorothy's face teemed with expectation.

Ruth understood the desperation to not be alone. "Of course."

Dorothy searched Ruth's face. "Not too many flowers?"

Ruth shook her head. "It's pretty. You made it so nice."

"Yes, I did. Should we start planning our trip to Pennsylvania? We could go to Hershey first."

Dorothy's house looked nothing like her drawing, of course, a 1940s California ranch with a top floor added in the '80s, but it was full of comforting things that she imagined a mother should have—clean dish towels embroidered with vegetables, extra blankets folded in a linen closet that smelled of clean cotton, books, framed pictures of people, matching dishes, and plenty of toilet paper.

Later that evening, when Dorothy dozed to people bantering on FOX News, Ruth picked up her purse and climbed the stairs to Dorothy's bedroom. She opened the top dresser drawer, took out a long maroon velvet box, removed the sapphire bracelet from her purse, and laid it inside, and returned it to the drawer.

The following week, Ruth took a whole stash of jewels back to the jewelry store in Santa Monica. The manager greeted her with a slight bow, then ushered her to a back office, where she was offered coffee and pastries by the gemologist.

Ruth bit into a doughnut, then opened her purse. Both men shifted in their seats, eyes bright and eager. She lined up the pieces across the table.

The gemologist picked up a large diamond pendant and inspected it. Frowning, he put it under something resembling a microscope. "This is a CZ." His expression changed to something Ruth was more accustomed to. "It's fake, worth about twenty-five dollars."

And so it went, down the line. Everything was glass, crystal, or CZ.

The gemologist leaned back and sighed. "The settings are nice; much of it is eighteen karat. Whoever made these put some effort into making them look authentic."

The manager turned a different shade, embarrassed. "The other pieces. Do you have them with you? The ruby?"

Ruth gathered the jewelry in a pile, her face hot and mouth dry. A familiar feeling swept through her body. Over the years, she'd never been able to identify it, but now she knew, because every memory, every painful moment of her life had been accompanied by this feeling, shrinking, as if something were pulling her down from the inside, as if her heart were collapsing. She knew, while grabbing another doughnut, that it was the physical sensation of shame.

The gemologist cleared his throat. "All these pieces look fairly new, probably made within the last ten years."

Ruth lowered her head. The carpet, orange, was matted with disturbing brown specks. On Halloween, 1951, Ruth was dressed as Glinda, the good witch. Children had swarmed in costume, laughing, excited, acting out. Ruth had taken regal strides down the sidewalk, waving her wand. Her classmates, their mothers, and a few teachers stopped to watch. Miss Miller had dabbed Ruth's lips with pink lipstick. Ruth had slept on rollers to create corkscrew curls. Even her nails had been meticulously painted because Miss Miller said no detail would be overlooked. Ruth had never felt beautiful until that moment. Then the world went dark and wet, and her head swayed under a heavy weight. Kids squealed with laughter. Opening her eyes, looking through a hole, two holes, she saw Pepto Bismol–pink satin. Everything was orange and slimy. Above the voices, a familiar cackle rang out. Wobbling with the weight of her head, she teetered and tripped, then fell with a hollow thud.

The gemologist said, "Did your mother buy these herself?"

Ruth whispered, "Yes."

"Did she happen to shop at Carson's?"

Ruth lifted her head. "It's all from there."

The gemologist looked away, as if to spare her. "I'm sorry, but the owner filed for bankruptcy and took off after several high-profile lawsuits. He's probably out of the country by now. It seems that Mr. Halabi was not an honest man."

Ruth looked back to the carpet, where she noticed, embedded in the loops, the black-mottled shell of a sunflower seed. On that Halloween day, a pumpkin had been smashed over her head. She lay in a pile of orange slime and grotesque chunks. Gelatinous seeds stuck to her face and neck. Her brother, wearing a pink satin jumpsuit and demented Peter Rabbit mask, had picked up her crushed silver crown and pressed it deep onto her head. The combs dug into her scalp. Miss Miller's crucifix flashed inside her eyelids, an orange light, like a bar sign at night. The worst part was not the pain or humiliation, but that no one helped. Even the mothers didn't bother. He was sixteen. They'd been afraid. Ruth had cleared her eyes of pumpkin guts and staggered away.

Ruth picked up the sunflower seed and set it on the gemologist's desk next to the pile of fake jewelry. The gemologist, the store manager, and Ruth stared at it. Ruth said, "Are sunflowers called sunflowers because they're yellow and look like the sun, or because they need a lot of sun to grow?"

Ruth noticed a split in the sunflower shell, opening like an oyster, the seed meat still inside. Back then, on Halloween, the yellow car, ever present, had witnessed it all, parked on the street under the large palm tree. Ruth had moved toward the car. She wasn't crying, she recalled, because it had felt normal to be demeaned, and even though the feeling was unpleasant, normal was comfortable. When she got closer, she could see that the man's eyes had flooded with pain. She'd wanted to help him, tell him it was OK, that she was used to it. He'd called to her, "Let me help you."

Ruth spit pumpkin on the street. "Help? No one has ever helped me." The man held out a package of yellow Peeps. Ruth stepped closer, accepted the Peeps, and said, "What's the color of your car?"

The man looked through the windshield at the glossy hood. "I think they call it Moonlight Cream."

Ruth scanned the car, the chrome eagle still flying. "Like a butterscotch sundae when you stir it up."

The man looked better now. He smiled. "Yes, like that. What would you call it?"

Ruth narrowed her eyes. A pumpkin seed slipped down her cheek. She said, "Paradise."

He said, "Paradise?"

Ruth nodded. "It feels nice."

The man handed Ruth a couple of Dairy Queen napkins. "They don't know who you are."

She took them and wiped her cheek. "Who am I?"

He seemed to relish her face as if eyeing a pie. "You're a queen, remember?"

Ruth corrected him. "I'm a witch. Glinda."

His eyes moved to the Peeps. "Well, Glinda needs a necklace." Inside, something caught sunlight. Through a small tear, she pulled a necklace from the package. A dazzling yellow stone glimmered back at her. He said, "A little sunshine for the good witch." Ruth could not look from the stone. He went on, "It captures sunshine, which bounces around inside until it's thrown out the center." Although Ruth had seen him many times before, she now noticed that he was not a particularly attractive man, balding, ruddy-skinned. A funny tooth protruded in front like a spare that should have been stored in back, behind a molar. He looked at her with such intention that Ruth wondered what he saw. He said, "You're my Sunshine Girl, Ruth." Ruth looked from the stone into the man's hazel eyes, and her painful reality melted away. "It's called Sun Drop. Wear it inside your dress and don't show it to anyone because it will burn their eyes. But you can look at it as much as you want because you and I, we have gold flecks in our eyes, which is rare. If a person has the flecks, their eyes will not be harmed." Ruth wanted to get into that car and drive for days, eating Dairy Queen and seeing the world, all the colors it could offer, but instead, she'd thanked the man and walked home.

Ruth suddenly pushed the jewelry into her purse like spare change, picked up a glazed doughnut, and turned to leave the jewelry store.

"Wait!" the gemologist called.

Ruth stopped.

"May I see the pendant you're wearing?"

Ruth touched the stone. "It's nothing. A toy."

He kept staring. "Can I see it?"

Ruth reached behind her neck and released the clasp. "It's a prize from a candy package. It's just sentimental." She handed it to him.

The yellow stone broke light into a starburst of colors, a firework. The jeweler handled it with care, held his tool to his eye, and smiled. "This is no toy."

Ruth scratched her neck. "A man on the street gave it to me when I was a kid; it's nothing."

"It's a fancy yellow diamond. Vivid. The cut, Ideal. Polish, Excellent. About four carats. It appears to be flawless."

CHAPTER 25

TICKLE ME PINK

Ruth had returned the fake jewelry to Dorothy's dresser. Anything purchased after 1996 wasn't worth much. She occasionally looked at a few older pieces, jade brooches, a string of well-worn pearls in a green velvet box, Carson's circa 1950, but none of it appealed to her, and what was the point? She practically lived there.

Ruth was hanging clothing in Dorothy's closet when Dorothy stepped from her bathroom wearing a powder-blue dressing gown. She held her wrist to Ruth's face. "What do you think of this?"

Ruth sniffed. "Very nice."

Dorothy sniffed her wrist. "It's *Chanel Coco Mademoiselle*. The fragrance lady called it a man magnet."

Ruth folded some clothing.

Dorothy sat on her chaise lounge and put her feet up. "She worked at Chanel headquarters for years. Now she's the fragrance expert at Neiman's."

Ruth stuffed clothes into the closet.

Dorothy pointed. "I'll wear that plum dress."

Ruth laid it on the chaise—*Grape Gummy Bear*. "When did Robert ask you out?"

Dorothy wiggled her toes. "Last week. I stepped out to get a flyer off the door, and he was doing the same thing. I hate the solicitors. We should get a sign for that. A nice gold one. They make attractive ones now."

Ruth turned to Dorothy. "What are you two going to do?"

Dorothy's smile spread wide. "Well, first we're going to dinner, and then he's taking me to a movie."

Ruth moved to the window. "I thought you didn't care for Robert in that way."

"He's all right."

Ruth looked out at the sky. He would ruin everything.

Dorothy said, "I might still remarry, you know. I've had plenty of men interested over the years. Robert and I had a nice Christmas. I'm not sure why it took him three months to ask me out, but I do like his accent."

Ruth dropped her eyes to the horizon, to a spot of blue. "I think he's hard to understand."

Later that day, Ruth opened the front door. Robert wore a crisp white shirt under his tweed dinner jacket. His hair was neatly combed to the side like a newly plowed field; the trails remained as evidence of his efforts. Dorothy stepped into the foyer. Chanel Coco, lips lush, colored deep plum to match her dress, she glittered with jewelry. A diamond pendant, the first one the jeweler had dismissed as "fake," almost made Ruth feel sorry for her. A ring, which Dorothy had described as "the rarest green, so green it looks almost fake," reinforced this feeling of pity. Ruth marveled for a moment, as she fondled her own diamond pendant, how pity felt from this side, from the pity-giver, and concluded that pity is a horrible thing, whether giving or receiving.

Robert presented Dorothy with a bouquet of hot-pink roses.

"Why, Robert, are those for me?" Dorothy reached for the flowers, but Robert handed them to Ruth with a smile.

Robert took Dorothy's hand and bowed to kiss it. "Aye, the hands that play such beautiful music."

Dorothy curtsied. "My goodness, Robert!"

Robert said, "You like pink?"

Dorothy batted her lashes. "Yes! I love pink. And such a wonderful pink they are! I would say amaranth pink." She kept looking at Robert. "Ruth, put them in a nice vase and set them on the table."

Ruth took the roses to the kitchen—*Strawberry Starburst*—then returned.

Robert said, "I'm taking you to a place called Bloom. Where all the celebrities go."

Dorothy giggled.

"And then some new film. It was at that Robert Redford film show, Sundance. It's in all the news." Robert pulled a paper from his breast pocket. "Let's see, here." He tipped his dark glasses up on his forehead. "*Once*. It's called *Once*."

Ruth had already seen the film, alone. She hadn't liked it too much. Full of relationships that didn't work out, love lost, and that kind of thing. There weren't many words, either, lots of music and singing. All that artsy stuff. The guy and girl liked to play music together, and the guy gave the girl a piano. That's it. Except for the girl's daughter, Ruth did wonder about her— Jane, her tiny violet hand and helpless heaving chest, the knife, the scar on her tender head, her own bloody feet, and the mop turned pink.

In the foyer, Robert and Dorothy still stood talking and smiling.

Ruth said, "I can drive you, like a chauffeur, so that you don't have to worry about parking. I can wait in the car while you eat. Might be nice not to drive."

Ruth pulled up to the restaurant to let Dorothy and Robert out. "I'll be parked here in the lot when you're done." But Dorothy had already sashayed to the entrance, allowing a restaurant worker to open the heavy door with thick brass handles.

Robert said, "Thank you, Ruth," then nodded, shut the car door, and hurried to follow Dorothy.

The restaurant's modern décor, dark and mysterious lighting, and hostess in a short black dress and strappy red heels seemed to make Robert uneasy. Wearing his dark glasses, Robert slogged, legs spread wide and hands outstretched. The hostess pushed away the gold upholstered chairs to widen the path. Dorothy took Robert's arm and wrapped it in hers, careful to make it appear as though he were leading.

A handsome, young waiter welcomed them to a quiet table against the back wall, near a window with a view of a vegetable garden, where chefs collected various herbs in wicker baskets. The waiter pulled back Dorothy's chair. Dorothy smoothed her dress over her hips and buttocks, then sat. The waiter expertly pushed her chair back toward the table. Dorothy looked up at him as she rode the chair, wheels smooth across the dark carpet. She offered him a coy smile while grazing him head to toe with her eyes. The waiter tried the same with Robert, but he sat abruptly, bouncing on the cushion, then scowled.

"Are we celebrating something special?" The waiter had moved to the side, with his hands clasped loosely.

Dorothy deferred to Robert, but he busied himself feeling around for his napkin until the waiter finally draped it across his lap.

Once composed, Robert said, "I'd like to start with two glasses of your best champagne." Beneath his dark glasses, a smile spread for Dorothy.

Dorothy radiated joy, but she tried not to smile too big since Judith had said it made one look foolish. "How nice."

The waiter left, then returned to set down two bubbling glasses.

Robert said, "Irene hated champagne."

"Who could hate champagne?" Dorothy took a small sip.

"She was very particular with her wine and food—and most everything else. She was a sensible woman, but she took things to extremes." Robert lifted his glass. "She liked my accent. Said it made her feel far away. She didn't like it here. But I did. I wanted to be a Californian."

"I can't imagine living anywhere else." Dorothy turned to the window. "Eugene was so easygoing. I couldn't make him mad if I tried. And sometimes I tried. He was sweet, though. Such a pleaser. Usually, that type is hiding something, secrets. Those quiet and obedient kids, they were the ones with the problems. But not Eugene, what you saw was what you got."

Robert removed his glasses. "Do you think they knew each other from school?"

Dorothy admired the flatware. "Who knows?" The knife was so large she could see her reflection, lips rhubarb, eyes smoky. The blurring of her face flattered in a glamorous way, like the cover of a good mystery.

Robert rubbed the corner of his eye. "Something felt odd to me. Remember your Fourth of July party, where they both acted peculiar when they met?"

Dorothy turned the knife to catch a new angle of her face. "It doesn't matter now." Dorothy watched the sous-chefs pluck cherry tomatoes through the window. Long ago, she'd decided her life would be whatever she wanted it to be. If something didn't fit into her story, she simply removed it. Ruth was just her assistant, nothing more.

Robert's eyes glazed, and he seemed to focus on the thoughts inside his head. "No, I guess it doesn't matter now." He raised his glass. "To dinners out!"

Dorothy still gazed out the window, then reached out absently to tap her fingernail on the glass, as if testing its reality. "And to movies, in the theater."

Just as Dorothy was about to comment on the lovely color of the eggplant she spied in the garden, her view was abruptly obstructed. Ruth's head popped up behind the glass.

Ruth, squinting, cupped the sides of her face, the smoking butt of a cigarette held between two fingers. The sun behind Ruth was still relatively high, so it was impossible for her to see the dark setting inside the restaurant. Yet, she seemed to try. Her eyes darted around with brown-streaked teeth shown gruesome, and her head bobbed around like that of a caged animal. She took a drag of her cigarette and then tried again. Desperate and frustrated, her face pinched and torqued.

Dorothy had pulled her hand from the window and cleared her throat. "Oh dear!" Dorothy covered her mouth with her fingertips. She swallowed away her disgust, then looked at Robert, whose eyes were wide with shock. "She can't see us."

Robert leaned away from the window. "No, I don't believe she can, the poor girl."

Persistent, Ruth smashed her mouth and nose against the glass, leaving an opaque smudge.

Dorothy straightened her rings. "I don't think she wanted us to go to dinner. She's jealous." She continued to watch Ruth struggle like someone trapped, drowning in a sinking boat.

Robert said, "Should we ask her to join us?"

Dorothy looked at Robert as if he'd given her the greatest insult. "She's my maid!"

Robert's face drooped, and his mouth gaped open. "I'm sorry. I just feel kind of sorry for her."

Dorothy had given up jealousy years ago. She had no reason to be envious of anyone, ever. She was beautiful, rich, healthy, and popular. She'd fulfilled nearly all of her goals and dreams. She was, even at that very moment, drinking expensive champagne and anticipating the service of a fabulous dinner, paid for by a man who, she could tell, was desperately in love with her.

Ruth's tongue projected from her mouth as a by-product of her efforts to see inside. Dorothy recalled a student she'd had, very smart, very determined, who always stuck his tongue out a little, just peeking from the corner of his mouth, when he'd almost solved a problem. Dorothy had thought it so cute, the little boy, trying with all his might. But he did not have a scar on his tongue, like Ruth. On the tip, a white spiral—the scar expanded and contracted with the muscularity of an invertebrate sea creature. Dorothy looked away to the beautiful waiter pouring ruby-red wine into an oversize glass across the aisle, then up to the faint glint of the brass lighting, linear and modern but still attractive, because pity had welled up inside, and she did not like the feeling.

Robert grimaced. "She is quite strange. I wonder about her upbringing."

Ruth moved a few feet down, in front of the next window, where she repeated her struggles like a fly bumping glass. The couple seated there, alarmed, asked the waiter to do something about the homeless person. "Maybe she's hungry?" the woman suggested.

Ruth dashed away.

Robert retrieved Visine from his coat and put a few drops in each eye. Frowning at the menu—no spinach salad, no lentil soup, and so many kinds of beef—in frustration, he fumbled the oversize book with such fury that silverware fell to the floor in a chorus of alarming clatter.

"Butter lettuce?" Dorothy suggested. "They can put the dressing on the side. They always put too much on anyway."

"Exactly! That is precisely why I go without. Ah! Angus beef. It's from Scotland."

Dorothy nodded while still reading the menu. "That's what I was thinking."

Robert closed his menu. "A very sensible choice."

Dorothy looked up from her menu and noticed the fancy bar with lots of mirrors. Ruth slithered by. "There's Ruth again!"

Robert tried to twist around, but Ruth was gone. "Maybe she was using the restroom." He ordered a nice French red from the Languedoc-Roussillon region.

They both ate dry salads and Angus beef. Dorothy complimented Robert on his choice of wine, his knowledge of beef, and his insistence on butter with bread, not olive oil. For dessert, Robert ordered the "Baked Alaska for Two with Passion Fruit and Matcha Ice Cream Swirl." Dorothy had never tasted passion fruit.

The fire alarm rang out. Robert's face pinched in anguish; he covered his ears. But with no flames or smoke, diners looked around with question.

Ruth ran out the door.

The manager announced that the building would have to be cleared for investigation. People filed out, but Dorothy would not stand.

"It's probably nothing." Dorothy wanted her Baked Alaska.

Robert stood and put on his glasses. The manager offered to assist them out.

Dorothy remained seated. "We want our dessert," she said, using her authoritarian voice.

The manager assured her they would bring everyone in once it was safe.

Dorothy pursed her lips, then said, "We have another engagement."

The manager rubbed his forehead. "I'll try to bring it out to you."

Once Dorothy got her dessert, Robert and Dorothy walked through the parking lot to find Ruth. Ruth had parked in a far corner of the lot. Robert opened the back door for Dorothy, then hobbled, gripping the Baked Alaska, to the other side and slid in. The car smelled of hamburger grease and french fries. Ruth crumpled her In-N-Out Burger bag and tossed it onto the floor. A jumbo chocolate milkshake with a chewed straw sat in the cupholder.

In her strictest teacher voice, Dorothy asked, "Why were you in the restaurant?"

Ruth took a long, hard suck on her straw until it made a sound resembling a Shop-Vac sucking water. "I needed to use the bathroom." Ruth pressed the accelerator and swung the car sharply through the lot.

Dorothy fell against Robert. Sarcastically, she said, "Right before the fire alarm went off?"

Ruth's voice came out flat. "I guess, with all that excitement, you two will want to go home."

"Of course not!" Dorothy yelled. "Take us to the movie." Tipsy and bold, she smiled up at Robert.

"Your fragrance is nice," Robert said, as if to diffuse tension.

Ruth pressed on, sucking her milkshake violently.

Robert held Dorothy's hand as they walked into the theater. Ruth trailed behind. Once inside, Ruth said she'd see *A Night at the Museum*. Pouting and sulking, she headed for the snack counter.

Dorothy was having too much fun to let another woman ruin it. "Ruth is just like Eugene, so even-keeled, so easygoing."

Robert narrowed his eyes and scratched his head. "There's something about her."

Ruth disappeared down the dark hallway with a tray of soda, popcorn, and Swedish Fish.

Dorothy flung her hand. "She's had a hard life."

Robert watched Ruth receding down the hallway. "Irene had toes like that."

Dorothy admired her own glossy toenails, painted the color of good red wine. "She does have ugly feet. That strange second toe. There are people who can fix that. I have nice feet, size five." She wiggled her toes.

Robert kept watching Ruth walk away.

Dorothy leaned from side to side to see her feet. "Shoe salesmen always marvel at my feet. One time, I bought fifteen pairs. You can't believe the service I got—everyone gathered around to admire them. They know me at Saks and keep my size well stocked."

On the way home, Dorothy and Robert sat close while Ruth drove with ferocity.

Robert leaned toward the front seat. "How did you like your movie, Ruth?"

Ruth said, "It was OK."

Robert leaned back, gripped his seat belt, and turned to Dorothy. "Did you enjoy the film?"

Dorothy turned her head away. "It was different."

"Aye, quite strange. I haven't seen too many movies, but I thought you might like the part about the piano."

Dorothy looked out the window, where car lights flashed through darkness. "The couple was quite bohemian."

"I think that's what people like these days. Kind of rough around the edges, as you Americans say. I read they weren't even real actors, just musicians."

"It seemed that way." Dorothy straightened her rings. "They were so plain, no makeup. Nothing like the old movies. The girl could have been pretty, but she's no Elizabeth Taylor or Carole Landis."

Robert said, "Carole Landis?"

"She died young. I met her at a party once. She got jealous when all the men were talking to me. That's where I met Eugene."

Robert raised his brows. "You do run in fancy circles."

Dorothy smiled, but a wave of melancholy threatened her. "I did, once."

"You've used the word *once* twice in your last two comments." Robert took Dorothy's hand.

"Did I?" Dorothy sighed. "It feels that way, as if 'once upon a time' was a long time ago." She wasn't sure what had brought on this feeling. Too much wine, perhaps?

Ruth chewed the last of her Swedish Fish, then picked them from her teeth.

Robert said, "I read that the couple fell for each other while making the film."

Dorothy's hand warmed inside Robert's. "I could tell they weren't acting, as if we were watching something private." The melancholy intensified, weighed her down. Reality.

Robert adjusted his hand around Dorothy's. "They wanted it to seem realistic."

Dorothy looked at Robert. "Realistic to whom?"

Robert cleared his throat. "You know, down and dirty."

As they whizzed by, the Hollywood sign loomed in the distance, lit from below. Dorothy said, "This is real to me."

Robert shuffled his body closer. "Sitting here with you seems real enough to me."

Dorothy gazed back at the hills, at the dark shadows and smear of light. "What do you think the girl said when the boy asked if she still loved her husband?"

"She said, 'No, I love you.' I learned a little Czech in school."

Dorothy faced Robert. "But he didn't understand, did he?"

Robert shook his head. "No, I'm afraid not."

Ruth stopped at a light, forcing Dorothy's and Robert's seat belts to lock up.

Dorothy rolled down the window. Robert's face dropped with alarm, as if open windows in moving cars were scandalous.

The clear night air, infused with sweet citrus blossoms, brought Dorothy back to 1946, when she first stepped from the train. The exotic scent, the bright sun, and swaying palms had mesmerized her, as if she'd landed in Oz. Aunt Hedda, the good witch, had smiled under her giant sunglasses and waved her hand high above her head, with a filmy scarf afloat on the breeze.

Ruth swung onto the highway.

Dorothy's stomach spun, so she faced the open window.

Wind blew over her face. "It's delightful to hear the ocean and see the stars, smell the citrus." Content once again, Dorothy lingered in the sensation.

Robert held his hair down with both hands. He grimaced as if he were in pain. "Let's stop to take it in properly!"

"Yes! Wonderful! Ruth, pull off up here."

Ruth pulled into a parking area that served a small beach. She opened her door and stuck her leg out.

Dorothy glanced over. "Ruth, stay with the car."

Ruth retrieved her leg and slammed the door while Dorothy and Robert got out of the car.

Dorothy said, "Bring the Baked Alaska." Her heels crunched the sand covering the boardwalk.

Robert picked up the Baked Alaska. "Will Ruth be joining us?" Ice cream dripped from the corners of the box down his pants and across his shoes.

Dorothy shouted, "No!"

Robert eyed a bench. "Will this be suitable?"

Dorothy and Robert sat. A young couple walked hand in hand along the shore, their pants rolled. The dark waves shimmered. A few stars flickered. The cool ocean breeze christened their faces with moist brine. The waves crashed and pulled to reveal a luminous reflection of moonlight on smooth ivory sand. The color was nice, moonlight cream. Eugene had said it many times, but Dorothy never knew what he meant.

Dorothy said, "I haven't been to the beach in forty years."

Robert scuffed his shoe across the gritty pavement. "I've never touched the sand."

Dorothy grabbed his forearm. "What?" She kicked off her heels.

Robert's chest heaved. His breath became audible.

"It's only sand." Dorothy placed her foot on the beach. It sank in, but once she felt steady, she stepped the other in next to it.

Robert stood. "Be careful, Dorothy!"

With the gritty sand massaging her feet and the breeze against her face, Dorothy was overcome with a feeling of liberation, like stepping off that train, as if she had been born again to become something other than a Midwest-middle-class plain Jane. She wouldn't be *mid-* anything. Looking to the stars, she wiggled her toes and dug her feet deeper.

"Dorothy! Where are you going?" Robert stepped to the edge of the sidewalk. He hovered inches from the sand, as if it were the ocean itself.

Dorothy moved toward the water.

Robert paced like a caged polar bear.

Dorothy raised her arms high above her head. "It's wonderful!"

Robert sat back on the bench to remove his shoes. He stood, picked up the Baked Alaska, gingerly stepped across the sidewalk, and dipped his black-socked toe into the sand before taking a cautious step. The other foot came down. He was walking, prancing, maybe, toward Dorothy.

"You're supposed to take your socks off." Dorothy laughed. Robert's socks had holes at the big toes where his thick yellow nails poked out. She would suggest her pedicurist later.

Robert struggled to keep his balance as he tried to remove a sock.

"You're going to have to sit down."

Robert tried to crouch but fell back, a plume of hair flying up like a cockatiel's feathers. His lips pursed into a beak. Dorothy bent down as best she could with her weak knee and grasped his sock. Robert's leg went into the air as he rolled to his back with a heaving sound, all while trying to keep the Baked Alaska upright. Dorothy yanked the sock but was unable to release it because Robert's toenail was hooked around the hole.

Robert wiggled from side to side in the sand. "Dorothy, I can't!"

"I've almost got it!" Dorothy pulled until she was propelled backward. She examined the sock. A scaly yellow nail clung to the hole.

Robert relaxed his body. "The stars! I've not seen them from this angle since I was a boy." He rolled to sit. Digging his feet in, he said, "It tickles!"

Dorothy dug her fingers through the meringue topping of the Baked Alaska and popped it into her mouth. The ice cream, now a pool of liquid sloshing around the bottom of the box, dripped from her fingers. Robert's face filled with horror, but then he laughed and dug a piece out.

Dorothy headed toward the ocean. She needed to feel everything: the air, the sand, the water. Her twenty-six-year-old self welled up. The possibilities, the parties, the glamour, her new name, Mrs. Fiske. Jewelry and clothes, the endless supply of money, everything beautiful and extravagant and smelling sweet.

The only thing missing was a child.

Dorothy glanced back toward the car. Ruth's dark silhouette, a shadow, watched. Dorothy waved, but Ruth remained still. She dropped her hand and imagined her life without Ruth. A bit of sadness jeopardized her elation. She'd enjoyed their time together, but some people are unlucky and get hurt. What could she do about it? She'd seen her own lot in life, a middle-class minister's wife, and had changed it by expecting more, believing she was worth more. Distracted by moonlight on water, she dispelled any underlying feelings of pity.

"What on earth! Dorothy, you're approaching the water!" Robert struggled to stand. He marched after her. "Ahh! It's too much on my feet." He laughed. "Like scratching a bloody itch!"

Dorothy looked back at Ruth once more. A phantom. *A servant, that's all.* Cold water surprised her feet. "Oh! It's freezing, Robert."

Robert let the water lap at his toes. "Aye!"

Dorothy grabbed his arm. "I must be drunk."

Robert held her up. "Then so am I."

Dorothy rested her head against his chest. "Will this kill us?"

Robert placed his hand on her head and hugged her closer. "It might."

The ocean air, rich and complex, full of primal, exotic scents and moist, vibrant sensations carried from distant lands, Hawaii, Tahiti, Acapulco, swirled around them.

Dorothy looked up at Robert. "Who were you waiting for at the restaurant all those nights?"

Robert returned her gaze. "For you."

Dorothy puckered her lips and fluttered her eyes. "I can read faces, but I can't read minds. You should have asked me."

"I didn't think you'd oblige, but when you invited me for Christmas dinner, I thought it was permissible."

Dorothy backed out of Robert's embrace. "Why three months? I thought we had such a nice time."

Robert took Dorothy's hand. "I had a wonderful Christmas. I thought of it often. Afterward, I sent you many requests. I mailed you letters, dropped them in your slot to make sure. I even asked Ruth to relay my invitation. Did you not receive them?"

CHAPTER 26

THE BOOK OF RUTH

Although Ruth had been spending most of her time at Dorothy's house, she still checked on Marbit daily while out running errands. Ruth had been leaving her window open because it was easier for Marbit to come and go as he pleased. However, numerous other pigeons had also made themselves at home. Pigeons were everywhere—huddled on the sofa, lined up across the counter, wandering around the floor, and a pile lay in Ruth's bed. The apartment was painted in white splatters of poop, and a few nests had been built in the space above the kitchen cabinets. The stench was stifling, bearable only because of the open window.

Ruth looked around. *Pigeon guano was a highly valuable fertilizer in sixteenth-century Europe, and coops were guarded against thieves.* Marbit flew in with a paper, a note, in his feet. He dropped it on the table and then waddled to a pile of Fruit Loops that Ruth had poured out for him.

Ruth stared at the paper for a moment. It was crumpled and dirty, not a nicely rolled scroll as she'd seen on TV when a pigeon brings a message to someone. Just as she was reaching for the note, her door flung open and Urth ran in, panting.

Droplets of sweat congregated above her upper lip, and one of her eyes was swollen, the lid black and purple.

"Ruth, where have you been?" Urth stomped her foot. "Listen, you've got to stay out of that house. You understand?"

Ruth turned away and watched Marbit eat.

"Dorothy. She's evil. Surely you've seen it. Making you dress up like a maid, driving her around like a chauffeur, and then pretending to be your friend. Why are you so stupid, Ruth? She's just using you to make herself feel important. She's toying with you. She knows who you are, and she's playing the long game."

Ruth stood. "I *am* her maid! And she pays me."

Urth moved closer, wading through pigeons. "It's all part of her plan, Ruth." Urth reached out her hand.

Ruth stepped away. "I like it there. It's where I belong."

Urth tried again, reaching to touch Ruth's arm. "You belong here. Eugene may have been your father, but you were a mistake. He didn't want you, and your mother was crazier than a pet coon. Dorothy is not your kind. And I'm telling you. She's dangerous."

Ruth sat back down.

Urth pushed pigeons away, then sat in the other chair. "This place is disgusting, Ruth!"

Pigeons are very clean animals and do not spread disease.

Urth ate a Loop from Marbit's pile. Marbit didn't notice, tossing his loops into the air and catching them with his beak like a circus trick. "I'm trying to help you, Ruth. I'm trying to save you. She wouldn't even let you out of the car at the beach. Remember? She hates your clothes and everything about you. She thinks you're hideous."

Ruth looked up from the table. "How did you know about the beach?"

Urth patted the back of Ruth's hand. "I told you. I see things. Visions. I'm here to protect you." Urth smiled. "I'm your angel."

Ruth sniffled. Marbit pecked at her hand resting on the table. "I don't care. I want to be in Eugene's house. I want to live there."

Urth leaned back in her chair and sighed. "I understand. I do. It's hard to accept things that happen to us. Bad things. My man beats the shit out of me, and what do I do? I stay. People call me a lunatic for it, but I do it anyway. We all have an idea of how things should be, even if it's not possible."

Ruth looked away and nodded.

Urth put her elbows on the table and leaned in. "And we don't give up on that dream even if it kills us or hurts everyone around us. Am I right?"

Ruth nodded again.

Urth straightened her back with authority. "OK, Ruth. You win. I've changed my mind. I'm going to help you to get what you want. But you have to do exactly what I say. Because if you don't, well." Urth shook her head. "I don't even want to think about it."

Ruth felt the dry streak on her cheek where a tear had fallen. She looked back to Marbit, then to the note, still crumpled on the table. Ruth looked up at Urth.

Urth shifted her eyes to Marbit.

Marbit kept eating.

Ruth reached out and brushed Marbit's cheek with her finger.

Urth stood and moved into the kitchen. "Where is it, Ruth?"

Ruth turned around to watch Urth. Panic rose in her throat, squeezing.

Urth opened every cupboard. Pigeons flew from the counter. "Where do you keep it, Ruth? I know you still keep a little of Miss Miller's special tea sugar on hand in case you're in a situation. I understand. If someone is in a lot of pain or if someone is hurting you. It's a smart idea. I'd do the same."

Ruth stood. "No!"

Urth stopped and turned to Ruth, her face stern. "What did I say? What did I just tell you, Ruth?"

Ruth shifted her eyes to the small tin canister on the counter.

Urth followed her eyes. "Ah, of course, just like Miss Miller."

Ruth felt dizzy. She looked back to Marbit. His friend had flown in and was eating alongside him. Ruth whispered, "Please. There has to be another way."

Urth picked up an old carton of McDonald's french fries near the sink. "Trust me. This is what you want. You can't see it yet, but it will give you exactly what you want."

Ruth whimpered. "When I'm at Dorothy's, nobody feeds them." Ruth turned back to Marbit. "David said God didn't make us to live alone but to be in families. His family would have been his fellow priests, and me, I hope. Did it rain that day? Did he slip? Maybe you were there, flying by. Never mind. I don't want to know."

Urth rattled around the remaining fries in the carton. "Stop talking to that rat, Ruth. I'm starting to think you're crazy."

Ruth took the crumpled paper from the table, sat, and opened it.

SUGAR

TEA

POTATOES

Marbit had brought her this message. He understood what had to be done. Ruth glanced back to Urth, who was sprinkling white powder on the remaining fries. "My family is Dorothy. I see it clearly now."

Marbit flapped his wings, then ran across the table toward Ruth. He jumped onto her lap. "I put the jewelry back. I don't care about any of it, except for my necklace, the one Eugene gave me. But I liked it better as a toy. It's worth the same to me. Its realness has made no difference. Reality is whatever we want it to be. Dorothy taught me that."

Urth replaced the baggie of white powder in the canister and pressed down the lid. "Stop talking to that rat. It's weird, Ruth, really weird."

Ruth nuzzled her face against Marbit. "Is it Dorothy's fault that she hates anyone who's different? Someone had to teach her that. We're not born hating. It's not her fault that she's losing her mind, seeing things. Who's to say something isn't really there? If something is in my mind, it's real to me. My bad thoughts are real. They have power. People die when I think things; even if I don't want them to, they die."

Urth sat down with the fries.

Tears fell down Ruth's cheeks and onto Marbit's back. He pecked at them. "I wonder if all that Agatha Christie, all those murders, changed my mind. Growing up, I thought that's how people die—murder. It never seemed strange to me."

Urth touched Ruth's arm. "This will take care of it, Ruth. Trust me."

Ruth looked to the fries, then up at Urth. "It kind of looks like McDonald's salt. Their salt is really fine and powdery, so it sticks better to the fries."

Urth smiled. "Yes, it does."

Ruth said, "Dorothy doesn't need Robert. She has me. Am I not enough? Why does there always have to be a man?"

Urth held out the fries to Marbit, who was still sitting on Ruth's lap. "Now you're getting it, Ruth. Here you go, little fella. You like fries? There's extra salt on it."

Marbit greedily snatched at the fries.

Ruth said, "Sometimes I wonder about the color of pigeon blood." She looked at Urth. "What's so beautiful about it?"

Urth set down the carton, stood, and placed her hands on Ruth's head, massaging it. "Remember when David said God is always good and he knows what we need, right when we need it?"

Ruth felt Urth's thumb trace the ridge of her scar.

Ruth nodded. "Yes! That's what he said." Ruth looked at the

blue shimmer of Marbit's neck. "Their eyes, both of them, that color, azure, that blue-green mix, him and me. Why did such a beautiful thing about them both come from a monster, two monsters?"

Urth whispered. "You're not a monster, Ruth. You're good, very, very good."

Marbit bounced away with the carton. He had it over his head. Ruth and Urth laughed.

Urth said, "He's so cute."

Ruth suddenly felt sick. "My children. I loved them even though they were half-him. At the time, I didn't want them. I left them, but not for good, not forever. Impossible. An unwanted child is still a child. A child God loves, right? David knew God loved him."

Urth stroked her hair. "Shhhhhh. It's all going to work out."

"He slipped from that cliff, didn't he?" Ruth turned to look up at Urth.

Urth gazed out the window with her warm hands still on Ruth's head.

Ruth said, "Eugene loved me enough to watch me all those years. And then I watched him. We just never got our timing right, but he cared enough to watch." Ruth turned in her chair to see Urth straight on. Urth's face was serene and glowing in the sunlight. "I want Dorothy to know who I am. Why should I hide anymore? Was it my fault I was born? Good mothers love their children no matter what they are or where they came from, mistake or not." Ruth stood to face Urth. "Does this make me a good mother?"

Urth shifted her gaze to the table. Marbit was crouched down, and his head was drooping.

Ruth sat down with her back to Urth. "I'm afraid of my thoughts. They do things on their own. I can't help it. Paul, from the Bible, says something like that. I memorized it because it seemed like God was speaking directly to me." Ruth recited the verse, "For I do not do what I want, but I do the very thing I hate. For I know nothing good dwells in me, that is, in my flesh. For I do not do the good I want, but the evil I do not want is what I keep on doing."

Ruth waited for Urth to respond but the room was strangely silent. A siren wailed by from the street below. She waited. "Urth?" Ruth spun around in her chair. She stood. Her eyes searched all around the room, but Urth was gone. When Ruth finally looked back to the table, at what had happened, she shrieked and collapsed to the floor.

CHAPTER 27

RAW SIENNA

Aweek after Dorothy and Robert's beach date, Ruth watched Dorothy walk over to Robert's house to personally deliver a handwritten invitation to join her for afternoon tea. Dorothy had spent much of the morning writing it out with her calligraphy pens. Shortly thereafter, Robert played something lively and uplifting, and so Ruth knew he had accepted.

Later that day, Dorothy clipped around the house. "Ruth! Ruth!"

Ruth folded clothes in the small laundry room adjacent to the kitchen. She'd heard Dorothy calling but continued to shake out the sheets and towels with loud, snapping whacks. Ruth could not endure another conversation about Robert's infatuation with her or watch Dorothy shake her head with pity, again, at how he had never had a "real woman."

Dorothy stepped into the doorway. "Ruth! I need you. Robert is coming to tea this afternoon, and I want you to wear your maid uniform."

Ruth looked away into the blue-gray lint ball she'd pulled from the dryer vent. "All right."

Dorothy held out a shopping list. "I want clotted cream and lemon curd. Make sure the scones are fresh. Ask for the ones in the back. And a box of those Scottie-dog cookies." Dorothy let that last request hang in the air as she searched Ruth's face.

"Scottie-dog cookies?" Ruth recalled how she àlways bit the head off first because it would be less painful to lose one's head and die instantly than to endure the slow death of having legs and tail severed. Head consumed, the body would look like a mouse, or a rat, with the dog's tail becoming an ear. She'd nibble around the circumference, feet, then tail/ear, until all that was left was a little buttery circle that could be anything, or nothing at all.

Dorothy tilted her chin down. "Yes, you know, shortbread, from Scotland. I'm sure you've seen them."

Ruth would not give her the satisfaction of reacting. "All right, let me finish this load, and then I'll go."

Ruth went to Gelson's and purchased everything on Dorothy's list. When she opened her trunk to load the groceries, she moved the clear plastic Ziploc bag containing the dead body of Marbit, leaking blood from his beak, to the side. As sad as it made her to see him this way, sacrifices must be made, as Urth had said. Ruth understood now, and she would follow through with what needed to be done.

An elderly woman struggled with her bags in the parking space next to Ruth's car. Ruth tucked Marbit to the side of the trunk before offering to help.

The old woman said, "Your hand is bleeding, dear. Let me get you a tissue."

Ruth noticed the bright red blood smeared across the back of her hand. *Beautiful.* "I'm fine." Ruth wiped her hand across her pants.

Ruth returned home to find Dorothy waiting in the living room, sitting erect in a French chair.

Dorothy said, "Did you get it all?"

The blood Ruth had failed to wipe away had dried into the cracks of her hand. "I think so."

"Did you polish the silver and check the cups for stains? He's coming at three. You need to get dressed. Get your hair fixed in a bun. What happened to your hand?" Dorothy followed Ruth into the kitchen, then watched her unload the bags.

Ruth felt her skin tighten and her jaw clench. *Steady.* She took two bottles of Visine from the grocery bag.

Dorothy eyed the bottles. "What's that for?"

Ruth set the Visine on the counter. "I bought it for Robert. I didn't want your tea to be spoiled by his eyes."

Dorothy nodded. "How very thoughtful of you, Ruth."

While Dorothy primped, Ruth went back to her car to retrieve Marbit.

Robert arrived two minutes early, wearing his tweed jacket and dark glasses. Ruth watched him approach up the walkway from the living room window—hair slicked. Dorothy had stood behind Ruth but hurried away when she saw him.

"I'll be in here," Dorothy called from the dining room.

Ruth opened the door before Robert could ring the bell. He stepped inside, holding a bunch of orange tulips wrapped in tissue.

"Hello, Ruth." Robert smiled.

Dorothy suddenly appeared in the entrance to the dining room as if a curtain had been raised and Dorothy was on stage and ready to perform. She sauntered into the entryway, accepted the tulips with a sly smile, then handed them to Ruth. The black stamens—*spider legs*—and obnoxious orange petals sent rage through Ruth's body. A feeling she should have felt back then but, powerless, had shoved down and sealed the lid tight. *Clouds.* But now, it rebelled, demanded release, fed up with silence and restraint.

Dorothy led Robert into the living room. "Won't you sit down, Robert?"

Robert chose a stiff chair. "What a lovely day for tea."

Dorothy sat on the sofa and crossed her ankles. "I have tea every day at this time."

"You are a proper lady indeed." Robert laced his fingers.

Dorothy cleared her throat. "Do you think it's dim enough for you to remove your glasses?"

Robert adjusted his glasses. "I'd prefer to keep them on at the moment, but I could possibly remove them later."

Dorothy fixed her loose earring. "Tell me more about your career. It sounds fascinating."

"It was terribly boring. I wished I could have made a career in music, but it seems I have ended up with an audience of one." He smiled.

Dorothy grinned. "I am your greatest fan."

Robert leaned forward, reaching out his hand. "And I am yours."

Ruth couldn't listen anymore. She went to the kitchen.

Ruth's hand shook as she lifted the eight-inch chef's knife from the drawer. She'd not held a sharp knife in decades. Afraid of its power under the direction of her bad thoughts, Ruth twisted and turned the blade, gripped the handle tight, watched her fingertips turn red and her knuckles white, and then focused on the sharp point. Touching it with the fingertip of her left hand, she pressed, feeling the pain, wondering how much pressure was necessary to break through the outer layer of skin. She thought of Jane and how that rusty knife had, in fact, saved Jane's life, releasing her from the tight tunnel, freeing her into the world, where she would learn to survive without her mother. And perhaps that rusty pocketknife had also saved her own life as well. Such irony to think—Ruth pressed harder until a drop of her own blood appeared on her fingertip—that the monster, so cruel, wretched, and inhuman, had created then saved that life and that she, Jane's mother, had done nothing but provide the vessel and then grieve at the loss. Ruth put her bloody finger in her mouth. But she loved Jane (and David, too) and hoped, still, to find her someday so that she could tell her the truth— that she, Ruth, loyal Ruth, loved her children.

Ruth poked the tip of the knife into Marbit's throat with little effort. She sliced it from chin to tail, down its belly. The bright blood poured onto the countertop. It ran, spreading with haste, as if running from something. Ruth touched the blood with her fingertip, then let a drop fall onto the back of her ring finger. The blood made its way into the dry crevasses of Ruth's knuckle. The color was undeniably perfect, a living gem.

Ruth dug out the liver and mashed it into a paste (the liver is a filter for toxins), mixing in enough blood to achieve the desired consistency. She formed it into an attractive mound and sprinkled it with salt and pepper and a sprig of thyme.

Returning to the living room with the large silver tray packed with scones, cucumber sandwiches, small crystal bowls filled with dark-red jam, thick clotted cream, silky lemon curd, and her specialty, pâté, smiling, Ruth said, "Here we are!" She set down the tray. "I wanted to make something very special." Ruth paused and gazed into Dorothy's eyes. "My mother's family was from Spain, although she grew up and lived right here." Ruth looked at Robert. "Anyway, her mother, my grandmother, used to make fine pâté from a rare wild bird that roamed free on her extravagant estate in northern Spain. Robert, I recall you mentioning your fondness for pâté, yes? At Christmas, I believe?"

Ruth waited for them to react, but Robert and Dorothy both stared at Ruth as if they were surprised she was capable of stringing so many words together at once.

"Anyway, the rarest of the rare, the bird was called El Peep back then. Now, in America, it's called something else." Ruth flung her hand away as if it didn't matter. "The feathers are bright yellow, and the meat is very sweet and tender. El Peeps only lived on my family estate. The neighboring castles tried to breed them, but the Peeps always returned home."

Ruth pushed the tray to the center of the coffee table. Robert and Dorothy stared at the raw-sienna lump.

Robert said, "Yes, I do recall this bird." He reached for a cracker. "But it seemed to come from a fairy tale, a book." He closed his eyes as if trying to remember. "My mother read me many fairy tales when I was a child. Grimm's . . . maybe it came from Grimm's."

Dorothy shook her head. "No. There was no yellow bird in any of *Grimm's Fairy Tales*."

Robert opened his eyes. "Hmmm. Are you certain? What about 'The Golden Bird'?"

Dorothy seemed to think a minute, staring at the lemon curd. "No. The bird was golden, not yellow. There is a spectacular difference between gold and yellow."

Ruth placed a napkin on Robert's lap and continued with the story. "Anyway, my mother's family only ate one Peep a year, and they never killed it. Every Good Friday, one sacrificial Peep would make its way up the grand stone stairs of my grandmother's castle, lay down, then die, as if he knew that three days later, on Easter Sunday, he would be resurrected as Peep pâté."

Dorothy's eyes turned into glowing blue moons.

"I could hardly believe it, but Frank, Gelson's butcher, had a Peep imported especially for Penelope Cruz. I think she had some connection to my family, and that's how she knew about how special they are. Anyway, she had to leave suddenly for Madrid and couldn't pick up her order, so Frank gave it to me."

Dorothy looked at the maroon lump on the tray and then back at Ruth, to a gray feather hanging from her elbow.

Ruth removed the feather and stuck it into the pâté as decoration. "There we go. This Peep was a bit older, so some of his feathers had turned gray."

Dorothy's lips parted, and she gasped.

Ruth said, "The older meat is actually much better, more flavorful. Dorothy, it's delicious, but I know you don't eat pâté under any circumstances. You've mentioned this many times—no yogurt, no pâté." Ruth placed her hand gently on Robert's shoulder. "So I made it for Robert."

Robert looked from Dorothy to Ruth and then back to Dorothy. "Well, I'd love to try it. Sounds lovely!"

Ruth began serving. She had pre-poured tea into the cups while preparing the tray.

Dorothy scoffed. "Ruth, you need to pour the tea out here because the milk goes in first."

Ruth covered her mouth. "I'm sorry, Dorothy. I forgot."

Robert said, "It's quite all right. I don't take milk, and I always add sugar after the tea is poured."

Ruth returned to the kitchen. She'd set aside a couple of pastries for herself. Bits of conversation drifted in—Dorothy laughing, Robert telling a joke about a pig and a sheep. Sometimes lonely old people managed to find each other. Robert appeared well. His skin held color, and his legs seemed fairly strong, whereas Dorothy had slipped some the past month, her knee weaker, the stairs more challenging. Ruth went to her snack cabinet and opened a bag of Double Stuf Oreos.

"Ruth!" Dorothy shouted.

Ruth hurried to the living room, wiping crumbs from her chin.

Dorothy tapped the rim of her cup. "We'd like our tea refilled."

Ruth bowed slightly, "Of course."

Robert had removed his glasses, a sure sign things were going well. Ruth pushed down a rising emotion. She wasn't sure what it was, exactly, but it felt frightening and potent. She pushed harder, biting her tongue, clenching, but her once-reliable methods weren't working.

Ruth stared at Robert's empty cup. When Ruth was just

eleven, her brother had shown her those magazines where the women's insides were showing between their legs, as if they'd been cut open. He'd threatened to do the same, again, with his pocketknife, if she didn't take the money from Miss Miller's jar.

Ruth filled Dorothy's teacup first. "Oh dear, the water has gone cold."

Dorothy took a sip. "It's fine."

Ruth didn't move. The strange feeling rose in her chest again. It coursed through her arms and legs, reckless and torrid. She fixated on Dorothy's painted lips, the color, red orange. Dorothy had called it *Alani*, Hawaiian for "orange tree."

On a Saturday afternoon in 1957, Ruth read one last Christie book to Miss Miller. She'd delivered her son a month before, unassisted. When Ruth finished reading, Miss Miller asked for tea with a special kind of powdery sugar. Before drifting off for a nap, she'd told Ruth to leave, to go far away. Ruth waited until dusk, but Miss Miller didn't wake. Strychnine? Cyanide? Two of Christie's favorites. Ruth removed Miss Miller's glasses and covered her with a throw. She boxed up the Christie books and hid them in her own basement before returning for the money jar. At the time, it had not seemed strange. She had been trained for this. Tears would wait. Glancing back at Miss Miller, her hand exposed, the Inca Rose, a firm raspberry just a day from sweetness, the cabochon dome a swirl of watermelon and guava flesh, like candy, Ruth wiggled it from her finger. Her son, still unnamed, and in the care of her boyfriend, would wait, too. The only adult she'd ever trusted had told her to leave, and so she did, on a one-way flight to Honolulu, to the only place she knew of, the Niumalu Hotel (renamed Hawaiian Village Waikiki Beach Resort), the chocolate mint wrapper still her favorite bookmark, and not as a guest, but as a maid.

Dorothy's harsh voice rang out. "Ruth. Ruth! Go back to the kitchen."

Ruth blinked a few times to reorient herself, then took

Robert's cup and disappeared into the dining room before Dorothy could protest, but she heard Dorothy's low voice proclaim, "She's so odd."

Looking up, Ruth saw the chandelier crystals quiver. She touched the sharp end of the center shard.

Dorothy's voice drifted into the dining room. "She made all that Spanish castle stuff up. She comes from a very low-class home, never had parents, got pregnant. Her son killed himself. The papers said he was a Satan worshipper. He had an upside-down cross tattooed on his neck. His picture was in the paper when he died. Probably a good thing. Can't have those people running around, especially here in the Palisades."

Robert said, "Sometimes people jump to conclusions. These journalists always want to make a story more sinister."

"Yes, there was a whole article about it. She also has a strange tattoo on her tongue, like a coiled snake"—Dorothy's voice went down an octave—"a symbol." Dorothy paused. "I've been trying to save her. She knows nothing about Jesus."

Robert said, "She seems very nice, very stable to me."

Dorothy scoffed. "I'm not so sure."

Ruth's breath seized with the cruel words uttered from Dorothy's mouth. Was it shameful to be so sad that, to find relief, one must jump? Satan worship? The inverted-cross tattoo —the Cross of Saint Peter—she'd asked, and he'd explained how Peter, the martyr, felt unworthy to be crucified like Christ and how he, too, had felt unworthy. Then, eyes averted, David had spoken of a priest. Weeping, nauseous, she'd turned, unable to absorb his words because mothers are desperate to spare their children the pain they've known.

Ruth peeked around the entrance to the dining room, where she had a partial view of Dorothy and Robert.

Robert said, "Does she live here now?"

Dorothy flipped her hand in the air. "Mostly, but I'm getting rid of her. She takes my jewelry, then, strangely, puts it back."

Robert took a handkerchief from his breast pocket and

wiped his nose. "Is that so? She seems to do a good job. I'd never want to move into one of those homes where people just go to die. I'd rather have live-in help if I ever got to that point."

Dorothy lowered her voice to a whisper. "Well, I'm certainly not at that point. She's my maid, not a caregiver." Dorothy paused. Her teacup clinked in the saucer.

Robert chuckled. "Maybe I'll hire her when I can't make my tea anymore."

Dorothy frowned, then recovered. "My jewelry, I think she looks at it in her room for a while, you know, kind of pretends. She's a child, no education." Dorothy pursed her lips, then crossed her legs and rolled her ankle in slow circles. "And besides, if I were to remarry . . ." Dorothy straightened her rings. "I wouldn't want her here."

Ruth's body tightened, as if strangled, and then something sank, like a dead thing in water. Her soul? She couldn't breathe. Her chest ached. Grasping a chair, she steadied herself against the spinning room. She would not go back to her apartment. A tear fell, but she hastily wiped it, scolding herself. There was no supply room to cry in, no bed to hide under, no Miss Miller to run to, no Moonlight Cream car to lean against.

"Ruth!" Dorothy shouted. "You see?" she continued, her tone hushed. "She's dim-witted. Can hardly read. It's pathetic."

Ruth hurried to the kitchen to heat more water. What did she expect? Dorothy was Dorothy, and she knew better than anyone what that meant. To think she would be anything different was foolish. But she had felt something and was sure Dorothy had, too. Something pleasant. Love?

She worked to prepare the tea. Dazed, hardly aware of her body moving, her hands reached for the Visine. *Looks like a pumpkin threw up on her.* Tears. *Cover her ugly face.* Wipe. Scolding herself. *No one wanted her, like a piece of trash.* Pouring. *She's stupid, too. My parents just took her for the money.* Squeezing the little bottle. *She's nasty. I know—you've got to close your eyes.* Stirring.

Ruth smoothed her apron, fixed her bun, and smiled before

lifting the tray to enter the living room. She set down the tray on the coffee table and presented Robert's full teacup, nodded, then turned back to the kitchen.

Dorothy said, "Ruth! You did it again. You must pour the tea out here!"

As a child, Ruth never knew where to be or what to do. Everything had always been wrong, so she had eventually concluded that *she* was wrong. But she was not a child now.

Dorothy pushed away the cup. "Take it back to the kitchen and do it right."

Ruth's eyes settled upon Dorothy's angry, twisted face while her own was fixed into pleasant indifference, a look she'd practiced in the mirror. She would not take the cup. It would remain.

Dorothy raised her finger in the air and shook it at Ruth. "Take the cup, dump it out, and bring back a fresh, empty cup with a full pot of tea!"

Ruth shifted her gaze to Robert, then to the tray.

Robert said, "The pâté was delicious! The finest I've ever eaten."

Ruth smiled. He was a nice man, and so a part of her, the part that was Eugene, urged her to take the cup. She reached for it.

Robert held his hand over the rim. "No. This is a perfectly good cup of tea, and I will not have it thrown out on account of outdated decorum. We are in California, not England, for heaven's sake!"

Late that evening, after Robert went home, Dorothy sat at the kitchen table, watching Ruth wash the dishes as if nothing were wrong. Ruth had managed to clean up the mess in the kitchen earlier—blood and feathers—while Dorothy and Robert played "Heart and Soul," as a duet, in the den.

Dorothy tapped her fingernails on the table. "The tea went well. Don't you think? Careful with the china, Ruth."

Ruth silently wiped at the cups, refusing to look at Dorothy.

"I'm thinking of marrying Robert."

Ruth looked up. "Did he ask you?"

Dorothy smiled. "No, not exactly, but he will."

Ruth wiped harder.

"We'll live here, of course." Dorothy sighed. "My house is so much larger, with the second story."

Ruth went to the floor with the rag, erasing invisible dirt while watching Dorothy circle her ankle around.

Dorothy stomped her foot in front of Ruth's face. "Ruth! Don't use my good dishrag on the floor. Is that blood? What's gotten into you?"

Ruth stood and rinsed the rag. Dingy water ran through her fingers.

Dorothy resumed tapping the table. "Get my coffee."

Just good for messes.

Dorothy let out an easy laugh. "It will be so fun to plan the wedding."

The next day, Robert stayed silent. Dorothy played a few of their favorite songs, including "Moonlight Sonata" and "Prelude to the Afternoon of a Faun," but there was no reply.

Dorothy sat at her piano, gazing through a gap in the curtains. "Do you think Robert is upset with me?"

Ruth handed Dorothy a bowl of popcorn. "Why would he be?"

Dorothy peeked through the curtains. "I'm concerned."

Ruth walked toward the doorway. "I'll go check on him."

Dorothy nodded while still staring at the window.

Ruth returned after a few minutes. "Robert is lying on his sofa. He's dead."

Ruth called an ambulance.

Dorothy sniffled in the living room.

A few days later, after hearing a knock, Ruth opened the door. Dorothy stood behind her.

A handsome man in a suit revealed a badge, then stepped inside. He handed Dorothy a large, thick envelope. "This was leaning against the door."

Dorothy handed it to Ruth without looking.

The detective shifted his weight. "Sorry to bother you ladies, but I'd like to ask a few questions regarding the death of your neighbor, Robert McClure."

"What happened?" Dorothy asked.

The detective ignored her question. "Was Mr. McClure using Visine when he was here?"

Dorothy said, "He always used it. What does that have to do with anything?"

Ruth moved into the dining room and set the envelope on the table, noticing that it was addressed to her. It appeared to be from a law firm, something with "estate planning." She opened a drawer in the buffet and slid it under a stack of tablecloths, then stepped back to watch Dorothy and the detective.

The detective's eyes searched around the living room. "The coroner determined he was poisoned with tetrahydrozoline."

"Poison!" Dorothy swayed. "What's tetrahydrozoline?"

The detective tapped his temple. "Eye drops."

Dorothy wavered on her heels. The detective led her to the sofa. He sat in a stiff chair facing her.

Ruth wasn't sure what had done it, the pâté or the eye drops. Maybe a little of both?

The detective took a small pad and pencil from his breast pocket. "I understand he was here the day prior, having tea?"

"Yes," Dorothy said, pale and weak. "I've never heard of eye drops killing people."

The detective was handsome in that Old Hollywood way, a

swoop of hair, big white teeth. Dorothy seemed to notice this. Recovering, she straightened her back, crossed her legs, and circled her foot around seductively.

The detective said, "He ingested them."

Dorothy's mouth hung open. "What? Why in the world?"

The detective scribbled on his pad. "We found several empty bottles in his bathroom trash bin."

Dorothy placed her hand over her heart. "Robert would never, never do that!"

The detective leaned in close. Dorothy swooned.

"That's why we're here, ma'am." The detective wore no ring. "May I speak with your maid?"

Dorothy gazed into his blue eyes, surrounded by bronze California-touched skin. She pushed her hair from her forehead. "Yes, of course." She turned her head to the dining room. "Ruth, we'd like some refreshments."

Ruth stepped into the living room. She'd been questioned about mysterious deaths before. She laced her fingers and let her hands hang in front of her body. "I worked for years in a nursing home. I've seen it happen many times."

"Seen what, exactly?" The detective asked.

Ruth moved farther into the room. "Desperate old people ready to be done. They talk, you know, among themselves, about how to do it. How to make it discreet."

The detective set down his pad and pencil. "Sit down."

Ruth sat in a chair opposite the detective. "It's pretty well known in that community that Visine can be used as a poison. Some of the residents would start complaining of dry eyes to their loved ones, or me. It was a code word, *dry eyes*, so I'd get it for them. At first, I didn't realize what they were doing."

The detective snapped back, "But then you knew?"

Ruth perused the detective's face before settling on his eyes. "I knew before their eyes went dry." Ruth paused, waiting for this to sink in. "They'd either get it from me, or they'd get it from their children." Ruth shrugged. "What's the difference?"

The detective's expression changed, sadder, as if he'd lost someone.

Ruth crossed her ankles and looked at Dorothy. "They're all so old, no one cared. Most of the family were waiting on the inheritance or for the bills to stop. Most didn't even want to pay for an autopsy. Many were cremated with no service, but I cared. I cared about them like I care for Dorothy, who is just like a mother to me."

Dorothy smiled and blinked thoughtfully, then caught her breath.

The detective watched Dorothy's mouth. "What is it? Do you remember something, Miss Fiske?"

"It's just—" Dorothy shook her head and looked down. "You wouldn't understand."

The detective lowered his head, as if trying to see Dorothy's face. "I'm a detective—everything is important, whether you think it is or not."

Dorothy looked up and sharpened her gaze. "Yes, that is what Poirot always said." She turned to Ruth. "Right, Ruth? It's all important."

Ruth nodded.

The detective's hand moved to the edge of the chair. "What do you remember?"

"Well, that night after Robert left"—Dorothy's eyes wandered around the room—"he played a song on the piano. I can hear perfectly. Right, Ruth?"

Ruth nodded again.

Dorothy pulled at her earring. "I don't use hearing aids."

Ruth addressed the detective, adding, "Her ears are remarkably keen for her age."

Dorothy sat taller and cocked her head with pride.

The detective's face turned a shade darker. "What did you hear?"

Dorothy lifted her toes off the bed of her sandal, which

created the sound of peeling tape. "It made sense at the time. I thought he was saying good night."

The detective gripped the chair and leaned in. "Go on. What do you remember?"

Dorothy wiggled her fingers in front of her. "He played a song."

Ruth felt a deep sense of satisfaction, like the moment before revealing a winning hand. Perfect timing. Fantastic luck. When things go well, they can go really well. It happens rarely, but it happens, and today was her day.

Dorothy looked toward the den. "He played that Andrea Bocelli song. Blind from birth and still such a good-looking man." Dorothy paused, looked at the ceiling. "The irony. I love irony, don't you? I know Ruth does, too. Irony makes life so interesting. The serendipity of how strangers can meet but aren't really strangers, or how beautiful things can come from the most unfortunate people. Right, Ruth?"

Ruth had read all about Bocelli in the *Palipost* last week. He was coming to perform in LA, such flawless timing. "Yes, I do. It makes everything feel connected."

The detective shifted with agitation. His hair wilted.

Ruth said, "Did you know his parents were told to end the pregnancy? Because of the birth defects, the blindness?"

Dorothy looked at Ruth. "Is that so?"

The detective's face contorted with confusion. "What are you talking about?"

Ruth ignored him. "Can you imagine if they'd gone through with it? What a terrible loss that would have been. Sometimes, the most beautiful people, the most famous and talented people, are flawed and unwanted." Ruth shook her head. "Oh, the irony."

Dorothy watched Ruth with caution. "I didn't know you liked opera, Ruth."

"Oh yes. I love opera. There are lots of things you don't know about me, Dorothy."

The detective desperately moved his eyes back and forth between the women. "Tell me! What did Robert McClure play?"

Dorothy turned to the detective. "My goodness. We were having such a nice talk. There is no need to get upset. He played 'Time to Say Goodbye,' of course."

EUGENE

Lincoln had been spending more time under the floorboards. Was he mad?

Eugene tried to coax him out with his favorite candies, even put a few of Dorothy's best pieces of jewelry out on the floor. He peered into the air vent with a flashlight and then realized it might scare Lincoln or hurt his eyes. Kneeling down to the floor, then falling to one side on his hip, legs twisted, knees torquing, Eugene leaned toward the vent. "Lincoln, are you there?" He rattled a candy wrapper, opened it, and waved it over the vent to entice him. "Do you know what I've done?" Eugene waited a moment, then ate the candy himself. He felt tears well up and his throat tighten. "It was very bad, but I couldn't stand it, someone hurting her."

Eugene managed to hoist himself from the floor by gripping his bookshelf. He sat in his comfy leather chair and waited because he had nothing else to do. Closing his eyes, he listened, hoping to hear Lincoln's toenails scraping along the inside of the metal ductwork that had become his passageway home. Eugene imagined Lincoln had a nice nest in there, warm and cozy and full of interesting decorative items.

Eugene heard only the faint ticking of the brass mantel

clock Dorothy had placed over the fireplace in the living room when they were first married. The clock had always been too loud. That constant ticking had nearly driven him mad because, with Dorothy out shopping all day, it was oftentimes the only sound he heard. The sound made Eugene sad. The ticking away of time was never a reassuring feeling. It always felt like a loss, like everyone was just marching toward death.

Eugene opened his eyes. From this seated position, he could only see blue sky in the frame of his window. A puffy cloud that looked like a delicious dollop of whipped cream floated by. He imagined rainbow sprinkles on top. Inspired, Eugene took a piece of paper from his desk, glue, scissors, and a few popsicle sticks. He crafted the materials into an old biplane (he was skilled) and sent it sailing across the room and into the blue sky of the window. For a moment, the plane dipped and turned in the frame as if it might make it, soar away into the cream cloud, but then it hit the glass and fell to the ground. "You'd do the same thing, Lincoln. You'd protect your children at all costs. I know you would."

CHAPTER 29

MAUVELOUS

A few weeks after Robert's death, things seemed back to normal. Dorothy didn't appear to mind that he was gone. Sometimes, when she played her piano, she would pause to look out the window, but she would quickly resume her playing with vigor, as if shaking away any feelings of loss. Ruth found her behavior somewhat odd, to brush away loss so easily. But Dorothy had always been good at staying focused on pleasant things.

Ruth set the tea tray down in the living room in front of Dorothy, who sat on the sofa. The doll in the corner was now wearing a lavender dress and matching hat. A light-blue stone, aquamarine, hung from a gold chain around her neck.

Dorothy was dressed in an evening gown from, perhaps, the 1940s. Pink taffeta was fashioned into a fitted bodice, escalating to puffy sleeves and finished with a long, full skirt. Dorothy's hair was extra poufy, and her lips were painted a rich purplish red —*mauve?* Ruth followed her gaze. She seemed to be watching Akio through the six-inch gap in the drapery. A pleasant smile settled across her face, as if she were pleased with him. Her mind seemed adrift, eyes soft. One hand, bent at the wrist, dangled from the arm of the sofa; the other relaxed across her lap.

Ruth looked to Akio, the drips of sweat, the mangled hand, and the dingy dampness of his white cotton shirt. The petals fluttered, caught in the breeze, flew upward, confetti, like a party. Ruth looked back to Dorothy; yes, from her seated angle, she was witnessing a party.

Dorothy turned to look at Ruth, still smiling, still relaxed. "Ruth, I have something to tell you."

Ruth took a step back. She wasn't sure why Dorothy was dressed up. Ruth was unable to interpret the strange look in Dorothy's eyes—sharp and excited, they darted around Ruth's face. Ruth couldn't determine her emotion as good or bad. And this made Ruth nervous because it had always been one of her strengths. It had protected her and kept her one step ahead of the world and its dangers. But now, she had no idea.

Dorothy stood, then arranged her full skirt around her body so that it hung straight. "Let's take tea in the den today."

Ruth picked up the tray and followed Dorothy into the den, where Dorothy sat in her chair and arranged her skirt, spreading it across the arms of the chair in a semicircle like a little girl dressed up for the first time.

Ruth thought about what to say. "You look very pretty today, Dorothy."

Dorothy smiled with her lips closed and pushed her hair in place, as if she'd not heard.

Ruth began preparing the tea. "Did I forget about a special engagement you had today?"

Dorothy didn't answer. She continued to fawn over herself, straightening her rings, smoothing the taffeta, rolling her ankles to admire her matching mauve pumps.

Ruth added a smidgen of milk to Dorothy's cup, placed one sugar cube inside, then poured from the Fiske silver teapot without a stray drop. The fragrant steam swirled in front of Dorothy's face. Ruth precisely aligned a pressed napkin, a silver teaspoon, a jam knife, and a fork next to a dessert plate from Dorothy's wedding china. She arranged scones, preserves, clotted cream, and lemon curd artfully within reach; set her own place; then sat in Eugene's chair.

Dorothy smiled. "Very good, Ruth, very, very good."

Ruth swiftly made her own cup, her hands moving with ease and precision, little sound, no mess.

Dorothy cleared her throat, as if about to give a speech. "You will now be my lady's companion." Dorothy's face radiated pride. "It's a promotion."

Ruth set her cup in its saucer with a faint tink. Uneasiness diffused through her mind, as if things might turn perverse. "What's a lady's companion?"

Dorothy broke open her scone. "A lady's companion is the highest rank for someone of the working middle class." She spread cream. "To be accurate, many lady's companions are of the upper echelon but have come into misfortune, like widows or spinsters. I'm making an exception in your case, which I'm entitled to do. Companions live in the family's quarters and are given a small allowance."

Ruth held her cup. "Do I live in the family's quarters now?"

"Yes, your bedroom, on the main level, would be considered a family area. Maids, as you were before, don't often live in the house, or they may live below stairs." Dorothy took a bite.

"Below stairs?" A vision of a dungeon with rats, steel bars, and dripping water took hold of Ruth's mind.

"The basement." Dorothy looked at the floor as if a basement lay just beneath. "There will be some restructuring, some training."

Ruth chewed her scone with restraint. Her mouth felt too dry to swallow. Dorothy's behavior, her talk, had become stranger since Robert's death. Things scampered across doorways, caught from the corner of Dorothy's keen eye, or pitterpattered down hallways, picked up by her astute ear.

Her obsession with decorum, fashion, food, and manners

had reached an impressive pinnacle. Her pattern was to delve deep into the past—Waikiki, Judy's emerald bedroom, Carole's petal silk gown—then swing sharply into a present that was unidentifiable to Ruth and unique to Dorothy's perspective alone. Dorothy did not appear to be living in 2006, but sometime much earlier. Yet her memories seemed to hover anywhere between 1945 and 1965.

At that moment, as best as Ruth could determine, they were living in 1906, and not in California, but in a grand manor house in rural England. And so it was not entirely a surprise when Dorothy appointed her as a "lady's companion."

Dorothy smoothed her dress. "I will create a formal list of your new duties, but your primary purpose will be to serve tea, which you've nearly mastered; escort me to social engagements; learn the finer arts of music and art; and provide me with conversation."

Ruth prepared her scone. She liked the lemon curd best. The pale color reminded her of happy things—soft, fresh Peeps with wings and the shiny car called Moonlight Cream.

"There will be some fancy sewing involved. My gowns must be maintained." Dorothy placed her hand on a beaded evening gown and a sewing box she'd set next to her chair. "You will still do light dusting, but we'll hire a staff—a scullery maid, a footman, a housekeeper, and a chef, for all the real cleaning, washing, and cooking. It will be your duty to hire and manage them. I'll determine their wages, of course, but they will never speak to me directly. They will always address you as 'ma'am.'"

Ruth nibbled her scone, let the lemon coat her tongue. "Yes, ma'am."

Dorothy stirred her tea. "You need not refer to me as ma'am. As my companion, you will address me as Lady Fiske in public, but in private, you may still call me Dorothy."

Ruth had played along with the mysterious moving of things and formal afternoon teas, among a few other emerging oddities, but Dorothy had headed into new territory. Ruth was up for the challenge—full-time role play in the Edwardian era. She bowed her head slightly. "I'm greatly honored to be your lady's companion. Thank you for entrusting me with this prestigious position."

Dorothy nodded. "You're entirely welcome. You've been a loyal servant to me all these years. It's time you were given a suitable position among the family. Eugene will be relieved that I have a proper companion. With all the hunting trips and diplomatic meetings, he expressed his concern just yesterday for my well-being, given the frequent solitude I experience in his absence."

With the mention of Eugene, Ruth's stomach fluttered. Dorothy's delusion was worse than Ruth had thought. "Eugene is a good man. You've said it yourself many times."

Dorothy nodded, as if it were a well-known fact. "I still want you to clean the chandelier, though. I wouldn't trust that with just anyone."

Ruth noticed the light changing, so she gathered the dishes.

Dorothy was thinking. The absence in her eyes, the dismissal of her surroundings, signaled the shift. Ruth wondered what year they were in.

Dorothy handed Ruth the sewing box and gown. "Have you gotten to *Funerals Are Fatal*?"

Ruth fumbled through Dorothy's meager sewing supplies.

Earlier, Ruth had watched Dorothy pull the beaded gown from her closet, where the hem tore on the sharp corner of the bifold door. Several beads had bounded across the floor. Early 1960s, Ruth had guessed. A strange color, chartreuse with teal beading. "Yes, Christie was real clever in that one."

Dorothy dabbed the corners of her mouth with her napkin. "Cora's lady's companion didn't work out so well."

Ruth picked lightly at a loose bead. "No. She went crazy."

Dorothy watched Ruth's fingers. "Dressing up like her mistress. It reminds me of that movie *All About Eve*. You said you like to dress up, too. Remember? And I told you I used my mother's lingonberries for blush."

Ruth chose teal thread. "Lingonberries are a nice color, such a deep and rich red when they're ripe."

Dorothy seemed to be thinking; her eyes wandered around the wall. "It was quite gruesome how the companion used a hatchet on Cora while she slept."

Ruth found scissors at the bottom of the sewing box. She pulled them out by the orange plastic handle. "Yes, a hatchet. Eight or nine blows, I think."

Dorothy shook her head and pursed her lips. "What a horrible way to go."

Ruth tested the scissors in the air, opening and closing them like the beak of an impressive waterfowl feeding. The sound sliced the air like the sharpening of a blade. "Why do all sewing scissors have orange handles?" Ruth continued to cut the air. The bird swallowed a fish. "Who would choose orange?"

Dorothy watched. "You've always seemed very stable to me, Ruth. Are there mental problems in your family?"

Ruth cut the thread. "A few. My mother went crazy at the end. It happens." Ruth looked up at Dorothy. "I'm not sure about my father. I never knew him." Ruth looked back to the thread. "I bet he was a very nice man, though."

Dorothy watched Ruth fiddle with the thread, then shifted her gaze to Eugene's slippers, still tucked under the coffee table. "My mother's brain softened near the end. She thought the nurses in the hospital were trying to kill her because they were Black." Dorothy eyed Ruth as she struggled with the needle. "Haven't you ever sewed?"

Ruth looked up. "I've had some experience, but not with this type of material."

"Silk can be difficult to work with." Dorothy cleared her throat. "But you've got all day tomorrow."

Ruth ran the thread across her tongue. Dorothy's eyes focused there. Ruth realized what it might have looked like from

Dorothy's view, the teal line of thread gliding across her scar. She felt nothing, of course, but tasted something bitter and smelled the rancid perfume of previous hands that'd handled the thread.

"What do you think made the companion kill her mistress like that?" Dorothy's eyes settled upon the scissors.

Ruth straightened the thread. "She was bored. The monotony, day after day, listening to Cora rattle on about nothing. Boredom is dangerous. People can spend too much time in their own heads." She rolled the thread between her fingers to create a knot. "She was also pretty upset to lose her tea shop."

Dorothy folded her hands with caution. "What were your dreams and aspirations, Ruth?"

"I didn't have any." Ruth pulled the needle through the tiny hole of a bead. "I guess it would have been nice to be an artist or architect. Maybe have a little sweets shop. I drew a few sketches of it a while ago." Ruth let out an agitated laugh, but it sounded like the sudden release of air from a pinched balloon. "I'd have named it 'Sweets.'"

Dorothy's face turned darker, and she tightened her lips as if she'd just spotted a rat. "You draw?"

Ruth pulled the dress closer to her face as she tried to attach the bead. "A little."

Dorothy brightened. She slapped both of her hands on her thighs, causing the taffeta to rustle. "Perfect! We'll make it part of your day. First, music. I've ordered a harp for you to accompany me on the piano; then you may draw. Tea will remain at four o'clock."

Ruth looked up. "Harp?"

"It's a small one. I can teach you to start. As you advance, we'll hire a professional." Dorothy stood and shifted her gown before walking to the piano. She played something slow and romantic. Distant, her eyelids lowered, hands graceful and confident, pleasantly lost, like a child deep in play, where imagination is more real and interesting than anything shared with others.

Ruth took her sketchbook and pencils from her purse. She drew the Dickens village from several angles, as viewed from a scaled person's eye level, a virtual tour. She added her own house, a small cottage on the edge of town, creamy yellow—Moonlight Cream—with black shutters and a pale-blue door, the color of Dorothy's eyes. Bloodred tulips edged the walkway, and several large trees, oak and maple, shaded the front porch, where a small gathering of wicker furniture waited for visitors.

A pleasant feeling enclosed Ruth when she drew, maybe the same feeling Dorothy felt when she played piano. It felt far away, as if time were arbitrary and the world was simply what one determined it to be.

As she drew, the Inca Rose of Miss Miller's ring caught light from the window. Ruth had always kept it hidden in her apartment because she'd been afraid to break it. Miss Miller had said the stone was quite fragile, not suitable for a ring, especially if rough work were required, but regardless, she'd made it a ring so that she could admire it while worn and always remember her migration west. Ruth had decided to wear it that day because it looked nice with the filmy white tea dresses that Dorothy had recently required her to wear indoors, consistent with the revealed state of Dorothy's current Edwardian world.

Dorothy stopped playing. "Where did you get that ring?"

Ruth touched the hidden hinge with her thumb. "It's nothing. A family friend gave it to me when I turned eighteen."

Dorothy leaned to inspect it. "It's pretty." Her eyes shifted to the sketchbook. "What are you working on?"

Ruth turned her book around for Dorothy to see. "Your village."

Dorothy took the pad, cocked her head, then paused. "Drawing isn't new to you."

Ruth caressed the Inca Rose with her fingers. "No. I've always liked to draw."

Dorothy's face opened with expectation. "We still need to plan our trip."

Ruth had long since dismissed the trip as just talk.

Dorothy looked up, her face optimistic. "I've got a wonderful idea! Let's go to England instead. We'll stay in the best manor houses. Many of them are luxury hotels now. We'll have proper tea served to us every day and stroll through Kensington Gardens. We can see the Crown Jewels." Dorothy's face shone in the light from the window. The fine white hairs along her cheeks glistened.

Ruth smiled and straightened her ring, realizing where she'd picked up that habit. "That sounds like such fun." Beneath the stone, the tiny portrait of old Mr. Miller remained, and on the other side, directly under the stone, like the left page of a book, was Ruth's own addition. "Maybe we could go on an Agatha Christie tour. Visit places from her books. See her grave."

Dorothy stood. "We can see *The Mousetrap* in London! Let's go this summer." Dorothy hurried to a small secretary desk and flipped it open to reveal various compartments stuffed with papers. "I wonder if Eugene's travel agent is still working. She booked our trips to Hawaii." Dorothy rummaged around, then paused before pulling a small slip from a pile. She blinked as if the paper might do something, then turned to Ruth. "I wonder why he kept this." A muscle in Dorothy's jaw poked out, signaling an abrupt change of mood.

"What is it?" Ruth stood.

Dorothy held out the slip.

Ruth took it, then ran her thumb across the lettering. The words were printed, but her name was signed in blue ink.

It's been my pleasure to serve you.
Safe travels home.
Please come stay with us again.

Aloha Nui Loa,
Hawaiian Village Waikiki Beach Resort housekeeping
staff

Ruth

Dorothy snatched the paper from Ruth's hand. "I've decided to call you Tiffany from now on."

Ruth watched the slip of paper as Dorothy folded it into a tiny square. At the Waikiki Beach Resort, back in 1957, Ruth was not entirely surprised when she saw the familiar face, the driver of the Moonlight Cream. He had led her there, after all, with a piece of chocolate. And the irony! Leaving the impersonal note for him, a maid in a hotel, and then finding him again, with a note, twenty years later, slid across the table at a Denny's by her newly found mother. "Tiffany? Why Tiffany?"

Dorothy threw the note into a small brass waste can. "I always wanted a daughter named Tiffany."

Dorothy, eyes averted, shuffled to the piano. "Keep to your drawing."

Ruth sat. Dorothy's profile, prominent against the hazy fading light seeping through the sheers, took shape as Ruth worked her pencil. The afternoons had become sullen and dull without Robert's piano to reply. Ruth missed the music, the secret language. Her hands had moved of their own accord, just following Urth's instructions. She lacked memory of ever making the decision to go through with it. Sure, she had prepared—made the pâté, bought the Visine. It was a nice gesture to have some on hand.

Dorothy played "Afternoon of a Faun" as if she were unsure of the notes, which was not true, of course. This allowed Ruth time to capture the subtleties of her essence. Her hand moved the pencil across the paper, creating a pleasant sound and gentle vibrations of fine labor. The very same absence of mind that had overtaken her while canceling lives returned. Ruth was not angry or distressed, so it was a curious thing to observe her own mind as it worked in this strange way. Disconnected, an awareness outside her body, as if watching someone else.

Dorothy gathered more energy as the music developed. Her face lifted, eyes expanded, back straightened. Was she thinking of Robert? Imagining his reply? Or maybe their trip. Tea in a castle. Ruth captured what mattered.

Ruth paused to stare at the tip of her pencil. Miss Miller had painted to pass time. Her best work came as her eyesight waned. Abstract, a style Ruth found intimidating, yet intriguing, as if seeing a reflection of private thoughts in all its beauty and horror. She'd taught Ruth about filtering, its importance. Accuracy, too. "Always tell the truth, Ruth." Ruth would never flatter. But genuine beauty actually existed in a miniature old woman with never-ending dreams and the self-assurance of God himself, who tenderly played a seventy-five-year-old piano—a gift from parents who hoped it would prove useful in securing a proper marriage and faith in the Lutheran church.

Dorothy finished the piece, her face content, satisfied, as if she'd taken an ocean breeze or fresh air while rambling through the English countryside. "Can I see?"

Ruth turned her sketch, then looked at a stain on the carpet. Miss Miller had said, "Forget what you're trying to draw and just draw what you see; then it will be what it is." It made no sense to Ruth at the time. She'd thought she had always drawn what she saw, or what she saw in her head, or maybe what she wanted to see. "Forget it's a red apple. It's not an apple, and it's not red—it's a unique sphere with infinite colors. There are no lines, only this thing, and not this thing. Draw that, and it will become an apple." But now, Ruth saw.

Dorothy's eyes filled. "Artistic talent and madness go hand in hand." She took a tissue and blotted at her nose, which had turned an exceptional shade of pink—*Piggy Pink*. "Is this how I really look?"

Ruth was uncertain of the origin of Dorothy's tears. "I draw what I see."

Dorothy's round, blue pools spilled to her cheeks, not from sadness, it appeared, but from joy, from love. Ruth had rarely, if ever, had this look directed toward her. She had seen it in movies, of course, when a mother joyfully cries with pride for her child—not for what the child had done, although her sketch was pretty good, but out of pride that the child had been entrusted into the mother's care by God, and that it was that mother's honor to raise the child and participate in the child's life. Ruth felt her own eyes moisten.

Dorothy wiped under her eye. "You must think I'm lovely, Tiffany?"

Ruth looked at her sketch. "This is how I see you." She returned her eyes to Dorothy, whose face had shed its pretense like that first day in Dorothy's bedroom when Dorothy had become vulnerable while speaking of Eugene. "If it's lovely, then, yes, but you are very lovely in many ways, Dorothy, not just how you look. You have been so very lovely to me, trusting me as your companion and treating me as part of your family."

Dorothy reached out to touch Ruth's hand, covering the Inca Rose. "Well, you are. You are part of this family."

CHAPTER 30

PACIFIC BLUE

A month later, Ruth dabbed her feather duster around Dorothy's bedroom while Dorothy picked through a collection of jewelry spread across her dresser. Although Ruth had moved in with Dorothy, she still kept her apartment. A part of her was still uncertain as to her security in Eugene's house. Dorothy frightened her at times. She could not predict Dorothy's behavior from day to day. And Ruth had no idea what would happen to the house and estate when Dorothy died.

Dorothy had insisted that Ruth's hair be colored blonde. Ruth had also endured a series of chemical peels and microdermabrasion treatments to erase her pockmarks. Her new teeth would be ready the following week. Dorothy had scheduled another eye lift for herself because loose skin was drooping and threatened to impair her vision, she said. She wanted Ruth to get a tuck around the eyes, too, but Ruth refused to be cut.

Dorothy inspected a necklace. "I need you to take down the details for my funeral and reception."

Ruth turned. "Dorothy, what's wrong?"

"Nothing. I'm perfectly well." Dorothy flicked her hand. "Get a pen and paper."

Ruth set down her duster and returned with the implements.

Dorothy watched as Ruth removed the pen cap with her teeth. "I want a high-quality white coffin with a marble finish and polished brass trim. The lid must have a very tight seal. The cheap ones leak. I don't want bugs and worms to get in."

Ruth scribbled, "white, marble, brass, tight, no worms."

Dorothy dug through her closet, pulling and pushing, trying to part the garments that were packed so tightly that the hangers were useless because the clothing seemed to hold itself up from the sheer lateral force of their encapsulation. Dorothy yanked at a turquoise silk dress, pulling a wad of material out. "This will match my eyes."

Ruth pushed the bifold door open wider. "Dorothy, I think your eyes will be closed."

Dorothy chuckled. "Of course. You're so funny." Threads popped and fabric ripped as Dorothy pulled the dress free. A hanger flew out and hit the ceiling. "But maybe we could somehow keep them open."

Ruth watched the hanger land on the floor. Dorothy was serious, so Ruth proceeded with caution.

"In Victorian times, they used to display the deceased upright." Dorothy placed her palm on the wall. "The coffin would be set on end, leaning against a wall, so the person was sort of standing."

A disconcerting mist descended upon Ruth, cool and damp, obscuring, like a macabre Victorian-themed film.

Dorothy sat on her chaise and laced her fingers. "Maybe my eyes will naturally open when I'm upright, like those baby dolls."

Ruth never had a baby doll but tried to imagine how little girls practiced being mothers, recalling how actual motherhood had been violently forced upon her with a real baby at fifteen.

"You know, the ones where the eyes close when they lie down." Dorothy balled her hands, then flicked her fingers open as if flinging water. "Then pop open when you lift them up."

Ruth flinched. "I'm not sure a dead person's eyes would look particularly attractive."

"That's a good question for the funeral parlor." Dorothy pointed at Ruth's paper. "Note that under a heading entitled, 'Questions for Funeral Parlor.'" Dorothy patted the top of her head. "See how my hair is puffed up on top?" Dorothy's white-blonde hair held firm, molded, spread, and sprayed in an attempt to hide the pink scalp several inches below.

Ruth leaned in.

"Come closer." Dorothy tipped her head forward. "You'll need to make sure the thin spots are covered. That's where the puffing comes in. They need to tease it. I also want it freshly colored when they prepare my body."

Ruth stepped back. "Maybe we should ask if they do that."

Dorothy glanced at herself in the mirror. "Sure they do. I had Eugene's color touched up."

Ruth wrote, "hair coloring, teasing."

"I've already purchased the plot next to Eugene. I've secured a mausoleum with fluted pillars holding up a pediment. The tympanum will have a relief sculpture of my profile. They need a photograph." Dorothy turned around. "Maybe we could send them your drawing."

Ruth looked up. "Sure. I made it for you."

Dorothy turned back to the mirror and picked at her hair. "Cherubs will be perched on each corner. I think this place is trustworthy, but you never know when you prepurchase if they'll take your money and stick a plain old headstone in the ground. And that's exactly why I'm telling you all this. You need to make sure they do it right."

Ruth wrote, "cherubs, columns."

"My name, Dorothy Anderson Fiske, will be carved into the tympanum under the relief. Each letter should be six inches high. If you don't check, they'll try to save money and make the letters smaller."

"Six-inch letters."

"Under my name, the inscription will read, 'A Beautiful, Humble Pilgrim of Christ.'" Dorothy's face, firm and steady, jaw set with certainty, solidified, to Ruth's astonishment, Dorothy's conviction. This notion had not yet struck Ruth with such clarity, until now. Dorothy considered herself a good person.

Ruth watched as Dorothy's lips moved, how she kept checking herself out, how she flipped her hands around, so proud of their smallness. Ruth heard nothing but her own inner sounds—air moving through her nostrils, a slight ringing in one ear. She had also wanted to be good, had wanted people to consider her a "good person." She'd imagined people saying: "That Ruth, always helpful, always on time, always doing the right thing." Many times she'd tried to believe it. *Believe and it will be yours.* From the Bible, or Wayne Dyer? No matter. The ringing got louder, followed by a sharp stab in that ear. She cupped her ears and closed her eyes to make it stop. Dorothy had done it, Ruth thought. She'd created this reality—*a beautiful, humble Pilgrim of Christ*—she believed it, and so it was.

Ruth opened her eyes to find Dorothy pointing at the paper on Ruth's lap with her raspberry fingernail. "Write it down. You need to have it all down."

Ruth bowed her head and wrote, "A Beautiful, Humble . . ." Maybe Dorothy was a good person. Who was she to judge? Some people had an easier time being good.

Dorothy turned to touch her drapes. "I had these custom-made thirty years ago. Mulberry silk, the finest in the world. The purebred worms only eat mulberry leaves. I've tried to get more fabric, but they don't make it anymore. My coffin will be lined with them."

Peach, cantaloupe, papaya. A coffin cocooned with worm excrement.

Dorothy felt the fabric, pulling, rubbing it between her thumb and fingers, as if she were Julie Andrews planning the children's new play clothes.

The Sound of Music. Ruth loved that movie, the singing and dancing, how the children got a new mother. She scribbled, "silk drapes for coffin."

"It'll be a custom charge, of course, but it's the best color with the dress and my complexion."

Ruth looked up again. "Your complexion?"

"My peaches-and-cream skin tone." Dorothy looked into her mirror. "I'll have to write down all the makeup, or better yet, I'll buy duplicates and have them in a bag marked for you. It will say 'funeral makeup.' But most important . . . Tiffany?"

Ruth's mind drifted to the Austrian Alps, and she silently sang "The Hills Are Alive."

Louder, Dorothy said, "Tiffany?"

Ruth switched over to "So Long, Farwell."

"Tiffany, this is important." Dorothy clapped her hands. "Pay attention. I'll have my jewelry instructions written out for you. Are you listening?" Dorothy clapped again, right next to Ruth's ear.

Through the window, Ruth considered the grapefruit tree and blue sky beyond. David hadn't had a funeral because she'd been nearly broke. Her old boyfriend, the one who raised him, had also died. So David was cremated, paid for by the state.

Ruth touched the drapes. "Dorothy? What if I go first?"

Dorothy went back to the mirror. "I guess that's possible, with your smoking." She pondered her reflection.

Ruth looked beyond a half mile of thoughtfully planted vegetation to the place where the bluff dropped. Sometimes, Ruth went down to the beach to sit in the sand near the spot where he'd forgiven her, where she'd convinced herself he was doing all right.

"Tiffany! My jewelry. Are you listening?" Dorothy grabbed Ruth's arm. "Don't bury me in it, for heaven's sake. That would be an incredible waste. People at the funeral parlor, the cleaning crew, anyone could take it right off my body. This happened to someone I knew. The body showed up at the wake bare of jewelry, and nobody knew what happened to it."

Ruth turned back to the sparkling stones and shiny metal scattered across the dresser. She'd touched every piece, worn it, returned it. She knew what was fake, what was real, but it all looked the same to Dorothy. Reality was irrelevant. It equally evoked the same emotion, feeding her pride and vanity, raising her value.

Dorothy squeezed Ruth's arm. "So you need to stay with me the whole time. And at the very last minute, right before they seal me up, you need to take all my jewelry off."

Ruth said, "What should I do with it?"

Dorothy smiled and reached to squeeze Ruth's hand. "It will all be yours."

Fake or real, Ruth's heart swelled.

Dorothy took Ruth's other hand. "The house, too. I know you won't change anything. You'll take care of it and keep the chandelier clean. Actually, you're getting everything, which is a lot when you include Esther's estate, although I still haven't heard from her attorney." Dorothy looked at her jewelry lying on the dresser. "I need to call him." Turning back to Ruth, still grasping her hands, she said, "Now you understand your training. You will become upper class, Tiffany." Dorothy glanced at Ruth's chipped fingernails. "We still have a lot of work to do."

"Dorothy, I don't know what to say." Ruth continued to hold Dorothy's hand, and at that moment, she felt a surge of hope, a Peep with wings, believing that things might come together. All the suffering could end. In having this home, her father's home, everything would be set straight. This is exactly what she'd planned, and the next step, the easiest step, was helping Dorothy along. There are so many ways to die when you're over eighty, so many. Ruth had thought about a few scenarios: a little slip down the stairs, some extra-sweet tea to obscure the bitterness, or an improperly hung chandelier.

Ruth gently squeezed Dorothy's hand. But what good was it if Dorothy was gone? Ruth didn't want to be alone anymore.

"You're entirely welcome. We'll plan the reception tomorrow. The champagne needs to be Dom Pérignon Rosé, and I want coconut filling for the truffles." Dorothy sighed. "It's a shame I'll miss it." She released Ruth's hands. "And no one wears black. You know how I feel about that."

Dorothy spent the next two hours getting ready for the day. She wanted to go to Carson's.

Ruth drove slower than usual. She would need to act surprised when they arrived. She parked on the street in front of the store, which was dark, the windows covered with brown paper.

Dorothy stared out the window. "What's happened?"

Ruth slowed to a stop. "It looks closed."

"Yes, I can see that!" Dorothy tried to get out of the car, but her door seemed too heavy. "Tiffany!"

Ruth jumped out and hurried around to let her out.

Once on the sidewalk, Dorothy stood in front of the door. Her face sank. "How can this be? He must have moved."

Ruth bent over to peek in a window between sheets of brown paper. "Looks empty." She tried the door.

Dorothy crossed her arms. "It's obviously locked."

Ruth stepped back.

"He could have called." Dorothy touched the door handle. Her hand shook. "He has the bracelet, Eugene's bracelet." She finally looked at Ruth. Her eyes fearful. "He was going to clean it and fix the clasp." Dorothy's wedding ring dazzled synthetically in the sunlight. "He called a couple of weeks ago. He offered a free cleaning service for his best clients, and I still needed the clasp fixed. He even came to pick it up. You'd gone out. I'd given him a few other older pieces as well." Dorothy bowed her head and grasped her own wrist. "He came into my bedroom, into my private quarters."

A storm stirred in Ruth's chest, windy and violent. "Esther's ruby ring?"

Dorothy struggled to swallow, then nodded.

Ruth threw her hands in the air. "Thief! He's a rotten thief! To steal from you like this!" Words flew from Ruth's mouth. "He sells you fake stones and steals the real ones!"

Dorothy's head popped up. "Fake stones?"

Ruth paused to swallow. "I heard this rumor and didn't want to upset you, but after this. Snake!"

Dorothy examined her four-carat diamond ring with a sour, pinched look on her face. "Eugene traded in my real ring for this." Eyes glazed; she twisted it around her finger. "This was the first thing." Large pink stones pulled her earlobes, revealing a small flicker of light through the holes in her flesh. Around her neck, a thick chain sparkled. Sunlight filtered through her hair revealing pink scalp beneath. She brightened. "He couldn't have been doing this for ten years. Certainly, he would have been caught. Many of my things are probably good."

"We'll get your real stuff back." But Ruth looked away.

As Dorothy examined the ground, her face shifted with disbelief. "I thought we had a relationship. I trusted him." She wandered away, down the sidewalk, then paused at a storefront with big glass windows and a fancy sign. AVIANO, a coffee shop where beautiful people drank lattes from white mugs topped with swirled foamy hearts. "Years ago, this was a photography shop. I used them for our wedding."

Through the window, Ruth noticed a case filled with sweets. "Should we get some coffee?"

Dorothy moved toward the door. "That sounds nice."

Once inside, Dorothy ordered her regular black coffee. Ruth ordered a mocha with extra whipped cream. They sat at a table near the window.

"I can't believe it costs ten dollars for coffee." Dorothy took a sip, leaving a bright-pink lipstick mark on the rim. "It's good, though." She looked at the window. "The photographer also took my engagement picture."

Ruth licked whipped cream from her lips. "I'd like to see it."

Dorothy finally smiled. "It's that one on my dresser in the crystal frame. He liked it so much, he put it in that window for advertising. It was a very large portrait. Many people commented about how wonderful I looked. How I was so photogenic and should have been a model."

Ruth smiled. "So you were famous!"

Dorothy laughed. "I guess I was." Familiar brightness returned to her eyes.

Ruth wondered if Dorothy's way—her perpetual optimism, her refusal to accept or mere acknowledgment of the bad—was the best approach. Delusion was her drug, and maybe that was OK. Don't happy people claim it's all how you look at things? Wayne Dyer said so. Mr. Halabi *had* moved. Dorothy *did* have a relationship with him. And Dorothy *was* famous—in the Palisades.

Several young mothers in yoga pants and ponytails walked in with babies. They laughed and fawned over the children, engaged in high-pitched chatter about feeding, baby music classes, and chemical-free toys. Dorothy and Ruth watched in silence until Ruth crunched into her croissant.

Dorothy said, "Is it fresh?"

"Very." Ruth stretched her tongue far to the side to get the chocolate she felt on her cheek.

Looking back at the mothers, Dorothy's face hung pale like a dead fish. Her eyes followed each woman back and forth, memorizing them. "Tiffany, remember when you were little?"

Ruth paused midbite, waited, then answered with caution, "Yes."

Dorothy's gaze still floated away. "You were such a sweet child."

Ruth searched Dorothy's eyes for a speck of reality on which to anchor the conversation, but reality to Dorothy was just that, reality to Dorothy, so Ruth smiled and nodded. "I hope so. I hope I didn't cause too much trouble."

Dorothy finally looked into Ruth's eyes. "With your pretty green eyes and beautiful skin, like a Spanish princess. The skin came from me, of course—the texture, I mean. I'm much whiter. But your eyes are from your father." Dorothy sneaked another glance at the women.

"Dad did have nice eyes." Eugene's eyes weren't pretty, but soft and gentle, nothing like her own, except for the gold flecks.

Dorothy fixed her gaze on the babies, plump and wiggly, dressed in baby-boutique wear. Their wondrous eyes, exposed only to beauty, beautiful parents and homes, beautiful coffee shops and clothing, wandered around in content amazement. A baby girl, bedazzled by her mother's diamond, gummed it as if it might taste just as pretty. Dorothy pressed her lips and closed her eyes, as if to prevent collapse from an internal tide. "He was a good man. I guess that can be enough."

Ruth, pulled by the same powerful undertow, clenched her jaw to keep her face from breaking into anguish at the beauty that shuffled and squirmed next to them, beauty that couldn't be bought. "You always made me such nice birthday cakes."

Dorothy came up for air and looked toward the ceiling. "Yes, I did, didn't I?" She blinked several times. "Which one did you like best?"

Ruth didn't hesitate. She could see it perfectly. "The cake shaped like a doll. It was pink and blue and swirly inside."

"Oh yes! It looked like a wedding cake, didn't it?" Safely back in delusion, Dorothy chuckled before sipping her coffee.

"And you and Dad bought me that dollhouse." Ruth felt better, too. The storm had passed, and life was sunny again because they wanted it to be.

Dorothy's face glowed. The color had returned. "Yes, it was so big. And the lights actually worked!"

Ruth pictured it. The one she'd seen in the Sears catalog

she'd fished from the trash, thrown there after her brother told her there was no Santa. "Yes, it was wonderful. Remember the tiny pots and pans, the cat, the little loaves of bread, and the teeny toothbrush?"

"And the teeny-tiny books and perfume bottles." Dorothy smiled at the memory. "I wonder what happened to it?" Dorothy looked out the window. "It's probably out in the garage somewhere. We could look for it, but it's hard to find anything with Eugene's old car in the way."

Ruth's stomach flopped. "What car?"

Dorothy looked back to the window and flicked her hand. "Just an old, ugly, yellow thing he bought after we married. He'd drive it around with nowhere to go. Just loved driving it."

Ruth picked up crumbs, then licked her finger. "I'd like to see it." A toddler ran by with something that looked good. "Could I have one of those cake pops?"

Dorothy noticed the pastry display, colorful packages on a stick. "Aren't those cute! Of course, Tiffany." She opened her purse and handed Ruth a five-dollar bill.

Ruth sat back down with a pink-and-white pop.

"You did so well in school, so smart, and married well, too. But he was like your father, with that heart trouble." Dorothy hesitated. "What was his name? Your husband?"

Ruth admired her pop. "Harrison."

"That's right. I saw Harrison Ford jogging once, very handsome. He was really eyeing me."

Ruth took tiny bites to make the pop last longer. "You and Dad made things so nice for me. Thank you." She touched Dorothy's hand.

"Tiffany, your father loved you. I love you. We were so happy you finally came after all those years of trying."

No one had ever told Ruth this. But now, in a rewritten past, a new present, and a promising future, she was loved.

Dorothy sank as if swept under again. Ruth patted the back of her hand. "What is it?"

"I was thinking of all the people we've lost. My father, Mother, Judith, Eugene, Esther, then poor Robert, Harrison, and your son. What was his name?"

Ruth didn't hesitate. "Tom, like Tom Cruise."

"Yes, Tom. Oh my word, my mind. He was so good-looking." Dorothy sipped. "It seems that everyone is dead. It's only the two of us now."

Ruth twirled her pop stick between her fingers. David's beautiful face. Ruth had seen joy there, or maybe just contentment, which was OK, too. He'd fallen, slipped. Accidents happen. The dirt was loose from the rain. It had rained the day before. She was sure of it. Ruth scraped her teeth along the cake-pop stick, trying to get the last of it.

Dorothy closed her eyes tight, then blinked a few times. "My eyes are dry."

Ruth stopped. Dorothy's bloodshot eyes struggled against the bright lights and air-conditioning draft.

Dorothy blinked furiously. "Not that! I'd never do that. Keep me alive at all costs. Do you understand?"

"I will." Ruth did not want to be kept alive at all costs. Dorothy had not seen how it goes, how the end becomes ugly.

Dorothy's Caribbean eyes twinkled in the warm sunlight passing through her famous window. A sinister smile spread, sweet and sassy, like lemon curd on a cream scone set before her at an Edwardian tea party in her gazebo. The magnetic power of Chanel Coco Mademoiselle drifted across the table, her body becoming heated with emotion as she said, *"And then there were none."*

That evening, back at the house, sitting in the den, Dorothy read to Ruth from a faded copy of *Twelfth Night*, stopping to explain when Ruth seemed confused.

Ruth yawned.

Dorothy closed the book. "Should we watch a movie

instead?" She flipped through the channels. "Look. *Blue Hawaii!*"

Of all the old movies, this is the one she found? Ruth couldn't believe the irony. God worked in mysterious ways.

On the screen, the waves crashed and the palms swayed. Ruth smelled bleach and jasmine, the scent of the hotel soap she replaced daily, keeping the hardly used pieces for herself.

Dorothy leaned forward, eager. "Have you seen this one?"

Ruth thought a moment. "No." True. She'd never seen it on a screen.

Dorothy focused on the TV. "There's Angela again. She's been in so many movies. People don't give her enough credit. Everyone only thinks of *Murder, She Wrote*. Angela asked me to play a minor role in *Murder, She Wrote* once. We'd been in close communication. Did I ever tell you that?"

"I think you did." Ruth dismissed Dorothy's delusion while watching the screen as the plane door flung open, revealing Elvis (Chad), back from the war. On the runway, his girlfriend watched, jaw dropped, arms crossed, as he passionately kissed a stewardess.

Dorothy said, "What do you think of Elvis? Did you like him? You would have been about the right age."

Yes, I liked him. I was there, cleaning his room. He sang to me and said my eyes were nice. "He was all right."

Dorothy said, "In 1957, when Eugene and I went back to Honolulu for our anniversary, he was staying in our hotel for a concert. It was a luxury hotel, extremely expensive. Nothing you've ever seen."

Ruth smiled. God, the irony. It was too much. "Yes, you mentioned it. That must have been exciting."

The movie was at the part where Chad's girlfriend loses her bikini top in the waves while he performs Hawaiian music with a few nearly naked locals rowing a boat.

"I had a bikini like that. You have to be quite bosomy for it to work." Dorothy inspected Ruth's chest.

Ruth's thoughts escaped. "It was made in 1961, in Kauai."

Dorothy looked back at Ruth, her face questioning. "Yes. I think you're right."

Ruth watched as Chad flirted with teenage girls on tour. They danced at a luau, kicked sand, mingled at a tiki bar, spilled drinks. Chad sang "Can't Help Falling in Love." His girlfriend swooned. Angela appeared.

Dorothy said, "Chad's mother, Angela, is a wealthy woman who wants Chad to take over the pineapple business. They always make her look so old. She's older than me."

The contrast between Angela's character and her real self was something Ruth thought of from time to time, especially since their encounter at Gelson's. She was a gifted actress. Dorothy was right about that. After four years at the Waikiki Beach Resort in Honolulu, Ruth had moved to Kauai in 1961 to work at the Coco Palms Resort. The staff had rushed around, giddy. Elvis was coming to make his first movie, and they'd be using the beach and hotel for the set.

Ruth watched as, in the movie, distraught over Chad's refusal, a teenage girl drove to the beach and dramatically threw herself to the waves. Chad pulled her from the water. Hysterical, the girl claimed no one liked her. Chad told her to straighten up, but she continued to sob. "My parents are always trying to get rid of me, sending me away," she said. Chad took her over his knee. "All you need is a good ole spanking," which he proceeded to give her. The girl's legs kicked, and her curls bounced like those of a child. In the next scene, the girl was socializing normally, cured of her depression.

Ruth cringed.

"See, Tiffany." Dorothy crunched a piece of popcorn. "These classic movies, the old times, they were right about a lot of things. All this blubbering about depression, jumping from cliffs, when a good old spanking is all kids need."

Ruth inhaled a dry popcorn kernel, coughed, thought it might come back up, but it didn't, so she swallowed continuously to encourage its slow creep down her esophagus. Old people say ridiculous things. But it still hurt.

Dorothy turned to Ruth. "You need to stop smoking."

Ruth fixed her eyes on a bit of spittle clinging to her hand. In 1961, she'd watched the filming of *Blue Hawaii* while cleaning a nearby lanai. Frantic, the director had looked around. "Where are all the wedding guests? The extras!" Panicked, people shuffled around, bumping into each other. Elvis stood with his arms crossed. Angela fanned herself in a chair. "We need more people at the wedding!" Elvis looked at Ruth. "What about that one? The one with dark hair and those eyes." Ruth, holding a broom, scanned the watchful crowd. Elvis winked. The director turned, looked her up and down, nodded, then summoned her with a wave of his hand.

On the TV, a crowd gathered around as Chad and his girlfriend floated down a river on a flowered raft, holding hands, in Hawaiian wedding attire. Angela insulted the bride's grandmother.

Dorothy laughed. "Angela's so funny. She can play any role."

In the movie, young Ruth, wearing a blue and white muumuu, a scented flower in her hair, and professional makeup, walked along the shore. One in a crowd of a few other maids and professional extras. She liked being called an extra. It felt extravagant.

Ruth pulled a fuzzy blanket over her lap. Strange to see herself at twenty-one, looking as pretty as she could, in a movie with Elvis and Angela, like watching a memory. Her memories made public—better this one than the others. Dorothy would never recognize her. Ruth hardly recognized herself.

Dorothy's face remained attentive. "Everyone looks so pretty in the movies." She sighed.

Ruth looked into her popcorn bowl. A few old maids remained. Back then, before they'd shot the wedding scene, Angela had approached Ruth. So nervous—all she had to do was walk in a crowd, but still. Angela had touched her shoulder.

"If you close your eyes and pretend it's real, it will be." When they'd fixed Ruth's hair, her diamond necklace, the Sun Drop, fell to the ground. Angela picked it up. Her eyes widened. "This is beautiful." She handed it back. "They can be so rough with the brushes. Sorry about that, dear." Concerned, Ruth grasped the stone in her fist, then searched Angela's face. "Do your eyes feel all right?"

Dorothy flipped off her shoes. "I should've been in the movies. I'm exceptionally photogenic."

On the TV, Ruth watched herself stroll along the water's edge, smiling, for real, until she walked off the screen and the movie ended with a kiss.

Dorothy rubbed her palms together. "What a nice movie. I wish they made them like that today. Good quality, smart lessons, happy ending. Children would be better off."

The movie was horrifying. A part of Ruth wanted to tell Dorothy everything, but what would be the point? It would be hurtful, at the very least, and she didn't want to hurt Dorothy. She didn't want to hurt anyone. Even with all the pain she'd endured, she still wanted to do good, whatever that meant. To want a mother and father, a home, was not bad. Was it wrong to leave her son? Of course. People repeat what they know. Miss Miller had said, "Go." So she went, like Eugene. She'd long since forgiven him for leaving her as a newborn and then again at Irene's funeral. How scary to face your grown child as a stranger. All those old people? They wanted to die. She was certainly not alone in that opinion. Robert, yes, wrong. The little orange bully who hurt David, wrong. But what kind of mother doesn't protect her children? Although she did know a couple. She had no excuse, unless she blamed her past, which she would not do.

A few years after *Blue Hawaii*, in 1964, Ruth had returned to LA. She'd wanted to find her son. From her car, she'd watched her old boyfriend holding David's hand, walking him to school. A swoosh of flaxen hair fell over his seven-year-old eyes. David smiled, skipped, and swung his arms like little boys should. Her old boyfriend hugged him before he ran onto the school grounds. Ruth drove away.

Dorothy said, "You seem tired. Why don't you go to bed?"

Ruth went to her room and changed into her yellow satin nightgown. She lay on her bed, facing the Dickens dolls. In the dim blue light from the moon shining in, their stretched mouths changed from joyous singing to frightful screaming, like the art book on the coffee table, the one Dorothy had explained—Munch, Norwegian, anxiety in the modern world. *The Scream*, she'd said. *Yes, that's it.* Something every educated person should know. But to her, anxiety didn't look like that. To Ruth, anxiety looked more like a child with her mouth shut.

Dorothy's muffled voice seeped in from the locked room next door. Ruth listened for a minute, then got out of bed. She figured Dorothy had piled the room high with things she couldn't part with, typical hoarding, and had been embarrassed for her to see.

Was she singing? Ruth pressed her ear to the wall. Yes, something soft and slow. Ruth put on her robe and walked down the hall. The door was shut, but a dim light glowed from the crack beneath. She listened again. Turning the knob, she pushed open the door to peek.

Dorothy stood in the middle of the room with her back to the door. She swayed slightly and continued to sing in hushed tones. Beyond her was a fancy white crib dripping with pink and ruffles. A mobile floated above, the fuzzy pastel stars, a moon, a sun, were all drifting. A changing table stocked with diapers, a silver baby brush, a pink rocking chair, and a white fluffy bunny were artfully positioned throughout the space. Lacy dresses on pink satin hangers lined the open closet. Dorothy's small frame kept a steady rhythm—"Rock-a-Bye-Baby."

Dorothy stepped to the crib. The face of a blonde baby doll appeared over her shoulder. Its eyes flipped open. Ruth's hands turned cold and sticky. Her chest caught midbreath. Dorothy patted the doll's back. "There, there, Tiffany," she said, then set it in the crib and covered it with a fuzzy yellow blanket. Dorothy remained, head tilted. She fixed the doll's hair, closed one eye that was stuck open, then placed her tiny hands on the rail, gripping, her rings lined up, clinking as she adjusted her grip.

Ruth held her breath and tiptoed back to her room. She pushed the lock button on the door and got into bed. Turning away from the window, from the dolls, she tried to listen over the sound of her own heart pounding. Ruth wanted to be back in her own dirty bed, her part of town, where people were poor and drunk and outwardly crazy. Dorothy had seemed harmless, their game, a way to cope, but this was too much. Jolted back into reality, Ruth reviewed the facts—it was 2006, she was a caregiver for old people, and Dorothy had lost her mind.

Ruth rubbed the Inca Rose under the sheets. Colorado, the mines, Mother Cabrini, the Queen of Heaven Orphanage. Ruth thought of how Cabrini miraculously cured an infant of blindness, qualifying her for sainthood. To distract herself, Ruth frantically thought about all she'd read, how Cabrini had saved orphans, mostly girls. An image of Miss Miller came to mind— she was breathing deeply, the white collar of her dress moving up and down, teaching Ruth how to calm herself. Miss Miller had a way with words and stories, just like her sister, like Agatha. Her father left her, too. Illegitimate. A bastard. Ruth breathed. But Miss Miller did good; she found her way with no parents at all. Ruth thought about living on that mountain in Colorado with the giant Jesus. It was still there; Ruth had done research— the shrine, the church, a little farm, the healing spring, the convent. Miss Miller was right. The stained-glass windows of the chapel had come from that school in Burbank, Villa Cabrini Academy. Someone had saved them. She would be so happy! Ruth's heart slowed. Miss Miller had been just like a sister and a mother. Ruth thought about being that for someone, how good it would feel. Was she too bad to be a nun?

Ruth's thoughts were interrupted by the sound of a door

closing. Dorothy's feet clicked down the hall. The footsteps stopped. Ruth watched her door. The knob wiggled. "Tiffany? Are you awake?"

Ruth crouched deeper under the covers. She was a girl again, hiding from people she lived with.

Dorothy's voice sounded low and stern. "Tiffany? Were you up?"

Ruth braced herself. *Candy clouds.*

"The belt to your robe is in the hallway, lying on the floor." Dorothy rattled the door handle again. "Tiffany! You lost your belt! The robe's no good without the belt."

Ruth's breath turned short and shallow while she tried to remind herself that Dorothy was a harmless old lady.

Dorothy knocked hard, the sound sharp, bone against wood. "Bad girl, Tiffany. You're a very bad girl!"

Ruth got up and began throwing her clothes in her bag. She'd go back to her apartment and never come back. Ruth paused, panting. Urth appeared in her mind—laughing and scolding, sneering, then screaming. *Betrayed.* Urth had killed Marbit and had made her kill Robert. Evil, pure evil. Tricked, like Satan, a liar. David had warned her of this, but she'd been weak. Ruth thought of living in her apartment without Marbit. Sorrow overtook her. She collapsed over her bag and whispered, "God, forgive me." A moving image of a white dove descending on the head of Jesus in the Jordan River played in Ruth's mind like a film. She lifted her head, got up, and set her bag by the door before returning to bed. She'd go to Colorado. Sneak out early, leave no note, before Dorothy awoke. She'd be a nun.

CHAPTER 31

EUGENE

After weeks with no Lincoln in sight, Eugene was sick with worry. He'd tried every candy, every shiny trinket, even vegetables, but there was no sign of him.

He pulled a book from his shelf, *Baby Farm Animals*, and sat down. A moment later, Lincoln poked his snout from the opening in the floor. "There you are! I've been worried. Come sit." Lincoln climbed up onto the twin leather chair. He looked thin. Eugene withered. "Are you feeling OK?" Lincoln tore the wrapping from a Twix left on the seat.

A few moments later, Eugene heard a tiny sound coming from the vent. A wiggly pink snout popped up from the edge of the hole, then another, and another. Three miniature Lincolns crawled out and sniffed around with hesitation. Lincoln jumped down from the chair to attend to them.

Eugene's heart swelled with delight. He could not remember such joy, except once, maybe twice. The first, flying in that plane, and the second, seeing his own gold-flecked eyes blink back at him while his palm rested on her dark, fuzzy head. Holding her, inhaling her essence, that unexplainable gush of love he'd felt, he realized, had been Dorothy's greatest longing.

At that moment, he still believed he could change her mind,

that Irene, a Spanish beauty, would marry him. The hope had carried him, allowed him to be happy, as a new father should be.

Weeping for joy as Lincoln nuzzled her babies, saliva and mucus dripped from his face. Wiping with his shirt, continuing to cry, he said, "I found her, Lincoln. I found her, but I got scared and ran."

Eugene touched the head of a baby rat with one finger. "Esther knew everything. We were close. She wanted to raise her, was more than willing, but it would have ruined our reputation. It might have killed Mother." He kicked at the rug. "The Fiske name was preserved, while Ruth, my baby Ruth, was discarded."

CHAPTER 32

SHADOW

The following morning, Dorothy sipped coffee at the breakfast table tucked into one corner of the kitchen. Ruth opened a bakery box while looking out the sink window. Dark figures moved around inside Robert's house. It was for sale. People were looking.

In 1968, Ruth had driven by the house where she'd grown up. She'd stopped to watch her brother's shadow moving from room to room from the safety of her car window. She'd wanted Miss Miller's Christie books, which she'd hidden in the basement. The sight of her brother had still caused a violent storm inside, but she had to get the books. At the time, she'd thought they were the most valuable thing she owned.

Very early that morning (four o'clock), Ruth had opened her eyes, dressed, and lifted her bag. But after looking around the sweet room, she set her bag down and sat on the bed. While digging her feet into the fuzzy rug and fondling the comforter, still warm from her own heat, she felt compelled to open the little drawer of the bedside table. Inside she found an old Bible with a well-worn black leather cover. She examined the gold edges of the pages, which were dingy near the back where

Christians spent most of their time. But Ruth opened it to the book of Ruth, near the front. She knew right where it was. Just three pages, sandwiched between Judges and 1 Samuel. Easy to miss, the book had been described as out-of-place, obscure, maybe even a bit random. But Ruth knew it well. In the story, Ruth, loyal Ruth, accompanied her widowed mother-in-law, Naomi, to return to her home, the land of Judah. Ruth read silently until she came to the passage she wanted, then she read aloud, "Do not press me to leave you or to turn back from following you! Where you go, I will go; where you lodge, I will lodge; your people shall be my people, and your God my God. Where you die, I will die—there will I be buried. May the Lord do thus and so to me, and more as well, if even death parts me from you!" Ruth had looked up into the dark cave of a hooded doll—The Ghost of Christmas Future—and she realized that she couldn't leave. Dorothy would be lost. Someone would put her in a home, and then what? She'd wither and die.

Ruth turned from the window to watch Dorothy, who sat slouched in her robe, her eyes puffy and dreamy. Ruth took a deep breath and let it out slowly. Dorothy could never live in a home. Ruth wouldn't, either. She licked a bit of doughnut glaze from her finger. *Dorothy needs her things. She needs to live in her house.*

Ruth continued preparing breakfast. She felt Dorothy watching as she cut a cinnamon bun in half with a spatula. The previous night, when she had managed to sleep, horrific dreams tormented her. Dreams of Dorothy picking the lock to her room with a pocketknife and the baby doll next door crying all night. In her dream, when Ruth finally went to check, the baby had a bloody cut across her head.

Dorothy said, "The pieces would be much neater if you'd use a knife."

Ruth focused on the bun. "I've got it with this."

Dorothy cleared her throat. "I've been meaning to tell you something for a while now."

Ruth looked up.

Dorothy's face appeared pale and frightened. "There are people coming into the house at night. A woman and a girl. They crouch down on the side of my bed and grin up at me with black beady eyes and long, pointy noses."

Back in familiar territory, in a world of Dorothy's imagination, Ruth said, "Do they talk?" Ruth noticed Dorothy's pug nose, realizing how perfectly it matched the other shapes of her body.

Back then, in 1968, when her brother had eventually gone out, Ruth sneaked into the house, got her books, and put them in her trunk. She was about to drive away, then stopped. Her brother had returned with bottles of liquor. He was thin and wiry, old for thirty-two. Ruth stayed with her car, hidden across the street in the shadow of a large palm tree. An hour later, a pretty teenage girl with a long, dark ponytail had come and gone from the house. Ruth guessed the girl to be about fifteen. *A child will look for her mother or father.* Ruth's body had tensed. A strange sensation engulfed her, a heaviness in her pelvis. She'd wanted to follow the girl, to look at her face, at her eyes. Ruth had assumed her brother had left Jane with the Catholics. Did he leave a name? His or hers? Either way, she'd had no authority with which to inquire. Ruth started her car. Was the girl on foot? Ruth had pulled onto the street and passed the Moonlight Cream (yes, it was!), but she was so distracted by the girl that she did not realize it until the car was already in her rearview mirror. The last time she'd seen it, she was just eleven.

Dorothy set down her cup. Her face tightened. "Yes, the intruders tell me to get out, that I'm to get out!"

Ruth licked the spatula when Dorothy wasn't looking.

"And sometimes they crouch at the end of my bed and peek over with their black eyes staring at me." Dorothy squinted. "They're very unattractive, sort of ratlike."

Ruth separated the layers of her cinnamon bun. "Dorothy, that sounds awful. Who do you think they are?"

"I think it's Irene, but I don't know who the girl is."

Ruth looked up to study the air vent in the ceiling of Dorothy's kitchen. A week later, after getting her books, Ruth had heard about her brother's unfortunate death. Carbon monoxide. At the time, she had been as surprised as anyone. She'd concluded that her bad thoughts were to blame. But now, remembering the Moonlight Cream, it dawned on her—Eugene had still been watching. The authorities concluded that a rodent, most likely a pack rat, had made a nest in the exhaust vent that served the furnace to her old house. It had been jammed full of leaves, grass, sticks, and paper trash, including an enormous wad of candy wrappers. The rat had had a certain affinity for snack-size Baby Ruth candy bars, but back then, Ruth had no reason to associate them with Eugene.

Distracted until Dorothy's kitchen air vent ticked, then exhaled a cool breeze across her face, Ruth poured coffee until it overflowed from the rim of her cup. She looked back at Dorothy, who'd seen her accident. "What else do they do?"

Dorothy frowned. "Last night, the girl took the book from my night table and hit me in the shin." Dorothy pulled up her nightgown. "See, the bruise is forming."

A fresh pink bruise appeared on Dorothy's shin, along with red splotches, purple veins, spidery red ones, and brown spots.

Ruth wiped the spilled coffee, then opened the freezer for ice. "Does it hurt?" Ruth wrapped the ice in a clean dishrag, then crouched to dab Dorothy's shin.

Ruth marveled at the variations of Dorothy's skin, the colors, the shapes. The death of her brother had somewhat lightened Ruth's load. She'd developed a weak faith in the possibility of an overarching moral authority—or was it the enduring power of her dark thoughts? Although at the time, she had wondered because her thoughts had not stuffed that pipe with candy wrappers. Eugene had protected her. He'd waited until she'd fetched her books, let a week pass, and then did what needed to be done, no blood, nothing gruesome, just an everyday accident, bad luck. Like a puzzle or a good mystery, the pieces finally fit. With the motive and suspect now realized, Ruth looked around the kitchen and saw Eugene everywhere. He'd loved her, and now, here she was, right where he'd wanted her to be, in his home, using his dishes and sitting in his chairs. Ruth's eyes watered at this thought. Still inspecting Dorothy's leg, Ruth wondered what it had looked like as a fifteen-year-old girl.

Ruth closed her eyes and saw the young girl's dark ponytail bouncing as she walked from her brother's house. She'd have been about the right age. Had she been looking for her parents? Confused and restless, she was no doubt desperate to understand why her mother had left her. And Ruth had let her go, again.

Dorothy whimpered. "It hurts a little."

Ruth pulled up a chair, sat, and continued to press the ice gently on Dorothy's bruise. Back then, she had felt unfit, or maybe unworthy, to approach the girl. But more simply, like Eugene, when the moment came, she was just too scared. "How long have the intruders been coming?"

"Years. They come every night, and in the morning, they're gone. One time, the older one bit my toe."

Ruth lifted Dorothy's foot onto her lap to check her toes. "Every night?"

Dorothy nodded, her face shaken and pale.

Ruth rubbed Dorothy's foot. "We lock the doors, so I'm not sure how."

"Well, they get in." Dorothy's eyes darted around the tightly drawn curtains.

Ruth lifted Dorothy's other foot onto her lap and massaged it gently. She thought of how Jesus had washed his disciples' feet. "My son, David, told me that Jesus came to serve people. It seems ironic, God serving us, but I guess he was teaching us what love looks like."

Dorothy seemed not to hear Ruth. She twisted her body and tried to pull the curtain to close a small gap.

Ruth worked her thumb into Dorothy's arch. "I've always liked my work, serving people. I feel closer to God when I'm serving people."

Dorothy finally gave up fiddling with the curtain and leaned back in her chair. "You're good at it. Some people are just made for that type of work, and others are not." She folded her hands in her lap. "But you shouldn't have listened to your son so much. He was a Catholic."

Ruth looked up. "He loved God. Isn't that enough?"

Dorothy, frustrated, turned and gave the curtain one final yank. "Tiffany, you've never even been to church. You don't know what you're saying."

Ruth watched a flicker of light reflect off Dorothy's red toenail. "You're right. I haven't. Not that I remember, at least." She looked into Dorothy's eyes. "Could I go with you sometime?"

Dorothy looked away. "I'm not sure you'd feel comfortable in my church. It's mostly people who live in the neighborhood."

Ruth waited a moment to see if Dorothy would turn back to her. "But I do live here now, don't I?"

Dorothy let out a weak laugh and watched her feet as she wiggled her toes. "Yes, Tiffany, but it's different. I'll give you a Bible to start reading on your own, and then we'll see."

"I've already read the Bible." Ruth looked down at Dorothy's foot. "But I guess you can never read it too much."

Dorothy was silent, so Ruth looked up to find Dorothy's lips tight and her eyes hard and slightly narrowed.

Ruth placed her hand across Dorothy's ankle. "David said I should read it, so I did. And then Esther and I used to talk about it sometimes, and that's when I started realizing some things."

Dorothy didn't move or speak. Her face was blank.

"Parts of my life started making more sense. I've been realizing lately how good can come from bad. We can't see it when it's happening, but then when you look back at things, you know. It's like some of the bad stuff starts to make sense."

"There is no tolerance for superstition within Christianity, Tiffany. That's where the Catholics lead people astray with the rituals and the saints and the rosaries. Maybe it's better if you don't think about these things too much."

Ruth realized the topic was hopeless, so she returned to their original conversation. "What book did the intruder, the girl, hit you with?"

Dorothy fondled her ring. *"Blithe Spirit.* I'm rereading it because Angela is going to be playing the part of Madame Arcati on Broadway soon." Dorothy's face lifted. "I'd like to see that. Wouldn't it be something?"

"Maybe we could go." Ruth said this without much thought. "After England."

Dorothy gazed into her ring. "Yes, what a wonderful time that would be."

Ruth set Dorothy's foot down with extreme care. The ice melted on the table, and the water ran out, colorless, reminding her of Marbit's bright blood running across the counter and onto the floor.

Ruth ate her bun, relieved that nothing about the previous night had come up. She would try to forget it, too. Everyone has secrets.

Dorothy reached down to dab at her shin. "They also took the belt to your robe and left it in the hall."

Ruth closed her eyes a moment to remind herself that Dorothy was, at best, senile, but more likely, deranged. That word, deranged, seemed harsh, truly mean. The word permeated Ruth with sadness and guilt. Dorothy couldn't help it. Irene couldn't, either. Eugene tried his best, too. People are really flawed and broken, Ruth realized, as if she were the first person to come to this conclusion. "Yes, I noticed it on the doorknob this morning. Was that you?"

Dorothy slurped her coffee, then set down the cup, her hand wobbly. "I put it there last night. You were already sleeping."

Ruth wiped up the water with the rag. "Thank you. I wouldn't want to lose it. It's such a beautiful robe."

Dorothy straightened her own robe and tightened the belt. "And quite expensive. The intruders must have realized it."

CHAPTER 33

THE BOOK OF RUTH

Ruth smelled her apartment as soon as she got off the elevator. She just needed to pack the last of her things because she was moving in with Dorothy, permanently.

Urth moaned through the wall in a chorus of clanking metal and scraping percussion of heavy items dragged across a gritty floor. Ruth grabbed the remote from the couch and turned up her TV. The pigeons remained, increased in number each day, it seemed, but now they just made Ruth sad. Urth pounded on the wall until Ruth's drawings shook. She turned the TV louder. *The Price Is Right* theme music, the trumpets and drums, reverberated in Ruth's head. "Bobby Lou Webb, come on down!" The audience clapped and cheered as contestants hugged each other and ran down the aisles with big yellow name tags, hands raised in victory.

Eugene's painting of the rat fell to the ground, where the frame broke open.

Rage electrified Ruth's body. She ran to the door and swung it open. She felt brave enough to confront Urth, but Urth was standing right outside Ruth's door. Urth stepped forward, pushed Ruth aside, and walked in. Urth stood near the table, looked at a few boxes on the floor, then turned back to Ruth. "You moving out for good?" Urth moseyed around the living room, stroking her long braid that draped in front of her shoulder. With a snotty look on her face, she said, "You got just what you wanted, thanks to me."

Ruth folded her arms. "I'm part of the family. I'm a Fiske."

Urth harrumphed.

Ruth put her hands on her hips. "I care for Dorothy, and she cares for me. Nobody's perfect. I need a real home. I need Dorothy, and she needs me. The things she says about David aren't true. None of it's true."

Urth put her hands on her hips, as if to mimic Ruth, then laughed. "Oh, Ruth, he jumped. He was crazy, just like your mother, your father, Dorothy, and guess what? You're crazy, too."

Ruth dropped her arms. "He slipped."

Urth shook her spiked orange fingernail in the air and said, "There is no forgiveness for suicide."

Ruth watched the pointy nail, curved and bladelike. An image of Freddy Krueger came to mind. "He liked standing on the edge, to see the ocean. I told him the truth about his father. I thought he could handle it. He was upset that night. We'd gone to dinner. He liked fried chicken. We went to KFC, and he wasn't eating much. He usually ate two breasts and two legs, extra crunchy, with—"

Urth stepped up and slapped Ruth across the face. "Ruth, shut up!"

Ruth felt nothing. She laughed because it was nothing. A slap, ha! A teeny, little slap. "With honey mustard, he liked a lot of honey mustard."

Urth slapped Ruth again. It stung a little. "The next day, he just slipped. He was startled, that's all. Maybe a bird, maybe a plane, or a squirrel had scared him." Ruth reached up to touch her face. It felt good to be slapped because she knew she was alive and grounded in her body. "Something just startled him, that's all, with the rain and the mud . . ."

Urth pushed past her to dig into a box of Lucky Charms. "Ruth, stop making up your own version of what really happened. You won't even admit you were raped." Urth crunched more cereal. "It was your fault, you know. Your shirts were too tight and your skirts too short."

Ruth felt her stomach sink inward. She had always felt embarrassed that her clothes didn't fit.

Urth held up a crystal ball marbit, then popped it into her mouth. "You're embarrassed. And so ashamed."

Shame was too mild a word. There was no word for how Ruth felt. *Rape.* She screamed. "Stop! Don't say that word. Don't ever say that word again!"

"Rape! Rape! Rape! Ruth was raped!" Urth made a digging sound with her hand deep in the cereal box. "You were a little girl, your parents were young, and Irene didn't love Eugene. They got rid of you because you were going to ruin their lives. So why would you think either one of them would want you to show up later? And besides, they're dead, Ruth. I think you forget that sometimes."

Dizzy, Ruth sat on the couch and sucked air in short, fast breaths. *Breathe like Miss Miller.* Ruth looked down at her hands resting on her knees. "I do feel like I did something. It's a sick sensation." Ruth wiped a tear from her cheek and looked up. "Why didn't I scream? Miss Miller could have heard and called the police or something."

Urth poured herself a bowl of cereal. "It wouldn't have helped. He would have just come after you again. You got with bad people. People want money, Ruth. Eve needed money, and it made her mean. Your brother was just creepy and bad. I don't know why or how, but he rubbed his badness all over you and tried to make you bad, too. And I'm sorry to say, Ruth, but he did make you bad. You can see this, can't you? I'm not telling you something you don't already know."

Ruth looked out the window at a long, dark cloud dividing the sky. "Maybe I am bad, but it's not my fault. And if it's bad to want love and a home, then I guess I'm bad. If God is David's real father, then God is my real father, too. God will help me to be good."

Urth sat at the table and popped cereal bits into her mouth one by one. "You can't be good. You're just not. You're a murderer, Ruth." Urth slashed her throat with an orange talon. "You murder people."

Ruth pulled her eyes from Urth's orange nails and looked back at the window. Marbit's friend, with the feathered feet, stood on the sill. She moved her head around the window, looking inside, looking for Marbit. Ruth felt heat rise into her head. A sudden explosion of energy rushed through her arms and legs. She felt her face twitch. Rubbing her tongue over her bottom teeth, with the scar tissue creating a scraping sound inside her head, she said, "Look what you've done! You've left her alone. You witch! You killed Marbit and left her alone." Ruth stood and pointed at the window. "Look at her. She's so sad and scared. She's got no one to be with, no one to care for her, no one to love her!"

Urth turned to the window and laughed. "It's a bird. A stupid flying rat." She threw the cereal box at the window. Lucky Charms flew everywhere, then fell to the floor. Marbit's friend flew away. Urth turned back to Ruth, then shifted her eyes to Eugene's fallen painting. She shook her head. "Just like Eugene, just like your worthless father, painting rats."

A funny feeling came over Ruth, as if she were underwater or floating in a cloud. A certain calmness cocooned her body. She sat back on the couch, crossed her legs, and rested her arms leisurely across the back cushions. "Urth, I've changed my mind. I'm going to stay with you." Ruth leaned forward. "Will you help me unpack?"

Urth's face dropped. "What?"

Ruth placed her hands in her cardigan pockets and rolled

her lighter wheel. "Yes, I think you're right. We're meant to be together. We're the same. Yin and yang. Soul sisters. Two sides of a coin. Dr. Jekyll and Mr. Hyde. Two peas in a pod. Twins."

Urth started slowly pushing the fallen cereal together with her foot, forming a pile.

Ruth walked to the table, sat in the chair, and lit a cigarette. "Everyone is broken, Urth. Everyone. But we have each other. When one is weak, the other is strong. We'll help each other."

Urth looked up from the floor. Her face appeared vulnerable, as if a child had emerged from somewhere hidden inside.

Ruth rested her hands on the table. "How did it all go so wrong? When God made us, he made us in his image. Can a perfect God make something that is imperfect? That breaks and dies and does bad things? David said the evil in the world is our own fault because God gave us a choice, and we chose wrong. We wanted to be left alone, and so he did; he left us alone and look at the mess we've made. God expects a lot from us, but he is merciful. But I feel no mercy. Do you? I see mostly bad. I see good people get hurt and bad people get away with things. So we need to help each other."

Urth nodded with hesitation.

Ruth leaned in. "People will do anything for love. Dorothy thought love would come out of wealth and status. Eve thought from fame. Eugene wanted Irene, but Irene was running from her own demons. She probably wanted a father, too. I suspect something went wrong there. David wanted to know his birth father. It all boils down to the same thing. Robert wanted love. He cried out through that piano and darkened his world with those glasses. Esther wanted to marry. She wanted a child, too. Why? To love. God created this world to be beautiful and perfect, but it's just a bunch of lonely people desperate to have love, and no one is getting anywhere." Ruth reached out and grabbed Urth's hand. "I don't want to be alone anymore."

With a weak voice, Urth said, "You're not alone. You have me."

Ruth looked to the window. "Yes." The dark cloud had moved on. "Eugene loved me. I'm sure of this now. I knew we were alike. We thought the same." Ruth squeezed Urth's hand. "A parent will do anything to protect their child, anything. Knowing what he did, even if it was very bad, makes me valuable." Urth's face had weakened with confusion, the hardness now gone. "I feel truly valuable. When someone is willing to protect you at all costs, to save you even if it means sacrificing themselves, that's true love."

Urth squeezed back, her nails digging into Ruth's wrist. "We'll make dinner. We'll go out to the movies."

Ruth felt nothing. She focused again on the clear blue sky. "That's what Jesus did. He laid down his life for his friends. Love is not really about me. Love is about them." Ruth turned her face to the ceiling. "God, forgive me for everything, but mostly for not seeing you all along. All the people you've put in my path, I could have helped them more. If I'd understood how simple it was—just love—I could have loved them, all of them." Ruth choked. "Even him." Ruth looked down at Urth's orange talons clutching her wrist. "But *him*." Ruth swallowed hard. Her eyes burned. "I'm not sure if I can—God will just have to love him for me." Ruth shook her head and whispered to herself, "But there is good because without him, my children, my babies, would not be."

Urth loosened her grip. "Ruth, you have me, remember? I'm a goddess. You don't need Jesus. He only helped people in the olden days."

Ruth lowered her head. "Jesus, help me find Jane. I'll grab her and hold her until she sees who I am. I'll tell her everything. How I named her after a book hero, an orphan who had a hard time but found love. She'll know how she came into this world and how it wasn't my fault she was left and how I was just a girl myself and how sometimes people do bad things, but good, very good, things can come from them. I'll teach her how all things work for good. Because without David, I'd never have found you. Even the bad can be good. Like the movies, even the bad can look beautiful, be beautiful, sometimes."

Ruth looked up to Urth's face, then stood. "You're right. I need you. I need you to come with me."

Urth pushed her chair back with a screech. "Where are we going? Shopping? Out for lunch? I've got money."

Ruth walked toward the door. "Come with me."

Urth ran over. "What kind of food do you want? American food?"

Ruth left her apartment and walked down the hall. When she reached the elevator, she pushed the down-arrow button. Urth, beads rattling, followed her inside. Ruth pressed the "B" button, which lit up with an orange glow. Ruth fixated on the button; the shade of red orange was particularly upsetting, almost neon, but dirty, *Dirty Neon*.

Urth looked. "The basement? Why'd you push 'B'?"

Ruth smiled. "I want to show you something first."

Urth fumbled with her bracelets. "I like french fries with mayonnaise. Don't you?"

The elevator doors opened, and Ruth stepped out. She turned back to Urth, still standing in the elevator, and smiled. "Come on, Urth. I want to show you where they filmed *Nightmare on Elm Street*. Remember that one? From 1984. I was here. It was Johnny Depp's film debut. I like his exotic look, don't you?"

Urth remained in the elevator. She steadied herself with the handrail. "I don't want to see it, Ruth. I don't like horror movies."

Ruth motioned for her to come, scooping the air with her whole arm. "I know you don't, but come anyway. It'll be fun to see it again. Let's see where Freddy Krueger did all his nasty business." Ruth stepped back to the elevator, grabbed Urth's hand, and pulled her out. "It's still considered one of the best slasher movies ever made. In fact, I believe the term slasher movie came from this film." Ruth dragged Urth by her wrist as Urth took baby steps against the resistance. "Come on. It's a part of American film history. Not too many people get to see the actual boiler room."

Urth, now committed, moved closer to Ruth. "He had knives for fingers. I don't like knives."

"I know you don't." Ruth grabbed Urth's hand. "We can hold hands if you're scared."

Urth stuck close to Ruth, holding her hand and practically resting her chin on Ruth's shoulder. Ruth felt warm moisture form between their skin while her free hand rolled the lighter wheel in her left pocket.

Urth's hand began to shake. "Freddy had all those horrible scars."

Ruth squeezed. "We all have scars, Urth, but many times they are hidden."

Urth said, "What's the worst thing that's ever happened to you, Ruth? The very worst."

Ruth squeezed again. "Shhhh, Urth. It's time to let go of those things. It's time to move on."

They walked through the gloomy, dank corridors scented with dirty iron and fire, where a conglomerate of metal pipes and ladders lined the walls and ceiling. Water left shiny trails down the cement wall, which shone dimly against a couple of small, high windows that allowed faint light to filter in. Ruth led Urth to a large cylindrical boiler that groaned and hissed. There was a small wheel the size of a dinner plate, painted red, attached. Ruth felt heat from several feet away. She turned to look at Urth, whose face was pale and stiff.

Ruth smiled and nodded. "Here it is. Here's the spot."

Urth pulled back while still gripping Ruth's hand. "What spot?"

Ruth chuckled. "Where Freddy did his dirty work, of course."

Urth backed away. "I want to go to lunch."

Ruth still gripped Urth's sweaty hand. "Freddy wasn't real, you know. Even in the movies, he was just in those kids' dreams.

He killed all those kids, and then the parents of those murdered kids killed him. Burned him up. That's where he got all those scars on his face. Do you remember that?"

Urth pulled back, but Ruth was stronger. "No. I don't watch horror movies."

Ruth yanked Urth closer. "But you saw this one. I know you did, or you wouldn't be scared."

Urth started to cry. "Ruth, why are you doing this to me?"

Ruth rolled her lighter. "If those kids didn't believe in Freddy, then he'd disappear. Remember? He wasn't real because he was actually dead."

Urth's lip trembled in the low light. "But if something is in your mind, then it *is* real. You told me that."

"Yes, I did, but I can decide what's in my mind. I decide, Urth." Ruth released Urth's hand and gripped the red wheel with both hands until it turned.

Urth steadied herself against a nearby wall. "Ruth! What are you doing?"

Ruth gave the wheel another turn. "Let's see how this thing works." The boiler roared, and the orange flicker of flames shone through the crack around a small door with a simple latch. Ruth turned the latch, and the door swung open. A series of pipes ran through the open flames. Ruth turned back to Urth. "See, Urth, the water goes through these pipes and is heated with the flame."

"Ruth, I'm leaving. You're crazy. You need help." Urth turned to go.

Ruth grabbed her by her braid and yanked her back. "Not yet."

Urth screamed and fell back against Ruth. Ruth gave the braid a firm yank, and it detached from Urth's head. A clip dangled from the end. What remained on Urth's head was a few overly bleached clumps of frizzy, shoulder-length hair. Urth's face shook and contorted. One purple eyelash fell to the ground. Ruth watched Urth's cheeks quiver and eyes spill over with tears.

Hundreds of lies. Decades of shame. Countless moments of humiliation, rejection, and sorrow were gradually revealed in Urth's face as if floating to the surface of a dark lake.

Ruth grabbed the remaining clumps of Urth's hair and shook her head back and forth. "You're not real!" Ruth spun her in circles by her hair. Urth wailed. Round and round as if playing a schoolyard game, Ruth chanted, singsong style:

"You are the earth and I am the sun.
You thought messing with me would be so much fun.
I know who you are, trying to cause me such strife.
But you are not real, unlike that knife."

Ruth spun faster. Behind Urth, the fire inside the boiler flashed with each spin. The orange flame, *Dirty Neon*, sent shocks of rage coupled with waves of elation through Ruth's body as she realized her power. Ruth held Urth's hair with one hand while she pulled the Sun Drop diamond from beneath her shirt with the other. Holding it up, she shouted:

"I'm the sun and you are the earth.
I made you real and I gave you birth.
But today you will burn
With each coming turn.
Today you will die
A death for each lie."

Ruth let go of Urth just as she passed by the open door to the boiler. Urth fell back, shrieking, into the flames. Ruth leaned closer. "Hurt, your name is Hurt!" Ruth flinched as her hand brushed the hot metal, but she stayed close to the flame to watch Urth melt. "You'll never hurt me again!" Urth shrank away like paper burning to ash. And then she was gone.

Ruth looked at her hand. A blister was forming, but nothing too bad. When she looked up, toward the elevator, a dark, bulky figure blocked the walkway. A mask covered his face. He grasped something long and pointy.

Ruth backed away. Acid rose in her throat. She hated horror movies. She hated to be scared. "Please, no!"

The figure came closer and held up his weapon. Ruth still could not see his face.

Ruth shouted, "No! Please don't! I've changed. I'm good now."

The man laughed and kept walking toward her.

Ruth crouched on the floor and wrapped her hands around her head. She whispered, "It's not my fault." She crouched lower. "God is changing me." She felt a hand on her arm, then flinched. "The bad part is gone."

"Another lookie-loo." The man laughed.

Ruth peeked up between her bent arms and saw a large wrench hanging from a normal human hand.

"You live here, right?" The man tried to grab Ruth's hand and help her up. "Everybody wants to see *the* boiler room."

Ruth took the man's hand and stood. He wore a white air-filter mask, which he pulled down to his chin.

"Terrible dust down here." The man sneezed violently. "Are you satisfied? Did you see what you wanted to see?"

Ruth, embarrassed, said, "My mother wanted to see the boiler room. She loves horror movies." She brushed off her pants and tried to fix her hair. "I told her I'd take some pictures." Ruth realized she had no camera.

The man smiled. "Is that right?"

Ruth said, "Yes, she's very strange. Most old ladies don't like movies like that, but she's a huge fan of slasher movies."

The man peeked into the boiler. "Uh-huh." He turned the red wheel to lower the flame. "Why don't you run along now? Fun's over down here."

Ruth nodded and hurried back to the elevator, got in, pushed the number three button, and waited for the familiar jolt of the old elevator to leap into action, then hold steady, as if it were a tamed animal. She exited on her floor, walked down the hall, then paused a moment at Urth's door. It looked different than the other apartment doors. There was no number, no lock, and the door was narrower. Ruth turned the handle and pushed it open.

The small, dark room was lined with shelving holding various boxes and buckets. One corner served as a storage area for several mops and brooms. A small window traversed by a jagged edge of broken glass was near the ceiling. Ruth noticed a nest up on the high shelf, hugging the wall, her wall, blue on the other side, where her drawings hung. *Pigeons' nests are composed of hardened pigeon poop, which turns into a cement-like material, perfect for keeping the babies safe on high cliffs and during windstorms.* Ruth stepped into the room and spotted a ladder. She opened it gently, but it still created a terrible screech, which caused an image of Eugene to appear in her head, followed by the very recent memory of Urth's last sound.

Ruth set the ladder, tested its steadiness, and climbed toward the nest. She heard a faint cooing as she approached the level of the shelf. She leaned over and saw a single feather-footed pigeon, Marbit's friend, sitting in the nest. The bird cocked her head and cooed. Ruth became thick with sadness when she looked into that pigeon's black eye. The pigeon stood, as if to show her what she had. Between her feet sat two pale-yellow, lightly speckled, *Moonlight Cream*, eggs the size of a Cadbury Creme Egg. *Pigeons mate for life.* Ruth looked back to the mother. *Both mother and father pigeons sit on the nest and produce baby pigeon food, called crop milk.* "I'm terribly sorry for what she did, but she's gone now; Urth's gone. I killed her, and no one will ever hurt you or your babies. I promise."

CHAPTER 34

RAZZMATAZZ

Ruth gave up her apartment to move in with Dorothy permanently. A couple of months later, a young family moved into Robert's house. His piano room served as the nursery. Dorothy could see the pink crib from her piano bench. A mobile of pastel farm animals, a cow, pig, horse, and sheep, drifted above. There was no goat—*God will separate the sheep from the goats*—which Dorothy appreciated.

Last week, the baby could finally stand while holding on to the side rails. She pulled and pushed as if trying to break out. Dorothy loved her spirit. Sometimes the baby howled. She really put on a show, with her red face pinched and feet stomping. Dorothy found this adorable. Once tired, she'd plop down, crouch up, and fall asleep with her cute rear end in the air. Dorothy often tapped the window to get her attention. The baby, her fat cheeks loose like an old man's jowls, would tilt her head with wonder, grasp the rails, and jump, jump, jump, then pause and smile, as if she knew Dorothy were watching. And Dorothy was, of course, watching, smiling and sad all at once.

The baby had seven onesie pajamas, three pink, two yellow, and two white (one with pink hearts). She took her bottle at seven with a book in the rocking chair (sometimes Dorothy could read the titles). Lights went out by seven thirty, but a soft yellow glow remained from the night-light shaped like a moon.

Dorothy imagined what it would feel like to rub her back, touch her fuzzy head, and breathe her baby scent. She nearly broke, aching to hold her, feel her weight and heat, and bury her face in the folds of her neck. Dorothy watched what her life could have been behind two panes of glass and two sets of drapes.

Sometimes she wondered if they should have adopted. It was Inga who told her adoption was risky. Why had she chosen to listen to her mother for that particular piece of advice but nothing else?

She stepped to the Dickens village. Tiny Tim had fallen over. How? The intruders would not leave her alone. Playing tricks. She straightened Tim, replacing the tiny cane beneath his arm, then wiped dust from the roof of the Old Curiosity Shop. Tiffany needed to dust the village more thoroughly.

Sitting at the piano, 7:28 p.m., she played "Rock-a-Bye-Baby" with one hand while admiring the blue-stoned ring on her finger. Real or not, it looked good. It was real enough.

The Tony Awards would be starting soon. Angela Lansbury had been nominated for her recent Broadway performance in *Blithe Spirit*.

She made popcorn and got a Coke and settled in to watch. Liza Minnelli performed "But the World Goes 'Round."

Liza was rusty, her voice breaking and her dance moves wobbly—nothing like Judy.

Angela won best actress; she wore a white pantsuit, with pearls around her neck and dangling from her ears. A flash on her wrist caught Dorothy's attention. She leaned closer to the TV. Angela approached the stage, hobbling a little, as if her knees hurt, yet laughing and giddy. "Oh, God! Who would have thought? Who knew at this time in my life I should be presented with this lovely, lovely award. I feel deeply grateful. I can't believe that I'm standing here. Bless you all. I am the essence of happiness and gratitude and joy, and being back on Broadway and back with all you Broadway actors, it's the greatest gift I can imagine in my old age. Thank you for having me back."

With a close-up view of Angela holding the microphone, Dorothy could see a familiar pattern in the diamonds of the bracelet she wore—triangles, circles, and squares. *Cornflower Blue sapphires inside the circles?* It slipped under the cuff of her jacket.

Dorothy stood. "Tiffany! Come quick! My bracelet!"

Dorothy left the den. Click. Click. Click. Click. "You can get the top crystals later." She was about to enter the dining room when she heard a jarring and familiar squeak, followed by the shattering crash of breaking glass. The sound sent a wave of panic through her body. The screech of the ladder was forever connected with the stopping of one's heart. She paused to look at her reflection in the mirror hanging askew in the hall.

And then there was one.

Turning away from the mirror with hesitation, Dorothy continued down the short hallway. She paused again to look back over her shoulder, where lights from the TV flashed against the walls and the audience at the Tony Awards clapped. Dorothy steadied her hand on the corner leading into the dining room, then slid around it.

Ruth lay flat on her back beneath the fallen chandelier. Crystals, whole and fragmented, were scattered across the floor, catching the last of the evening light and reflecting it back across the walls in shades of pink and red. The drapes had been pulled wide open. The sky, nearly sunset, swirled orange and fiery red. Ruth seemed to be looking, too, with her eyes rolled back and her mouth gaping open, screaming silently.

Pieces of plaster, yellowed, crumbling, hung, then fell, from a jagged hole in the ceiling. A wire, frayed, the blue insulated covering chewed away, swayed.

Dorothy peered into the space between the ceiling and the floorboards of Eugene's office, then looked back at the rug, where the crystals twinkled like diamonds. It was so beautiful that, for a moment, she forgot what had happened.

Ruth groaned.

On top of the fallen chandelier sat an amber-colored, crystallized mass. Dorothy took a step closer.

Ruth whispered, "Dorothy."

As Dorothy got closer, the scent was strong and foul, like that of a zoo enclosure. Curious items were tucked inside, leaves and twigs woven together, shiny things.

"Nine-one-one," Ruth choked out.

Dorothy held her breath, crunched over a few crystals, reached in, and pulled something from the nest. Fabric with metallic ribbons, pink, black, silver, a bow, lace. She lifted it and let it twirl in the air, a piece of her lingerie, the crotch and part of the front of her wedding panties.

Ruth stared up at the fragment dangling overhead. She couldn't breathe.

Dorothy set the panty fragment aside and reached for a sterling-silver baby spoon, without a scratch, a gold earring, a brass key, a paper-clip chain. More jewelry. Rings, a bracelet, two necklaces. Dorothy dug deeper. Several tiny sample perfume bottles, coins. The bottom was carpeted with shiny red, blue, and silver wrappers of miniature candy bars.

Ruth's eyes rolled back. "Lady Fiske. Please."

Dorothy's breath quickened as she dug through the treasure chest. She pulled the whole thing toward her, causing fragments of grass, leaves, and pieces of crystallized urine to fall onto Ruth's face. She found a photo of a slender, young, dark-haired woman standing, smiling, on a college campus. A Spanish beauty. Dorothy inspected her hair and skin, tried to see the color of her eyes. She looked happy. Eugene must have taken the photo. He had smiled, too, no doubt. Dorothy threw it aside. It didn't matter, it never mattered, because she was the one who married him, and her name was Fiske.

A bolt. A crystal cabinet knob from her bathroom. Copper

wire. A keychain with miniature rhinestone sunglasses she'd bought for a friend but couldn't part with.

A river of blood ran beneath Ruth. "Blood is a beautiful color, don't you think, Tiffany? A truly gorgeous color."

Ruth whispered, "Don't let me die."

Dorothy looked at Ruth's face. "But that's what we do. We turn away, we wait, we leave the room, we put a little bottle on someone's nightstand, we make tea. Isn't that right, Tiffany?"

"It wasn't all fake," Ruth said, her voice like gravel. "The black pearl is real; the living gem is real. I'm real."

Dorothy touched Ruth's head. "I wouldn't use the word *murder*, exactly. Sometimes it's the best choice. We both know that, right? Sometimes it helps everyone."

"Dorothy, I care for you. I love . . ." Ruth gasped, then winced.

"Hush now. Close your eyes and wait for Jesus. If you've never asked him to live in your heart, then you'll need to do that now. It's never too late. God is merciful. Confess all you've done, and he will forgive you."

Ruth closed her eyes and thought about all she'd done, but she didn't know what parts were bad and which were good, so she thought of it all, her whole life in tiny broken pieces, a collage. Still, like a painting, or a series of frozen images. No stories. No sad beginnings or happy endings. No words, only color, shape, light, and dark.

"Do you see Jesus yet?" Dorothy knelt down and took Ruth's hand. "I'll hold your hand until he comes, and when I feel you let go, I'll know he's there."

Behind her closed eyelids, Ruth walked down the cobblestone street. To her right was Bob Cratchit. She waved. Ahead was the Old Curiosity Shop. She smelled something roasted and sweet. Chestnuts? Roast turkey? Plum pudding? Tiny Tim dropped his crutch and ran. He smiled. She waved. She passed a wooden sign, SCROOGE AND MARLEY, the charming buildings blending together, their quaint storefronts fused into a pleasant mess of loveliness. A candy shop with a jar of swirly rainbow sticks. A black iron lantern. A tabby cat. A plump woman in a white apron sweeping. The bakery, doors flung open, released the aroma of yeast and sugar. Ahead was the Toy Shoppe, with a blue dollhouse in the window. Was hers in Dorothy's garage?

Her own house, past the church, stone, black shutters, with a holly-berry wreath hung on the door. Christmas. The voices of carolers lifted in the distance. Candles lit the windows. Dusk approached. A light drifting of snow floated around. Ruth stuck out her tongue to catch the sugar flakes.

Dorothy touched the chandelier. "You did a nice job on the top crystals. I can see them well now." A red, jagged line ran from the corner of Ruth's mouth to her ear. Dorothy wiped it away, then noticed the stone lying in the hollow of Ruth's neck.

In 1953, Mr. Carson, a pleasant-looking man with silver hair and red cheeks, had kissed Dorothy's hand and offered her a wide grin. "How are you enjoying the Sun Drop?" Dorothy had pulled her hand away.

Dorothy recalled her confusion. "Sun Drop?"

Mr. Carson had smiled. "Yes, your diamond pendant. Stunning, wouldn't you agree? I told your husband to be sure to explain its rarity. Fancy Vivid Canary, internally flawless, and nearly four carats. I was able to source it from a private collection. It's believed to be cut from the same stone as *the* Tiffany Yellow Diamond."

Humiliated, Dorothy had stood in his store among all the clerks with raised brows, forced to admit, "I don't know what you're talking about. When did he purchase it?" Dorothy's eyelid had twitched wildly before she whispered, "Eugene never gave me a yellow diamond pendant."

Mr. Carson, realizing his misstep, cheeks transforming into maraschino cherries and perspiration sprouting from his forehead, had said, "Oh yes, I'm so sorry. I've confused Mr. Fiske with someone else," then turned quickly to help another shopper.

Dorothy tore the necklace from Ruth's neck. "It was you. The Tiffany Diamond."

Ruth gulped air, confused, hoping the stone might burn her eyes, then coughed a spray of blood across Dorothy's cheek.

Dorothy touched the Inca Rose on Ruth's hand. "A poison ring. Isn't that ironic." She swiveled it open to find the face of adolescent Eugene in the lid, behind the stone. And on the other side was the portrait of a man she didn't recognize. "Look at Eugene. You can't see his teeth, he still had hair, and he wasn't fat yet." Cocking her head, she said, "But who's this?"

Ruth closed her eyes. She approached a church with a bronze cross upon the steeple. She climbed the steps and pushed through the heavy door into the entryway, where her nose filled with the scent of incense. She looked up; colorful light shone through stained glass. Ahead, the suffering Christ, head bleeding, side pierced, gazed down at her. She felt the undeniable presence of a father, of Eugene—kind, soft, and quiet.

"I made a good home for you here, didn't I?" Dorothy looked down at Ruth. "You're smiling. And your face is bright and shiny. Do you see him? Has Jesus come for you?"

Ruth looked back at the figure of Christ, but only the cross remained. A warm weight descended upon her shoulders. Turning to look, she saw that his fingers rested there, but she was not afraid.

Dorothy fixed her eyes to the center of the chandelier. The pointed shard, the crystal weapon, had disappeared into Ruth's chest, just below her heart. "Did I ever tell you about the time they took out my rib? My father held my hand. That's what I remember most. But Mother, well, she couldn't even be in the room. But I'm not leaving you, Tiffany. I'll never leave you." Dorothy gave Ruth's hand a gentle squeeze.

A faint draft dried Ruth's tongue. She felt the pull of Dorothy's dining room floor. With no space in her chest, her breath barely moved. Had David known he was dying when he hung from the branch? Was he scared, alive or dead, staring at water and sky? Or did he see the face of God, Pigeon Blood, the one he sought. Was her last confession to him—*a product of violence*—the thing that became too much?

Something drifted from the gaping hole in the ceiling, a paper airplane folded from yellowed newsprint. Dorothy reached up and caught it. Unfolding it, she found an article from the local paper with a photo of an old biplane. Seated inside were the pilot and a boy. Standing next to the plane was another boy, younger, maybe six. Both boys held tiny parachutes, and from them hung candy bars. Dorothy read the caption then held the photo in front of Ruth's face. "See here." Dorothy pointed to the older boy sitting in the copilot seat. "Paul Tibbets. This was his first ride in an airplane. Later, Tibbets was the pilot for the *Enola Gay*. Remember, he dropped the bomb. Hiroshima." Dorothy paused to notice blood bubbling up and spilling from the side of Ruth's mouth. "He got to ride in that plane and drop candy, Baby Ruth candy, over the side to a crowd of people at a horse race in Miami because his father was the principal distributor for Baby Ruth candy in Florida. It was a promotional stunt."

Ruth moaned.

"And do you know who that other little boy is?" Dorothy held the newspaper closer to Ruth's face. "Eugene. I told you Eugene flew with Paul Tibbets. He got to drop Baby Ruth candy bars from the sky. The Fiskes had all the connections. Eugene's father knew Otto Schnering quite well. Mr. Schnering founded the Curtiss Candy Company in Chicago. Invented the Baby Ruth in 1921, the same year Eugene was born. Did you hear me, Tiffany? So Eugene got to be in that plane. Of course, no one knew at the time that Paul Tibbets would be a hero."

In the darkness of Ruth's closed lids, Akio clipped gingerly with tiny, sharp shears. Pink petals fell. White linen swayed. She looked up; candy fell from the sky as she swallowed the iron bubbling in her throat. Drowning, she was drowning like Esther.

Dorothy looked again at the nest. "I knew Eugene was

eating all the Baby Ruths from the Halloween candy. He denied it, but we know the truth now. Don't we, Tiffany."

Ruth saw the plane swirling above, a crowd cheered below, horses thumped, and children reached with fingers spread as Eugene threw white parachutes over the side. *How wonderful!* Ruth gasped.

Dorothy scoffed. "He was a clerk. He wanted to be a pilot, but the army made him a clerk. He just typed."

In her mind, Ruth reached to the sky, arms wide. Pounding hooves, palm trees, a bright sun made her squint, but she still caught the glint of the plane.

Dorothy squeezed Ruth's hand. "Do you see Jesus yet? He'll be coming. I'll hold your hand. Keep asking and he'll come. He loves you, Tiffany. He died for you."

Ruth slipped. Dorothy's hand squeezed harder. Her pretty house with the blue door, candles flickering, faded into darkness. The Ghost of Christmas Future remained faceless under his hood. Eugene, whipped-cream chin, the offset teeth. Sapphire bracelet. Peach Jolly Rancher riding the ocean breeze. *Children will look for their mothers.* A spot of blue. *How did you know Irene?* Agatha. Fun Dip.

"There's a lot of blood. It's a good color on your lips." Dorothy took a tissue from her pocket and lifted the dry husk of a rat from the nest by its tail. "Look. A dead rat. A pack rat." She looked closer. "With a tiny penny around its neck." Dorothy turned the rat, twisting from the tail. "It's an exact replica. See, there's Lincoln."

Dorothy let go of Ruth's hand.

Ruth fell.

A white parachute jerked Ruth's body. She floated. Scottie-dog cookies. Urine. Diamonds. Dog-poop pralines. *Please Murder Me.* Judy. Carole. Angela. Elvis. The ladder. Cheetos. Ruby ring. Ruby slippers. Earl Grey with milk. Princess Diana. Hershey, Pennsylvania. Tiny Tim. *Blue Hawaii.* Baby doll. *The Scream.* Ruth's foot caught. The parachute floated below. Saint Peter.

She hung upside down with the Royal Blue ocean above and the Cornflower sky below.

Ruth stirred, then opened her mouth.

Dorothy leaned in. "Go ahead, Tiffany. It's all right. What's that? I'm listening."

As blood spilled from her lips, Ruth whispered, "Just like the movies . . . even the bad can be beautiful." Ruth choked, her voice barely audible, submerged beneath the pool of iron in her throat. "Jesus turns the bad to good." With one final breath, Ruth whispered, "Dorothy—God loves you."

But Dorothy had become fixated on a sparkly, red-eyed pigeon charm she'd pulled from the rubble—an early gift from Eugene. "Of course he does."

As if watching a movie, Ruth saw herself as God had intended, a living gem, before the world had defiled her. Pigeon Blood—*Like seeing the face of God.* Whipped-cream clouds. Marbit. Crooked smile. Giant Jesus. Rainbow sprinkles. Black pearl. Tiny parachute. Emerald eyes. *Hello, Lincoln.* Moonlight Cream. Mother Cabrini, Sun Drop. Baby Ruth.

Ruth let go.

Love, Eugene.

EPILOGUE

Mr. Halabi had taken Judith's bracelet to London and sold it to an independent jeweler for $58,000; then it sold again at auction for $62,000 to a collector of deco jewelry. This collector sold it to a woman whose grandmother had had a similar one, but the other granddaughter got it. The unlucky granddaughter paid $70,000, pretending it was Granny's. With a financial downturn, she sold it to a small independent shop specializing in estate jewelry for $40,000.

When Angela went to visit this small shop, looking for a special piece for the Tony Awards, where she might be on stage, she noticed it immediately, recognized it. That elegant Old Hollywood look. When she tried it on, she knew it was the very thing because she wanted something with history, with a life of its own. And it reminded her of the Palisades, of someone she knew once, not someone close, but someone she remembered because she'd received letters for decades commenting on *Murder, She Wrote*, complimenting her acting, making suggestions for future plots, and even offering a few makeup tips.

It wasn't until she returned home and got her magnifying glass that she read the inscription engraved inside: *My darling Judith, in honor of our son Eugene Fiske, 1921.* Initially stunned.

She'd fixed the clasp. The coincidence, the smallness of the world, struck her as remarkable, or at least the smallness of a world occupied by those who come into possession of $75,000 bracelets. Puzzled as to why Mrs. Fiske would part with it, she decided to wear it to the Tonys, then, upon her next return to LA, would inquire about her.

The whereabouts of the Crimson Flame is another story.